A LITERARY HISTORY OF SPAIN

A LITERARY HISTORY OF SPAIN

General Editor: R. O. JONES
Cervantes Professor of Spanish, King's College, University of London

THE MIDDLE AGES
by A. D. DEYERMOND
Professor of Spanish, Westfield College, University of London

THE GOLDEN AGE: PROSE AND POETRY
by R. O. JONES

THE GOLDEN AGE: DRAMA
by EDWARD M. WILSON
Professor of Spanish, University of Cambridge
and DUNCAN MOIR
Lecturer in Spanish, University of Southampton

THE EIGHTEENTH CENTURY
by NIGEL GLENDINNING
Professor of Spanish, Trinity College, University of Dublin

THE NINETEENTH CENTURY
by DONALD L. SHAW
Senior Lecturer in Hispanic Studies, University of Edinburgh

THE TWENTIETH CENTURY
by G. G. BROWN
Lecturer in Spanish, Queen Mary College, University of London

SPANISH AMERICAN LITERATURE SINCE INDEPENDENCE
by JEAN FRANCO
Professor of Latin American Literature, University of London

CATALAN LITERATURE
by ARTHUR TERRY
Professor of Spanish, The Queen's University, Belfast

A LITERARY HISTORY OF SPAIN

THE GOLDEN AGE
PROSE AND POETRY

The Sixteenth and Seventeenth Centuries

A LITERARY HISTORY OF SPAIN

THE GOLDEN AGE PROSE AND POETRY

The Sixteenth and Seventeenth Centuries

R. O. JONES

Cervantes Professor of Spanish, King's College, University of London

LONDON · ERNEST BENN LIMITED

NEW YORK · BARNES & NOBLE INC

First published 1971 by Ernest Benn Limited
Bouverie House · Fleet Street · London EC4
and Barnes & Noble Inc. · 105 Fifth Avenue · New York 10003

Distributed in Canada by
The General Publishing Company Limited · Toronto

Printed in Great Britain

ISBN 0 510-32261-1

ISBN 0-389-04191-2 (USA)

Paperback 0 510-32262-X

Paperback 0-389-04192-0 (USA)

For
LAURA, SARAH
and DEBORAH

FOREWORD BY THE GENERAL EDITOR

SPANISH, the language of what was in its day the greatest of European powers, became the common tongue of the most far-flung Empire the world had until then seen. Today, in number of speakers, Spanish is one of the world's major languages. The literature written in Spanish is correspondingly rich. The earliest European lyrics in a post-classical vernacular that we know of (if we except Welsh and Irish) were written in Spain; the modern novel was born there; there too was written some of the greatest European poetry and drama; and some of the most interesting works of our time are being written in Spanish.

Nevertheless, this new history may require some explanation and even justification. Our justification is that a new and up-to-date English-language history seemed called for to serve the increasing interest now being taken in Spanish. There have been other English-language histories in the past, some of them very good, but none on this scale.

Every history is a compromise between aims difficult or even impossible to reconcile. This one is no exception. While imaginative literature is our main concern, we have tried to relate that literature to the society in and for which it was written, but without subordinating criticism to amateur sociology. Since not everything could be given equal attention (even if it were desirable to do so) we have concentrated on those writers and works of manifestly outstanding artistic importance to us their modern readers, with the inevitable consequence that many interesting minor writers are reduced to names and dates, and the even lesser are often not mentioned at all. Though we have tried also to provide a usable work of general reference, we offer the history primarily as a guide to the understanding and appreciation of what we consider of greatest value in the literatures of Spain and Spanish America.

Beyond a necessary minimum, no attempt has been made to arrive at uniform criteria; the history displays therefore the variety of approach and opinion that is to be found in a good university department of literature, a variety which we hope will prove stimulating. Each section takes account of the accepted works of scholarship in its field, but we do not offer our history as a grey consensus of received opinion: each contributor has imposed his own interpretation to the extent that this could be supported with solid scholarship and argument.

Though the literature of Spanish America is not to be regarded simply as an offshoot of the literature of Spain, it seemed natural to link the two in our history since Spanish civilisation has left an indelible stamp on the Americas. Since Catalonia has been so long a part of Spain it seemed equally justified to include Catalan literature, an important influence on Spanish literature at certain times, and a highly interesting literature in its own right.

The bibliographies are not meant to be exhaustive. They are intended only as a guide to further reading. For more exhaustive inquiry recourse should be had to general bibliographies such as that by J. Simón Díaz.

R.O.J.

PREFACE

IN THIS VOLUME spelling in quotations has been generally modernised except for certain phonetic features which it was desirable to retain.

This volume should be read in conjunction with the third volume of this literary history—*The Golden Age: Drama, 1492-1700*, which covers the same period under another aspect.

King's College,
London,
March 1971

R.O.J.

CONTENTS

LIST OF ABBREVIATIONS

Actas II	Actas del Segundo Congreso Internacional de Hispanistas (Nijmegen, 1967)
BAC	Biblioteca de Autores Cristianos
BAE	Biblioteca de Autores Españoles
BBMP	Boletín de la Biblioteca de Menéndez Pelayo
BH	Bulletin Hispanique
BHS	Bulletin of Hispanic Studies
BRAE	Boletín de la Real Academia Española
BSS	Bulletin of Spanish Studies
BUG	Boletín de la Universidad de Granada
CC	Clásicos castellanos
C Ca	Clásicos Castalia
FMLS	Forum for Modern Language Studies
HR	Hispanic Review
MLN	Modern Language Notes
MLR	Modern Language Review
NRFH	Nueva Revista de Filología Hispánica
RABM	Revista de Archivos, Bibliotecas y Museos
REJ	Revue des Études Juives
RFE	Revista de Filología Española
RFH	Revista de Filología Hispánica
RH	Revue Hispanique
RLC	Revue de Littérature Comparée
RLM	Revista de literaturas modernas
RN	Romance Notes
SPh	Studies in Philology
Sym	Symposium
ZRPh	Zeitschrift für Romanische Philologie

Chapter 1

THE RENAISSANCE IN SPAIN: I

THE SIXTEENTH AND SEVENTEENTH CENTURIES are rightly called Spain's Golden Age (Siglo de Oro) in literature and the other arts. What sort of Spain was it that gave birth to those centuries of such extraordinary artistic achievement?

At the beginning of the sixteenth century Spain was now unified at last: unified politically by the dynastic marriage of Isabella I of Castile and Ferdinand of Aragon, and also by the conquest of Granada, the last Islamic kingdom in Spain, in 1492; unified in religion by the option of conversion or exile imposed on Jews in 1492 and Muslims in 1502, with the Inquisition to watch for backsliders and other manifestations of heterodoxy. Ferdinand and Isabella, the *Reyes Católicos* (a title conferred by Pope Alexander VI in 1494), had brought order to Spain after a long period of rebellion and civil war. Not only that: the union of their kingdoms created what was without question the strongest power in Europe, now poised for a leap forward in influence and culture. As Antonio de Nebrija wrote in 1492: 'no queda ya otra cosa sino que florezcan las artes de la paz'.

On the death of Isabella in 1504 she was succeeded by her daughter Juana, married to the Archduke Philip the Fair, heir of the Emperor Maximilian. Juana, already unstable, became insane on the death of Philip in 1506. The succession passed to their six-year-old son Charles who in 1516, on the death of Ferdinand (who had been acting as regent), became Charles I of the united Spanish kingdoms. He was to be elected Holy Roman Emperor in 1519, becoming Charles V of the Empire. By his accession and subsequent election Spain was plunged irrevocably into a European involvement which had far-reaching consequences for her over the next two centuries.

Granada fell to the armies of Ferdinand and Isabella in 1492. In October of that year Columbus made his first American landfall. For him the lands he found were the Indies; the name survived the discovery of his error. The discovery of the New World was the most momentous event of the entire Renaissance period ('The greatest event since the Creation of the world' said the Spanish historian Francisco López de Gómara in 1552) but the effect on Spain at large was not immediate. The imagination was not at once quickened, as far as we can tell from the evidence of literature. The main interest at first seems to have been in the American gold which Columbus brought back: indeed, the hope of gold was to remain a driving force of the *conquistadores*. The early voyages were in the main exploratory; the conquest began in earnest in 1519 with Cortés's overthrow of the Aztec empire of Mexico. The energies and aspirations born of seven centuries of re-conquest of Spain were now diverted to a new continent. In spite of their all too frequent cruelties and destruction of the cultures which they overran, it is hard not to find in oneself some admiration for at least the heroism and verve of the *conquistadores*; and though Spaniards perpetrated much that is hateful, one must finally respect the vastness of Spanish enterprise in legislation and administration in their new empire. Crimes and errors were committed, but there were also attempts to protect the new-found peoples from exploitation and injustice. The outstanding figure in the campaign for justice was the Dominican Fray Bartolomé de las Casas (1474-1566), who fought untiringly for the rights of the Indians, urging the renunciation of force, slavery, and forcible conversion to Christianity. In spite of nationalistic attempts to denigrate him, his work remains a monument to the nobler side of Spain. Las Casas's principles were embodied in Vitoria's famous lectures *De Indis* delivered at Salamanca in 1539, from which sprang the modern conception of international law. Las Casas found, however, an uncompromising opponent in the classical scholar Juan Ginés de Sepúlveda (1490?-1573) who invoked the authority of Aristotle in support of his claim that the Indians were to be regarded as natural slaves and so could be legitimately conquered and enslaved by Spaniards, as members of a higher civilisation. In 1549 the Council of the Indies was moved to recommend to the king that the matter be put before a meeting of theologians and jurists. Accordingly, a Council was summoned to meet in Valladolid in 1550 to hear Las Casas and Sepúlveda debate. Charles went further: he ordered all conquests in the New World to cease until it should be decided how conquest should justly be conducted. 'Probably never before or since has a mighty emperor—and in 1550 Charles V, Holy Roman Emperor, was the strongest ruler in Europe with a great overseas empire besides—ordered his conquests to cease until it was decided if they were just.'[1] Unfortunately the Council broke up without reaching a decision and the controversy continued. Future legislation, however, was to go some way in the direction of the principles upheld by Las Casas. Conquest was not long interrupted.

Spain reshaped the life of her American dominions. America, in return, was to have an immense effect on the destiny of Spain. For one thing, Spain was able to sustain almost continuous warfare in the sixteenth century because of the rising tide of silver imports from America; but these same imports contributed through inflation to Spain's economic instability. The imports were in any case increasingly inadequate to finance Spanish foreign policy (the royal treasury was bankrupt three times in the reign of Philip II: in 1557, 1575, and 1597) and actually began to decrease from the beginning of the seventeenth century. Inflation and high taxation made an unpropitious climate for commerce; Spanish trade, including the increasingly important trade with America, passed more and more into the hands of foreigners. Spanish industry, active and enterprising in the first half of the sixteenth century, was eventually crippled by high home prices, and its export trade was to wither completely. Agriculture did not suffer less; partly because under pressure from the Mesta, the immensely influential sheepfarmers' corporation, legislation favoured sheep against arable; partly because the heavy burden of taxation drove peasants off the land in search of a better life elsewhere. The depopulation of the countryside was a major cause of concern from the later years of the sixteenth century.

That Spain was a profoundly religious country scarcely needs saying; but some of the ways in which religion informed Spanish life call for at least some mention. The alternatives of conversion or expulsion with which Jews and Muslims were confronted induced many thousands of people useful by their learning or their labour to emigrate, but also left Spain with a considerable population of nominal converts, many of them indifferent, some hostile, to the Christian Church. The Inquisition watched zealously. Many New Christians (or *conversos*) suffered death, pain, or ignominy at its hands; many more must have suffered silent agonies of fear lest they arouse its suspicions. The presence of the New Christians had indeed an insidious effect on society as a whole. New Christians were debarred from certain honours, offices, and professions; and in any case to be known as one was in itself shameful. Many therefore concealed their origins, so that there was a skeleton in the cupboard of many apparently Old Christian families. The question of *limpieza de sangre* became in these circumstances a source of secret anxiety that acquired the dimensions of a national neurosis which only a few enlightened souls were able to rise above. The national obsession with honour—the craving for and aggressive susceptibility over social esteem—has been attributed by Américo Castro to this national anxiety; though his thesis must be qualified by the reflection that Spaniards were not wholly different from other nations who lacked this anxiety over *limpieza de sangre*.[2]

Spanish society at the beginning of the sixteenth century was dominated by the aristocracy and it was to remain so. Though Ferdinand

and Isabella broke the independent power of the lawless nobles of their day, and though under Charles V and Philip II the influential administrators and secretaries of the Crown were commoners, the nobility remained the dominant caste. The aristocracy were immensely wealthy; as landowners they may be said to have *owned* Spain; and their economic power received no effective challenge from the small middle class, whose power was undermined in the sixteenth century and eventually overwhelmed by economic disaster in the seventeenth. The dominance of the aristocracy left its stamp on the forms and ideals of society as a whole. Nobility was held to be incompatible with labour or trade, and contempt for these (assisted by a fear of one's *limpieza de sangre* being put in doubt) played an unfortunate though incalculable role in Golden Age Spain. The aspiration to be or to be thought noble became a national mania. This was particularly marked in Castile, where the mercantile spirit found its shallowest soil. It was a Spain nourished on aristocratic ideals which lent herself enthusiastically to the warlike policy of Charles V and Philip II. Spaniards went to America not to plough or mine: that was for the Indians; they went to live as *hidalgos* on what land they could acquire. The secular literature of Golden Age Spain was in the main to reflect aristocratic ideals and conduct. The exemplary heroes and heroines of fiction and drama were usually *hidalgos* (except where an idealised peasantry was depicted—as in the seventeenth-century drama—as an example of unassuming though independent humility). When members of other classes take the leading role they are usually other than exemplary, as in the picaresque novels. Even Spain's counterpart of *The Pilgrim's Progress*—Gracián's *Criticón*—is not about a commoner like Bunyan's Christian but about *hidalgos*. Humbler readers were evidently content to enjoy vicariously the life of an idealised aristocracy, and no doubt identified themselves with it. The aristocratic cast of Spain is especially marked in the seventeenth century when the aristocracy, having loyally served the Crown throughout the sixteenth century, now moved into positions of governmental power as the weak Philip III and his weaker successors handed over all effective government to their noble favourites.

As they had been from time immemorial, the extremes of wealth and poverty were widely separated: in this the Golden Age was an age of splendour and misery. The class struggle was not absent: it played some part in the revolt of the *Comuneros* (1520-21) and, more markedly, in the simultaneous revolt of the Valencian *Germanías*; but thereafter until the economic crises of the seventeenth century inflamed old frictions, Spain, in comparison with other European countries, enjoyed a remarkable cohesion. Religion no doubt played a part in this: under the vigilance of the Inquisition Spain did not know religious dissension (and, perhaps equally important, social discord could not cloak itself in religious dissent). This was a society whose members were capable of astounding feats of self-sacrifice and endurance in war and exploration and for their faith, but who were jealous in honour and sought the bubble reputation with an obsession which struck foreigners and even some Spaniards as perverse. As in the rest of Europe, it was a society most of whose members were familiar with hardship. Famine was frequent: more frequent than history books declare. In a bad but poignant poem Juan del Encina described how famine in Andalusia in 1521 reduced some to cannibalism:

> Y en Niebla con hambre pura
> otra madre a un hijo muerto
> también sacó la asadura
> y en sí la dio sepoltura,
> que diz que la comió cierto.
> ¡O cosa de gran mancilla,
> horrible de gran mancilla,
> de gran compasión y duelo,
> que se me eneriza el pelo
> en contalla y en oílla![3]

Famine carried off the poor; not even the rich were immune to the pestilence which periodically haunted the land. Violence increased the hazards of daily life. Impulsive vengeances and quarrels on points of honour were frequent: *hidalgos* carried the sword for use. At sea, corsairs added to the dangers of nature; and corsair raids made life hazardous for those who lived round the coasts. The precariousness of life no doubt fostered temperaments of mingled emotionalism and resignation, and Spaniards of the Golden Age probably knew wider extremes of elation and dejection than most modern readers of their literature.

The Renaissance cannot be rigorously defined in such a way as to permit a sharp boundary to be drawn between it and the Middle Ages. This is especially true of Spain, whose Renaissance, though it derived its impulse from Italy, acquired a character of its own in which medieval and newer elements mingled. Rather, then, than attempt a fruitless definition it seems best to describe the innovations and changing emphases of the Golden Age and allow the Renaissance to define itself as the sum of those changes. This will in turn entail a refusal to mark a clear-cut division between 'Renaissance' and 'Baroque', segments of one arch which spans the gulf between what we recognise as the Middle Ages and the modern world.

Whatever else is indistinct about it, the European Renaissance was primarily a general revival of interest in classical civilisation. Humanism, the study of the classical writers, was not, however, a movement antagonistic to Christianity (though there were exceptions to this). The ideal that in general animated Renaissance Europe was a desire to make a synthesis of the best in classical thought with Christianity.

Indeed, the Renaissance may be said to have been in some respects a Christian revival. In the same way as, in secular literature, humanists thought of themselves as reaching back over the distorting centuries that lay between in order to get at purer sources of knowledge and inspiration, parallel trends appeared in the fifteenth century in the sphere of religion. Many Christians, less and less content with the institutionalised Christianity of the official Church, felt called to return to the doctrinally simpler and more heartfelt creed of the early Christians. From this soil sprang not only the Reformation but a more general though less radical impulse (as in Spain) to religious renewal and reform.

In some respects, Spain had enjoyed a close association with Italy in the fifteenth century. Alfonso V of Aragon had conquered Naples in 1443 and chose to live in his new kingdom. Though the dynasty divided on Alfonso's death, one line taking the kingdom of Aragon, the other Naples, a bond persisted. In any case, trade between Catalonia and Italy established and maintained contact between them. Some Italian cultural influence entered the Iberian peninsula by this route (though less than is commonly supposed[4]). Castilians were also discovering Italian culture for themselves, though inevitably the discovery was confined to relatively few. The main outside cultural influences continued to come to Spain from France, Burgundy, and Flanders. Economic forces ensured this predominance of the North—for example, the wool trade was a bond between Castile and the Low Countries. For the full reception of the Italian Renaissance in Spain we have to wait for the generation of Garcilaso de la Vega in the sixteenth century. Significantly (perhaps) it was in Garcilaso's lifetime that Fernán Pérez de Oliva (*c.* 1494-1531) composed his *Diálogo de la dignidad del hombre* (first published at Alcalá, 1546) which, though it does not contain anything essentially new, nevertheless gives a refreshingly optimistic view of man by stressing his potentialities rather than his limitations—as if the author had caught a dim and distant glimpse of the headier vision recorded by Pico della Mirandola in his *Oration on the dignity of man.*

Under the influence of Italy, humanism began to take firm root in fifteenth-century Spain. Isabella's active patronage of learning attracted Italian scholars to Spain, among them Peter Martyr (Pietro Martire d'Anghiera) and Lucius Marineus Siculus, both of whom taught Latin at Court (Marineus after twelve years, from 1484 to 1496, as Professor at the University of Salamanca). Spaniards in their turn went to Italy to study. One was Elio Antonio de Nebrija, or Lebrixa (1444-1522), who studied for twelve years in Italy and returned to teach at Salamanca where, with a long interruption of nearly twenty years, he was professor from 1476 to 1513, being then appointed to the Chair of Rhetoric at Alcalá. He devoted himself indefatigably to the propagation of Latin ('desarraigar la barbaria de los ombres de nuestra nación,' as he puts it in the prologue to his Spanish-Latin dictionary). His Latin grammar (*Introductiones latinae*; Salamanca, 1481) was followed by his *Dictionarium latino-hispanicum* (Salamanca, 1492) which superseded the monumental *Universal vocabulario* of Alfonso de Palencia which had appeared only two years before. Nebrija devoted himself not only to Latin: his *Gramática sobre la lengua castellana* (Salamanca, 1492) was followed by his Spanish-Latin dictionary, *Interpretación de las palabras castellanas en latín* (Salamanca, *c.* 1495). In the dedication to Isabella, Nebrija speaks of the double opportuneness of his Spanish grammar (the first of any modern European language): in that Spain's new subjects will wish to learn the language of their conquerors, since language follows power ('siempre la lengua fue compañera del imperio'); and in that Castilian is now at its zenith ('por estar ya nuestra lengua tanto en la cumbre, que más se puede temer el decendimiento della que esperar la subida'). Nebrija doubtless reflects in this the mood of confidence verging on arrogance at Court.

Nebrija was not alone in his educational work. There were other excellent Latinists; and the study of Greek was initiated in Spain by the Portuguese Arias Barbosa, a professor at Salamanca from about 1480 and the first Professor of Greek in the Peninsula. There was to be no lack of classical scholars to build on the foundations laid by these.

The rising European fervour for religious reform helped, through the person of Cardinal Francisco Jiménez de Cisneros, the cause of learning in Spain. Cisneros was not only a reformer of abuses, though he was that also: he applied himself vigorously to the reform of the Spanish clergy, including the monastic orders, which he attempted to lead back to a more ascetic life (with sufficient success to induce four hundred Andalusian friars to choose North Africa and conversion to Islam rather than give up their concubines). But Cisneros's programme was positive as well. Seeing clearly that the reform of the clergy entailed the reform of education, he founded in 1498 at Alcalá de Henares (where a college had existed since the thirteenth century) a university designed to be a new instrument of ecclesiastical education. The new university, which opened in 1508, was not intended as a humanistic centre: theology was to be its heart; but the strongly represented liberal arts, necessary as a prelude to theological and biblical studies, gave humanism a powerful impetus. Chairs of Greek and Hebrew were instituted. Leading scholars were invited to teach there. Among those attracted was Nebrija.

The first fruits of the new university were not long in coming. In 1517 the printing of the great Polyglot Bible (known as the Complutensian from the Latin name of Alcalá) was finished (though publication was not authorised until 1520 and the work was not on sale until 1522). Its begetter was Cisneros, who as early as 1502 had assembled a group of biblical scholars at Alcalá for the purpose, intending that the new Bible, in Hebrew, Aramaic, Greek, and Latin, should incorporate all the latest advances in scholarship and textual criticism (though in some respects the criteria employed proved to be very conservative). The result is a monument to the quality of Spanish scholarship, to the new university press at Alcalá, and to the energy and enthusiasm of Cisneros himself. The Complutensian Polyglot was in its turn superseded by another Spanish enterprise, the Antwerp Polyglot Bible published in 1569-72 under the direction of Benito Arias Montano (whose textual criteria were this time to be radical enough to alarm authority).

In 1517 Cisneros invited Erasmus to go to Spain. Though in the event Erasmus, reluctant to face the long journey to a country which meant little to him, was never to go, he was destined to exercise a profound if short-lived influence in Spain, particularly at and through the University of Alcalá. Erasmus, now at the height of his European fame, represented a movement of reform and spiritual renewal within the Catholic Church. His doctrines were not wholly original, but his untiring activity as scholar and propagandist made him the focus of a peculiar interest—hatred or admiration according to the quarter. Essentially he stood for a laicisation of Christianity. Not all Christians now were satisfied to believe blindly and to observe the forms and ceremonies of a religion whose doctrines might be discussed and taught only by a minority of priestly initiates. Erasmus devoted his life to an attempt to arouse the spirit of Christ in men by leading them back to the words of Christ—and not only of Christ but of Paul, who for Erasmus was the great expounder of the inwardness of Christianity.

Erasmus's doctrines—his insistence on an inward piety instead of outward ritual and ceremony, on personal familiarity with the Scriptures, his appeal to Christians to live in peace as members of the spiritual body of Christ—were influential among the Flemings around Charles V before he came to Spain, and entered Spain under their auspices. Erasmus's doctrines also appealed to many Spanish intellectuals, above all at the University of Alcalá, where in the 1520s Erasmian ideas were to flourish. Various of Erasmus's works were reprinted there at the university press, beginning in 1525. Translation into Spanish had already begun: *Querela pacis* had appeared as *Querella de la paz* in 1520 (Seville). A translation of *Enchiridion* was published in 1526 at Alcalá.[5] Translations of the *Colloquia* began to appear in the Peninsula in 1527.

The Spanish Erasmian movement was to remain strongest at Alcalá, but the number of translations (and reprints of them) indicates a more widely diffused interest. Erasmianism, proved, indeed, a subtly pervasive influence in some areas of Spanish religious life. It gave some impetus to the Illuminist or *alumbrado* movement, a pietistic movement born of the fifteenth-century religious ferment in Italy and the Netherlands, and one which exercised some attraction on Spanish *conversos*, who doubtless found in inner devotion a religious way more congenial than the organised ritual of the Church. From about 1523 the influence of Erasmus is perceptible in the more literate members of the movement. Illuminism was already condemned by the Inquisition; its association with Erasmianism helped to bring the latter under attack. The opportunity was not resisted by the religious orders, inflamed by the anti-monastic satire of Erasmus. Although Erasmianism had many important adherents in Spain, including the Inquisitor-General himself, the antagonism proved irresistible, and as the fear of heresy and the concomitant suspicion of foreign ideas increased, the works of Erasmus came under ever-sharper attack. A movement of traditionalist reaction was gathering itself during the very years of Erasmus's greatest popularity in the Peninsula. From 1529 individual Erasmians began to be drawn into the Inquisition's net, charged not with Erasmianism but Illuminism or 'Lutheranism'. Erasmianism faltered as a liberal force in the increasingly unpropitious atmosphere; eventually Erasmus's doctrines were condemned and his most influential works put on the Spanish Inquisition's index of prohibited books in 1559. Thereafter, in the closed world of Counter-Reformation Spain, his influence is hard to detect.

The thought of one of the greatest of Spanish humanists, Juan Luis Vives (1492-1540), shows the influence of Erasmus, but Vives did not contribute to the propagation of this influence in Spain since he himself spent most of his life abroad. His *converso* origins, recently discovered, are sufficient explanation of this.[6] Another Spanish Erasmian, Juan de Valdés (1490?-1541), one of the most attractive figures of his generation, was also to prefer to live outside Spain. In 1529 he published anonymously his *Diálogo de doctrina cristiana* in which Fray Pedro de Alba, archbishop of Granada, is shown teaching the true spirit of Christianity—as understood in Erasmian terms—to Antronio, an ignorant and superstitious priest, and to Eusebio, a monk. The work—written in the easy but elegant colloquial style we shall meet again in the author's *Diálogo de la lengua*—breathes the very spirit of Erasmus. The insistence on personal experience of the liberating power of faith and love means that for Valdés, as for Erasmus, outward forms of worship are unnecessary, but he does not oppose the practices of the Church: he preaches conformity not strife, in this following Erasmus's ideal for Christendom, *pax et unanimitas*. The book was denounced to the Inquisition. Though it was still a period of relative tolerance and there is no reason to suppose that Valdés would have been proceeded against, he evidently judged it wiser to run no risk. The rest of his life was spent in Italy, much of it in Naples, where he became the centre of a group of like-minded Christian radicals. He continued writing, but not for Spaniards, and of these writings little has survived. His influence survived for a time his death in 1541 but amidst the hardening orthodoxies of the sixteenth century there was little room for the humane, undogmatic piety he professed.

Juan's twin brother Alfonso (1490?-1532) put Erasmianism to a different use in his two dialogues written in justification of Charles V, in whose Chancery he served as Latin secretary. The dialogues can be fully understood only in their historical context. Valdés was active in the imperial campaign to bring peace to Europe under the authority of Charles, who in the 1520s was regarded (not only in Spain) as an instrument of God destined to bring a new era of peace. Political ambitions and religious aspirations fused into a confused hope of a restoration of Christian unity, of a general reform of the Church, and of the establishment of peace under the rule of Charles. This mood very naturally suited Charles and was fostered by his Chancery, but the mood was not created by propaganda: it goes back to the religious fervour of the turn of the century, and probably had roots in the latent millennialist expectations which had periodically burst to the surface in medieval Europe. An almost Messianic hope came to be focused on Charles (not one shared by Erasmus himself, it must be said).

The defeat and capture of François I at Pavia in 1525 seemed to many to be a step towards this long-desired universal peace. The sack of Rome in May 1527 by the imperial army assembled to confront Pope Clement VII produced consternation and dismay. Was Charles after all the bringer of peace?

The line taken by the imperial Chancery was that the event was an act of divine retribution on the warlike head of a Church gravely in need of reform; a belief doubtlessly held sincerely by many. Alfonso de Valdés made it the substance of a dialogue, *Diálogo de las cosas ocurridas en Roma*, which was probably written in the summer of 1527 and circulated in manuscript before being printed, probably in 1529. In it Valdés puts his Erasmian convictions at the service of the emperor.

The speakers are Lactancio, a young gentleman of the emperor's entourage, and an Archdeacon, an old acquaintance just back from Rome full of horror at the sack of the city, which he witnessed. Lactancio undertakes to exonerate the emperor.

His argument is heavy with ideas drawn from various of Erasmus's works. Proceeding by way of an indictment of the Pope for plunging a peaceful country into war with all its miseries, Lactancio broadens his attack into a general denunciation of the Church for its rapacious pursuit of money—for baptism, for marriage, for confession, for death. To the Archdeacon's objection that without money there would be no Church Lactancio retorts:

> ¿Como que no habría iglesias? Antes pienso yo que habría muchas más, pues habiendo muchos buenos cristianos, dondequiera que dos o tres estoviesen ayuntados en su nombre, sería una iglesia. Y allende desto, aunque los ruines no edificasen iglesias ni monesterios, ¿pensáis que faltarían buenos que lo hiciesen? Y veamos: este mundo, ¿qué es sino una muy hermosa iglesia, donde mora Dios? ¿Qué es el sol, sino una hacha encendida que alumbra a los ministros de la Iglesia? ¿Qué, es la luna, qué son las estrellas, sino candelas que arden en esta iglesia de Dios? ¿Queréis otra iglesia? Vos mismo. ¿No dice el Apóstol: *Templum* [*enim*] *dei sanctum est, quod estis vos*? ¿Queréis candelas para que alumbren esta iglesia? Tenéis el spíritu, tenéis el entendimiento, tenéis la razón. ¿No os parece que son éstas gentiles candelas? (p. 102)[7]

This is the heart of Erasmus's doctrine: that religion is of the spirit. Lactancio presses the point: the defilement of churches is nothing to the desecration of human bodies, temples of the Holy Ghost, in war; and if relics were desecrated, most of them are in any case false. He quotes a long list of ludicrous examples.

> El prepucio de Nuestro Señor yo lo he visto en Roma y en Burgos, y también en Nuestra Señora de Anversia, y la cabeza de San Juan Bautista en Roma y en Amians de Francia . . . Pues de palo de la cruz dígoos de verdad que si todo lo que dicen que hay della en la cristiandad se juntase, bastaría para carga una carreta. Dientes que mudaba Nuestro Señor cuando era niño pasan de quinientos los que hoy se muestran solamente en Francia. Pues leche de Nuestra Señora, cabellos de la Madalena, muelas de San Cristóbal, no tienen cuento. (p. 122)

True devotion consists in loving Christ and living by his teaching. The Archdeacon, a reasonable man, owns himself convinced at last.

As well he might, for this is a work of unusual intelligence, written with wit and verve. The argument is set out with lucidity and logic.

The style is a model of clarity and even elegance: the elegance of idiomatic colloquial Castilian at its best.

In 1528-29, after England and France had declared war on Charles, Valdés wrote a more comprehensive attack on the emperor's enemies in his *Diálogo de Mercurio y Carón*, formally suggested by Lucian and Pontano but original in all important respects. In it we find Charon complaining that times are too peaceful for his liking; Mercury reassures him: all Christendom is in arms, mainly through the emperor's enemies. Mercury's account of the un-Christian state of Christendom is interrupted periodically by the arrival of souls to be ferried across by Charon. These give Valdés further opportunity for satire and for the restatement of the Erasmian view. Most of the souls are ignorant of the real teaching of Christ; some are shocked to find themselves on the way to damnation after a lifetime of every observance enjoined by the Church. A few truly Christian souls appear: an ordinary citizen, a king, a bishop, a married woman, a friar, and so on, all of whom tried to live according to the teaching of Christ, humbly and without ostentatious piety. The undisputatious reasonableness in the pursuit of goodness held up for admiration by Valdés is precisely the ideal set forth by his brother Juan.

The second dialogue is written with the stylishness and colloquial ease of the other. Erasmus has been well studied: Alfonso's style has his master's plainness, economy, and clarity. *Mercurio y Carón* seems to arouse more admiration than the other dialogue. *Roma*, however, has the greater verve. Lactancio's arguments and polemical style are more vivid; and the work in general shows more clearly the heat of its author's feelings.

Erasmus did not write for entertainment but for instruction; indeed, he seems to have had little interest in secular literature for its own sake. His somewhat puritanical spirit is discernible in the attitude to secular literature taken by his followers. The most extreme position was taken by Vives, who in various works—e.g. *De institutione feminae christianae, De disciplinis, De ratione dicendi*—attacks a wide range of secular writing for its lies and immorality, including (to take Spanish literature alone) *Amadís* and its sequels, *La Celestina, Cárcel de amor,* and secular love-poetry. A scarcely less extreme position is taken by certain others. Juan de Valdés is more discriminating: in his *Diálogo de la lengua* (see below, pp. 24-6) he too attacks romances of chivalry, but distinguishes between good and bad; and throughout his remarks he shows the same balanced discrimination. His criterion is verisimilitude or credibility—'los que escriben mentiras las deben escribir de suerte que se lleguen cuanto fuere posible a la verdad, de tal manera que puedan vender sus mentiras por verdades'.

The general pressure of the literary influence of Erasmus in sixteenth-

* *

century Europe was in the direction of the exemplary, the morally profitable, and the true (or at least the true-to-life). The trend of the times was in any case in the same direction. Verisimilitude was a concept of growing importance throughout the period, largely owing to the rediscovery of Aristotle's *Poetics* in fifteenth-century Italy (a Latin translation was published in 1498) and the series of commentaries on it by sixteenth-century literary theorists. Neither did Erasmus create the desire that literature should be morally profitable. Humanistic interest in classical literature extended to the moral profit to be derived therefrom. As in matters of doctrine, Erasmus was the articulate voice of a great body of existing opinion: he did not invent all he expressed.

However, it is undeniable that Erasmus gave a strong though not precisely measurable impetus to the movement. In one field in particular —the compiling of proverbs, apophthegms, miscellanies of all sorts— Erasmus's influence and example were to have innumerable progeny. In 1500 he published his first collection of proverbs, *Adagiorum Collectanea*, succeeded in time by his larger *Adagiorum Chiliades* (first edition 1508) which went into many editions, each larger than the last. Each adage had its expository essay. Adages interested Erasmus not only as stylistic models but as repositories of the accumulated wisdom of the past. These books were joined in 1531 by Erasmus's collection of apophthegms (in imitation of Plutarch). Both kinds of book fed the unappeasable European appetite for miscellaneous information of all sorts, which the encyclopaedic miscellanies (again imitated from classical models, such as the *Attic Nights* of Aulus Gellius and the collection of *memorabilia* by Valerius Maximus) were designed to cater for more directly. Spain had her representatives in all these fields.

Though in Spain interest in proverbs preceded Erasmus (the marqués de Santillana had been a collector) his example stimulated that interest. A number of collections appeared in the sixteenth century. The best known and the largest is *La filosofía vulgar* (Seville, 1568) by the humanist Juan de Mal Lara (1524-71), a pupil of Hernán Núñez (1475?-1553), known as *el comendador griego* from his accomplishment as a Greek scholar, whose own collection was printed in 1555 (Salamanca). Erasmus had drawn his adages from the classics; his Spanish imitators took their proverbs from the people about them. Mal Lara printed a thousand in his *Primera parte* (he was not to write more), all classified and each with its expository essay, in imitation of Erasmus, containing a wealth of anecdote and precept. In his preamble he speaks with impressive reverence of his subject:

> Es grande maravilla, que se acaben los superbos edificios, las populosas ciudades, las bárbaras pirámides, los más poderosos reinos, y

que la Filosofía vulgar [*i.e. proverbs*] siempre tenga su reino dividido en todas las provincias del mundo. (p 90)

And the value he attached, and was attached by his age, to these humble sayings may be judged by:

> Los refranes aprovechan para el ornato de nuestra lengua y escritura. Son como piedras preciosas salteadas por las ropas de gran precio, que arrebatan los ojos con sus lumbres, y la disposición da a los oyentes gran contento, y como son de notar, quédanse en la memoria. Entiéndense muchas cosas de la lección de los refranes, hay grande erudición en ellos, sabiéndolos sacar, y glosándose de la manera que yo tengo hecho, y así aprovecharán tanto, que el mismo provecho dará testimonio de mi trabajo para utilidad de todos. (p. 92)

Apophthegms were collected by Melchor de Santa Cruz in his *Floresta española de apothegmas o sentencias, sabia y graciosamente dichas de algunos españoles* (Toledo, 1574) and Juan Rufo in *Las seiscientas apotegmas* (Toledo, 1596). Erasmus had drawn on classical literature; the apophthegms in these books are modern, and Spanish. Such things have largely lost their savour; something of their sixteenth-century appeal can be seen in the fulsome *Discurso* with which Fray Basilio de León introduced Rufo's book:

> Llegó a mis manos, antes que se imprimiese, el libro de Las Apotegmas del Jurado Juan Rufo, con el cual verdaderamente me juzgué rico, pues lo que enriquece al entendimiento es del hombre riqueza verdadera . . . Allégase a esto la agudeza de los dichos, el sentido y la gravedad que tienen, la filosofía y el particular discurso que descubren.

Spain produced her share of miscellanies, the first of which was to become one of the most widely read books in Europe: Pero Mexía's (or Pedro Mejía's) *Silva de varia lección* (Seville, 1540), a large work which in 127 chapters (to which Mexía added later twenty-two more) ranges over ancient and modern history, the properties of things, natural curiosities, origins and inventions, famous and varied deaths, questions such as why men once lived longer, the truth about tritons, why sight is the noblest sense (together with an account of famous blind men)—anything and everything which Mexía, drawing as much on previous compilations as on original sources, judged to be of interest to his contemporaries. He had not misjudged: the work went into thirty-three editions in the sixteenth and seventeenth centuries. In 1552 a French translation appeared, to be frequently reprinted in its turn; an Italian translation came out in 1556; and from the French was made the English translation of 1576. The book undoubtedly responded to the curiosity of Renaissance Europe, its appetite for sheer fact; and by keeping his chapters short and avoiding systematic order ('... hame parecido escrebir este libro así por discursos y capítulos de diversos propósitos, sin perseverar ni guardar orden en ellos, y por esto le puse por nombre *Silva*, porque en las selvas y bosques están las plantas y árboles sin orden ni regla ...') he was doubtless able to attract the kind of inconstant reader who wished only to dip for amusement and be satisfied with the illusion of nourishment. Another such miscellany is Antonio de Torquemada's *Jardín de flores curiosas* (Salamanca, 1570), composed in dialogue form and less miscellaneous than Mexía's book. It too enjoyed a wide European diffusion.

The dialogue or colloquy also enjoyed a European vogue in the sixteenth century, mainly owing once again to the example of Erasmus. Mexía published a volume of *Diálogos* (Seville,1547) treating rather dully of a miscellany of subjects, natural and social. Pedro de Luxán's (or Luján's) *Coloquios matrimoniales* (Seville, 1550) dealing with matrimony, motherhood, and allied subjects, are much more lively, as are Torquemada's *Coloquios satíricos* (Mondoñedo, 1553) on a variety of social vices and abuses. Erasmus's serious educational enterprise had worthy successors in Luxán and Torquemada, who treat of serious subjects, sometimes seriously, sometimes lightly, always entertainingly.

The naïve humanistic spirit represented by the miscellany is to be found again in one of the most celebrated figures of sixteenth-century Spanish letters, Fray Antonio de Guevara (1480?-1545), whose copious writings are interesting and irritating in equal measure.

Guevara was a younger son of one of the branches of the ancient and noble family of Guevara. (As he boasted in one of his epistles: 'primero hubo condes en Guevara que no reyes en Castilla'; I, 10.) He was brought up at the Court of Ferdinand and Isabella and was page to Prince Don Juan until the latter's death in 1497. In 1504, perhaps because of the death of his protector, his uncle Don Ladrón de Guevara, the young Guevara retired from the world into the Franciscan order. In 1521 he returned to Court as Court Preacher. In 1526 he became Royal Chronicler. In 1528 he was named bishop of Guadix, and in 1537 bishop of Mondoñedo (neither of them a lucrative bishopric). Guevara seems to have been active and conscientious in his pastoral duties; in spite of his worldliness his piety does not seem open to question. But he was not by nature a contemplative. He was a courtier as well as a friar; and no doubt he shared the general warlike mood when he accompanied the emperor on the Tunis expedition in 1535. He was a learned man: his work testifies to voracious reading in the classics, and his frequently arrogant tone indicates that he prided himself on his standing as a scholar as well as a man of letters.

Guevara was in many ways an eccentric of letters, but he managed to earn, and for a long time retain, not just a national but a European esteem. His work is very various. In this lay a good part of the reason for his popularity. His work has indeed the character of a vast miscellany, stuffed with curious information (much of it of Guevara's own fabrication), improving tales and *sententiae* drawn from the ancient authors, advice, injunction, and example concerning a wide range of human experience; the whole clothed in a style whose mannered artificiality kept generations of readers attentive to Guevara's endlessly inventive discourses and homilies.

Guevara's first work was his *Libro áureo de Marco Aurelio*, begun in 1518, published first anonymously and without Guevara's permission in 1528 (Seville). This entirely fictional account of Marcus Aurelius (which Guevara claimed in his prologue not to have composed but to have translated from a Greek manuscript newly discovered by him in Florence in the library of Cosimo de' Medici) was then absorbed in the much larger *Libro llamado reloj de príncipes, en el cual va encorporado el muy famoso libro de Marco Aurelio* (Valladolid, 1539). The *Libro áureo* is a miscellany of anecdote and sententious wisdom woven round the figure of Marcus Aurelius. It is in the main didactic in character, but Guevara's imagination ran away with him to the extent of attributing to Marcus Aurelius a number of wholly unedifying amatory letters (love-letters seems too intimate a term for these rhetorical works) addressed to various women of Rome, and portraying a very different man from the grave Stoic philosopher revered by Renaissance Europe. The letters were omitted by Guevara from *Reloj de príncipes*, but continued to be printed in the editions of the *Libro áureo* alone. They must have contributed a good deal to the popularity of that work, which at times has something of the character of a historical novel.

Reloj de príncipes is a work intended for the instruction of princes and men in general. The work is divided into sections among which the material from the *Libro áureo* is distributed. The work was an immediate and immense success. There were to be at least twenty-five Spanish editions of the *Libro áureo* and sixteen of *Reloj*, and more than fifty-eight editions in French, Italian, English, German, and Latin. It was in fact one of the most widely read works of its century. The reasons are not far to seek. Guevara provided miscellaneous erudition allied to bold (some would say shameless) and entertaining invention, the whole serving a moral end. If his wisdom does not rise at its highest much above commonsense, in its very banality it expresses the ethos and aspirations of its age. The repeated praise of peace and the repeated injunction to princes to remember their Christian duty to preserve peace; the warnings of the silent passage of time; the calls to abjure the temptations of the world; these were themes which, if they did not satisfy the subtler minds of the age, were found edifying by the less subtle spirits which made up the majority of the literate. Antique dress helped to cloak the banality: 'all tyrants die at last'—this consoling reflection seems to acquire the dignity and timelessness of wisdom itself when traced by Marcus Aurelius in the half-obliterated inscription on the weathered tomb of the tyrant Periander. Conquest is cruel and rapacity unjust; these truths (so relevant in any case to the contemporary debate concerning the conquest of America) must have seemed to acquire a deeper significance for the sixteenth-century reader when eloquently urged before the Roman Senate by the 'Villano del Danubio', whose entry is described by Marcus Aurelius as follows:

> En el año primero que fui Cónsul, vino un pobre payés de las riberas del Danubio a pedir justicia al Senado contra un censor que hacía muchos desafueros en su pueblo. Él tenía la cara pequeña, los labios grandes, los ojos hundidos, el cabello erizado, la cabeza sin bonete, los zapatos de un cuero de un puerco espín, el sayo de pelos de cabra, la cinta de juncos marinos, y un acebuche en la mano. Fue cosa de ver su persona, y monstruosa de oír su plática. Por cierto, cuando le vi entrar en el Senado, pensé que era algún animal en figura de hombre, y de que le oí, le juzgué ser uno de los dioses, si dioses hay entre hombres. (p. 119)[8]

This episode is one of Guevara's most skilful inventions and for a long time indeed many were convinced that Guevara had drawn it from some authentic ancient source. The Antiquity which Guevara portrays in this book is largely invented, but even an invented Antiquity served the purpose which he shared with the serious humanists of his time: to show that, since all wisdom is one, the classics are reconcilable with the Christian revelation and that to study them is to learn a wisdom the more laudable for being unaided by revelation. In the *argumento* Guevara wrote:

> La ignorancia de los antiguos no fue sino una guía para acertar nosotros; y porque ellos erraron entonces, hallamos el camino nosotros después. Y para más gloria suya y mayor infamia nuestra, digo que si los que somos agora fuéramos entonces, supiéramos menos que supieron; y si los que fueron entonces fueran agora, sabrían más que sabemos. Parece esto ser verdad: porque aquellos sabios, con su diligencia, de las veredas y sendas cerradas hicieron caminos, y nosotros, con pereza, de las carreras llanas y caminos abiertos hacemos prados. (p. 17)

Another ten years passed before Guevara published again. Most of his remaining works came out together in 1539 (Valladolid): *Una década de las vidas de los X Césares, Menosprecio de la corte y alabanza de la aldea, Aviso de privados y doctrina de cortesanos, Libro de los inventores del arte de marear y de muchos trabajos que se pasan en las galeras*, and the *Epístolas familiares* (of which a second series appeared in 1541). The *Década* is based on material drawn from ancient sources but much embroidered by Guevara. Once again he invented freely. The book was widely read but it did not enjoy the success achieved by others of his works. Certainly not as much as his *Epistles*, whose popularity throughout Europe in the sixteenth and seventeenth centuries rivalled that of the *Libro áureo*.

The *Epístolas familiares* (which contain 112 items, not all true epistles) have few precedents in Spanish: only the epistles of Hernando del Pulgar resemble Guevara's in any important respect. The *Epístolas familiares* have a wide range of subjects: ancient history, inscriptions, love, marriage, old age, government, famous harlots, Holy Writ, and so on. They are in fact another miscellany, and one containing again Guevara's characteristic mixture of erudition and falsification. It is now impossible to decide how many of the epistles were sent as real letters and how many were composed as literary exercises. Many have the ring of authenticity (though this is a fallible criterion); but however that may be, their value for the student of literature rests not on their authenticity but their intrinsic interest. By this test they are more vigorously alive than any other work by Guevara. There are moments of tedium, and Guevara's feats of brazen invention tax the most refined sense of humour; but through the collection taken as a whole the personality of the author shines: proud to the point of arrogance, vain, garrulous, ready with unsolicited advice, widely read but without a scholar's conscience, and interested in everything. In their variety and discursiveness the epistles have something of the character of essays: they formed indeed part of the reading of Montaigne, whose *Essais* derive from the sixteenth-century miscellanies. The epistles of Guevara enjoyed the European celebrity of his other works, and were almost as frequently reprinted in French, English, and Italian translation as in the original Spanish.

The epistles dealing with public affairs, such as those addressed to the bishop of Zamora, Juan de Padilla, and María de Padilla as leaders of the *Comuneros* (together with the harangue which Guevara delivered to the *Comuneros* at Villabráxima), have a strong historical interest, whether or not they were written and sent in the form in which Guevara prints them. The epistles in which he airs his varied and sometimes fraudulent erudition often have an eccentric appeal as their vain author struts before us. However, for most present-day readers it is unquestionably the more down-to-earth epistles in which Guevara depicts and comments on everyday life which have the greatest attraction. In a letter reprehending the Governor Luis Bravo for falling in love when old, Guevara writes sternly:

> A tal edad como la vuestra, falso testimonio os levantáis en decir que padecéis dolor y morís de amores, porque a los semejantes viejos que vos no los llamamos requebrados, sino resquebrajados; no enamorados, sino malhadados; no servidores de damas, sino pobladores de sepulturas; no de los que regocijan al mundo, sino de los que ya pierden el seso . . .
>
> En tal edad como la vuestra, no sois ya para pintar motes, tañer guitarras, escalar paredes, aguardas cantones, y ruar calles; como sea verdad que las mujeres vanas y mundanas no se contentan con ser solamente servidas y pagadas en secreto, sino que también quieren ser recuestadas y festejadas en lo público.
>
> En tal edad como la vuestra, no se sufre traer zapatos picados de seda, media gorra toledana, sayo corto hasta la rodilla, polainas labradas a la muñeca, gorjal de aljófar a la garganta, medalla de oro en la cabeza y de las colores de su amiga la librea . . . (1,220)[9]

He follows this up with another letter to the unfortunate governor instructing him in the style of life proper to an old gentleman of sixty-four. The first letter had evidently had its effect:

> Muy noble señor y enamorado caballero:
> En las palabras de vuestra carta conocí cuán presto llegó a vuestro corazón el tósico de mi letra, y huelgo mucho de haberos tirado con tan buena yerba que abastó para os derrocar y no para haceros caer . . . Decís, señor, que a la hora que leístes mi carta quemastes la empresa de vuestra enamorada, rasgastes las cartas de amores, despedistes el paje de los mensajes, quitastes la habla a vuestra amiga y distes finiquito a la alcahueta. (1, 224-5)

All Guevara's advice is eminently sensible: keep clean, warm, calm, contented.

> Sea, pues, la conclusión: que los viejos de vuestra edad deben mucho trabajar de traer la ropa no grasienta, la camisa bien lavada, la casa tener barrida y la cama que esté muy limpia; porque el hombre que es viejo y presume de cuerdo, si quiere vivir sano y andar contento, ha de tener el cuerpo sin piojos y el corazón sin enojos. (1, 230-1)

In another epistle he pressed advice and admonition on an excessively young married couple. His tone is the opposite of romantic.

> Las propriedades de la mujer casada son que tenga gravedad para salir fuera, cordura para gobernar la casa, paciencia para sufrir el

> marido, amor para criar los hijos, afabilidad para con los vecinos, diligencia para guardar la hacienda, cumplida en cosas de honra, amiga de honesta compañía y muy enemiga de liviandades de moza. Las propriedades del hombre casado son que sea reposado en el hablar, manso en la conversación, fiel en lo que se le confiare . . . [etc.] (I, 364)

His lengthy and on the whole sound advice is punctuated with vivid vignettes—of the shrewish wife, the overbearing husband, and so on. He writes with a celibate's relish:

> La mujer brava es muy peligrosa, porque embravece al marido, escandaliza a los deudos, es malquista de los cuñados y huyen de ella los vecinos; de lo cual se sigue que algunas veces el marido le mide el cuerpo con los pies y le peina el cabello con los dedos. A una mujer furiosa y rencillosa, por una parte, es pasatiempo oírla reñir, y por otra parte, es espanto de ver lo que se deja decir, porque si se toma con ella una procesión de gentes, ella les dirá una letanía de injurias. Al marido dice que es descuidado; a los mozos que son perezosos; a las mozas que son sucias . . . [etc.] (I,375)

It is not unlikely that here Guevara is offering a corrective to the 'romantic' view of woman given in the fictional writing of his day. (We know that he deplored the falsifications of literature: he denounced *Amadís* and its successors in his *Aviso de privados*.)

Another of Guevara's works which gained him his European fame also came out in 1539: *Menosprecio de la corte y alabanza de la aldea*. This is a simpler work than those already discussed. Its theme is what its title declares. Guevara denounces the Court in terms which were traditional, probably following (amongst other models) Aeneas Silvius's *De curialium miseriis*. His eulogy of country life is entirely prosaic and down-to-earth: life in the village is more comfortable and healthy, food is cheaper and better, a man is not surrounded by flatterers and scandal-mongers. Though village life is recommended for its virtue too, the emphasis is on homely comforts:

> El que mora en el aldea toma también muy gran gusto en gozar la brasa de las cepas, en escalentarse a la llama de los manojos, en hacer una tinada dellos, en comer de las uvas tempranas, en hacer arrope para casa, en colgar uvas para el invierno, en echar orujo a las palomas, en hacer una aguapié para los mozos, en guardar una tinaja aparte, en añejar alguna cuba de añejo, en presentar un cuero al amigo, en vender muy bien una cuba, en beber de su propia bodega, y sobre todo en no echar mano a la bolsa para enviar por vino a la taberna. (p. 72)[10]

A man may go about dressed as he pleases:

Es previlegio de aldea que cada vecino se pueda andar no solamente solo, mas aun sin capa y sin manteo, es a saber, una varilla en la mano, o puestos los pulgares en la cinta o vueltas las manos atrás. No pequeña sino grande es la libertad del aldea, en que si uno no quiere traer calzas, trae zaragüelles; si no quiere traer capa, ándase en cuerpo; si le congoja el jubón, afloja las aguejetas; [etc.] (pp. 74-5)

Sometimes the rhetoric may ring hollow, but the list of edible birds and beasts has an air of honest emotion:

El que mora en la aldea come palominos de verano, pichones caseros, tórtolas de jaula, palomas de encina, pollos de enero, patos de mayo, lavancos de río, lechones de medio mes, gazapos de julio, capones cebados, ansarones de pan, gallinas de cabe el gallo, liebres de dehesa, conejos de zarzal, perdigones de rastrojo, peñatas de lazo, codornices de reclamo, mirlas de baya y zorzales de vendimia. O no una, sino dos y tres veces gloriosa vida de aldea, pues los moradores della tienen cabritos para comer, ovejas para cecinar, [etc. etc.] (p. 89)

Guevara's remaining works were not to be so popular. *Aviso de privados* is a practical work, giving advice on the accomplishments and manners which find favour at Court. It is a humdrum work, conceived within far narrower horizons than (for example) Castiglione's *Cortegiano*. His *Libro de los inventores del arte de marear* is equally practical, being largely an account, drawn from Guevara's own experiences, of conditions at sea and how to make oneself comfortable on shipboard. He spares no realistic detail:

Es privilegio de galera, que las camas que allí se hicieren para los pasajeros y remeros no tengan pies ni cabez señalados, sino que se echen a do pudiesen y cupieren, y no como quisieren, es a saber, que a do una noche tuvieron los pies, tengan otra la cabeza: y si por haber merendado castañas o haber cenado rábanos el compañero se le soltare algún (ya me entendéis), has de hacer cuenta, hermano, que lo soñaste, y no decir que lo oíste.

Es privilegio de galera que todas las pulgas que saltan por las tablas, y todos los piojos que se crían en las costuras, y todas las chinches que están en los resquicios, sean comunes a todos, anden entre todos, y se repartan por todos, y se mantengan entre todos; y si alguno apelare deste privilegio, presumiendo de muy limpio y polido, desde agora le profetizo que si echa la mano al pescuezo y a la barjuleta, halle en el jubón más piojos que en la bolsa dineros.[11]

The book is racy and informative: possibly its author's liveliest work.

Guevara's last two works were purely religious: *Oratorio de religiosos y ejercicio de virtuosos* (Valladolid, 1542) and *Monte Calvario*

(Part I Salamanca, 1542; Part II 1549). Both found favour: *Oratorio* was printed eleven times in the sixteenth and seventeenth centuries, the first part of *Monte Calvario* eighteen times and the second nine times.

Guevara's books owed much of their success to the heady Ciceronian rhythms of his style. On every page of Guevara we find rhetorical accumulations of words and phrases, balanced antitheses and cadences, and rhyming cadences. As an example of both accumulation and balanced final cadences:

> ... puercos para salar, lanas para vestir, yeguas para criar, muletas para emponer, leche para comer, quesos para guardar; finalmente, tienen potros cerriles que vender en la feria y terneras gruesas que matar en las Pascuas. (*Menosprecio*, p. 89)

In this example we find balanced cadences with the added embellishment of assonance:

> Débese también mucho apartar de los hombres viciosos, holgazanes, mentirosos y maliciosos, de los cuales suelen estar los pueblos pequeños muy llenos; porque si las cortes de los príncipes están llenas de envidias, también en las aldeas hay muchas malicias. (*Menosprecio*, p. 63)

Guevara's pen seems on occasion to run away with him and his lists at times grow absurd. One of his tricks, a vacuous use of *aun* to round off a period, is particularly tiresome.

> O cuánto es honrado un bueno en una aldea, a do a porfía le presenta las guindas el que tiene guindalera, ... truchas el que tiene red, besugos quien va al mercado y aun hojaldres quien amasa el sábado. (*Menosprecio*, p. 90)

However, these are extreme cases; and though Guevara's style is always mannered the effect is usually more palatable. His contemporaries took great relish in it, and it is thought that English Euphuism has its origin in Guevara.

Not all his contemporaries took pleasure in his work. The indignation of one, Pedro de Rhúa, led him to write remonstratory letters to Guevara (beginning in 1540) and finally, in exasperation, to burst into print with *Cartas de Rhúa lector en Soria sobre las obras del Reverendísimo señor Obispo de Mondoñedo dirigidas al mesmo* (Burgos, 1549). Pedro de Rhúa, evidently a humanist of considerable learning, takes Guevara to task for both his style and his invention of spurious authorities in his epistles and historical works. He begins mildly enough, purporting to be quoting the opinion of others on Guevara's style and his frequently expressed pride of birth:

> ... unos la copia llamaban lujuria o lozanía de palabras; otros al ornato notaban por afectación; otros, los matices de las figuras, como

> son contenciones, distribuciones, exposiciones, repeticiones, artículos, miembros, contrarios, y los otros primores del bien hablar de que muy a menudo usa Vuestra Señoría, les parecían ejemplos de quien lee los preejercitamentos de Aftonio o el cuarto de la retórica *ad Herennium*; otros decían que tan frecuentes figuras acedaban toda la oración. A unos les era odiosa la muy repitida conmemoración de su noble y antigua prosapia como arrogancia . . . (f. 4ᵛ)

In a later letter Rhúa attacks Guevara's airy display of erudition:

> Escrebí a Vuestra Señoría que entre otras cosas que en sus obras culpaban los lectores es una la más fea e intolerable que puede caer en escritor de autoridad, como Vuestra Señoría lo es: y es que da fábulas por historias y ficciones proprias por narraciones ajenas; y alega autores que no lo dicen, o lo dicen de otra manera, o son tales que no los hallarán sino *in afanis* . . . y el lector, si es idiota es engañado, y si es diligente pierde el tiempo . . . (f. 57ᵛ)

Guevara's reply to the charges does not suggest that he was much put out.

> . . . son muy pocas las cosas que ha notado en mis obrillas y serán sus avisos para remirar lo hecho y enmendar lo venidero. Como, señor, sabéis, son tan varios los escritores en esta arte de humanidad que fuera de las letras divinas no hay que afirmar ni que negar en ninguna dellas; y para decir la verdad, a muy pocas dellas creo más de tomar en ellas un pasatiempo . . . No haga vuestra merced hincapié en historias gentiles y profanas, pues no tenemos más certinidad que digan verdad unos que otros . . . (f. 54ʳ)

It is hard to know what to make of Guevara. He was undoubtedly pious: his life as well as his works give evidence of that. Yet he was willing to lie (his inventions deserve no other word). He had erudition but not the scholar's conscience which should go with it. Are we to put his aberrations down to a sense of humour? This is at least as satisfactory as the allegation that Guevara, being a younger son and so unable to achieve glory and riches, tried to make up for his disappointments by his writings.

> Su obrar y su escribir serán en adelante un esfuerzo continuo para llenar la vasta oquedad de su aspiración, buscando en las letras lo que otros alcanzaban con las armas, la riqueza y el poderío . . .[12]

His inflated style and air of omniscience certainly suggest self-importance; but if indeed he envied power, military glory, or wealth, there had been nothing to prevent him joining the many *segundones* who sailed for America; and the Church was no bad road to influence and even wealth if he had cared to exploit it. Speculation about Guevara's secret dreams and frustrations is fruitless. What stares us in the face is his determination to make his mark as a man of letters; and if we remember that (in spite of distinguished exceptions) among men of his class letters were not given great importance, Guevara's pedantry may then seem to be a counter-affirmation of the dignity of letters in the face of a Philistine majority. When thinking of Guevara's court circle we should put men like Garcilaso de la Vega out of our minds: a man like Alonso Enríquez de Guzmán is probably much more representative. In his very readable memoirs he reveals himself as a man obsessed with three things: lineage, honours, money. He quotes some scraps of Latin, once quotes a line by Boscán, and includes some execrable verse by himself; but it is obvious that literature and learning played no part in his life. Faced with men like these Guevara's attitude becomes more comprehensible. In a society which in general still prized arms above letters, Guevara affirmed his own allegiance in these words:

> . . . mas yo loo y nunca acabaré de loar, no a los que hallaron armas para emprender guerra, sino a los que buscaron letras para deprender ciencia. ¡Cuánta diferencia vaya de mojar la péñola en la tinta a teñir la lanza en la sangre, y de estar rodeado de libros o estar cargado de armas, de estudiar cómo cada uno ha de vivir o andar a saltear en la guerra para a su prójimo matar!
>
> No hay ninguno de tan vano juicio que no loe más los ejercicios de la ciencia que no los bullicios de la guerra, porque, al fin fin, el que deprende cosas de guerras no deprende sino cómo a los otros ha de matar y el que deprende ciencia no deprende sino cómo él y los otros han de vivir.[13]

Probably Rhúa was not the only one to be outraged by Guevara's cavalier ways. The important Erasmian group, dedicated to truthfulness in literature and a plain style, must have shared Rhúa's sense of outrage, since Guevara would have offended them as much by his style as by his frivolity (not to say his lies). Erasmus favoured a plain and clear style and opposed the Ciceronian flourishes affected by many humanists. He set an attractive example of the first in his own writings, but in addition, not content with passivity, carried the war into the other camp with his satirical dialogue *Ciceronianus*. Guevara's style, at its most florid, is a parody of Cicero; but it reflects a naïve ambition to emulate the most revered of Latin stylists. There does not appear to have been an open stylistic war in Spain between Ciceronians and anti-Ciceronians, as there was in some other countries, but the antagonism was there. Guevara may stand for one party; the Erasmian literary ideal is to be seen in *Diálogo de la lengua* by Juan de Valdés, which was written probably in 1535 (though not printed until 1736).[14]

Valdés stands for morality and verisimilitude in fiction and for plainness in style.

> El estilo que tengo me es natural, y sin afetación ninguna escribo como hablo, solamente tengo cuidado de usar vocablos que sinifiquen bien lo que quiero decir, y dígolo cuanto más llanamente me es posible, porque a mi parecer en ninguna lengua stá bien el afetación. (p. 154)

Everything he says of style is an elaboration of this central doctrine, which he applies to poetry no less than to prose.

> Por buenas [coplas] tengo las que tienen buena y clara sentencia, buenos vocablos, acomodados a ella, buen estilo, sin superfluidad de estilo . . . (p. 166)

For examples of good style he appeals to the *refranes*, on the ground that the genius of Castilian is *vulgar*. One of his interlocutors, Pacheco, interrupts enthusiastically to say that he has often thought of compiling a book of Spanish proverbs

> como uno que diz que Erasmo ha hecho en la latina, alegando todos los refranes que hallase y declarándolos lo menos mal que supiese, porque he pensado que en ello haría un señalado servicio a la lengua castellana. (p 15)

When asked if he approves of the spelling *l'arca*, *l'alma*, etc., Valdés replies:

> No me parecería mal si se usase, pero como no se usa yo por mí no lo osaría decir ni escribir. (p. 45)

Valdés the Erasmian appealed in religious matters to personal experience and to commonsense as his criteria. Regarding language we find him expressing an analogous doctrine: for his criterion he takes, not a book with all its artificialities of style, but examples of plain spoken Spanish. Juan's work, religious and literary, is all of a piece, the product of a sensitively empirical and toughly independent mind.

His own style has all the vividness of good colloquial Castilian. When the other speakers, who are discussing style, come upon Valdés, one of them cries:

> Pues habemos cogido y prendado a Valdés, aun no le dejemos de ninguna manera sin que primero le examinemos hasta el postrer pelo. (p. 18)

Valdés submits to their interrogation good-humouredly:

> Ora sus, vedme aquí más obediente que un fraile descalzo cuando es convidado para algún banquete. (p. 20)

On another occasion:

> Asperáos un poco, que aún os queda la cola por desollar. (p. 192)

Reference was made earlier to Don Alonso Enríquez de Guzmán. His presence is a salutary reminder that the Renaissance in Spain (as elsewhere, with the possible exception of Italy) touched only the surface of society. How could it not, when that society was composed principally of priests, peasants, and warriors? Enríquez de Guzmán showed no interest in literature or learning. He was pious, but his piety was not of the kind to affect his life: the Spanish Erasmians belonged to another moral universe, of which Enríquez de Guzmán gives no sign of having heard. He had a passionate concern for his honour, but saw nothing dishonourable in theft when penniless. His account of his quarrelsome and violent career in Spain, Flanders, and Peru gives us a deeper insight into the realities of his age than all that which is studied as 'literature'. Enríquez de Guzmán is a warning to the literary historian not to get his categories mixed: literature is about life but must not be confused with it.

Some of the most vigorous writing of the sixteenth century—and the next—is to be found among the historians, such as (to name only a few): Gonzalo Fernández de Oviedo (1478-1557), *De la natural historia de las Indias* (Toledo, 1526) and *La historia general de las Indias* (Seville, 1535); Bernal Díaz del Castillo (1492-1581), *Historia verdadera de la conquista de la Nueva España* (Madrid, 1632); Diego Hurtado de Mendoza (1503-75), *Guerra de Granada* (Lisbon, 1627); Francisco López de Gómara (1512-72?), *La historia de las Indias y conquista de México* (Saragossa, 1552); Francisco Cervantes de Salazar (1514?-75), *Crónica de la Nueva España* (New York, 1914).

NOTES

1. L. Hanke, *Aristotle and the American Indians* (London, 1959), p. 57.
2. Américo Castro, *De la edad conflictiva*, 2nd ed. (Madrid, 1963). See a critique of Castro's thesis by A. A. Parker in *Renaissance Quarterly* (1968).
3. See R. O. Jones, 'An Encina Manuscript', *BHS* (1961), 229-37.
4. See Peter Russell, 'Arms versus Letters: Towards a Definition of Spanish Fifteenth-Century Humanism' in *Aspects of the Renaissance. A Symposium*, ed. A. R. Lewis (Austin and London, 1967), pp. 47-58.
5. There is a modern edition edited by Dámaso Alonso (Madrid, 1932).
6. M. de la Pinta Llorente and J. M. de Palacio, *Procesos inquisitoriales contra la familia judía de Juan Luis Vives* (Madrid, 1964).
7. The best editions of Alfonso's two dialogues are those by J. F. Montesinos in Clásicos castellanos 89, 96; my references to the 1946 edition of *Roma* and the 1947 edition of *Mercurio*.
8. *Libro áureo*, ed. Foulché-Delbosc, *RH* (1929).

9. *Epístolas familiares*, ed. J. M. de Cossío (Madrid, 1950), I, 220-1.
10. *Menosprecio . . .*, ed. M. Martínez de Burgos, CC 29 (Madrid; my refs. to 1952 ed.), p. 72.
11. Quoted from R. Costes, *Antonio de Guevara. Son Oeuvre* (Bordeaux, 1926), p. 123.
12. A. Castro, *Semblanzas y estudios españoles* (Princeton, 1956), p. 55.
13. *Reloj de príncipes*, ed. A. Rosenblat (Madrid, 1936), p. 109.
14. ed. Montesinos, CC 86 (Madrid; my refs. to 1946 ed.).

Chapter 2

THE RENAISSANCE IN SPAIN: II

AS REGARDS POETRY, the European literary Renaissance meant more than anything else the discovery of Petrarch—the Petrarch of the *Canzoniere*—and his successors. Although from early in the fifteenth century individual Spanish poets had been aware of and sometimes intensely interested in the poetry of Petrarch (Santillana, for example), that poetry had not markedly affected Castilian poetry either in form or content (Santillana's sonnets being a striking exception). The newer Italian poetry was not to be felt as a living influence until the third decade of the sixteenth century. Boscán tells the story in his dedication to the duquesa de Soma prefixed to the second book of his poems published in 1543.

> Porque estando un día en Granada con el Navagero, el cual por haber sido varón tan celebrado en nuestros días he querido aquí nombralle a vuestra señoría, tratando con él en cosas de ingenio y de letras y especialmente en las variedades de muchas lenguas, me dijo por qué no probaba en lengua castellana sonetos y otras artes de trobas usadas por los buenos autores de Italia, y no solamente me lo dijo así livianamente, mas aún me rogó que lo hiciese. Partíme pocos días después para mi casa, y con la largueza y soledad del camino discurriendo por diversas cosas, fui a dar muchas veces en lo que el Navagero me había dicho. Y así comencé a tentar este género de verso, en el cual al principio hallé alguna dificultad por ser muy artificioso y tener muchas particularidades diferentes del nuestro. Pero después, pareciéndome quizá con el amor de las cosas proprias que esto comenzaba a sucederme bien, fui poco a poco metiéndome con calor en ello. Mas esto no bastara a hacerme pasar muy adelante si Garcilaso con su juicio, el cual no solamente en mi opinión mas en la de todo el mundo ha sido tenido por regla cierta, no me confirmara en esta mi demanda.[1]

This encounter took place in 1526 when Andrea Navagero, poet and classical scholar, was present, as Venetian ambassador, at Charles V's triumphal entry into Granada. Navagero's great prestige as a man of letters doubtless made his encouragement the more persuasive. Garcilaso, in his enthusiasm for the new literary experience which Italy afforded, was led to reject earlier Spanish literature root and branch. In a prefatory letter written for Boscán's translation of Castiglione's *Il Cortegiano* (Barcelona, 1534) he wrote:

> Y también tengo por muy principal el beneficio que se hace a la lengua castellana en poner en ella cosas que merezcan ser leídas, porque yo no sé qué desventura ha sido siempre la nuestra, que apenas ha nadie escrito en nuestra lengua sino lo que se pudiera muy bien escusar . . .[2]

The precise scope of Garcilaso's words cannot now be determined, but it is reasonable to suppose that he was referring amongst other things to that poetry in traditional Spanish metres which both he and Boscán turned their backs on. Before the extent and quality of this poetic revolution can be appreciated, we must look again at the poetry which the revolutionaries now felt to be superseded.

The change of feeling was relatively recent and sudden. In 1496 Juan del Encina wrote in the 'Arte de poesía castellana' with which his *Cancionero* opens:

> . . . porque según dice el dotísimo maestro Antonio de Lebrixa, aquél que desterró de nuestra España los barbarismos que en la lengua latina se habían criado, una de las causas que le movieron a hacer arte de romance fue que creía nuestra lengua estar agora más empinada y polida que jamás estuvo, de donde más se podía temer el decendimiento que la subida; y así yo por esta mesma razón creyendo nunca haber estado tan puesta en la cumbre nuestra poesía y manera de trobar, parecióme ser cosa muy provechosa poner en arte y encerrarla debaxo de ciertas leyes y reglas, porque ninguna antigüedad de tiempos le pueda traer olvido.[3]

The words have an arrogant ring: Encina writes with the assurance of a poet within a secure tradition, but his words—addressed to the young prince Don Juan—also reflect the cultural self-centredness of a recently unified country aware of her strength and ready for empire. Encina's words refer to a wide range of theme and style. Fifteenth-century doctrinal poetry is at best a sober pleasure, but as regards the Castilian courtly love-lyric something of Encina's arrogance is justified, for within the narrow conventions of that lyric were written some of the most beautiful and intense poems in the language.

The Castilian courtly love-lyric, a late outgrowth of the European literature of courtly love, formed part of the ritual of gallantry that was an important part of life at Court. Many of the poems written in this tradition are as pallid and jejune as we might expect from this account of their origin, but many—surprisingly numerous—have an obsessive intensity which can still startle. In the work of these Castilian poets of the late fifteenth century we find a narrowing and an intensification of the European courtly-love tradition. They used an extraordinarily small vocabulary and an extraordinarily narrow range of rhetorical devices, these being chiefly three: oxymoron, antithesis, and polyptoton (repetition of a word or forms of a word), all three expressive of the tormented obsession of the lover, helpless in the grip of contradictions, willing his own martyrdom but yearning for release, thrown from extreme to extreme of joy and pain, hope and despair. The rhetorical devices are not empty: they express the central experience of this kind of love.

The courtly lyric brought to this degree of narrow intensity in the last decades of the fifteenth century was maintained at this level in the early sixteenth by younger men like Garci Sánchez de Badajoz, the story of whose love-induced madness (for which he appears to have been for a time in chains) gave him a romantic aura similar to that which clung to the fourteenth-century poet Macías. The poetry of this tradition has scarcely any individualised traits: impersonality is its hallmark. Even in those poems where Garci Sánchez seems to allude to his imprisonment it is difficult to claim a sense of personality for his poetry.

> Como el que en hierro ha estado
> y después se vee suelto,
> y se halla tan atado
> para andar, que aprisionado
> estaba más desenvuelto:
> así yo, que os he mirado,
> soy tan vuestro, tan no mío,
> tan sujeto a os adorar,
> que aunque me fuese tornado
> mi franco libre albedrío,
> no podré libre quedar.[4]

The narrow virtuosity of this kind of poetry was manifestly a very self-conscious art, deliberately cultivated.[5]

This was not the only or even the dominant poetic mode of the opening years of the sixteenth century. There were other kinds of verse: moralistic, religious, and allegorical verse abounded. All three were combined in one compilation which was evidently popular in the early years of the century: Juan del Encina's *Cancionero*, first published at Salamanca in 1496 and reprinted in 1501 (Seville), 1505 (Burgos), 1507 and 1509 (Salamanca), and 1516 (Saragossa). The taste for Encina's poetry was not exhausted by this: in 1521 he published his *Tribagia*, a verse-account of his pilgrimage to the Holy Land, written in *arte mayor*: an obviously deeply-felt work whose pedestrian plod testifies all too clearly to Encina's almost total loss of his poetic powers coincident with his taking Holy Orders. However, as so often, literary history disconcerts the literary critic: this poem was to be Encina's longest-lasting claim to fame: long after Encina's other verse was forgotten, *Tribagia* was reprinted in 1606, 1608, 1748, and 1786.

Encina's lyric poetry has retained its appeal, and many of his poems, especially those in which he captures something of the freshness of folk-song, are among the most delightful of the period. But he is disappointingly dull in his more serious verse: his *Triunfo de la fama*, *Triunfo del Amor*, his to-order religious verse (all these in his *Cancionero*), the *Tragedia trobada* written in 1497 on the death of Prince Don Juan, *Tribagia*, and so on. Amongst his most attractive works are his nonsense poems, the famous *Juicio* and *Almoneda* and even more famous *Disparates*. Taking his work as a whole, Encina was somewhat a better musician than poet: the sixty-one pieces by him preserved in the so-called *Cancionero musical de Palacio* are inventive and often moving.[6]

Among the more interesting minor poets of the period was Pedro Manuel Jiménez de Urrea (1486?-1535?), an Aragonese nobleman whose *Cancionero* (Logroño, 1513) contains some good poems in traditional style and some tentative imitations of Petrarch.

This then was the poetry on which a youth born at the beginning of the sixteenth century was brought up. One of the major literary events of his life would be the publication of the *Cancionero general* (Valencia, 1511), a massive compilation of predominantly fifteenth-century poetry of all kinds: a representative anthology which stands as a majestic monument both to its compiler, Hernando del Castillo (otherwise unknown to us), and to the high quality of printing in Spain. The work was clearly an immediate commercial success. A revised edition (with additions and deletions) was brought out in 1514 (Valencia). This was reprinted in 1517 (Toledo), 1520 (Toledo), and 1527 (Toledo), with just one poem added in this last edition. A considerably revised new edition appeared in 1535 (Seville); a number of litanies of love and other love-poems using the language of religion were now cut out and a considerable number of new poems (mainly religious, mainly pedestrian) were added. This version was reprinted in 1540 (Seville). A considerably changed new edition was printed in Antwerp in 1557 and reprinted there in 1573. The editors of the successive editions made attempts to bring the *Cancionero general* up to date by including recent work, but it retained its fundamentally fifteenth-century stamp; so that we have the curious phenomenon that for the greater part of the sixteenth century the best-known single collection of poetry was a compilation of mainly fifteenth-century work. Generations of poetry-readers were brought up on it. It helped to ensure that the *cancionero* lyric did not die, but survived to flower again in the seventeenth century.

From the *Cancionero general* were extracted other collections, in the main collections of love-poetry. There was a notorious exception, the celebrated *Cancionero de obras de burlas provocantes a risa* (Valencia, 1519), containing the section of *obras de burlas* printed in the *Cancionero general* (including the indecent and diverting 'Pleito del manto'), to which was added what at least in conception is one of the most ingenious poems in the language: the *Carajicomedia*, whose (doubtless pseudonymous) author 'fray Bugeo Montesino' gives a satirical account of the erotic career and final downfall of Diego Fajardo of Guadalajara, the whole being written in an excellent parody of the style of Mena's *Trescientas*, complete with erudite notes (in imitation of Hernán Núñez's edition of Seville, 1499) amplifying with solemn detail the account of Diego Fajardo's scabrous progress. Pornography is not what it was. The poem remains unrivalled.[7]

Poetry circulated more widely in humbler publications: the *pliegos sueltos* or chap-books (printed sheets normally folded twice to make a booklet of four leaves) which were printed in thousands and brought print within the reach of those who could not afford books. In the *pliegos* were reprinted poems of all kinds from the larger compilations, but also *romances*, folk-songs, etc., from other sources, including oral tradition. *Pliegos* were probably bought mostly by the less well off and the less literate; but they were not despised by men of greater learning and social standing: many were bought (for example) by the son of Columbus, Fernando Colón, whose lists of his purchases are a valuable source of bibliographical evidence for works which have long since vanished.[8] Some poets, and good ones, were printed only in the *pliegos*: one such is Rodrigo de Reinosa, of whose works no collected edition has yet been published, no doubt because of the indecency of some of them.[9]

The *pliegos* testify to the existence of a widespread popular taste for verse of all kinds.

> A fair quantity of what may justifiably be described as good poetry, lyrical, narrative, or satirical, was reprinted with the plebeian poems . . . We can thus learn that some of the best poetry composed in Golden Age Spain appealed to the ignorant as well as to the educated and cultured . . . There was a smaller gap—in some things—between the lettered and the ignorant than exists today.[10]

The *pliegos* were, then, in our period a powerful force for continuity. The earliest *pliegos* date from before 1510; *pliegos* continued to be produced in large numbers for the next four centuries, and some early poetry was still being printed in this form until relatively recently.

It is against this background that the poetic revolution initiated by Boscán must be seen. His and Garcilaso's innovations cannot be fully felt except by contrast with the previous state of Spanish poetry. The innovations provide, indeed, a striking contrast in a number of respects. The rhetorical and lexical range of the new poetry is far greater than that of the old. In love-poetry, Petrarch and the Italian Petrarchans being now the dominant influence, Petrarch's characteristic use of nature as the source of much of his imagery and as a backdrop for his self-analysis is imitated by Garcilaso and Boscán. This had an immensely liberating effect on the poets' imagination: the universe becomes their stage. By contrast, the poetry of their predecessors is claustrophobic in atmosphere. The new poetry is further enriched by the influence of the major Latin poets, above all Virgil and Horace. This vast enlargement of the language of poetry permitted deeper and more subtle exploration of states of mind and conduced to a more sensitive awareness of the outside world. The result is a poetry richer in texture and colour and so capable of more vivid sensorial effects, and capable too of greater conceptual complexity.

Juan Boscán Almugáver (b.1487-92, d.1542) was born into a family which belonged to what may be called the merchant aristocracy of Barcelona and himself used the title of *caballero*. As a youth he became *ayo*, or companion and moral tutor, to the young Don Fernando, the future duque de Alba. His life was passed almost entirely in court circles, where Boscán seems to have been considered a model of courtly accomplishment. It was hence entirely appropriate that Garcilaso should send Boscán a copy of Castiglione's *Cortegiano* with the suggestion that he translate it into Spanish. Boscán's excellent version duly appeared in 1534 (Barcelona) with Garcilaso's letter to Doña Gerónima Palova de Almogávar in which he praises his friend's skill and style:

> Guardó una cosa en la lengua castellana que muy pocos la han alcanzado, que fue huir del afetación sin dar consigo en ninguna sequedad, y con gran limpieza de estilo usó de términos muy cortesanos y muy admitidos de los buenos oídos, y no nuevos ni al parecer desusados de la gente. Fue demás desto muy fiel tradutor, porque no se ató al rigor de la letra, como hacen algunos, sino a la verdad de las sentencias, y por differentes caminos puso en esta lengua toda la fuerza y el ornamento de la otra, y así lo dejó todo tan en su punto como lo halló, y hallólo tal que con poco trabajo podrían los defensores deste libro responder a los que quisiesen tachar alguna cosa dél.[11]

Although he did not live to see his poetry published, Boscán arranged it for the press, dividing it into three books. The first consists of his poetry in the traditional Castilian metres (but not quite all he wrote in this manner: some has been printed subsequently[12]). At its best this verse is quite accomplished, as this *villancico* shows.

Si no os hubiera mirado,
 no penara,
pero tampoco os mirara.

Veros harto mal ha sido;
mas no veros peor fuera;
no quedara tan perdido,
pero mucho más perdiera.
¿Qué viera aquél que no os viera?
 ¿Cuál quedara,
señora, si no os mirara? (p.10)

Accomplished but without great distinction: the verdict is inevitable. He is better in the shorter pieces than in the longer: his talents tended always to run to diffuseness.

As we have seen, Boscán was persuaded to imitate Italian poetry in 1526. To do this, he had to learn to use the Italian hendecasyllable: an eleven-syllable line in which the accent falls normally on the second, sixth, and tenth syllables. He was perhaps assisted by his familiarity with the eleven-syllable Provençal line which was normal in Catalan lyric poetry (with a different accentuation, however, from the Italian line).

Boscán's verse never showed the suppleness of Garcilaso's. All the same, some of his sonnets have an awkward strength which can be impressive. The following sonnet (LXXXIV) shows an acute self-awareness expressed in a well-controlled flow of logically related images which describe the lover acceding to his own self-delusion.

Levanta el desear el pensamiento
con tal hervor, que todo'l mundo es mío.
Vuelven en seso todo el desvarío
la fuerza y la verdad del sentimiento.

Mi corazón do ama es tan atento,
que'l bien y el mal yo mismo me le crío,
tanto, que ya por puro amor confío
de sostener mis torres en el viento.

Cuanto entra en mí se muda todo luego
en el placer que del amor influye;
mi bien fingido pasa por verdad.

Esto no es mucho, pues que traigo fuego,
que cuanto toma luego lo destruye
y lo convierte en otra calidad.

Certain other sonnets—for example, 'Como aquel que en soñar gusto recibe' (CV), 'Como el patrón que en golfo navegando' (CVII)—exhibit the same qualities of insight into self, flashes of impressive imagery, and awkward articulation. Many of Boscán's best sonnets are in fact reworkings of sonnets by others: Petrarch, Ausias March, on at least one occasion Bembo; as if Boscán needed another's scaffolding. Left to himself, his imagination often fails in its flight and falls into bathos. He shows his strength and weakness in the sonnet 'Antes terné qué cante blandamente', in which he tells how the joys of love inspire his song. The sextet reads:

Yo cantaré conforme a l'avecilla,
que canta así a la sombra d'algún ramo,
que'l caminante olvida su camino,
quedando trasportado por oílla.
Así yo de ver quien me ama y a quien amo,
en mi cantar terné gozo contino.

The image of the singing bird is evocative, beautiful, and appropriate; the dull banality of the last two lines represents a collapse of imagination to which Boscán was peculiarly prone.

Another of his besetting faults is diffuseness, less evident in his sonnets (naturally) than in his longer poems. His *canciones* are for this reason generally broken-backed. His long *Leandro* (2,793 lines long), based on Musaeus's *Hero and Leander*, is enfeebled by diffuseness and impertinent interpolation. Even the *Octava rima,* which begins so promisingly, finally suffers the same fate. Bembo's elegant *Stanze* on which it is based are diluted intolerably (fifty octaves become 135). The poem begins well, with some of Boscán's best controlled lines:

En el lumbroso y fértil Oriente,
adonde más el cielo stá templado,
vive una sosegada y dulce gente,
la cual en solo amar pone'l cuidado.
Esta jamás padece otro acidente,
sino es aquél que amores han causado.
Aquí goberna, y siempre gobernó,
aquella reina que'n la mar nació.

Boscán could not keep this up: freed from the discipline of translation or close imitation his mind went woolgathering.

One of his most successful pieces is the least poetic: his verse epistle to Don Diego Hurtado de Mendoza, in which he describes his way of life, his marriage, and his ideals. It is not great poetry, but it is felicitously expressed and contains many passages striking for their pithiness.

In 1542 Boscán arranged for the publication of his poetry but died before printing was complete. His widow, Doña Ana Girón de Rebolledo, took up the task and in 1543 there appeared, printed by Carles Amorós of Barcelona, one of the most important volumes in Spanish literature: *Las obras de Boscán y algunas de Garcilasso de la Vega repartidas en cuatro libros*. The fourth book consisted of the work of Garcilaso, whose papers had on his death been entrusted to Boscán. The book, frequently reprinted, became the companion of every literate Spaniard of sensibility. Boscán and Garcilaso continued for years to be printed together, but towards 1570 the desirability of reprinting Garcilaso separately became evident. He had already acquired the status of a classic.

Garcilaso de la Vega was born, into one of the noblest Spanish families, in Toledo in (probably) 1501. He grew up at the royal Court. He became *contino* (member of the Court) of Charles V in 1520. Most of the rest of his life was to be spent in Charles's service. He served in numerous military campaigns, including the abortive expedition for the relief of Rhodes in 1522 and the Tunis campaign of 1535.

In 1525 he married. In 1526 he met Isabel Freyre, a Portuguese lady-in-waiting to the new Queen Isabel. Isabel Freyre was to be the subject of his finest love-poetry.

Garcilaso aroused the anger of the emperor in 1532 by attending the unauthorised marriage of a nephew without Charles's permission. He was first banished to an island on the Danube, but this was soon commuted to banishment at Naples: banishment, as lieutenant of the newly-appointed viceroy Don Pedro de Toledo, in a beautiful city which was a capital in its own right and one of the most flourishing centres of Italian humanistic and literary culture. There Garcilaso knew Spanish humanists such as Juan de Valdés, and Italians of the stature of Luigi Tansillo and Bernardo Tasso. Garcilaso was an admired member of the Neapolitan literary circles—and admired even further afield: he exchanged letters of mutual admiration with Pietro Bembo, the arbiter of Italian literary elegance in those years.

During the invasion of France in 1536 Garcilaso received his death wound in an attack on a fortified position at Le Muy on 19 September. He died in Nice on 13 or 14 October 1536.

He did not leave a great deal of poetry; no doubt some of his work is lost. What has survived consists of three eclogues, five *canciones*, two elegies (one of them an epistle to Boscán), another verse epistle to Boscán, thirty-eight sonnets (forty if we accept two attributed to him in one manuscript), and some verses in traditional Castilian metres. These last are of slight interest; some of them belong to the ritual of courtly badinage, an inheritance from the Middle Ages, which is one of the most tiresome features of the Renaissance.[13]

Garcilaso's most important work is in the new 'Italian' style. Both his style and his experience were gradually enriched as he assimilated the influence of the major Latin poets and of the Italians from Petrarch down to Sannazaro, Bernardo Tasso, and others of Garcilaso's own day. His eclogues are Garcilaso's most important achievement. Eclogue II is thought to be the first in chronological order, begun probably in 1533. It is a long poem of 1,885 lines, and in dialogue. It presents problems, of which the chief is the most basic of all: what is it about? Though it is a view which adds to rather than diminishes the problems, the love-struck shepherd Albanio who goes mad through grief is still sometimes taken to represent Garcilaso's friend and patron, the duque de Alba: hardly (in view of the humiliations suffered by Albanio) a flattering portrait to offer a grandee of Spain. Rather than impose an arbitrary interpretation we should try to discover the poem's 'meaning' from its internal structure, viewed in the light of whatever external evidence is available (and deemed relevant).

The poem concerns the misfortunes of the shepherd Albanio who, having loved the shepherdess Camila since childhood, is abandoned by her when he confesses his love openly. Meeting her again, he attempts to detain her by force and, when she escapes, loses his reason in his excess of grief. He attempts suicide but is restrained and tied up by his fellow-shepherds Salicio and Nemoroso. Nemoroso now tells of his own experience of love and how he was cured of a similar fit of 'amor insano' by the sage Severo, whose vision of the love and martial exploits (seen depicted on an urn) of the young Don Fernando de Toledo —to whom Fray Severo Varini was tutor in real life—he also tells.

The theme of the poem is love manifested and experienced in a variety of ways. The story, such as it is, concerns Albanio; but Nemoroso's account of the duke constitutes a third of the eclogue. Unless the poem is a chaos, we must be expected to seek some relationship between these two themes.

Albanio's plight seems clear, but it is helpful to approach it through some of Garcilaso's earlier poetry. His first three *canciones* were written before 1532. The first two, though expressive, fluent, and at times moving, are all the same relatively slight works which lack the vigour both of Garcilaso's later work and of Petrarch, their model. The third shows a more active imagination and touches deeper levels of feeling, but the poem remains a lover's complaint circumscribed by a narrow tradition. The rough vehemence of the fourth *canción* comes as a shock after the mellifluousness of its predecessors. Something deeper was at work in the poet. The poem describes a battle between reason and appetite or sensuality—a battle won by appetite, whose victory brings not relief but further suffering to the lover. The *canción* (which suggests the influence of Ausias March) can be labelled 'medieval' and perhaps conventional: certainly it has literary antecedents. But it has also the ring of authenticity: pretty certainly it expresses some deep emotional crisis in Garcilaso: a revulsion of feeling, however provoked, which made his former experience of love distasteful. The torment of mind of the sensual lover as described in *Canción* IV seems to be the very experience described by Albanio in Eclogue II. In the *canción* Garcilaso writes of the victory of appetite:

Corromperse
sentí el sosiego y libertad pasada,
y el mal de que muriendo estó engendrarse,
y en tierra sus raíces ahondarse
tanto cuanto su cima levantada
sobre cualquier altura hace verse;
el fruto que d'aquí suele cogerse
mil es amargo, alguna vez sabroso,
mas mortífero siempre y ponzoñoso. (72-80)

It is instructive to compare these lines with Albanio's description of how his love changed from childlike affection to something different:

basta saber que aquesta tan sencilla
y tan pura amistad quiso mi hado
en diferente especie convertilla,
  en un amor tan fuerte y tan sobrado
y en un desasosiego no creíble
tal que no me conosco de trocado.
  El placer de miralla con terrible
y fiero desear sentí mesclarse.
que siempre me llevaba a lo imposible;
  la pena de su ausencia vi mudarse,
no en pena, no en congoja, en cruda muerte
y en un eterno el alma atormentarse. (314-25)

Camila later accuses him thus:

¿Tú no violaste nuestra compañía,
quiriéndola torcer por el camino
que de la vida honesta se desvía? (817-19)

She eludes Albanio's rough attempts to detain her, and in his grief he goes out of his mind, believing that he has lost his body, which he believes he discovers at the bottom of a pool. In contrast with the general Italianate tone of the poem, he lapses into popular speech, which may be intended to express through stylistic discontinuity his deranged state. Salicio laments the change in him:

> Estraño enjemplo es ver en qué ha parado
> este gentil mancebo, Nemoroso,
> ya a nosotros, que l'hemos más tratado,
> manso, cuerdo, agradable, virtüoso,
> sufrido, conversable, buen amigo,
> y con un alto ingenio, gran reposo. (901-6)

Albanio's once noble mind has been overthrown by an ignoble desire. In dramatising his subject Garcilaso seems to be drawing an analogy between disordered values and disordered wits. Nemoroso tells how he was cured of a similar 'amor insano' by Severo:

> Tras esto luego se me presentaba,
> sin antojos delante, la vileza
> de lo que antes ardiendo deseaba.
> Así curó mi mal, con tal destreza,
> el sabio viejo, como t'he contado,
> que volvió el alma a su naturaleza
> y soltó el corazón aherrojado. (1122-8)

Albanio's distemper springs from a love which Camila seems to characterise as carnal. Albanio is certainly not held up for our admiration, but the poem does not turn away from all human love, only (it seems) from a concupiscent love which overthrows reason, breeds discord and even violence, and ends in unhappiness. A similar pattern of experience is described for us in one of the most influential works of the period, one which Garcilaso admired and which he induced Boscán to translate: Castiglione's *Il Cortegiano*. In Book IV of this civilised dialogue concerning the perfect courtier, one of the interlocutors is Pietro Bembo, author of a Neoplatonic treatise on love, *Gli Asolani*, whose main lines he follows in *Il Cortegiano*. Bembo contrasts the serenity of the 'spiritual' Neoplatonic lover with the torments of the sensual lover.[14]

> . . . porque no solamente en el cabo, mas aun en el principo y en el medio de este amor, nunca otra cosa se siente sino afanes, tormentos, dolores, adversidades, sobresaltos y fatigas; de manera que el andar ordinariamente amarillo y afligido en continas lágrimas y sospiros, el estar triste, el callar siempre o quejarse, el desear la muerte, y, en fin, el vivir en estrema miseria y desventura, son las puras calidades que se dicen ser proprias de los enamorados.[15]

Young men are easily misled by the senses, but age brings wisdom, and the wise courtier will choose the other path:

> Y así, con estas consideraciones, apártese el amor del ciego juicio de la sensualidad y goce con los ojos aquel resplandor, aquella gracia, aquellas centellas de amor, la risa, los ademanes, y todos los otros dulces y sabrosos aderezos de la hermosura. (p. 383)

Treading thus the path of true love:

> desta manera será nuestro Cortesano viejo fuera de todas aquellas miserias y fatigas que suelen casi siempre sentir los mozos, y así no sentirá celos, ni sospechas, ni desabrimientos, ni iras, no desesperaciones, ni otras mil locuras llenas de rabia, con las cuales muchas veces llegan las enamorados locos a tanto desatino que algunos no sólo ponen las manos en sus amigos maltratándolas feamente mas aun a sí mismos quitan la vida. (p. 388)

In all this the features of Albanio can be recognised. The vocabulary he employs—'deseo, pena, sufrir, muerte, congoja, tormento'—relates him instantly with the world of fifteenth-century *courtoisie* expressed in the *cancioneros*, in whose mould he is cast.

The long eulogy of the duque de Alba depicts the duke active in love and war. The account of his love by no means stresses its spirituality: perhaps he is to be excused by Bembo's exception in favour of youth (he was six years younger than Garcilaso):

> aunque el amor que reina en la sensualidad sea en toda edad malo, todavía en los mozos tiene muy gran desculpa, y quizá en alguna manera es permitido. (p. 374)

What, however, the duke does exhibit is discipline and purpose in contrast to the life of Albanio. Perhaps in this contrast is the episode's point: to depict love allied to reason, and strength tempered by love. The eulogy of the duke's harmonious life is prefaced by some of Garcilaso's loveliest lines, spoken by Salicio:

> Nuestro ganado pace, el viento espira,
> Filomena sospira en dulce canto
> y en amoroso llanto s'amancilla:
> gime la tortolilla sobre'l olmo,
> preséntanos a colmo el prado flores
> y esmalta en mil colores su verdura;
> la fuente clara y pura, murmurando,
> nos está convidando a dulce trato. (1146-53)

This scene of harmony and peace is appropriate to the life of love and duty which Nemoroso will describe. Evocation of nature in terms of love and harmony cannot but conjure up the ideas given typical expression by Bembo in these words, in which he describes love as the unifying as well as the generative force in nature: one of the most influential ideas of Renaissance Neoplatonism.

> Wherefore observe, you beautiful maidens, everything around you and see how captivating is the world, how many kinds of living things and what diverse things there are in it. None among them is born which does not receive from Love, as from its first and most holy father, its origin and birth . . . And this grass, even, which we sit upon, and these flowers, would not by their birth have made the ground so lovely and so verdant as they have done, perhaps to make us a more beautiful carpet of themselves, if most natural love had not joined their seeds and their roots with the earth in such a way that they, desiring temperate moisture from it, and it willingly offering it to them, had not with desirous accord come together for the act of generation, the one embracing the other . . . This so vast and so beautiful fabric of the world itself, which we perceive more completely with the mind than with the eyes, and in which all things are contained, if it were not full of Love, which holds it bound in its discordant bonds, would not endure nor would ever have existed for long.[16]

Nature is a spectacle of love and harmony in which human love, properly directed, can find its place. Salicio and Nemoroso have found that place; Albanio has not.

In this work, Garcilaso draws freely on ancient Latin and modern Italian poetry. One Italian work may have played a particularly important part in the conception of the eclogue. The 'urn' episode was clearly inspired by Ariosto's *Orlando furioso,* in which the fortunes of the house of Este are depicted in the prophetic tapestries surrounding the marriage-bed of Ruggiero and Bradamante. But the influence of the poem may have gone further: it seems probable that Garcilaso derived from the whole scheme of the *Furioso* the idea for his eclogue. In Ariosto, Orlando, a paragon among the knights of Charlemagne, obsessed with love of the disdainful Angelica, goes mad with jealousy. In him Ariosto is probably burlesquing the irrational and passionate conception of love associated with the literature of courtly love. To say this is to oversimplify a very complex work, but such an oversimplification may all the same suggest how *Orlando furioso* may have struck Garcilaso at a critical moment in his life. For Eclogue II is probably an expression of that same private conflict expressed in *Canción* IV, but now resolved as it was not in the *canción,* and given aesthetic distance in a fiction. If real people are to be sought in the poem, then Albanio must evidently be Garcilaso himself—the unredeemed Garcilaso in the grip of an unhappy passion.

This eclogue was probably the product of an intellectual perspective learned from Italy, and perhaps acquired in Naples itself. Garcilaso cannot be called a Neoplatonist: the term is too vast in reach; but it was a Neoplatonic theory of love which gave him his new perspective.

Albanio embodies the psychology of courtly love. In him Garcilaso seems to reject not just an ethos but the literary traditions which expressed it. Let us recall again some words of Garcilaso's quoted earlier (above, p. 29): 'porque yo no sé qué desventura ha sido siempre la nuestra, que apenas ha nadie escrito en nuestra lengua sino lo que se pudiera muy bien escusar . . .' He wrote this about the time he began the eclogue (late 1533). Among much else, he was doubtless dismissing the *cancionero* poetry of desire and despair which Albanio echoes.

Some time in 1534-35 Garcilaso wrote his next important work, Eclogue I, which shows a great advance in form and concentration. It was written in grief at the death in childbirth of Isabel Freyre. Sincerity is an irrelevant concept in criticism since we can judge only a work's effect, not the feelings which went into its creation; all the same this eclogue rings true: its pathos and vehemence make it one of Garcilaso's most moving works. This is not in conflict with the fact that (as we expect of poetry of the age) it is full of imitations of other poets, classical and Italian. It is in two main parts. After the dedication to Don Pedro de Toledo, the shepherd Salicio complains of the fickleness of Galatea, who has left him for another. He is followed by Nemoroso, who laments the death of Elisa. The poem begins at daybreak and ends at nightfall: a day marking a cycle of life. The poem presents a curious psychological difficulty: it seems strange that a man grief-stricken at the news of the death of a woman he loved should break out into new complaints of her earlier rejection of him. The larger grief could have been expected to eclipse the other. W. J. Entwistle proposed a solution which has its attractions: that Salicio's song was written earlier (perhaps in 1531) and on the composition of Nemoroso's song Garcilaso brought both parts together to form a single poem.[17] Salicio's maturity of style is an obstacle. We are left with a problem.

The poem presents no difficulties of interpretation: both laments are straightforward enough. Salicio describes how all nature seems alienated from him: birds and beasts go their appointed rounds, only he is left to weep apart:

> siempre está en llanto esta ánima mezquina,
> cuando la sombra el mundo va cubriendo,
>   o la luz se avecina.
> Salid sin duelo, lágrimas, corriendo. (81-4)

She who once had thoughts for him alone now whispers in the ear of another and winds her arms about his neck. Harmony for him is disrupted; no unnatural union can now seem impossible.

> La cordera paciente
> con el lobo hambriento
> hará su ajuntamiento,
> y con las simples aves sin rüido
> harán las bravas sierpes ya su nido,
> que mayor diferencia comprehendo
> de ti al que has escogido.
> Salid sin duelo, lágrimas, corriendo. (161-8)

Nemoroso's laments run a parallel course; he even echoes some of Salicio's phrases. For him too the harmonious course of nature is disrupted: cattle will not graze, weeds choke the growing wheat, thorns grow where once were flowers. He finds sad consolation in a vision of eternal union with Elisa beyond death, in the third sphere, the sphere of Venus (which it would be bigoted to insist on taking to be the Christian Heaven). The resigned tranquillity of the lines make them some of Garcilaso's finest; and they are followed by the last stanza of the poem, which provides a fitting close.

> Nunca pusieran fin al triste lloro
> los pastores, ni fueran acabadas
> las canciones que solo el monte oía,
> si mirando las nubes coloradas,
> al tramontar del sol bordadas d'oro,
> no vieran que era ya pasado el día;
> la sombra se veía
> venir corriendo apriesa
> ya por la falda espesa
> del altísimo monte, y recordando
> ambos como de sueño, y acabando
> el fugitivo sol, de luz escaso,
> su ganado llevando,
> se fueron recogiendo paso a paso. (408-21)

The tranquillity of resignation: this is the mood the eclogue leaves us with. Its emotional storms have subsided; Garcilaso has led the reader through Salicio's hot unreasoning complaints and Nemoroso's more sombrely dignified (and more moving) lament to the sad tranquillity of the close: no doubt the pattern of the poet's own life projected, perhaps discovered, in poetry. There is no 'thought' to be disentangled from this eclogue, but it is all the same poetry wrung from reflection.

It is appropriate here to turn to *Elegía* I, composed some time in

1535 on the death of the younger brother of the duque de Alba, Don Bernardino de Toledo, who died in Sicily after the Tunis campaign. It is a work which helps us to understand both Eclogue I and Eclogue III. In it, Garcilaso describes movingly the duke's grief, but soon the poem takes a different turn as he exhorts the duke to show the self-control expected of a leader of men:

> Tú, gran Fernando, que entre tus pasadas
> y tus presentes obras resplandeces,
> y a mayor fama están por ti obligadas,
> contempla donde estás, que si falleces
> al nombre que has ganado entre la gente,
> de tu virtud en algo t'enflaqueces. (181-6)

Grief is human, but must at last be restrained: 'el eceso en esto vedo y quito'. Not always did old Priam mourn for Hector; and Venus, after the first moment of grief at the death of Adonis, returned to normal life, seeing that her tears could not mend misfortune that was irremediable:

> los ojos enjugó y la frente pura
> mostró con algo más contentamiento,
> dejando con el muerto la tristura.
> Y luego con gracioso movimiento
> se fue su paso por el verde suelo,
> con su guirlanda usada y su ornamento;
> desordenaba con lascivo vuelo
> el viento sus cabellos; con su vista
> s'alegraba la tierra, el mar y el cielo. (232-40)

Garcilaso urges the Stoic doctrine that the mind must learn to suffer with fortitude, even without emotion, the accidents of fortune which are outside its control.

In 1536 Garcilaso wrote his Eclogue III, which in some ways is the hardest of his works for a modern reader: it lacks the apparent directness of Eclogue I, and its involved fiction demands of the reader a considerable effort of imagination.

After a careful description of the scene, in some of Garcilaso's most delicate poetry, four nymphs emerge from the Tagus, to weave their tapestry in the shade of the willows. The first is depicting how Orpheus reclaimed Eurydice from the underworld and lost her again. The second depicts Apollo's pursuit of Daphne and his grief on her transformation into a laurel. The third depicts Venus' grief on the death of Adonis. The grief of Orpheus is described in one line, Apollo's in two, Venus' in a stanza, as if we are presented with a crescendo of grief leading to the centrepiece of the poem, the fourth nymph's depiction of the death of Elisa and of the grief of Nemoroso, described in poetry never excelled by Garcilaso. Lines like these show Garcilaso's mature mastery of language.

> Todas, con el cabello desparcido,
> lloraban una ninfa delicada
> cuya vida mostraba que había sido
> antes de tiempo y casi en flor cortada;
> cerca del agua, en un lugar florido,
> estaba entre las hierbas degollada
> cual queda el blanco cisne cuando pierde
> la dulce vida entre la hierba verde. (225-32)

However, we are still far from the direct, personal quality of Eclogue I. Grief is represented in these four scenes, but the poetry is all the same not dominated by a sense of grief: there is a studied coolness which yields to some intensity of feeling in the depiction of Elisa and Nemoroso, but nowhere does passion break through, and the brief episode quickly gives way to new incidents and a quieter scene. The assured poise and skill of Garcilaso's writing forbid us to think that he attempted to express grief afresh and failed. Another sense must be sought. Reflection on the experience of reading the poem shows clearly that Garcilaso's subject in this eclogue taken as a whole is not grief. Its structure and artifice lead us to a different mood. We have three mythological scenes of undeniable force and beauty, yet conveying a sense of distance. Following them comes the account of Elisa's death conveying, in spite of its beauty, a similar effect. Garcilaso (it may be) is not trying to express intense sorrow but release from it, applying to himself the advice he pressed on the duque de Alba. The mythological episodes are not only a formal introit to the central episode but serve to give it distance as if it, too, belonged to the antique age of myth. Elisa's death is at last seen by Garcilaso in perspective. She, and the grief she caused him, belong to the past. The poem's elaborate fiction expresses this perfectly: we are not called on to witness a real death but its representation in tapestry: the poem is a work of art about a work of art. The nymphs will finally retire beneath the waters of the Tagus, taking their work with them, and leaving the scene as peaceful, as free from sorrow, as when they first emerged:

> siendo a las ninfas ya el rumor vecino,
> juntas s'arrojan por el agua a nado,
> y de la blanca espuma que movieron
> las cristalinas ondas se cubrieron. (373-6)

We can read the entire poem as an extended metaphor for the recollection of past sorrows which at last return again beneath the waters of oblivion whence they came.

Before they disappear, the nymphs are disturbed by the approach of two shepherds, Tirreno and Alcino, singing of their loves. Symbolism must not be pressed too far, but it seems likely here that they represent the poet's return to real life and love after his preoccupation with the past. The shepherds play here the part played by the introduction of Venus in *Elegía* I.

This eclogue is a remarkable achievement. In it Garcilaso conveys both his sorrow and his release from it. Like the other eclogues, it is an exploration of real experience, the record of a poet coming to terms with himself. Critics who see Eclogue III as pure art, as a flight from reality, have misread Garcilaso's finest work.

Some time during his Neapolitan period Garcilaso composed his *Canción* V, 'Oda a la flor de Gnido', a plea on behalf of his friend Mario Galeota addressed to Doña Violante Sanseverino. It is a very successful poem, imitated from Horace's Ode I, vi. Apart from its intrinsic poetic merits it has a further historical importance in that it introduced into Spanish the stanza-form in which Luis de León and St John of the Cross were to write some of their best poetry, and gave the stanza a name, *lira*, taken from the last word of the ode's first line: 'Si de mi baja lira'.

In Garcilaso's sonnets, which contain some small masterpieces, his poetic development can be very clearly traced: from the slight awkwardness of (say) 'Amor, amor, un hábito vestí' (XXVII), or 'En fin a vuestras manos he venido' (II), which probably belong among his earliest sonnets (the *cancionero*-like language of II supports the probability), to the emotional maturity and stylistic poise of sonnets like 'En tanto que de rosa y d'azucena' (XXIII). This is a reworking of the classical theme of 'Gather ye rosebuds while ye may', derived from Horace's Ode IV, x, and Ausonius' 'De rosis nascentibus' (containing the famous lines beginning 'Collige, virgo, rosas . . .'). In Garcilaso's sonnet the argument is set out with calm logic, each stage corresponding to a division of the poem: one proposition in each of the quatrains, the conclusion in the first tercet, the justifying generalisation in the last. The unhurried rhythm does not express urgency; the poem is a tranquil invitation to enjoy youth and beauty while they last: the note of fear of extinction struck by Góngora in his sonnet on the same theme, 'Mientras por competir con tu cabello' (probably an imitation of Garcilaso), is absent here. Garcilaso's tranquillity is that of a less anxious and more self-assured age.

The new poetry of Garcilaso and Boscán was rapidly accepted by their circle at Court, and (after publication) by the wider educated public. That Garcilaso had already acquired the status of a classic is shown by the square editions of his work, and commentaries on it, by Francisco Sánchez de las Brozas, *el Brocense* (1574),[18] and by Fernando de Herrera (1580).

However, though the new Italianate style gained ground very rapidly, it was not accepted immediately by all. Many remained attached to the older Castilian metres and the styles associated with them, either for nationalistic reasons or because they genuinely regretted the loss of the peculiar poetic experience which the older poetry offered. One of the stouter opponents of the new was Cristóbal de Castillejo. He was born between 1480 and 1490, served as page at the Court of Ferdinand and Isabella, and later entered the Cistercian order, whence he emerged in 1525 to become secretary to the Archduke Ferdinand, now king of Bohemia. Castillejo died in Vienna in 1550.

He wrote a considerable amount of poetry, much of it good. His subjects were very various—amorous, misogynistic, satirical, devotional; translations from Ovid; a poem in praise of *palo de las Indias* as a cure for the pox, etc. His *sermón de amores* and *Diálogo de mugeres* were printed in his lifetime (1542? and 1544 respectively). His complete works were printed in Madrid in 1573.

Castillejo's opposition to Garcilaso and Boscán is expressed in his 'Represión contra los poetas españoles que escriben en verso italiano', where the renegades are satirised; without, one must confess, excessive rancour. In spite of his attachment to the old metres and themes, Castillejo has been called (first by Menéndez Pelayo, faithfully echoed by others) a poet of the Renaissance. It is hard to see why, for he is clearly rooted in the older tradition from which Garcilaso turned away. His love-poetry has great charm and delicacy, but it belongs to the world of (for example) Juan del Encina. This poem is representative:

La vida se gana,
perdida por Ana.

Alegre y contento
me hallo en morir.
No puedo decir
la gloria que siento.
Un mismo tormento
m'enferma y me sana,
sufrido por Ana.

Do nace mi mal
se causa mi bien.
Padezco por quien
nació sin igual.

Por ser ella tal
mi muerte s'ufana,
sufrida por Ana.

Remedio no espero
de mi pena grave.
Perdióse la llave
do está lo que quiero.
Si vivo, si muero,
de mucha fe mana
que tengo con Ana. (II, 24)[19]

Even when he translates or paraphrases a Latin original, Castilejo's version sometimes strikes the characteristic note of the *cancioneros*. Here, in some lines from another poem to Ana, he paraphrases Catullus' *Carmen* LXXXV.

Mi alma os quiere y adora,
mas su pasión y fatiga
le dan causa que os maldiga,
y amándoos como a señora,
os tiene por enemiga.
Amo y quiero,
aborrezco y desespero
todo junto, y el por qué
preguntado, no lo sé,
mas siento que así muero. Ed. cit., II, 9)

He wrote some delicate poems in this style.

His *Sermón* and *Diálogo* are equally traditional: they are an outcrop of a misogynistic tradition well represented in fifteenth-century Spain, though Castillejo is more benign in his satire than some of his predecessors.

He is to be seen at his best in his translation of the song of Polyphemus to Galatea (Ovid, *Metamorphoses* XIII), which he turns into a richly sensuous poem in its own right. Here, it is true, Castillejo departs from Spanish traditions and, no doubt inspired by the classics, explores the world of nature. The poem is one of the most enchanting of its time.

NOTES

1. *Obras poéticas,* ed. M. de Riquer etc. (Barcelona, 1957), p. 89.
2. *Obras completas,* ed. E. L. Rivers (Madrid, 1964), p. 218.
3. Juan del Encina, *Cancionero* (1496), f.iir.
4. P. Gallagher, *The Life and Works of G. S. de B.* (London, 1968), p. 56.

5. See (for example) K. Whinnom, 'Hacia una interpretación y apreciación de las canciones del *Cancionero general* de 1511', *Filología* XIII (1968-69).
6. See Edward M. Wilson and Duncan Moir, *A Literary History of Spain: The Golden Age: Drama*, pp. 1 ff.
7. The *Cancionero de obras de burlas* was reproduced in facsimile by A. Pérez Gómez (Cieza, 1951) from the unique copy in the British Museum.
8. Extracts from Colón's lists have been printed by A. Rodríguez-Moñino in his facsimile edition of the *Cancionero general* (Madrid, 1958). For a brief account of Colón, see A. Rodríguez-Moñino, *Diccionario de pliegos . . .* (Madrid, 1970), pp. 72-4.
9. A selection of Reinosa's work has been published by J. M. Cossío (Santander, 1950).
10. E. M. Wilson, *Some Aspects of Spanish Literary History* (Oxford, 1967), pp. 19-20.
11. ed. Rivers, ed. cit., p. 218. Garcilaso's poetry will be quoted from an edition of his *Poesías castellanas completas* by E. L. Rivers (Madrid, 1969).
12. In Martín de Riquer, *Juan Boscán y su cancionero barcelonés* (Barcelona, 1945).
13. See for example Luis Milán, *El cortesano* (1561), reprinted in 1874 as vol. 7 of the series *Colección de libros españoles raros o curiosos*. See also his *Libro de motes de damas y caballeros* (Valencia, 1535; facsimile ed. Barcelona, 1951).
14. In the Neoplatonic system love, emanating from God, binds together the whole universe. True love in men is a desire to possess the beautiful, and since beauty is spiritual, being a reflection of the greater beauty of God, true love is directed not to carnal union (or at least not to this as an end in itself) but to the enjoyment of a spiritual beauty. The love of a man for a woman is a first step on a ladder which leads up to God. This doctrine is expounded by Bembo and, in a considerably different form, by Leone Ebreo (or León Hebreo) in his *Dialoghi d'amore* (composed *c.* 1502, printed 1535), twice translated into Spanish in the sixteenth century, the second time by Garcilaso de la Vega el Inca (1590).
15. I quote from Boscán's translation printed as Anejo XXV of the *Revista de filologia española* (Madrid, 1942).
16. Bembo, *Gli Asolani*, Book 2. My translation.
17. W. J. Entwistle, 'The Loves of Garcilaso', *Hispania*, XIII (1930).
18. Not to be confused with the other Francisco Sánchez (1550-1623), doctor and author of *Quod nihil scitur* (Lyon, 1581).
19. *Obras*, ed. J. Domínguez Bordona, 4 vols., CC 72, 79, 88, 91 (Madrid, 1926-28).

Chapter 3

PROSE FICTION IN THE SIXTEENTH CENTURY

A HISTORY OF SIXTEENTH-CENTURY SPANISH PROSE FICTION cannot be reduced to a neat scheme. The variety is such that any attempt to formulate a general theory must falsify the facts. There is no dominant genre, no single direction. Survivals of older forms of fiction are found side by side with innovations. A reading public eager for entertainment and evidently large enough by now to provide adequate rewards provided an encouraging milieu for the enterprise of writers and printers. The result was an extraordinary flowering of fiction of all kinds. Some of it is exemplary or didactic, but a great part is intended as pure entertainment; and the second category does not diminish (as one might expect it to) after the Council of Trent. All of it is, in widely different degrees of seriousness and competence, an exploration (and often an attempt at explanation) of the variety of human motivation and behaviour. To that extent the flowering of fiction reflects the curiosity concerning man which we associate with the Renaissance. Curiosity concerning the world which man inhabits is less evident: social realism was not on the whole a sixteenth-century preoccupation.

The literate were avid for entertainment; printers laboured to provide it. For many of both kinds an old book was as good as a new one. Some of the commercial successes of the sixteenth century were books of the fifteenth century or earlier. One such was *Grisel y Mirabella* by Juan de Flores, which was reprinted at least five times in the sixteenth century (and probably there were also editions now lost without trace). Diego de San Pedro's *Cárcel de amor* was reprinted at least sixteen times. Both works were translated into Italian, French, English, and other languages: of translations of *Grisel* there are forty-seven known editions in the sixteenth century, and of *Cárcel* at least twenty-seven. *Amadís de Gaula,* whose original version in three books probably goes back to the fourteenth century, was reprinted around thirty times, and from it was born a line of romances which became a dominant influence on the sixteenth-century European (not just Spanish) imagination. The continuing success of *Grisel* and *Cárcel* is not hard to explain: they treat of love, a perennially interesting human experience, in terms of fictions which, though far-fetched, had some relevance to a sixteenth-century reader. *Amadís* is a different matter: the reasons for the apparently anachronistic appeal of a fourteenth-century romance of knight-errantry are less obvious.

Down to the sixteenth century, French romances of the Arthurian cycle were still being translated into Castilian. *Amadís,* a native work inspired by Arthurian romance, was published in 1508 by Garci Rodríguez de Montalvo with the addition of a fourth book of his own, which he had evidently begun soon after 1492.[1] This obscure *Regidor* of the town of Medina del Campo left his mark on an age. The sheer quantity of sixteenth-century romances, and reprints of them, makes it obvious that they represent something central to sixteenth-century imagination and ideals.

Modern readers, influenced by *Don Quixote,* are very ready to believe that all the romances of chivalry are worthless and preposterous extravaganzas. On the contrary, *Amadís* is a work of great interest and artistic merit. It tells how 'no muchos años después de la pasión de nuestro Redentor y Salvador Jesu Cristo' King Perión of Gaul (meaning here a fictitious kingdom near Brittany) falls in love with the beautiful Helisena, daughter of Garínter, King of 'la pequeña Bretaña', and begets a child on her which is born in secret and cast adrift by his mother in an ark on the sea, bearing a letter which gives his name as 'Amadís Sin Tiempo, hijo de rey'. The child is found by a Scottish knight called Gandales, who brings him up as his own. Amadís proves to be the greatest and most virtuous knight of his time. He falls in love with Oriana, daughter of Lisuarte, King of Great Britain, and much of the story concerns the perfect love of these two, models of courtly lovers, who after many vicissitudes are rewarded for their constancy by marriage. Among their trials is the enmity towards Amadís conceived by Lisuarte, whose mind is poisoned by evil tongues. Virtue triumphs at last after many hazards and much bloodshed.

The book is rich in incident and has a multitude of characters. The marvellous and the supernatural play a great part: the plot is constantly complicated by the intervention of good and bad giants, enchanters (including Urganda la Desconocida, the protectress of Amadís), and so on. All this may easily hide from the reader that in fact *Amadís* is a coherent and well-constructed story, albeit slow-moving and digressive. There are many strands of narrative skilfully interwoven. The many combats necessarily have a certain sameness but on the whole monotony is avoided. Amadís is often in danger, and credible danger, so that suspense sustains interest. Though it would be absurd to look for the psychological depth of a novel by Henry James, there is clear characterisation of a simple kind. We can see this in (for example) the treatment of Amadís and his brother Galaor.

Amadís is the perfect knight; his love is immovably fixed on Oriana. The two make love on several occasions, but only after an initial promise of marriage (usual in the case of heroes of the Spanish romances). The tone of their lovemaking is set on the first occasion, when the lovers halt in a forest glade:

> . . . y Amadís tornó a su señora; y cuando así la vio tan hermosa y en su poder, habiéndole ella otorgada su voluntad, fue tan turbado de placer y de empacho que sólo catar no la osaba; así que se puede bien decir que en aquella verde yerba, encima de aquel manto, más por la gracia y comedimiento de Oriana que por la desenvoltura ni osadía de Amadís, fue hecha dueña la más hermosa doncella del mundo. (I, xxxv)

Galaor is very different: he flits from flower to flower (and—strangely in such a moral work—is nowhere much blamed for this). His affairs are casual, his approach direct. At a castle where he passes the night he is presented by a damsel to the beautiful lady of the castle with these words:

> Yo vos do al hijo del rey Perión de Gaula. Ambos sois hijos de reyes y muy hermosos: si vos mucho amáis, no vos lo terná ninguno a mal.
>
> Y saliéndose fuera, Galaor folgó con la doncella aquella noche a su placer . . . (I, xii)

Later, having rescued a damsel in distress:

> . . . estaban don Galaor y la doncella, que Brandueta había nombre, solos hablando en lo que oídes, y como ella era muy hermosa y él codicioso de semejante vianda, antes que la comida viniese ni la mesa fuese puesta, descompusieron ellos ambos una cama que en el palacio era donde estaban, haciendo dueña aquella que de antes no lo era, satisfaciendo a sus deseos, que en tan pequeño espacio de tiempo mirándose el uno al otro la su floreciente y hermosa juventud muy grandes se habían hecho. (I, xxv)

No doubt Galaor is intended to set off the superiority of Amadís, but also to provide the reader with some relief from the rigours of the courtly code. The contrast of character is part of the simple pattern of the book.

The sentimental novels of the fifteenth century and the medieval romances of chivalry were not didactic in the strict sense, but they offered examples of refinement and courtesy which were probably looked on as worthy of imitation. This was equally true of *Amadís*; though here there is positive instruction as well in the form of numerous asides and digressions. For example, in Book I, xiii, there is a digression on pride beginning:

> Aquí retrata el autor de los soberbios y dice: Soberbios, ¿qué queréis, qué pensamiento es el vuestro? Ruégovos que me digáis la hermosa persona, la gran valentía, el ardimiento del corazón, si por ventura lo heredastes de vuestros padres, o lo comprastes con las riquezas . . . Pues ¿dónde lo hobistes? Paréceme a mí que de aquel Señor muy alto donde todas las buenas cosas ocurren y vienen.

It is a long passage but not an irrelevant one because pride, presumption and arrogance are among the qualities on which Amadís wages war. Homilies and objurgations of the same kind recur throughout, giving the work something of the character of a textbook of knightly virtue. Montalvo probably added his share of such passages; certainly, Book IV, which is entirely his own invention, is particularly rich in moralising.

Whatever Montalvo's part, the text he transmitted to the sixteenth century created immense interest. There were about thirty editions between 1508 and 1587. Montalvo himself wrote a fifth book about Esplandián, the son of Amadís: *Las sergas de Esplandián* (1510, but possibly written before the beginning of the century). This went into nine, perhaps ten, editions by 1588. A sixth book, *Florisando,* by one Páez de Ribera, also appeared in 1510, to be reprinted only once. A seventh book, *Lisuarte de Grecia* (probably by Feliciano de Silva, who also wrote the ninth, tenth, and eleventh books), came out in 1514, and went into thirteen editions by 1587. And so on up to the twelfth book which ended the series in 1546.

Another independent series started early with *Palmerín de Oliva* (1511), closely modelled on *Amadís.* This went into at least ten editions by 1580. A second book, *Primaleón,* came out in 1512 and reached nine (perhaps ten) editions by 1588. But there are too many of these books for all to be mentioned.

> During the hundred years following the publication of *Amadís de Gaula,* some fifty new chivalresque romances appeared in Spain and Portugal. They were published at an average rate of almost one a year between 1508 and 1550; nine were added between 1550 and the year of the Armada; only three more came out before the publication of *Don Quixote.*[2]

And this without taking reprints into account: in all, over sixty romances (taking new and old together) were published in well over three hundred editions. There were even romances *a lo divino*: Pedro Hernández de Villumbrales, *El caballero del sol* (1552, not reprinted but translated into Italian and German); Hierónimo San Pedro, *Caballería celestial del Pie de la Rosa Fragante* (1554—this was put on the index of the Inquisition); Fray Jaime de Alcalá, *Caballería cristiana* (1570); Fray Alonso de Soria, *Historia y milicia cristiana del caballero peregrino, conquistador del cielo* (1601).

Plenty of intelligent people enjoyed the romances. St Teresa is said to have read them in her youth and, with her brother, to have written one. St Ignatius read them before his conversion to a religious life. When Diego Hurtado de Mendoza, one of the most brilliant men of his day, went to Rome as ambassador in 1547 it is reported that he took only two books to read on the way: *Amadís* and *La Celestina*. Men swooned on reading reports of Amadís's death. Some of the *conquistadores* read them: Bernal Díaz del Castillo, who fought with Cortés, wrote that when the Spaniards caught their first glimpse of the Aztec capital 'nos quedamos admirados y decíamos que parecía a las cosas de encantamiento que cuentan en el libro de Amadís, por las grandes torres, y cúes, y edificios que tenían dentro en el agua'. California was named after an island in *Esplandián*. When Prince Philip came to England in 1554 to marry Mary Tudor, one of his followers said of Philip's wonderment at the beauty of the gardens of the house at Winchester where Mary stayed to await him:

> ... que cierto al parecer que se hallaban en algo de lo que habían leído en los libros de caballerías ...

The romances had their detractors too: they were the object of a steady campaign of denunciation throughout the sixteenth century. In 1531 a royal decree forbade the importation of these works into the American colonies, partly because it was feared that the Indians might come to doubt the truth of Scripture by finding that books contained lies. In 1553 the ban was repeated, without effect. Equally ineffectually, the *Cortes* at Valladolid in 1555 banned the romances in Spain itself. The public was not to be denied its entertainment; the romances continued to be written, and to sell.

The romances were in fact far more popular than any other kind of fiction: more than *Lazarillo*, for example. For them to have had such a hold on the imagination of the reading public we must believe that they mirrored some important truth or aspiration of the time. To call them 'escapist' is to give no answer worth considering.

The cult of chivalry was an important fact in the life of the nobility in late medieval Europe, and in some respects was to remain so in the sixteenth century. For an explanation of the popularity of the romances we must, however, look beyond the nobility to the Spanish people's conception of its role or mission at this time. To speak of a 'people' has obvious dangers, but nevertheless there seems to have been a general mood of national self-confidence and crusading fervour. Regarding the second, there was in fact a widespread European mood of religious expectancy at the beginning of the sixteenth century, born of a sense of religious crisis which showed itself on the one hand in a desire for the reform of the Church and on the other in a Messianic crusading zeal. In 1510 a rumour circulated that the king of the Persians had been converted to Christianity and was going to join in the fight against the Turks. In Spain, Cisneros had repeatedly urged a crusade for the reconquest of the Holy Land. He settled instead for an attack on Oran in 1509, which he accompanied. Portugal was to mount an expedition against Azamor in 1513 amidst great popular enthusiasm, reflected in Gil Vicente's *Exhortação de guerra.*[3] All this may help to explain the reception of *Amadís*. The perfect chivalry of Amadís includes an unshakeable piety. He embodies the religious ideals which run through the entire history of chivalry. His story mirrored the expansionist and crusading mood of early sixteenth-century Spain.

This is even more true of *Las sergas de Esplandián*. The piety of Amadís is taken for granted as intrinsic to a perfect knight, but the emphasis is on the lover and righter of wrongs. His son Esplandián explicitly dedicates himself to Christ and war against the infidel, swearing never to draw sword against fellow-Christians. The book reads at times like a devotional tract, in which entertainment is subordinate to indoctrination. The story reaches its climax in a crusade against the Turks. Esplandián himself is only the most pious figure in a very pious story: for example, his grandfather Lisuarte decides to abdicate in favour of Amadís and Oriana in order to devote his last days to prayer in a monastic retreat.

Warlike piety is the keynote of the book. In this Montalvo gave the time-honoured fictions of knight-errantry a close contemporary relevance. He was doubtless a pious man; but he was also responding to the rising tide of Messianic fervour in late fifteenth- and early sixteenth-century Europe. The rumour of the conversion of the king of Persia shows the strength of the emotional tides. *Esplandián* was not just idle entertainment and was probably not received as such by its first readers. The very existence of the book gives a clue to the reasons for the popularity of these works. They embodied an ideal at once warlike and devout.

The initial appeal of romances of chivalry is not, then, very mysterious. Their continuing appeal may owe something to the accession of Charles to the throne in 1516 and the influences which through him and his Court entered Spain. He was duke of Burgundy, and seems to have thought of himself throughout his life as more Burgundian than anything else.[4] His education had been entirely on traditional Burgundian lines, which inculcated a profound piety, attachment to the ideals of chivalry, and a rigorously detailed court ceremonial. He bore the name of his grandfather, Charles the Bold, of whom it has been written:

> No one was so consciously inspired by models of the past, or manifested such desire to rival them, as Charles the Bold. In his youth he made his attendants read out to him the exploits of Gawain and of Lancelot . . .[5]

Philip the Good, his father, was the founder of the Order of the Golden Fleece. One of Charles's favourite books was *Le chevalier délibéré* by Olivier de la Marche, an allegorical treatment of human life in terms of chivalry. Charles induced Hernando de Acuña to turn it into Spanish verse, having already made a prose translation of his own. The work shows the kind of imagination to which the idea of chivalry appealed, and perhaps the spirit in which at least some of the romances were read by some readers.

Charles seems to have admired at least one romance, *Belianís de Grecia* (1547). (His admiration inspired Gerónimo Fernández to write the third and fourth parts published in 1579.) The hold that chivalresque fiction had on his imagination may be judged by an entertainment provided for him on his visit to the town of Bins in Flanders in 1549 during a tour of his northern European possessions in the company of Prince Philip. The entertainment took the form of a chivalresque spectacle which lasted two days. Knight after knight, failing to defeat a certain *Caballero del águila negra*, is imprisoned in a *Castillo tenebroso* until at last an unknown knight appears who gives his name as Beltenebrós (the name adopted by Amadís during his amorous penance in the *Peña pobre*), defeats his adversary, and proves that he is the knight for whom this adventure is reserved by drawing forth an enchanted sword from a stone. He sets forward and releases the captives from their prison. At last the identity of the victor is revealed: it is Prince Philip, who a few years later became king on the abdication of the Emperor Charles in 1556. Charles was tired and ill, but abdication was a rare event: in general kings did not relinquish power even when decrepit. Charles handed over power to Philip and retired to the monastery of Yuste as if in imitation of Lisuarte handing over to Amadís: was this perhaps Charles's last tribute to an ideal nourished by the romances of chivalry?

The chivalresque ideal was evidently a sustaining one until late in the sixteenth century. Spanish disenchantment after 1588 and the defeat of the Armada was the death of the romance of chivalry (though its themes lived on in drama and other forms), as if it was recognised that a dream was over.

But there is a danger of forgetting that these books were also works of entertainment. They vary a great deal in character and quality. Some are serious, some frivolous, some intelligent, some stupid. Some became favourites and were many times reprinted; of others there was only one edition. They appealed to all classes and had something for everyone. The best of them were carefully composed, and, contrary to first impressions, inventive, though always within the limits of a recognised convention. Their potency was that of a myth. A sympathetic reader can still be drawn into the timeless world of the romances as he follows some solitary horseman riding off into an idyllic landscape to encounter love, enchantments, and feats of arms:

> . . . y desta manera anduvo hasta tanto que el sol se quería poner, que se halló en un campo verde, cubierto de deleitosos árboles, tan altos que parecían tocar las nubes; por medio dellos pasaba un río de tanta agua, que en ninguna parte parecía haber vado, y tan clara, que quien por junto a la orilla caminaba podía contar las guijas blancas que en el suelo parecían . . .[6]

* * *

The romances of chivalry dominate sixteenth-century Spanish fiction, but other forms began, at first sporadically, to make their appearance, like the first mammals among the last of the giant reptiles. One of these is the pastoral novel.

Pastoral fiction began life in Spain in intimate association with the romances of chivalry. Probably in imitation of Italian pastoral fiction, notably Sannazaro's *Arcadia* (1504), Feliciano de Silva included in his *Amadís de Grecia* (1530) the story of the shepherd Darinel, who loves the disdainful shepherdess Silvia, who is in fact the abducted daughter of Lisuarte of Greece. For love of her, Don Florisel de Niquea, a son of Amadís of Greece (and hence her uncle) turns temporary shepherd. The pastoral element is continued in Silva's own continuation to this romance, *Don Florisel de Niquea* (parts I and II, forming the tenth book of *Amadís*, in 1532; the remaining parts in 1535 and 1551). Silva's affection for the amorous shepherd led him to introduce one in his *Segunda comedia de Celestina* (1534). Another pastoral episode is to be found in Torquemada's *Coloquios satíricos* (1553), of which the seventh *coloquio* is a story of pastoral love.

This growing interest in pastoral fiction, strengthened by the vogue of pastoral poetry, undoubtedly reflects (though to what extent is debatable) the almost mystical attitude to nature which we find in the Renaissance, a product of the fifteenth-century Florentine revival of Neoplatonism. For the Neoplatonists love was the controlling force of the universe: the nature of love, both 'cosmic' and human, became accordingly of profound interest. Marsilio Ficino's writings on love (his commentary on Plato's *Symposium*, etc.) were the first of a long line of such treatises extending down through the sixteenth century and beyond. Since nature was thought of as the manifestation of this cosmic love, bucolic literature came to be considered the appropriate vehicle for the discussion of love, and the shepherd—the typical inhabitant of the bucolic scene—the very embodiment of love. In his *De los nombres de Cristo* Luis de León represents the shepherd as of finer sensibility than other men and so an appropriate figure for the expression of love in poetry: 'no tenéis razón en pensar que para decir dél [*love*] hay personas más a propósito que los pastores, ni en quien se represente mejor. Porque puede ser que en las ciudades se sepa mejor hablar, pero la fineza del sentir es del campo y de la soledad'.[7]

Sannazaro's *Arcadia* consists of pastoral scenes and fragmentary stories interspersed with poetry. Feliciano de Silva's pastoral scenes were mere episodes. The first fully developed and unified pastoral romance or novel is *Los siete libros de la Diana* (Valencia, 1559?) by the Portuguese Jorge de Montemayor (1520?-61).[8] The book had an instant appeal, and it continued to appeal: there were twenty editions in Spain in the sixteenth and seventeenth centuries (fifteen of them before 1600), five in Antwerp, and fifteen elsewhere (all in Spanish). It was followed by numerous imitations; a second part (of very poor quality) by Alonso Pérez (1564); another by Gil Polo—*Diana enamorada* (Valencia, 1564); *La Galatea* (Alcalá, 1585) by Cervantes; Lope de Vega's *Arcadia* (Madrid, 1598); and many others: a total of eighteen romances up to 1633. Many apart from *Diana* were several times reprinted. The genre spread rapidly to other countries. *Diana* was first translated into French in 1578, into English (with Pérez's second part and *Diana enamorada*) in 1598. Imitations soon followed.

Works so alien to modern taste require an effort of imagination to understand how grown men could devote time to writing and reading them. Some were always thought bad: Cervantes, deeply attached though he was to the pastoral genre, was scornful of several of these works. But nearly all their authors were attempting something they thought serious and worthwhile. The pastoral novels are in fact a prolonged debate about the nature of true love, the trials of love, the endlessly varied complications that lovers may create or be victims of, and so on. The unreal setting allowed these by no means unreal questions to be presented and discussed in a 'pure' state, abstracted from the distractions of ordinary social life. The best of these works were not, at least in intention, 'escapist'.

Montemayor's *Diana* is an account of how the unhappy Sireno, made wretched by Diana's sudden change of heart and marriage to another—Delio—makes his way in company with a band of other unhappy lovers to the court of the enchantress Felicia, who is reputed to be able to cure all sorrows. She does in fact cure these by means of a magic potion which makes Sireno fall out of love with Diana and makes Sylvano and Selvagia fall in love with each other. Other cases resolve themselves. Diana, unhappy in her marriage, is the only one left disconsolate: partly because, being married, nothing can be done about her case, partly (no doubt) because her problems would be dealt with in the second part which Montemayor promised but did not write.

Pastoral fictions were often a literary disguise for real people. There may very well have been a real model for Diana, but Montemayor's book and its successors are primarily about the nature and complications of love. Montemayor's view of the matter proves to be a very traditional one. Love for him is a destiny against which it is useless for the lover to struggle; it is an irrational force, and indeed hostile to reason. Love almost inevitably entails suffering, which is good in that it both exhibits the lover's sensibility and ennobles him further. Jealousy is a natural concomitant of love. These views are familiar: they are typical of the literature of courtly love, and are the subject-matter of both *cancionero* love-poetry and the sentimental novels of the fifteenth century. Much of the verse in *Diana* derives in fact from the *cancioneros*.

Love which is irrational and over which the lover has no control can attach itself to any object and change that object with remarkable ease, so that fickleness is one of the lover's hazards, as Sireno knows, having been abandoned by Diana, who once loved him, in favour of Delio. The shepherdess Selvagia, recounting her own experiences, speaks of the 'desvariados casos de amor' (pp. 45-6),[9] a phrase fully justified by her own involved affairs. She receives a passionate declaration of love from a shepherdess at the temple and, the other being very beautiful, falls in love herself. 'Y después de esto los abrazos fueron tantos, los amores que la una a la otra nos decíamos, y de mi parte tan verdaderos' (ed. cit., p. 43) that they have no thoughts for the festivities. The stranger, Ismenia, later pretends to be a man in disguise, giving her name as Alanio, who is in fact a cousin with whom she is in love. She later tells Alanio of the escapade and he, curious concerning Selvagia, seeks her out and falls in love with her, and she with him when she learns the true story. Ismenia succeeds in rearousing Alanio's interest by feigning love for a shepherd called Montano who, seeing Selvagia later, falls in love with her. So Selvagia loves Alanio, who loves Ismenia, who by now really loves Montano, who loves Selvagia. This is representative of the kind of tangle which Montemayor creates and from which he is able to escape only by means of Felicia's magic potion (which appeared to Cervantes a blemish on the work).

The kind of love depicted in the book is represented as ennobling and a sign of a noble mind. All the lovers are in fact perfectly chaste. Another kind of passion is glimpsed briefly in a sudden attack by three wild men—

> tres salvajes de estraña grandeza y fealdad. Venían armados de coseletes y celadas de cuero de tigre. Eran de tan fea catadura que ponían espanto; los coseletes traían por brazales unas bocas de serpientes, por donde sacaban los brazos que gruesos y velludos parecían . . . (pp. 87-8)

These are un-courtly lovers, determined to take by force what the nymphs they love have refused them. The situation is saved by the opportune arrival of a beautiful armed shepherdess, who shoots the wild men. The stranger, Felismena, then tells the story of her own unhappy love.

Montemayor's conception of love is entirely medieval. It is curious therefore to find Felicia and others expounding the Neoplatonic doctrine of Leone Ebreo (see above, p. 49 n. 14), paraphrasing and quoting from a passage in *Dialoghi d'amore* where true and false love are distinguished. It is interesting that of all that work Montemayor selects passages which represent love as uncontrollable by reason (though born of reason), impetuous, and passionate, so that the lover is made

> enemigo de placer, amigo de soledad, lleno de pasiones, cercado de temores, turbado de espíritu, martirizado del seso, sustentado de esperanza, fatigado de pensamientos. (p. 199)

Leone invented an 'extraordinary reason' to which love *is* subject (this being simply the lover's subordination of that reason which seeks 'vida honesta' to the desire to obtain possession of the beloved). Montemayor omits this, perhaps to make more complete love's independence of reason. By stressing mainly the turbulent emotions associated with love, he is able to offer an appearance of fashionable Neoplatonism while leaving intact the older conception of love which is his real theme.

The success of *Diana* did not please everyone. One Padre Bartolomé Ponce de León conceived a great desire to meet Montemayor and when at last he did so scolded him for wasting his talent on a book of profane love.

> Con medida risa respondió diciendo: 'Padre Ponce, hagan los frailes penitencia por todos, que los hijos dalgo armas y amores son su profesión'.
>
> 'Yo os prometo, señor Montemayor—dije yo—de con mi rusticidad y gruesa vena componer otra Diana, la cual con toscos garrotazos corra tras la vuestra'. Con esto y mucha risa se acabó el convite y nos despedimos. (pp. xvii-xviii)

Ponce de León represents in this the literary puritanism which runs through the sixteenth century and is perhaps (though not certainly) accentuated for a time after the Council of Trent (1544-63). Moved by the flood of profane literature, Ponce de León himself duly wrote a pastoral novel *a lo divino: Primera parte de la Clara Diana a lo divino* (Saragossa 1599, perhaps earlier). The characters symbolise vices and virtues, the story being an allegory representing 'el discurso de nuestra vida'. The book is of little merit. Lope de Vega wrote another pastoral novel *a lo divino: Los pastores de Belén* (Lérida, 1612), which tells of the birth of Christ, and ends with the flight to Egypt. Lope (faithful to tradition) promised a second part but never wrote it.

Criticism of Montemayor's *Diana* did not have to wait for Ponce de León, however. Gaspar Gil Polo's *Diana enamorada* (Valencia, 1564) is in fact a criticism of the first *Diana*, of which it is a continuation. It is one of the most beautiful Spanish works of the sixteenth century, in both its prose and its verse.

Gil Polo makes clear his exemplary intent in his 'Epístola a los lectores':

> A este libro nombré *Diana enamorada*, porque prosiguiendo la *Diana* de Montemayor me pareció convenirle este nombre, pues él dejó a la pastora en este trance. El que tuviere por deshonesto el nombre de enamorada no me condene hasta ver la honestidad que aquí se trata ... y el fin a que se encamina esta obra, que no es otro sino dar a entender lo que puede y sabe hacer el Amor en los corazones, aunque sean tan libres y tan honestos como el de Diana; las penas que pasan sus aficionados y lo que importa guardar el alma de tan dañosa enfermedad ... Y aunque son ficciones imaginadas, leyéndolas como tales, se pueden sacar de ellas el fruto que tengo dicho: pues no se escribieron para que se les diese fe, sino para satisfacer a los gustos delicados y aprovechar a los que con ejemplo de vidas ajenas quisieren asegurar la suya. (p. 10)[10]

(The apology for *enamorada* may seem curious: the word could mean something little short of 'whore'.)

The story tells how Diana, having fallen in love again with Sireno, encounters a strange shepherdess who, hearing Diana sing of her unhappy love, debates with her on the subject of love. The stranger, called Alcida, offers to help her overcome her pain. Diana declares that she does not wish for relief at the cost of dismissing love from her heart, and in any case does not believe it possible to resist love. In both respects Diana expresses the traditional view embodied in the first *Diana*. The stranger retorts that love is indeed resistible, that the torments of lovers are of their own choosing. Her attack is clearly directed at a literary tradition, as when she describes in contemptuous terms the complaints of which love-poetry is full.

Delio, Diana's husband, now appears and instantly falls in love with

Alcida. Hearing another shepherd approach and recognising his voice, Alcida flees, hotly pursued by Delio. The newcomer, Marcelio, tells Diana of his misfortunes, which have led Alcida, to whom he was betrothed, to believe herself betrayed by him, so that she flees at his approach. The first book ends with the arrival of Berardo and Tauriso, two shepherds in love with Diana: ends, that is, with a complicated mass of material to work out (and to which more will be added). Diana loves Sireno, who is indifferent, but she is married to Delio, who has run off in pursuit of Alcida, who is fleeing from Marcelio. This is not only a complicated story but a varied collection of 'casos de amor'. Diana represents one conception of love, complicated by an unhappy marriage which prevents her seeking any solution; Alcida, representing a very different conception of love, is prevented by misunderstanding from finding fulfilment; the witless Delio is swept off his feet by a kind of love which, though similar to Diana's, he has not strength of mind enough to subordinate to duty. The writer's skill in starting so many hares at once is in part what we are expected to admire and be entertained by.

As in Montemayor's *Diana*, all the main characters make their way to the palace of Felicia, where all problems are resolved. But not by magic: the solutions are humanly credible; the changes of heart are carefully prepared and psychologically convincing. The union of Diana and Sireno is prepared for by the death of Delio. Alcida tells how, rebuffed by her, he was plunged by his 'loco amor' into despair and thence into a fever, accentuated by jealousy lest Sireno's love for Diana revive. He dies in a paroxysm of grief and frenzy. His death is a direct result of his disordered mind. His witlessness has been stressed on several occasions. Since Gil Polo's conception of love is based on reason, it is appropriate that it is the witless Delio who suffers most from the pangs of irrational love and jealousy.

Diana and Sireno (whose old love has in fact revived) are happily reunited. The work ends with a long speech on love by Felicia, who denounces irrational love in terms which echo Alcida's. (All this may have been found too severe to be entertaining: Felicia's account of love was omitted after the first edition.)

Gil Polo derived all his views on love from Bembo's *Gli Asolani*.[11] He makes as prominent a use of Bembo as Montemayor did of Leone Ebreo, but with this difference: whereas Montemayor borrows to lend fashionable colour to a psychology of love which really has nothing to do with Neoplatonism, Gil Polo's entire novel is designed to illustrate a theory of love made explicit at the very start. He went to the most uncompromising of the Neoplatonic treatises. Bembo teaches that true love is 'good and reasonable and temperate'. It is governed by reason.

It does not know perturbation, since the traditional sufferings of lovers are associated only with sensual love. True love is always calm, and the lover is not troubled by absence.

Diana enamorada, then, is a polemical work. Considering Montemayor to be a propagator of a false conception of love, Gil Polo attempts to arrest his influence by turning to an alternative version of Neoplatonic theory, a version whose austerity appealed to his own evidently puritanical cast of mind.

Cervantes's *La Galatea* (Alcalá, 1585) is another contribution to the debate about love as serious as Gil Polo's. Cervantes presents numerous 'casos de amor' and through them leads up to a central statement about love in Book IV when Tirsi, replying to an attack on love made by Lenio in terms which recall one of Bembo's interlocutors, Perottino, expounds Leone Ebreo's version of the Neoplatonic theory.

La Galatea is well contrived. Its many intertwined stories are skilfully managed. It has variety of characterisation, and in psychological truth it is a profounder work than Montemayor's. It came from a more serious mind. But his serious-mindedness was Cervantes's downfall in this first work of his: it is too sober and too wordy; in trying to give his pastoral world solidity he misses its magic.

Cervantes's interest in the nature and problems of love persisted throughout his life and is evident in all his works. It might be tempting to argue that after treating of love in the (almost) abstract manner of the pastoral novel he went on to situate love in real social contexts in his later works, and tempting to attribute this to his increasing maturity. The theory cannot be sustained. Not only did pastoral, in one form or another, creep into his later works, but Cervantes never abandoned the intention of writing a second part to *La Galatea*. He promised it in his prologue to the second part of *Don Quixote* (1615) and again—in one of the most poignant of literary documents—in the dedication of his *Persiles y Sigismunda* (1616) to the conde de Lemos, written on his deathbed. This ambition sustained over thirty-one years gives the measure of his attachment to the genre.

Arcadia (Madrid, 1598) was Lope de Vega's first venture into the novel. He declares in the prologue that he has novelised a subject taken from life: the work is in fact a fictional account of the ill-starred love of Don Antonio de Toledo, in whose service Lope had resided at Alba de Tormes until 1595. Lope himself appears under his favourite pseudonym of Belardo. The work contains a good deal of fine poetry, but it is disorderly in construction, as if Lope were unable to control his material. His lack of self-discipline is clear: he lards the shepherds' discourse with irrelevant pedantries which sometimes collapse into absurdity; as when in Book V we find this:

Si les costara amar a las mujeres, prosiguió Anfriso, lo que a las leonas el parto, ellas sin duda huyeran de segunda voluntad con el escarmiento de la primera. Eso deseo saber, replicó Frondoso. Pues sabe, dijo el pastor, que una vez le oí contar a Silvio, que las leonas tienen sus hijos veinte y seis meses en el vientre, donde en razón del tiempo crecen, y se les hacen dientes y uñas, con toda la perfección que después tienen. Pues estando así son tantos los saltos y movimientos que las martirizan y desatinan, y últimamente, rasgando las matrices y úteros, salen con espantosa ferocidad, dejándolas casi muertas, de donde nace que desde entonces no apetezcan la compañía de varón, si no es haciéndoles notable fuerza, con la cual no engendran, por estar impedidas y lastimadas.

Among the most notable of later pastoral novels are *El prado de Valencia* (Valencia, 1600) by Gaspar Mercader; *Siglo de oro en las selvas de Erifile* (Madrid, 1608) by Bernardo de Balbuena; *Cintia de Aranjuez* (Madrid, 1629) by Gabriel de Corral; and—perhaps the most notable for being the last—*Los pastores del Betis* (Naples, 1633) by Gonzalo de Saavedra.

A reader who wished to could find more realistic works than these. There was in fact a flourishing tradition of sixteenth-century realistic fiction in the form of the numerous imitations of *La Celestina* (or perhaps one ought to say: numerous humanistic comedies inspired by *La Celestina*). The chief ones are: *Comedia Tebaida, Comedia Hipólita,* and *Comedia Serafina,* all anonymous (probably published together; Valencia, 1521); *Segunda comedia de Celestina* by Feliciano de Silva (Medina del Campo, 1534); *Tercera parte de la tragicomedia de Celestina* by Gaspar Gómez (Medina, 1536); *Tragicomedia de Lisandro y Roselia,* published anonymously, but by Sancho de Muñón (Salamanca, 1542); *Tragedia Policiana,* anonymous (Toledo, 1547); *Comedia Florinea* by Juan Rodríguez Florián (Medina del Campo, 1554); *Comedia Selvagia* by Alonso de Villegas (Toledo, 1554). There were others; and the finest work of the series was reserved for the next century: Lope de Vega's *La Dorotea* (Madrid, 1632). All depict the progress of a love-affair assisted by the lover's servants and a *tercera* modelled in most cases on Celestina (in two cases it *is* Celestina). Some of the works end happily, others tragically. In nearly all of them the moral core of *La Celestina* is absent: they are written primarily for entertainment, despite the authors' stock claims to the contrary.[12]

Being derived largely from literature, these works are not wholly realistic. Nevertheless, they give a credible picture of certain aspects of sixteenth-century society. Many of the characters are stock types: the swooning lover, often ridiculed by his servants; servants in league with a bawd; cowardly braggarts; and so on. But the fact that they are conventional does not make them unrealistic. Men in love behaved then as now as if moonstruck; and some went melancholy-mad. The brothel scenes, the street fights by night, the unliterary lovemaking of servants and whores all carry conviction as being true to life. (Though it must be admitted that verisimilitude is undermined by the improbably pedantic and high-flown speeches uttered on occasion by servants and others—all in imitation of *La Celestina.*) Certain features of real life are portrayed in these works. Their eroticism (which has shocked some modern critics) is there for entertainment, but it would entertain only those who knew or imagined what the real thing was like: we are far from the unrealities of pastoral. Time and again the authors introduce gratuitous realistic touches—sometimes a whole scene—evidently because reality interested for its own sake. The physical details of Amintas's rape of Sergia in *Tebaida* (scene 10) are gratuitous, as is the whole incident: the interest is in its occurrence, not in its function or 'meaning'. In *Lisandro y Roselia* the boy Filirín sobs:

> Yo-yo ju-juro a San Juan yo-yo lo diga a mi padre que me pe-ela y-y me abofete-ea, y-y que me asiente co-con otro amo mejor.
> (III, i, p. 157)

A child speaks baby-talk, for the first time in Spanish:

> Ah senola mosa.—Senola, mi made dise que está alí la mujel de la ropa blanca, que tae lo que le mandaste! (III, iii, p. 177)

A whole scene (II, v) is devoted to the intricacies of legal debate, not to further the plot—that could have been done more economically—but evidently because it was expected to interest and please by its fidelity. These works manifest an interest in human variety for its own sake. The dwarf Risdeño in *Selvagia* (to take one example) is a brilliant invention.

These works are unjustly neglected. Some are poor things, but several are extremely interesting, and one or two are important works of art. This last is true of *Lisandro,* for example, which in many scenes has something of the intensity and skilful characterisation of *La Celestina* itself.

Another work of a similar kind remains to be mentioned: Francisco Delicado's masterpiece *La lozana andaluza* (Venice, 1528). Scarcely anything is known of Delicado. He was a priest; he read proofs of *Amadís* and *Primaleón* for Venetian presses (1533, 1534); published a treatise on the use of *palo de Indias* (lignum vitae) as a cure for syphilis (1529); and, above all, wrote *La lozana andaluza.*

The work is in dialogue like *La Celestina,* but the influence of the latter (if present) is almost solely formal. There is no love intrigue, no edifying moral. The work tells of the career of Aldonza, the *lozana* of the title, as prostitute and bawd in Rome. The work is undoubtedly highly realistic: Rome was notoriously one of the most immoral cities in Christendom. That the author's intention is partly entertainment is evident from the highly erotic character of the book, whose explicitness is sometimes startling. But more than entertainment is intended: the satirical element is strong (though intermittent), chiefly against the Church, particularly its wealth and the immorality of its priests, shown as assiduous customers of the prostitutes of the city. The story purports to take place before the Sack of Rome in 1527, references to which are inserted in the form of prophecies of destruction of the city as a punishment for its corruption. (No doubt the book was finished in 1524 as the author declares and subsequently retouched.)

The satirical intent is obvious; equally obvious is the author's affection for Lozana herself. She is depicted without malice, and she is allowed to retire peacefully on her earnings with her faithful Rampín, her lover and servant, to the island of Lipari ('y allí acabó muy santamente ella y su pretérito criado Rampín', as the heading of *Mamotreto* LXVI states). It is clear from an appendix in praise of women that Delicado had a soft spot for women in general and for Lozana in particular, of whom he says

> quiero dar gloria a la Lozana, que se guardaba mucho de hacer cosas que fuesen ofensa a Dios ni a sus mandamientos, porque, sin perjuicio de partes, procuraba comer y beber sin ofensión ninguna, la cual se apartó con tiempo y se fue a vivir a la ínsula de Lípari . . .

The primary feature of the book seems to be (however anachronistic it may appear to say so) delight in literary creation for its own sake. Creation of character, for one thing; as Delicado says at the end: 'Fenezca la historia compuesta en retrato, el más natural que el autor pudo . . .' He speaks of *retrato* throughout. The work is indeed above all else a portrait, both of Lozana herself and of the society in which she moves. Each page is heavy with *costumbrista* detail: about Roman life, about the stock-in-trade—chemical and human—of the Celestinas of the city, about food and drink and clothing. The book is a fascinating document, and in its own way a masterpiece. Regrettably, an isolated one: it had no detectable influence in Spain.

The sixteenth-century work of fiction most valued by modern readers is undoubtedly *La vida de Lazarillo de Tormes y de sus fortunas y adversidades*, published anonymously in three separate editions (Burgos, Alcalá, and Antwerp) in 1554. Various names have been proposed as the author's, the earliest being those of Diego Hurtado de Mendoza and Fray Juan de Ortega, both suggested in the early seventeenth century. Nothing approaching conclusive evidence has been adduced on behalf of either.

The book is a masterpiece of comedy (sometimes rather brutal comedy) and indeed one of the funniest books in the language, written in a sharp and witty style. It tells in the form of an autobiography the story of how Lázaro is as a small boy given by his mother to a blind man to be his guide; how he learns to fend for himself so that at last he is able to take a painful revenge on his master for his cruelties; how he passes from master to master until he is able to earn enough money as a water-seller to buy himself a second-hand suit and sword, whereupon he looks to higher things and becomes town-crier in Toledo, marrying the mistress of an archpriest.

The book is episodic. It contains some material which is clearly traditional. A fourteenth-century manuscript contains a marginal drawing of a blind man's boy drinking surreptitiously from his master's bowl through a straw, as Lázaro drinks from his master's jar in the first *tratado*. The pardoner's fake miracle in the fifth *tratado* resembles a story told in the fifteenth century by Masuccio Salernitano in *Il Novellino* in which two friars perpetrate a similar fraud: one denounces relics displayed by the other as false and then, as his accomplice prays for a sign to prove their authenticity, falls in a simulated fit. This version and that in *Lazarillo* may be variants of a European folk-tale. However, too much insistence on folklore can be misleading. The book indisputably contains traditional elements; but they must not distract attention from the book's striking originality, both in its form and in its representation of character.

The seven *tratados* of this short book are fundamentally—at least in appearance—the story of a local boy making good. Lázaro learns from his masters how to live. The lessons he learns from them he applies at last to his own affairs, and prospers. But the book is far from ingenuous: the reader must be alert to its ironies.

The book is a realistic picture of the kind of environment and people that Lázaro encounters. Spain, like the rest of Europe at that time, had a large population of beggars and paupers. Life was hard for others too: hunger in years of famine haunted the poor. There were enough poverty-stricken *hidalgos*, too proud to work and ashamed to beg, to serve as models for Lázaro's *escudero*. Many of the clergy were as hypocritical and immoral as the priests he describes. The Italian humanist and diplomat Navagero said in 1525 that 'the masters of Toledo and of the women in it are the clergy, who own magnificent houses and live like lords, in the lap of luxury, without anyone saying a word against them'. But the book's documentary value is distinct from its artistry: what matters to us most is what the author did with his material.

He was obviously a master of his craft. The portraits of Lázaro and his masters are economical but sharp and revealing. The style is racy and vivid. The author creates an ingenious pattern in Lázaro's relationships with his first three masters. He grows hungrier as they rise in the social scale, from beggar to priest to nobleman. His luck grows worse in another way: he runs away from the first, is thrown out by the second, and is deserted by the third. Other devices help to impose thematic unity on the work: for example, Lázaro's end—as town-crier one of his duties is to proclaim wine-prices—is foreshadowed by the blind man's words early in the story: 'Yo te digo que si un hombre en el mundo ha de ser bienaventurado con vino, que serás tú'.

In spite of the thematic coherence of the story, some have felt it to be too sketchy to be satisfying, and point to the inadequately filled gap in Lázaro's life between the end of the third *tratado* (when Lázaro is still a child) and his appearance as a man in Toledo at the end of the book. It has been suggested that the book is incomplete, perhaps through being published in haste. But the author manifestly did not set out to write a chronicle: he has traced the pattern of a life, without accounting for everything in it. We are shown Lázaro's early training, we are given a glimpse of his growing up, and we see his end. This is the diagram of a life, and to ask for more is to miss the point.

But in any case, the book's unity and artistry cannot be properly judged except in the light of the author's purpose. The book itself will guide us, by the ironies of Lázaro's many sententious remarks, the ironies of specific situations, and the overall pattern to which the author directs our attention in various ways.

Early in the first *tratado* Lázaro tells how his little half-brother runs in terror from his black father crying 'Coco!'—not realising that he himself is as black as his father. Lázaro reflects: '¡Cuántos debe de haber en el mundo que huyen de otros porque no se ven a sí mismos!'—a remark addressed to the reader, who may perceive the mote in the eye of his brother but be blind to the beam in his own. The hint that the reader will find the book's lesson as applicable to himself as to the characters in the story is irresistible. A little later, when Zaide's thefts on behalf of his new family are discovered, Lázaro reflects: 'No nos maravillemos de un clérigo ni fraile, porque el uno hurta de los pobres y el otro de casa para sus devotas y para ayuda de otro tanto, cuando a un pobre esclavo el amor le animaba a esto'. The overt sense is that if love can move even a brutish slave, it's not surprising that it can lead his betters into temptation; which implies that everyone is a helpless slave to love, so that nothing better can be expected even of the clergy. But the remark is clearly meant to be provocative, as if to say to the reader: 'Judge if you dare' (or, more evangelically, 'Judge not lest ye be judged'). Throughout the book Lázaro punctuates the narrative with *sententiae* which warn the reader to be careful at what he laughs, and whose underlying sense is 'Know thyself'.

From his first master Lázaro learns a painful and simple lesson: that life is a cut-throat business in which it is every man for himself. Of the blind man he says: 'que después de Dios éste me dio la vida, y siendo ciego me alumbró y adestró en la carrera de vivir'. His next master is a miserly priest who stands for shameless hypocrisy and effrontery. He is capable of offering the boy a plate of well-picked bones with the words: 'Toma, come, triunfa, que para ti es el mundo. Mejor vida tienes que el Papa'. At another time he remarks: 'Mira, mozo, los sacerdotes han de ser muy templados en su comer y beber, y por esto yo no me desmando como otros'—which Lázaro knows to be a lie, since he has seen his master gorging himself at funeral feasts: 'a costa ajena comía como lobo y bebía más que un saludador'. Lázaro's third master is a penniless *escudero* obsessed with the obligations of honour. His only care is for appearances. Lázaro reflects:

> ¡Grandes secretos son, Señor, los que Vos hacéis y las gentes ignoran! ¿A quién no engañara aquella buena disposición y razonable capa y sayo, y quién pensara que aquel gentil hombre se pasó ayer todo el día sin comer, con aquel mendrugo de pan que su criado Lázaro trujo un día y una noche en el arca de su seno, do no se le podía pegar mucha limpieza, y hoy, lavándose las manos y cara, a falta de paño de manos, se hacía servir de la halda del sayo? ¡Oh Señor, y cuántos de aquéstos debéis Vos tener por el mundo derramados, que padecen por la negra que llaman honra lo que por Vos no sufrirían!

Like nearly all Lázaro's masters, the *escudero* is not what he seems (the blind man's public prayers were pure showmanship).

His next master is a friar, evidently not a pattern of virtue, whom Lázaro soon leaves. He is then employed by a pardoner, whose irreligious frauds he recounts with relish. Then, employed by a chaplain, he becomes a water-boy and after four years of this moves on and up into the post of town-crier, marriage, and prosperity. His material prosperity is real enough, and his new post—however degraded it might appear to his betters—represents worldly success of a sort for a poor lad. At the same time, however, he has to put up with gossip about his wife's relations with the archpriest. He accepts reassurance easily enough, but we are left in no doubt of the truth. Lázaro, who professes to be happy so long as the matter is not alluded to, has acquired prosperity at the price of moral degradation.

Honour is an important theme in the book. Lázaro mentions it in his prologue, when he says (quoting Cicero) that 'La honra cría las artes'. He returns to the theme when he tells how, after four years as water-boy, he saved enough

> para me vestir muy honradamente de la ropa vieja, de la cual compré un jubón viejo . . . y un sayo raído . . . y una capa y una espada de las viejas primeras de Cuéllar. Desque me vi en hábito de hombre de bien, dije a mi amo se tomase su asno, que no quería más seguir aquel oficio.

Honradamente is a significant word and the sword a significant detail: both touches evoke the *escudero*. Even his words are echoed in Lázaro's *honradamente* and *hombre de bien*: 'Eres muchacho, y no sientes las cosas de la honra, en que el día de hoy está todo el caudal de los hombres de bien.' Finally, honour is referred to again when the archpriest reassures Lázaro in ambiguous terms concerning his wife's comings and goings: 'Ella entra muy a tu honra y suya.' Honour is, after all, profit. Lázaro ends where he began. He learnt to welcome his mother's lover because he brought food, just as now he accepts the archpriest's attentions to his wife for the sake of profit. We recall that the *escudero*, too, would have gladly accepted degradation—lying, fawning, backbiting—in order to please his master could he but find one. Honour is a social conspiracy in which Lázaro has learnt to play his part. This anatomy of honour as the world conceives it has an interesting parallel in the sixth dialogue of Antonio de Torquemada's *Coloquios satíricos* (Mondoñedo, 1553), in which the conventional notion of honour (as social esteem, the cult of appearances) is contrasted with true honour, which springs only from virtue. For Torquemada honour is the Devil's subtlest snare to tempt men to perdition. All classes are deluded by it—'veréis a cada uno, en el estado en que vive, tener una presunción luciferina en el cuerpo'. It is the contrary of Christian humility. The dialogue reads at times like a commentary on *Lazarillo*. In contrasting social and Christian values it makes explicit what is implicit in *Lazarillo*.

At the end of the book we can see Lázaro apply what he has learnt from his masters: the ruthless determination to win 'la carrera de la vida' which he learnt from the blind man; the hypocrisy of the priest of Maqueda; the cynicism of the pardoner (as when he swears by the body of Christ that his wife is as chaste a woman as lives in Toledo); the importance of honour as upheld by the *escudero*. Lázaro now embodies the values he has picked up along the road; he has been an apt pupil. The apparently haphazard structure of the book is brought to order by the last *tratado*, which draws the threads together. No *tratado* was complete in itself: each acquires its complete meaning only when we lay down the book. Lázaro could see through and mock the faults of others, but he is stubbornly blind to his own. Again the mote and the beam.

One is constantly struck by the frequency of Lázaro's allusions to God. He appears to attribute every piece of good luck and every clever idea to the direct intervention of God, as, for example, when he succeeds in avenging himself on the blind man in spite of his cunning 'porque Dios le cegó aquella hora el entendimiento'. Phrases of this sort are, of course, conventional, but their frequency may hint at something. Lázaro, we note, equates God with luck: the name has no moral connotation for him whatever. His pious phrases are unsupported by belief or action. He shares the hollow piety of a hollow society. His references to God are another aspect of the opportunism he has learnt from everyone about him. Lázaro is a victim of a society whose religion is a cloak for self-seeking. To say this is not to attribute anachronistically to the anonymous author a modern view of the importance of environment in the formation of the individual. An alternative formulation is possible, and indeed was made in a work contemporary with *Lazarillo*: Juan Maldonado's *Pastor bonus* (1549).[13] Maldonado, an Erasmian, arguing for ecclesiastical reform, shows how a vain and worldly clergy—from the bishop downward—can by its example corrupt the whole of society, whose members find no help in those who should guide them to better things. Ostentation, vanity, and self-seeking breed their kind. This is what we find in *Lazarillo*, which lifts the lid off a supposedly Christian society to show the reality within. It has often been suggested that the author of *Lazarillo* was an Erasmian. This is credible. Certainly, there is nothing of Erasmus's positive teaching present in the book, but the dissection of hypocrisy, the exposure of the un-Christian heart of an apparently Christian society, is very suggestive of an Erasmian origin.

The theme was not a new one. The essential novelty of *Lazarillo* is of another kind. No previous narrative offers what this one does: a portrait of a child in the process of becoming a man, an account of how he is moulded imperceptibly by the example of others, so that when we realise with a shock that his childish innocence has gone for good we cannot decide when and where the change took place. The answer is 'nowhere and everywhere': not at any one place and not in any one crisis, but as a result of an insidious influence that has surrounded him from his earliest days. That is why it is possible to hate the society he describes while retaining a feeling of pity, though mixed with derision, for Lázaro himself, this cuckolded town-crier who struts so complacently among the ruins of his innocence and boasts there of his good fortune. This portrayal of a man growing up is the anonymous author's great achievement. Its novelty is clearer if we turn to other sixteenth-century works of fiction, for example the romances of chivalry. In some of them we see a child born who will become a knight, and sometimes we see his death. But there is no sense of process. He already *is* from the start what the ideals of chivalry demand. He has adventures, but they do not mould his character. Lázaro's end mirrors his entire life.

In one trait he reflects his first master, in another the cool hypocrisy of the second, in another the obsessions of the squire, in another the cheerful blasphemy of the pardoner. The last *tratado* makes clear the formal and thematic unity of the whole work.

The printing of three editions in one year indicates that the book was an immediate commercial success. In 1555 a *Segunda parte* was published in Antwerp. In this Lázaro temporarily becomes a fish and has a series of submarine adventures. It is strange stuff, so strange that the possibility of an allegorical meaning cannot be disregarded.[14] Both parts were prohibited by the Inquisition's prohibitory index of 1559. In 1573 an expurgated edition appeared as *Lazarillo de Tormes castigado*, with all the irreligious jokes and episodes excised. This was several times reprinted in the sixteenth and seventeenth centuries. The original was reprinted a number of times outside Spain (though not again inside Spain until the nineteenth century). The book was popular elsewhere in Europe: it was translated into French as early as 1560 (and retranslated three times in the next century). An English translation by David Rowland of Anglesey was printed in 1576 (possibly 1568). The book, then, had its following; but it is disconcerting to the modern reader to realise that its popularity did not begin to rival that of the romances of chivalry, or even some of the pastoral novels.

The sixteenth century was one of experiment in prose fiction. One of the experiments was the first European epistolary novel: Juan de Segura's *Proceso de cartas de amores* (Toledo?, 1548). Nothing is known of Segura. His book is a sentimental novel of unhappy love whose novelty lies not in its theme but in the treatment of it. The entire work is in the form of letters between two unnamed lovers, who describe their feelings from the man's first diffident approach to the moment when the despairing girl's indignant family bear her off to an unknown destination. There are some pedantries and *longueurs*, but there are also poignancies. It is an interesting achievement, but with no immediate sequel in Spain.[15]

One of the oddities of the century is *El Crotalón* by 'Christophoro Gnophoso', sometimes (unconvincingly, on the slenderest evidence) identified with Cristóbal de Villalón, an uninspired humanist and pedagogue, and author of (amongst other things) an *Ingeniosa comparación entre lo antiguo y lo presente* (Valladolid, 1539), a *Gramática castellana* (Antwerp, 1558), and *El Scolástico* (unpublished in its entirety until 1967). *El Crotalón* (not printed until 1871) was written around 1553. It is a satirical dialogue in the style of Lucian between a cobbler and a cock who has been many people in his time: Pythagoras, Sardanapalus, a captain, a priest, a nun, and so on. This permits the author to range widely over all sorts and conditions of men, satirising all manner of human frailties and follies. The work has a strongly Erasmian tone. It borrows freely from many writers, ancient and modern, and is more curious than satisfying.

Another work sometimes attributed to Villalón (equally unconvincingly) is *Viaje de Turquía* which once again was not printed until modern times. It is a dialogue in which Juan de Votadiós and *Mátalascallando* question Pedro de Urdemalas (all three names belong to Spanish folklore) about his adventures in foreign parts, particularly about his captivity at the hands of the Turks, among whom Pedro was able to pass himself off as a doctor. He depicts vividly the customs of Turks and others, suggesting that the work was written by an eyewitness. It is clear from the treatment of religion that the author was an Erasmian. According to M. Bataillon he was Dr Andrés de Laguna (d. 1560), a celebrated and much-travelled medical man, author of an annotated translation of Dioscorides and other works; but the evidence, though persuasive, is far from conclusive.[16]

The rediscovery of the Byzantine novel, most notably Heliodorus's *Etheopica*, in the sixteenth century led to numerous European imitations. The first in Spanish was Alonso Núñez de Reinoso's *Historia de los amores de Clareo y Florisea* (Venice, 1552), a characteristic story of separated lovers, exotic adventures, and strange turns of fortune. The first part is a free adaptation of Achilles Tatius's *Leucippe and Clitophon*. Jerónimo de Contreras's *Selva de aventuras* (Barcelona, 1565), another vicissitudinous tale of frustrated love, follows the pattern of the Byzantine novels, but the action is more down-to-earth.

Both these books contain numerous intercalated stories. A growing interest in the *novella* or short story is one of the features of the sixteenth century, in fact. This is evident in the pastoral novels. The Italian *novellieri* Boccaccio, Bandello, Giraldi, etc., were the important influence in this development.

One isolated Spanish example is a masterpiece of the genre: the anonymous *Historia del Abencerraje y la hermosa Jarifa*. Four versions are known: one in Antonio de Villegas's miscellany of prose and verse, *Inventario* (Medina del Campo, 1565; but the privilege states that the author had applied for a licence to print in 1551); another intercalated in an edition of 1561 of Montemayor's *Diana*; a third printed in Saragossa (n.d.) apparently as an extract from a chronicle; and a fourth in a manuscript now in Madrid. Villegas's version is the best. The story is a simple one: it tells how the noble Moor Abindarráez is taken prisoner in a Christian ambush and prevented from keeping an assignation with his beloved Jarifa. Moved by the Moor's plight, his captor, Rodrigo de Narváez, gives him his liberty in order to see Jarifa. The lovers return to deliver themselves voluntarily to Narváez, who shows his generosity a second time by freeing them. The story is a deeply touching one of love and chivalry placed in the idealised and now exotic setting of the Andalusian frontier wars between Moors and Christians.

The enterprising Valencian bookseller Juan de Timoneda fed the demand for entertaining short stories, first with *Sobremesa y alivio de caminantes* (Saragossa and Medina, 1563), then in *El buen aviso y portacuentos* (Valencia, 1564), finally in *El patrañuelo* (Valencia, 1565). The first two are stories, pillaged from every quarter, reduced to brief anecdotes. The stories in the third are more ambitious but equally second-hand. They are baldly told. Timoneda was an enterprising middleman, not an artist.

Though it is not wholly a work of fiction, this seems the appropriate moment to introduce one of the most interesting works of its period: *Historia de los bandos de los Zegríes y Abencerrajes, caballeros moros de Granada, de las civiles guerras que hubo en ella, y batallas particulares que hubo en la Vega...* (Part I, Saragossa, 1595; Part II, Cuenca, 1619)—better known as *Guerras civiles de Granada*—whose author, Ginés Pérez de Hita (1544?-1619?), drew on historical sources, *romances* on the wars, and his own imagination to write a work which is best considered as a historical novel. It is written with vividness and verve. Local colour is exploited freely. Love and war intermingle so that the work acquires something of the character of a romance of chivalry. Numerous episodes and stories punctuate the main narrative, so that the effect is of an exotic abundance. Not surprisingly the work was many times reprinted and inspired a multitude of poems, plays, and stories.

NOTES

1. In editing the first three books (which of course he did not write) Montalvo abbreviated the text of the primitive *Amadís* (while at the same time making short interpolations of his own). For the evidence, see Rodríguez-Moñino, 'El primer manuscrito del "Amadís de Gaula"...', *BRAE* (1956).

2. Henry Thomas, *Spanish and Portuguese Romances...* (Cambridge, 1920), p. 147. Perhaps the finest Peninsular romance is the Catalan *Tirant lo Blanc* (Valencia, 1490) begun by Joanot Martorell and finished by Martí de Galba (see Arthur Terry, *A Literary History of Spain: Catalan Literature*). Cervantes admired it but the Castilian translation (1511) was not reprinted.

3. For this see M. Bataillon, *Erasmo y España* (Mexico, 1966), Ch. I.

4. Carlos Clavería, *Le chevalier délibéré de Olivier de la Marche y sus versiones españolas del siglo XVI* (Saragossa, 1950).

5. J. Huizinga, *The Waning of the Middle Ages* (Harmondsworth, 1955), p. 71.

6. From the first chapter of *Palmerín de Inglaterra* (1547—translated from the original Portuguese of Francisco de Moraes), much admired by Cervantes. The scene is England, the rider Don Duardos.

7. See below, pp. 78-9.

8. He was also the author of a considerable amount of verse, both amorous and religious, published in *Las obras de . . .* (Antwerp, 1554), subsequently republished (with additions) in two volumes: *Segundo cancionero* and *Segundo cancionero espiritual* (both Antwerp, 1558). The volume of religious verse was banned by the Inquisition in 1559. Montemayor also published translations of poems by Ausias March (Valencia, 1560). For these see M. de Riquer, *Traducciones castellanas de Ausias March en la Edad de Oro* (Barcelona, 1946).

9. My references to *Los siete libros de la Diana,* ed. F. López Estrada, CC 127 (Madrid, 1946).

10. My references to the edition by R. Ferreres, CC 135 (Madrid, 1953).

11. See R. O. Jones, 'Bembo, Gil Polo, Garcilaso. Three Accounts of Love', *RLC* (1966).

12. For the humanistic comedies in general, see (but with caution) the account by M. Menéndez Pelayo in *Orígenes de la novela* (Santander, 1943), vol. 3. For *La Celestina,* see A. D. Deyermond, *A Literary History of Spain: The Middle Ages,* pp. 166-70. See Bibliography for editions referred to here.

13. Bataillon, op. cit., pp. 328-38.

14. For an interesting interpretation, see M. Saludo Stephan, *Misteriosas andanzas atunescas de 'Lázaro de Tormes'* (San Sebastian, 1969). The interpretation often seems far-fetched; but so, undeniably, is the book.

15. The anonymous *Cuestión de amor* (Valencia, 1513), probably composed in Naples, is a prolongation of the fifteenth-century sentimental novel and has no sequel or influence. It was several times reprinted together with *Cárcel de amor*. For text and study see M. Menéndez Pelayo, *Orígenes de la novela.*

16. See Bataillon, op. cit., pp. 655-68 for Villalón, and 669-92 for *Viaje de Turquía.*

Chapter 4

LITERATURE AND THE COUNTER-REFORMATION

THE COUNTER-REFORMATION—the Catholic Church's response to the threat offered by Protestantism—was a phenomenon too complex to be briefly described. It was not a negatively conservative response to the challenge, but an attempt at the revivification of the traditional culture of Christendom, by a Church which aspired to mould and direct that culture in all its aspects. Humanism was enlisted and redirected. Education was rightly seen as a vital tool for the task the Church had set itself: the Jesuits were to prove particularly energetic in this field, so much so that by the end of the century they had acquired almost a monopoly of the lower levels of education. Many of the greatest figures in Spanish literature of the Golden Age were pupils of the Jesuits. Cervantes (who lavished memorable praise on the Jesuits in *El coloquio de los perros*) may have attended a Jesuit school; Lope de Vega certainly did. Through their famous *Ratio studiorum*—the elaborate rules which governed their schools from the end of the sixteenth century, prescribing an education based almost entirely on the classics—the Society of Jesus became indeed one of the greatest influences in moulding Spanish culture of the later Golden Age.

Before the Protestants could be won back or effectively countered, the Catholic Church needed to define its own dogma. This was done at the Council of Trent, where Spanish theologians played a leading role. Though now accentuated, neither the militancy of the Church nor its interest in education was new: the Church in Spain during and after Trent was following the same course as that laid at the beginning of the century by Cisneros. But there was an important difference between the two periods: between Cisneros and Trent came the Spanish Erasmian movement and the fruitful tolerance of those years, which exacerbated the traditional opposition. By the 1560s the traditionalists had won: under Philip II Spain was closed to new currents of ideas beyond her frontiers. Intellectual life did not immediately wither: for example, important contributions were made to economic theory in the later sixteenth century and in the seventeenth by men who used the language of scholasticism[1] but in general intellectual novelty came to be regarded with suspicion. The spiritual fervour and religious uniformity of later Golden Age Spain was accompanied by a closing of minds; if, indeed, the latter was not a condition of the former. A law of censorship which had existed since 1502 was strengthened in 1558. Before publication, a book now required the censors' *aprobación*, which was printed among the book's preliminaries. The importation of foreign books without a royal licence was now made a capital offence. The Spanish Inquisition published its first index of prohibited books in 1551, and in 1584 its first expurgatory index (i.e., an index of books permitted to circulate after the deletion of offending passages). It is fruitless to speculate how much Spain and Spanish literature were to lose, how many books were to remain unwritten, through such measures. The secretly heterodox were silenced; but within its doctrinal limitations Spanish literature was nevertheless to reach extraordinary heights.

There was a vast increase in the publication of religious books in Spain after Trent. Undoubtedly this marked an intensified fervour; but publications of all kinds multiplied as the presses increased in number and grew more efficient, and as a public used to books was created. That the absolute increase in religious publications was also a relative one is doubtful. If book production in Aragon was typical, the contrary is true. An analysis—necessarily assigning many books arbitrarily to one or the other category, and counting in all reprints—of J. M. Sánchez, *Bibliografía aragonesa del siglo XVI* (2 vols., Madrid, 1914), shows that in the period 1501-50 religious works amounted to 63 per cent of the total, and that this fell to almost precisely 50 per cent in the period 1551-1600. Too much reliance must not be placed on these figures (though no better ones are available) but they appear to be confirmed by the growing flood of profane literature which poured from the printing presses in the later sixteenth and the seventeenth centuries. Official ecclesiastical pressure was steadily in favour of a morally edifying literature and many edifying works were written, but confronted by the torrent of frivolous light literature in the seventeenth century, one would be hard put to it to say what general effect the Counter-Reformation can be said to have had on literature in Spain. The demand for edification encouraged the realistic portrayal of man in credible circumstances and hence perhaps favoured the rise of literary realism in the later sixteenth century whose culmination is seen in the best works of the picaresque tradition and in Cervantes; but even here it is wise to bear in mind that there was already a taste for realism long before the Counter-Reformation, and not always for edifying reasons, as *La lozana andaluza* reminds us.

Some of the finest writing of the sixteenth century is to be found in the works of ascetics and mystics. Among the first, three stand out: Fray

Luis de León, Fray Luis de Granada, and P. Malón de Chaide; and among the second, St Teresa and San Juan de la Cruz.

Fray Luis de León (1527-91) was born of partly *converso* ancestry in the town of Belmonte. He entered the Augustinian Order and studied at the University of Salamanca. He was a renowned Hebraist and biblical scholar. In 1572 he was arrested by the Inquisition on a charge of questioning the authority of the Vulgate and for circulating an unauthorised translation of the Song of Songs. He defended himself with eventual success, but was not released until 1576, with his health impaired. On release he was appointed to another Chair at Salamanca. Shortly before he died he became Provincial of his Order. His writings include original poetry (see below, pp. 103-10), verse translations from the Bible and the classics, and various devotional and edifying works (in Latin and Spanish) of which the best known are *De los nombres de Cristo* (Salamanca, 1583), *La perfecta casada* (Salamanca, 1583), *Exposición del Cantar de los Cantares* (not published until 1798), and *Exposición del Libro de Job* (finished in 1591, published in 1779).

De los nombres de Cristo is a dialogue (led by Marcelo, representing the author) on the significance of the names given to Christ in the Old and New Testaments: 'Pimpollo', 'Camino', 'Pastor', etc. It is based on a scholastic theory of language. As Fray Luis expounds it in *De los nombres de Cristo*, a thing is perfect in the degree in which it contains all other things, in this degree resembling the perfection of God, who contains all things. To resemble God is the aspiration of all things: 'el pío general de todas las cosas . . .' Man's mind can contain all things, not materially but through their names, contributing thereby to the unity of the universe.

> Consiste, pues, la perfección de las cosas en que cada uno de nosotros sea un mundo perfecto, para que por esta manera, estando todos en mí y yo en todos los otros, y teniendo yo su ser de todos ellos, y todos y cada uno de ellos teniendo el ser mío, se abrace y eslabone toda esta máquina del universo, y se reduzca a unidad la muchedumbre de sus diferencias; y quedando no mezcladas, se mezclen; y permaneciendo muchas, no lo sean; y para que, extendiéndose y como desplegándose delante los ojos la variedad y diversidad, venza y reine y ponga su silla la unidad sobre todo. Lo cual es avecinarse la criatura a Dios, de quien mana . . . ('De los nombres en general')

A word (Fray Luis goes on) ought to express as closely as possible the nature of what it names, which was indeed the case in the perfect first language spoken by Adam, from whose perfection all languages have since fallen away. Hebrew retained something of that perfection in its name for God: 'Porque, si miramos al sonido con que se pronuncia, todo él es vocal, así como lo es aquel a quien significa, que todo es ser y vida y espíritu sin ninguna mezcla de composición o de materia.' And the three signs forming the word symbolise the Trinity.

When in the presence of God, our understanding of him will be complete, but until that time no name can express his nature; hence the many names given to Christ in the Bible, each one expressing one aspect of his nature.

This, then, is the theory on which the book is founded. The rest of the work explores the inwardness of the symbolic names themselves. The book's range is necessarily limited by its nature, but it is nevertheless one of the most readable works of its time. Of particular interest are 'Pastor' and 'Príncipe de la paz'. The first is infused with Neoplatonism and the atmosphere of Renaissance pastoral as Fray Luis describes the innocence of the life of the (much idealised) shepherd amidst the beauties of nature, which is not only beautiful but morally instructive since the elements of which it is composed are a visible lesson in harmony or love (see below, p. 104). The same atmosphere and mode of thought pervade 'Príncipe de la paz', which opens:

> Cuando la razón no lo demonstrara ni por otro camino se pudiera entender cuán amable cosa sea la paz, esta vista hermosa del cielo que se nos descubre ahora, y el concierto que tienen entre sí aquestos resplandores que lucen en él, nos dan de ello suficiente testimonio. Porque ¿qué otra cosa es sino paz, o ciertamente una imagen perfecta de paz, esto que ahora vemos en el cielo, y que con tanto deleite se nos viene a los ojos? Que si la paz es, como San Agustín breve y verdaderamente concluye, *una orden sosegada, o un tener sosiego y firmeza en lo que pide el buen orden*, eso mismo es lo que nos descubre ahora esta imagen. Adonde el ejército de las estrellas, puesto como en ordenanza y como concertado por sus hileras, luce hermosísimo, y adonde cada una de ellas inviolablemente guarda su puesto; adonde no usurpa ninguna el lugar de su vecina ... [antes] se hacen muestra de amor ...

Passages like these read like a commentary on the poetry of Fray Luis, and can prove an important aid to its understanding since ideas are made explicit which are implicit there but not easy for the modern reader to divine.

The book is written in a style at once plain and elegant. In his dedication to Book 3, Fray Luis defends his having written in Castilian. He denies the superiority of Latin, but insists at the same time that good Spanish is not how the *vulgo* speaks but the result of painstaking care:

> ... que el bien hablar no es común, sino negocio de particular juicio, así en lo que se dice como en la manera como se dice. Y negocio que

> de las palabras que todos hablan elige las que convienen, y mira el sonido de ellas, y aun cuenta a veces las letras, y las pesa, y las mide, y las compone, para que no solamente digan con claridad lo que se pretende decir, sino también con armonía y dulzura.

Fray Luis the poet is visible in his prose not only in the vividness of much of his imagery but in this preoccupation with harmony of style.

La perfecta casada is a description of the perfect wife, written in the form of an extended commentary on *Proverbs* 31. Her virtues move him to rapturous eloquence.

> Y, a la verdad, si hay debajo de la luna cosa que merezca ser estimada y preciada, es la mujer buena; y en comparación con ella el sol mismo no luce y son obscuras las estrellas. ('Introducción')

Fray Luis's subject is the woman of flesh and blood, not the idealised abstraction of romantic fiction. She is shown about her daily tasks, cooking, cleaning, spinning. Commenting on verse 14 he writes:

> Y verá que, estándose sentada con sus mujeres, volteando el huso en la mano y contando consejas—como la nave que, sin parecer que se muda, va navegando—, y pasando un día y sucediendo otro, y viniendo las noches y amaneciendo las mañanas, y corriendo, como sin menearse, la obra, se teje la tela y se labra el paño y se acaban las ricas labores; y cuando menos pensamos, llenas las velas de prosperidad, entra esta nuestra nave en el puerto y comienza a desplegar sus riquezas; y sale de allí el abrigo para los criados, y el vestido para los hijos, y las galas suyas y los arreos para su marido . . .

Fray Luis's enthusiasm rises to an almost poetic eloquence. It is not surprising that in the past the book has been perhaps the most widely read of his works in prose.

Fray Luis de Granada (1504-88), a Dominican, led a more cloistered life than Luis de León, though he held high positions in his order and was celebrated as a preacher. His works were among the most widely known of the entire Golden Age: notably *Guía de pecadores* (Lisbon, 1556-57) and *Introducción del símbolo de la fe* (Salamanca, 1583). The first of these was read in Protestant countries and even by Far Eastern converts. It is an eloquently argued exposition of Christian doctrine and an exhortation to follow the path of virtue.

Introducción del símbolo de la fe has a far wider interest, which brims over the narrow banks of doctrine, especially in the first part, which is a meditation on the greatness of God as revealed through his works. The world (he declares) is not only for man's use but so that it may be enjoyed for its beauty. The manifold beauties of the universe are recounted in what reads at times like a hymn to creation. Fray Luis quotes and paraphrases Cicero's *De natura deorum* on how the majesty of the universe reveals the majesty of its creator, not only in the grandeur of the heavens but in the mountains and seas of Earth, and even in the smallest details of creation. All things proclaim God.

> Por cierto, Señor, el que tales voces no oye, sordo es; y el que con tan maravillosos resplandores no os ve, ciego es; y el que vistas todas estas cosas no os alaba, mudo es; y el que con tantos argumentos y testimonios de todas las criaturas no conoce la nobleza de su criador, loco es . . . ¿Qué hoja de árbol, qué flor del campo, qué gusanico hay tan pequeño, que si bien considerásemos la fábrica de su corpezuelo no viésemos en él grandes maravillas? (1, II)

Having stated his theme, Fray Luis now extols the various parts of the universe in turn: first the heavenly bodies in their spheres, then the sublunar world composed of the four elements (earth, air, fire, and water) whose peaceful coupling was ordained by God—

> y desta manera se traban y dan la mano unos elementos a otros, y hacen una como danza de espadas, continuándose amigablemente por esta forma los unos con los otros. (1, VI)

Then he describes in turn each element of Earth, enumerating the abundance of life with which its creator has filled it. He describes the infinitely varied fish of the sea:

> Pues ¿qué diré de las diferencias de mariscos que nos da la mar? . . . Y allende desto, ¿qué diré de las conchas de que se hace la grana fina, que es el ornamento de los reyes? ¿Qué de las otras conchas y veneras y figuras de caracoles grandes y pequeños, fabricados de mil maneras, más blancos que la nieve, y con eso con pintas de diversos colores sembradas por todos ellos? ¡Oh admirable sabiduría del Criador! ¡Cuán engrandecidas son, Señor, vuestras obras! (l, VIII)

He lists the creatures of earth, describing them with loving detail drawn from personal observation as well as from books, and drawing moral profit from them where he can:

> Porque el Criador no sólo formó los animales para servicio de nuestros cuerpos, sino también para maestros y ejemplos de nuestra vida: como es la castidad de la tórtola, la simplicidad de la paloma, la piedad de los hijos de la cigüeña para con sus padres viejos, y otras cosas tales. (1, XIV, §iv)

Next, Fray Luis describes man, first his body and its functions, then his mind and soul. Finally, he describes the six days of Creation to show how all the marvels of the universe came into being.

In all this Fray Luis is following the markedly Neoplatonic teaching of (amongst others) Hugh of St Victor and St Bonaventure, according to whom God's Providence may be read in nature's beauty and goodness: what Andrew Marvell called 'nature's mystick Book'.

The first part (undeniably the one of widest literary interest) tells, then, of the harmonious universe. Part 2 treats of the excellences of the Christian faith, Parts 3 and 4 of the mystery of the Redemption, Part 5 being a summary of the whole, with an appendix on how best to instruct the heathen. The whole work may be regarded as an encyclopaedia of the Christian religion.

Fray Luis's style is worthy of his theme. It is as expressively elegant as that of Luis de León, but more self-consciously rhetorical, showing the influence of Cicero in its frequent rhetorical questions, apostrophes, balanced cadences, and other devices.

Pedro Malón de Chaide (1530?-89), an Augustinian, studied at Salamanca under Luis de León and later taught at other universities before becoming prior of the Augustinian house in Barcelona. He wrote only one book: *La conversión de la Magdalena* (Barcelona, 1588), which, as he declares in the prologue, he had put aside and finally published only on the command of his bishop. It is intended as a morally profitable alternative to those 'libros lascivos y profanos' which corrupt and deprave.

> Porque ¿qué otra cosa son los libros de amores y las *Dianas* y *Boscanes* y *Garcilasos*, y los monstruosos libros y silvas de fabulosos cuentos y mentiras de los *Amadises*, *Floriseles* y *Don Belianís*, y una flota de semejantes portentos, como hay escritos, puestos en manos de pocos años, sino cuchillo en poder del hombre furioso? ('Prologo')

Girls scarcely able to walk carry a *Diana* in their pocket. Others read romances of chivalry in preference to Holy Writ. (In this literary puritanism he represents the age: Luis de León, believing—as he affirms in 'Monte' in *De los nombres de Cristo*—that poetry is 'una comunicación del aliento celestial y divino', held that only the sacred was a fit theme for poetry, anything else being corrupt and corrupting.)

The work is a discursive, digressive meditation on the life of Mary Magdalen, who is offered as a guide to the errant sinner. The first part starts with an account (of Neoplatonic inspiration) of the power of love, which is diffused downwards throughout the universe from its source in God, and is returned to him by his creatures to complete a circle of love.

> Es el amor un círculo bueno, que perpetuamente se revuelve del bien al bien. Necesariamente ha de ser bueno el amor, pues, naciendo del bien, vuelve otra vez a parar en el mismo bien donde nació; porque

> el mismo Dios es aquel, cuya hermosura desean todas las criaturas, y en cuya posesión hallan su descanso. (I, III)

The life of the Magdalen is one of love first misdirected into the paths of lust before finding its true object.

The book is written in a vivid style which moves easily between the colloquial and the ornately rhetorical, employing every device of language to bring the author's message home sharply to the reader. It is a style which reflects the preacher's art. That Malón de Chaide was very consciously preoccupied with questions of style is evident from his prologue, where, in justification of his decision to write in the vernacular, he alludes to *De los nombres de Cristo,*

> un librito . . . puesto por un muy curioso y levantado estilo, y con términos tan pulidos y limados y asentados con estremado artificio, en quien se verá la grandeza y majestad de palabras de que nuestra lengua castellana está como preñada, y que tiene gran riqueza y copia y mineros, que no se pueden acabar, de luces y flores y gala y rodeos en el decir . . .

This leads him on to a passionate (even nationalistic) eulogy of Castilian itself against its detractors. His care for language extends (unusually for that age) to orthography, which he believed should reflect actual pronunciation not etymology.

It is a book, then, which offers moments of varied and absorbing interest; but (it must be admitted) its *longueurs* are frequent and only the very devout would read the whole work for pleasure.

Mysticism (the experience of union with the divine), which if we exclude Ramón Llull had no medieval precedent in Spain, came to a late flowering there in the sixteenth century for reasons which are obscure. In the Middle Ages, Franciscan mysticism had developed a philosophy of love which was later to be influenced by the Renaissance Neoplatonists, according to whom true love, the pursuit of beauty, was an ascent of a ladder of love leading to the contemplation of God himself as the source of love and beauty together. Perhaps the sudden flowering of mysticism in Spain owed something to the direct influence of this doctrine; though then it has to be explained why this should happen in Spain in particular and not elsewhere. Whatever the reason, in the 1520s Franciscan mystical treatises began to appear in Spain, the most important being Francisco de Osuna's *Abecedario espiritual,* in six parts (1525-54), of which the most important is the *Tercer abecedario* (Toledo, 1527). This and Bernardino de Laredo's *Subida del monte Sión* (1535) were to have a great influence on St Teresa. Spanish mysticism reached its peak in St Teresa and in San Juan de la Cruz, but mystical treatises were to keep on appearing until the end of the seventeenth century.

St Teresa, or Santa Teresa de Jesús (1515-82), was born in Avila into a prosperous and respected family (though her paternal grandfather, a *converso*, had been obliged by the Inquisition to do public penance for relapsing into Judaism). She received little formal education. She was an active woman who, after becoming a Carmelite nun in 1534, devoted her life to the reform of the Carmelite Order. She founded her first convent of discalced Carmelites in 1562. Her most important books are *Camino de perfección* (Évora, 1583), *El libro de la vida* (Salamanca, 1588), *El castillo interior o tratado de las Moradas* (Salamanca, 1588), and *Libro de las fundaciones* (Brussels, 1610).

In all these works the personality of the author comes vividly before us. Being written for her fellow-nuns—in the main women of little education—at the command of her superiors, they are appropriately direct and colloquial in language. The spelling is capricious, reflecting popular pronunciation. St Teresa does not theorise but attempts to convey her experiences with the greatest possible vividness in a language rich in popular idiom and metaphors drawn from everyday life. Frequently the impression of a particular person in a particular time and place is communicated with artless immediacy. But not for its own sake: the intention is didactic: to reach the imagination of her readers the better to convey through reference to the familiar an unfamiliar world of experience. To take one example: in her *Vida*, describing the way of contemplation and prayer, she chooses an image which is (as she admits) commonplace enough—that of the garden to be made and tended. She describes how it is to be watered.

> Paréceme a mí que se puede regar de cuatro maneras: u con sacar el agua de un pozo, que es a nuestro gran trabajo; u con noria y arcaduces, que se saca con un torno (yo lo he sacado algunas veces): es a menos trabajo que estotro y sácase más agua; u de un río u arroyo: esto se riega muy mijor, que queda más harta la tierra de agua y no se ha menester regar tan a menudo, y es a menos trabajo mucho del hortelano; u con llover mucho, que lo riega el Señor sin trabajo ninguno nuestro . . .

Having thus touched the imagination of her readers, she can now apply the analogy, which in chapters 11-22 is made to yield instruction in the four levels of prayer.

The *Vida* (finished in 1562) is a spiritual autobiography of frequently striking insight into self, as vividly written as her letters. Deeply impressed with it, her confessors now instructed her to write a more systematic work on the spiritual life for the use of her nuns: she accordingly wrote *Camino de perfección* (begun in 1562). The *Libro de las fundaciones* (written in 1573) is an account of the founding of her convents, rivalling her *Vida* and letters in biographical interest.

Las moradas (written in 1570) is the most interesting of her spiritual works. It describes the seven 'mansions' or rooms of the castle of the soul. The soul in its progress towards mystic union passes through three mansions during the way of purgation, three more during the illuminative way, until it reaches union in the seventh and innermost mansion. The process is described with an abundance of metaphor. She describes (for example) the concentric arrangement of the mansions in terms of an edible palm sprout:

> No habéis de entender estas moradas una en pos de otra como cosa en hilada, sino poned los ojos en el centro, que es la pieza u palacio a donde está el rey, y considerad como un palmito, que para llegar a lo que es de comer tiene muchas coberturas, que todo lo sabroso cercan.

Telling how the soul must be mortified to the world before it can aspire to union she describes how a silkworm 'dies' in its cocoon to be reborn as a moth:

> . . . y allí con las boquillas van de sí mesmas hilando la seda y hacen unos capuchillos muy apretados, adonde se encierran; y acaba este gusano, que es grande y feo, y sale del mesmo capucho una mariposica blanca muy graciosa.

She urges her nuns to spin their cocoons out of prayers and penances; and the cocoon is Christ, in whom the soul is reborn. The everyday image has a beautiful appropriateness.

Not all her images are of this everyday nature: sometimes she displays an unusual quality of poetic imagination, as when, describing the mansion of 'oración de recogimiento', she speaks of this prayer as welling gently into the soul like a spring whose water, instead of flowing, grew into the very fabric of the mansion:

> Ansí como se entiende claro un dilatamiento u ensanchamiento en el alma, a manera de como si el agua que mana de una fuente no tuviese corriente, sino que la mesma fuente estuviese labrada de una cosa que mientra más agua manase más grande se hiciese el edificio . . .

Rarely can an experience so remote have been conveyed with such poignant effect. Her poetry, though good, is far less expressive.

San Juan de la Cruz (1542-91), christened Juan de Yepes, was born in the province of Avila like St Teresa. He graduated from the University of Salamanca, and entered the Carmelite Order in 1563. His association with the reform movement initiated by St Teresa led to his imprisonment in 1577 by the indignant inmates of an unreformed monastery in Toledo, where he was subjected to harsh treatment. He escaped after eight months, during which time he had composed most (perhaps all) of the poetry for which he is famous.

San Juan lives as a poet, and so it will be more appropriate to reserve the main discussion of his work for the next chapter. His prose-works are commentaries on his poetry and usually considered only in that light; but they have merits of their own and deserve study in their own right. For his poem 'Noche oscura' he wrote two commentaries: *Subida del Monte Carmelo,* too free-ranging to be of much assistance to understanding the poetry, and *Noche oscura,* which stops at the first line of the third stanza of verse. These, together with *Llama de amor viva* (both poem and commentary), were published at Alcalá in 1618. *Cántico espiritual* was published in Brussels in 1627.

San Juan's work embodies experiences as personal and profound as those of St Teresa. Necessarily, because of the nature of the experience, he is not less reliant on metaphor and simile than she, but the imagery gives evidence of a more literary culture than hers. For example, in his commentary on the line 'El canto de la dulce filomena' in *Cántico espiritual,* he writes:

> Lo que nace en el alma de aquel aspirar del aire es el canto de la dulce filomena; porque así como el canto de la filomena, que es el ruiseñor, se oye en la primavera, pasados ya los fríos y lluvias del invierno, y hace melodía al oído y al espíritu recreación, así en esta actual comunicación y transformación de amor, amparada ya la esposa y libre de todas las turbaciones y variedades temporales y desnuda y purgada de las imperfecciones y penalidades y nieblas naturales, siente nueva primavera en su espíritu . . .

The entire passage is literary in its associations: the very name Philomena indicates the literary origin of the scene. The passage is a beautiful one; but its beauty is wholly different in character from the colloquial directness of St Teresa's style. Commenting on the line 'Los valles solitarios nemorosos' he writes:

> Los valles solitarios son quietos, amenos, frescos, umbrosos, de dulces aguas llenos, y en la variedad de sus arboledas y suave canto de aves hacen gran recreación y deleite al sentido, dan refrigerio y descanso en su soledad y silencio. Estos valles es mi amado para mi.

There *are* such valleys but the tone of the passage suggests that he is describing a literary landscape of the kind he could have met with in Garcilaso or any other Renaissance writer of pastoral.

Inevitably, since his style is formed by the language of literature, the prose-work of San Juan does not set its author so vividly before us as does the work of St Teresa, who puts on paper the living speech of a sixteenth-century woman (as when she writes of recollections fluttering in the memory as being like 'mariposicas de la noche, importunas y desasosegadas'). The qualities of San Juan's prose are more subdued, less distinctive; but there are moments when his prose rises almost (though never quite) to the level of his poetry.

Of the other religious writers of the period perhaps the most interesting is the Franciscan mystic Fray Juan de los Ángeles (1536?-1609), whose best-known works are *Diálogos de la conquista del espiritual y secreto reino de Dios* (Madrid, 1595) and *Lucha espiritual y amorosa entre Dios y el alma* (Madrid, 1600).

The Counter-Reformation accentuated a phenomenon which before the end of the fifteenth century had little importance in Spain (though much in certain other countries): religious parody, or the rewriting of profane literature in religious terms. Poets like Fray Ambrosio Montesino recast numerous poems by others (commonly traditional or folk-poems); Juan del Encina recast several of his own. The practice grew in the sixteenth century, reaching its climax in the later years of the century and the beginning of the next. The movement petered out towards 1625. In that time countless poems were recast, or *contrahechos a lo divino*, as the phrase went. *Contrafacta*[2] were made of all kinds of poetry; though *villancicos*, *romances*, and other traditional forms predominated since these were sung and music played a crucial part in the movement. Almost all *contrafacta*, indeed, were composed to be sung to popular tunes.[3] Most of these versions were inevitably the work of mediocrities, but there are also many beautiful examples. Lope de Vega was one of many good poets who rewrote *a lo divino*.

Not only traditional poetry was rewritten in this way. One Sebastián de Córdoba brought out *Las obras de Boscán y Garcilaso trasladadas en materias cristianas y religiosas* (Granada, 1575), in which the complete works of these poets are refashioned. Córdoba made as few changes as possible in the originals so that the original voices are not entirely muffled; and in his poetry he expresses what seems a genuine love of the poetry: 'enamorado de su alto y suave estilo, vine a pensar si en devoción podrían sonar tan dulces'. He showed ingenuity and even a certain taste in his new versions, but inevitably the result is bound to be disconcerting to modern admirers of the two poets.[4]

The *a lo divino* movement caught up the words of popular dances (including 'indecent' dances like the saraband), and even games and pastimes were allegorised, as in Alonso de Ledesma's *Juegos de Noche Buena* (see below, Chapter 8). Nothing was thought inappropriate for transformation: in an age of faith there is no barrier between the profane and the divine: one can nourish the other. We are told in an illuminating anecdote that San Juan de la Cruz sang, as he danced holding in his arms an image of the infant Jesus snatched from a crib, the words of an old love song:

Si amores me han de matar
agora tienen lugar.

In this ecstatic interfusion of the secular and divine he seems to embody the spirit of an age.

The Counter-Reformation is alleged to have left its mark on poetry in another way. It has been argued that the influence of the *Spiritual Exercises* of St Ignatius, which comprise a systematic technique of meditation, can be observed in the religious poetry of the later sixteenth and seventeenth centuries.[5] In the exercises the meditator is required first to visualise clearly the subject of his meditation: the famous 'composition of place'. He then brings the 'three powers of the soul'—memory, understanding, and will—to bear on the principal points selected for meditation. Finally, the meditation ends with a colloquy addressed to God, or the Son, or the Virgin, 'speaking as one friend speaks to another, or as a servant to his master; at one time asking for some favour, at another blaming oneself for some evil committed . . .' Undoubtedly the Ignatian exercises were widely practised (even outside the Catholic countries) and must have contributed to forming the meditative patterns of those poets who came under their influence. Equally undoubtedly, their influence has been exaggerated: to see 'composition of place' in every sharply visualised scene in devotional poetry, or Ignatian colloquy in every poetic appeal to divinity, is indiscriminate. Only when all the Ignatian elements are united in one poetic meditation is it justified to allege the influence of the exercises; and such examples are uncommon. The famous anonymous (and undatable, though probably seventeenth-century) sonnet 'A Cristo crucificado' ('No me mueve, mi Dios, para quererte') is an example of a poem which may have been a text for meditation but is unrelatable to any particular scheme of meditation.

The Counter-Reformation has by some been held responsible for a distinctively 'Baroque' manner of perceiving and representing reality.[6] The evidence is at best dubious, and the arguments deployed are often vitiated by special pleading.

NOTES

1. See Marjorie Grice Hutchinson, *The School of Salamanca. Readings in Spanish Monetary Theory, 1544-1605* (Oxford, 1952).
2. B. W. Wardropper, *Historia de la poesía lírica a lo divino en la Cristiandad occidental* (Madrid, 1958), p. 6.
3. ibid., p. 7.
4. Córdoba's work has been reissued; edited by Glen R. Gale (Madrid, 1971).
5. See Louis L. Martz, *The Poetry of Meditation* (New Haven, 1954).
6. See, for example, Stephen Gilman, 'An Introduction to the Ideology of the Baroque in Spain', *Sym* I (1946).

Chapter 5

POETRY IN THE SIXTEENTH CENTURY AFTER GARCILASO

IN THE DEDICATION TO THE DUQUESA DE SOMA with which he prefaced his Italianate poems, Boscán wrote:

> De manera que este género de trobas, y con la autoridad de su valor propio y con la reputación de los antiguos y modernos que le han usado, es dino no solamente de ser recebido en una lengua tan buena como es la castellana, mas aun de ser en ella preferido a todos los versos vulgares. Y así pienso yo que lleva camino para sello. Porque ya los buenos ingenios de Castilla, que van fuera de la vulgar cuenta, le aman y le siguen y se ejercitan en él tanto, que si los tiempos con sus desasosiegos no lo estorban, podrá ser que antes de mucho se duelan los italianos de ver lo bueno de su poesía transferido en España. Pero esto está aun lejos . . . (ed. cit., p. 91)

Boscán saw clearly. The acceptance of the new style among 'los buenos ingenios de Castilla' was rapid. At first these *ingenios* were in the main courtier-poets of the circle of Garcilaso and Boscán, educated noblemen captivated by the prestige of Italian culture.[1] Diego Hurtado de Mendoza (1503-75), one of the most brilliant men of his age, was an early convert. His intimacy with Boscán is to be seen in the verse epistles in *terza rima* which they exchanged. The Portuguese Francisco Sá de Miranda (1481-1558), most of whose work is in Castilian, was another early convert. He became the first Portuguese poet to write in the new style, though he did not completely abandon the older style. He had a clearly first-hand acquaintance with the Italian poets, but Garcilaso was his model in much of his verse. He too wrote poetry inspired by Isabel Freyre, whom he knew at the Portuguese Court. He did not achieve full mastery of the new style: his poetry, though not without poignancy at times, is often faulty and wooden. Indeed, in general the first generation of those who followed the lead of Boscán and Garcilaso had an insecure grasp of the new manner. This is true of Diego Hurtado de Mendoza, who wrote some very fine poems in traditional metres but whose Italianate poems, particularly his sonnets, are often awkward and inexpressive. (His *canciones*, perhaps because being looser in form they were less cramping, are much more expressive.) Much of the best work of many poets like these was in the older manner, which was by no means eclipsed (as the successive editions of the *Cancionero general* show) and was to return to favour at the end of the century. Lope de Vega spoke with pride of the older poetry in the prologue to his *Isidro* (1599): '¿Qué cosa iguala a unas redondillas de Garci Sánchez, o don Diego de Mendoza?—perdone el divino Garci Laso . . .'

As the century went on, however, more and more of the poets who wrote for the educated turned to the new manner. Indeed, after Garcilaso, all those sixteenth-century poets (that is, who died or produced their best work before 1600) who seem to us the outstanding poets of their day, wrote mainly or wholly in the new style. And the new style descends from Petrarch. His presence is to be felt everywhere. The history of Spanish 'courtly' poetry (as distinct from that in traditional metres) in the later sixteenth century is in large part a history of the assimilation and adaptation of Petrarch. The victory of Petrarchism is not hard to understand, for Petrarch had created a poetic language which was both rich and flexible. It could express the deepest feelings, and be turned to lighter uses. For non-Italians who learned from Petrarch in the sixteenth century he meant a vast extension of sensibility.

Petrarch's characteristic imagery became the accepted poetic language of love (and some of it is with us still).[2] The lady being perfect, she can be described only through hyperbole: her eyes are brighter than the sun, her brow whiter than snow, her teeth more beautiful than pearls, and so on. Being an ideal, she is unattainable, even disdainful: she is all snow and ice, the lover all fire. The lover suffers alternate hope and despair, and so antithesis is central to the Petrarchan rhetoric, since Petrarch's own experience of love fell within what we term Courtly Love, though he enormously enriched its range of expression and sensibility. All nature, the universe, became the source of the Petrarchist's imagery. The images which sprang from Petrarch's inventive imagination to express the sufferings of love, the lover's acquiescence in his fate, his precarious joys—salamanders surviving fire, moths seeking destruction in a flame—became the themes for endless variations during the sixteenth and seventeenth centuries. In Italy, as later on elsewhere, Petrarchist poets sought to reanimate the tradition by seeking more startling new effects, so that there was a constant tendency towards more ingenious exploitation of the old themes, or the extension of imagery into new fields. To take one example: Petrarch's butterfly (or moth) blinded by Laura's bright eyes prompted throughout Europe numerous poems in the sixteenth century about insects drawn to their death by a lady's beauty: in Tasso a mosquito which bites her breast, in others (including later Lope de Vega) a flea.[3] But this cult of ingenuity was not to be a marked tendency in Spanish Petrarchism until the seventeenth century. In the sixteenth, poets were in general content with the familiar.

Poetry was not only a means of expression, but also a social accomplishment, especially in court circles, where Petrarchism took the place which earlier had been taken by the love-poetry in traditional metres collected in the *cancioneros*. There was in consequence much empty gallantry, but also a good deal of real poetry. Hernando de Acuña (1518-80?) is a typical example. He wrote copiously, almost exclusively in the new style. His sonnets, eclogues, and other poems do not often rise above a mediocre competence. A handful of sonnets stand out above the rest. The best remembered (justifiably: it is a vigorous work) is not a love-poem: it is 'Al Rey nuestro señor', the prophecy addressed to Charles V which promises the world 'un monarca, un imperio, una espada'. Acuña translated Olivier de la Marche's *Le chevalier delibéré* at Charles's command, and some of Boiardo's *Orlando* on his own account.

Far finer poetry was written by Gutierre de Cetina (before 1520-57?), about whom little is known. Like others he imitated and translated freely (mainly from Italian but in a few cases from the Valencian Ausias March, an influence not to be underestimated in sixteenth-century Castilian poetry). His much-anthologised madrigal 'Ojos claros, serenos' is charming, but he has much better, and sturdier, poetry than this. His sonnets are always fluent, and often inventive in imagery—within the limits of the Petrarchan manner. Some of them have an impressive logical strength in addition.

Gregorio Silvestre (1520-69) began in the old style and, as we are told in Pedro de Cáceres y Espinosa's prologue to Silvestre's *Obras* (1582), turned to the new when he saw its success. His verse is less mellifluous but more forceful than Cetina's, and his religious sonnets better than his love-sonnets. Some of his finest work is in the older style. Other poets of the second rank who contributed their quota to Spanish sixteenth-century Petrarchism are Jerónimo de Lomas Cantoral (*c.* 1538-1600), Francisco de Figueroa (1536-1617?), and Pedro Laýnez (*c.* 1538-84). The Portuguese Luis de Camões (1524-79) wrote a number of Castilian poems in both traditional and Italianate style. They are sensitive, imaginative, and skilful, though one would not deduce from them his great distinction in his own language. Luis Barahona de Soto (1548-95) is more interesting than most of the minor poets here mentioned. His lyric poetry includes a number of well-expressed love-poems in traditional style (including ten *Lamentaciones*), as well as poems in the Italian style. His sonnets are inferior to his elegies, and these to his *canciones* and five eclogues, imitations of

Garcilaso which capture something of their model's atmosphere. His incomplete *Las lágrimas de Angélica* (1586), an imitation of Ariosto, contains much beautiful poetry.

One of the most interesting of the minor Petrarchists of the period is the one about whom least is known: Francisco de la Torre, whose works were published by Quevedo in 1631 from a manuscript he came across. Nothing is known of the poet, but his style indicates that he wrote in the later sixteenth century. His poetry is entirely amatory. He shows a predilection for two settings: pastoral scenes (he has seven eclogues), and night. His numerous poems to night have been called romantic: they are certainly touching and evocative; but once again their themes derive from Italian Petrarchism (indirectly from Petrarch's 'Hor che'l ciel e la terra e'l vento tace').

Much sixteenth-century poetry was dominated, then, by a model. Poetic theory of the time made imitation a cardinal rule. Francisco Sánchez, *El Brocense*, in his commentary on Garcilaso (Salamanca, 1574) wrote:

> . . . digo, y afirmo, que no tengo por buen poeta al que no imita los excelentes antiguos. Y si me preguntan por qué entre tantos millares de poetas como nuestra España tiene, tan pocos se pueden contar dignos de este nombre, digo que no hay otra razón sino porque les faltan las ciencias, lenguas y doctrina para saber imitar.

This was the orthodox view (if we extend *antiguos* to include modern models deemed worthy of imitation).

Renaissance literary theory rested on an often loosely-held underlying belief that though poetry, like the other arts, had been defined by Aristotle as an imitation of nature, this meant imitation not of the fleeting particular aspects of nature but of the ideal or the principles beyond the visible and the ephemeral. Tasso gave this belief some degree of definition when he wrote in his *Discorsi* (1594) that the poet's images or representations are of 'subsisting things'. He goes on:

> But what things shall we say to be subsisting things—the intelligible or the visible? Intelligible things, surely, and once again on the authority of Plato, who placed visible things in the category of non-being, and only intelligible things did he place in the category of being.

It would be dangerously misleading to attribute this as a conscious belief to every poet of the time, but undoubtedly something of this attitude was general, even if only in the form of a belief that the poet was concerned with the ideal or the universal, not with the particular and local. This in turn supported the belief that poetry dealt in general propositions not the exclusively personal: a poem occasioned by a personal experience worked almost invariably towards a general conclusion, often a maxim or a *sententia* or a logical deduction. In this way even a lyric poem could be regarded as instructive or improving, thereby fulfilling Horace's dictum that the end of poetry was 'prodesse et delectare' ('enseñar deleitando', as the Spanish phrase went). This last note was to be accentuated by the Counter-Reformation.

The summit of the sixteenth-century Petrarchan movement in Spain is reached in the poetry of Fernando de Herrera (1534-97), known as *el divino*, who was born in Seville and spent his life there. He was of humble birth. By about 1565 he was the holder of a small lay benefice in the church of San Andrés. He was a member of a literary and artistic circle which met at the palace of the conde de Gelves, and which included many of the best-known figures of the cultural life of the city: Juan de Mal Lara; the painter and minor poet Francisco Pacheco; the historian Argote de Molina; Juan de la Cueva; and others. The condesa de Gelves, Doña Leonor de Milán, was the inspiration of Herrera's love-poetry. His love may have been partly a matter of courtly convention, but his poetry rings with a stylised passion, and Doña Leonor is represented in some poems as returning his love. Herrera appears to have given up writing poetry on her death in 1581. In the following year, perhaps as a tribute to her memory, he published his *Algunas obras* (Seville, 1582), the only volume of his poems published in his lifetime. (Pacheco brought out an enlarged and 'corrected' collection in 1619, but the authenticity of the changes he made is disputed.)

Herrera was a pure man of letters, unlike most of the other poets of his century. His fame was great in his own day, not only as poet but as historian and literary arbiter. Among his works are a *Relación de la guerra de Chipre y batalla naval de Lepanto* (Seville, 1572) and *Tomás Moro* (Seville, 1592). In poetry, he was attracted initially to the heroic: one of his lost works was a *Gigantomaquia*, on the revolt of the Titans. Another of his lost works was a history of the world.

Herrera published an edition of and commentary on Garcilaso: *Obras de Garcilaso de la Vega con anotaciones . . .* (Seville, 1580), a work of inestimable importance. His interest in literary theory was strong: an *Arte poética* was amongst his projects. His *Anotaciones* are more than notes to a modern classic: they are also an exposition of Herrera's view of poetry and poetic diction. His admiration of Garcilaso was immense, but not uncritical: he comments sharply on what seem to him examples of unpoetic diction and unworthy images. For Herrera the supreme quality in poetry is clarity:

> Es importantísimo la claridad en el verso, y si falta en él, se pierde toda la gracia y la hermosura de la poesía . . . porque las palabras son

> imágenes de los pensamientos, debe ser la claridad que nace della luciente, suelta, libre, blanda, entera; no oscura, ni intrincada, no forzada, no áspera y despedazada.... Cáusase la claridad de la puridad y elegancia.

The objective is praiseworthy. To attain it Herrera adopts an essentially aristocratic attitude to language since poetry, he believed, requires a diction far removed from ordinary speech. Commenting on the word *alimaña* in Garcilaso's *Canción* V he writes:

> Dicción antigua y rústica, y no conveniente para escritor culto y elegante. Porque ninguna cosa debe procurar tanto el que desea alcanzar nombre con las fuerzas de la elocución y artificio, como la limpieza y escogimiento y ornato de la lengua. No la enriquece quien usa vocablos humildes, indecentes y comunes, ni quien trae a ella voces peregrinas, inusitadas y no significantes; antes la empobrece con el abuso.

The word may have begun to sound archaic, though it was still good enough for Luis de León. It was almost certainly the ordinariness of the word which upset Herrera; just as he objected to line 363 of Eclogue III ('tener al pie del palo quien se duela'): 'Metáfora sacada de lugar humilde y odioso'. Of line 186 of *Elegía* I he writes: 'Aunque con este modo quiso moderar lo que decía, es humilde verso'. And on line 205 of the same poem: 'Común y humilde modo de hablar es el que usa aquí G.L.' These comments are in keeping with Herrera's reaffirmation of the old doctrine of the three styles of poetry: high, middle, and low. A style appropriate to one subject was inappropriate to another. This is a view to which in general Garcilaso himself would have subscribed, but doubtless without Herrera's inflexibility.

Comments such as these created resentment in at least one reader, whose riposte (which remained in manuscript until 1870) bears the title: *Observaciones del Licenciado Prete Jacobín, vecino de Burgos, en defensa del Príncipe de los Poetas Castellanos Garci-lasso de la Vega, natural de Toledo, contra las Anotaciones de Fernando de Herrera, Poeta Sevillano.* The very title breathes wounded Castilian pride: regional susceptibilities undoubtedly played some part in the controversy; but the critic—Don Juan Fernández de Velasco, condestable de Castilla—had much reason on his side when he ridiculed Herrera's frequent pedantry, irrelevance, and lack of logic. Herrera's reply (also unprinted until 1870) retracts nothing; indeed he asserts yet more firmly the legitimacy of his criticism of Garcilaso, 'porque más le sirvió el ingenio y naturaleza que el arte'. He reaffirms the doctrine of styles:

> Lícito es a todos ... usar alguna vez de voces vulgares y despreciadas

en sátiras y en epístolas familiares, pero en una canción levantada, en una elegía culta y en un soneto de argumento noble y amoroso, y en los poemas generosos y bien ornados, no es ni puede ser lícito, porque conviene que sean limpios y escogidos todos los vocablos con que aderezan y tejen sus versos los poetas más elegantes, y no se entorpezcan y afeen con la unión de voces bajas y humildes . . .

Herrera's best poetry is his love-poetry, whose language he draws from Petrarch, though the influence of Ausias March and the *cancioneros* is perceptible. The lady addressed is given a poetic name: variously, Luz, Lumbre, etc., which permits him the same kind of play with imagery and association as we find in Petrarch (Laura, *l'aura*, etc.). Luz can be associated with the sun, with fire, with the heavens generally: she both fits into the Petrarchan idiom and acquires a cosmic significance.

Being predominantly Petrarchan in inspiration, Herrera's poetry has little thematic originality: its originality lies in the vigour and colour with which Herrera suffused his borrowed idiom. He gives the old antitheses—fire/ice or snow, hope/despair—a new life. His imagery too is more vivid and more varied than that of most of his contemporaries. This is a good example:

Cubre en oscuro cerco y sombra fría
del cielo puro el resplandor sereno
l'húmida noche, y yo, de dolor lleno,
lloro mi bien perdido y mi alegría.
Ningún alivio en la miseria mía
hallo; de ningún mal estoy ajeno;
cuanto en la confusión nublosa peno,
padesco en la rosada luz del día.
En otro nuevo Cáucaso enclavado,
mi cuidado mortal y mi deseo
el corazón me comen renovado,
do no pudiera el sucesor d'Alceo
librarme de tormento no cansado,
qu'ecede al del antiguo Prometeo.

The lover mourns by night and day; but *luz* is also *Luz*: even her presence does not lighten his suffering since she is inaccessible to him. Grief will consume him like the eagle eating the liver of Prometheus; and Hercules himself could not release him: Luz will remain aloof.

Herrera valued energetic diction. Commenting on Cetina in his *Anotaciones* he wrote:

En Cetina . . . se conoce la hermosura y gracia de Italia; y en número, lengua, terneza y afectos ninguno le negará lugar con los

> primeros, más fáltale el espíritu y vigor, que tan importante es en la poesía; y así dice muchas cosas dulcemente pero sin fuerzas . . .

Just like those sculptors, Herrera goes on, who will model a beautiful youth 'no mostrando alguna señal de niervos y músculos'. Herrera has sinew and muscle in his best poetry. Sonnet IV opens:

> El sátiro qu'el fuego vio primero,
> de su vivo esplendor todo vencido,
> llegó a tocallo; mas probó encendido
> qu'era, cuanto hermoso, ardiente y fiero.

The image is forcible and vivid, and a striking variation on the familiar theme of the dangerous fires of love.

But vigour does not exclude mellifluousness: Sonnet XXVIII opens with the limpidity of Cetina at his best:

> Süave Filomena, que tu llanto
> descubres al sereno y limpio cielo
> . . .

On a few occasions Herrera achieves pathos also, as when, in *Elegía* III, he describes how Doña Leonor returned his love in one unguarded moment:

> Cuando del claro cielo se desvía
> del sol ardiente el alto carro a pena,
> y casi igual espacio muestra el día,
> con blanda voz, qu'entre las perlas suena,
> teñido el rostro de color de rosa,
> d'honesto miedo, y d'amor tierno llena,
> me dijo así la bella desdeñosa
> qu'un tiempo me negara la esperanza,
> sorda a mi llanto y ansia congojosa:
> 'Si por firmeza y dulce amar s'alcanza
> premio d'Amor, yo ya tener bien debo
> de los males que sufro más holganza.
> Mil veces, por no ser ingrata, pruebo
> vencer tu amor, pero al fin no puedo;
> qu'es mi pecho a sentillo rudo y nuevo.
> Si en sufrir más me vences, yo t'ecedo
> en pura fe y afetos de terneza:
> vive de hoy más ya confiado y ledo'.

Not all Herrera's poetry is amatory. He wrote too a number of heroic and patriotic odes. One of the best known is the *Canción* on the battle of Lepanto (1571) when the combined Christian fleets under the command of Don John of Austria defeated the Turks. For his ode Herrera adopted a deliberately biblical tone, no doubt reflecting the belief common in Counter-Reformation Spain that Spaniards were the chosen people to defend the Church. The poem is encrusted with paraphrases of the Psalms. The effect is often sonorous and majestic.

> Cantemos al Señor, que en la llanura
> venció del mar al enemigo fiero.
> Tú, Dios de las batallas, tú eres diestra,
> salud, y gloria nuestra.
> Tú rompiste las fuerzas y la dura
> frente de Faraón, feroz guerrero.
> Sus escogidos príncipes cubrieron
> los abismos del mar, y decendieron
> cual piedra en el profundo; y tu ira luego
> los tragó, como arista seca el fuego.

The solemn tone is maintained throughout.

In 1578 Herrera wrote another *canción* on the crushing Portuguese defeat at Alcazarquivir, in North Africa, where Sebastian of Portugal's ill-conceived crusade was abruptly halted, his army annihilated, Sebastian himself killed, and his body never found. Herrera sees the defeat as the chastisement of pride. Once again he assumes the mantle of the Psalmist and thunders with Miltonic grandiloquence:

> Ay de los que pasaron, confiados
> en sus caballos y en la muchedumbre
> de sus carros en ti, Libia desierta;
> . . .
> Y el Santo d'Israel abrió su mano
> y los dejó, y cayó en despeñadero
> el carro, y el caballo y caballero.

But to invoke Milton shows up Herrera's limitations. His grandiloquence is imposing, but it can ring hollow: he lacks Milton's imaginative range and density of language—the qualities that show in lines like these:

> While the Creator Great
> His constellations set,
> And the well-ballanced world on hinges hung,
> And cast the dark foundations deep,
> And bid the weltering waves their oozy channel keep.

The work of Francisco de Aldana (1537-78), one of the most remarkable Spanish poets of the sixteenth century but until recently one of the most undervalued, strikes a very distinctive note in Spanish poetry of the period. Aldana was born in Italy (probably Naples); in 1540 his family moved to Florence, where they lived under the protection of Cosimo de' Medici. There are many easily discernible traces in Aldana's work of his contact with Florentine Neoplatonism. He spent his life as a soldier. He fought and was seriously wounded in the Low Countries; and in 1578, as commander-in-chief of the Portuguese army, he was killed at Alcazarquivir beside King Sebastian, who had secured permission from Philip II for Aldana to accompany him. Aldana, like Sebastian, disappeared without trace.

Most of Aldana's poetry falls thematically within the general poetic repertoire of the period: amorous sonnets, many of them pastoral in setting; mythological verse (*Fábula de Faetonte*); an episode retold from Ariosto (*Medoro y Angélica*); religious poems (*Canción a Cristo crucificado*); verse epistles; etc. The distinctive elements are the vividness and originality of his imagery, the intellectual weight, and the concentrated vigour of his language. In reading Aldana, it is at once evident that he came from a milieu more interested in ideas than the majority of his Spanish contemporaries. (This must make us recall what Garcilaso owed to Italy.) There is also, in his amorous verse, an Arcadian sensuality whose guiltlessness is new in Spanish poetry. Some of these qualities can be seen together in one of his most memorable sonnets:

'¿Cuál es la causa, mi Damón, que estando
en la lucha de amor juntos trabados
con lenguas, brazos, pies y encadenados
cual vid que entre el jazmín se va enredando

y que el vital aliento ambos tomando
en nuestros labios, de chupar cansados,
en medio a tanto bien somos forzados
llorar y suspirar de cuando en cuando?'

'Amor, mi Filis bella, que allá dentro
nuestras almas juntó, quiere en su fragua
los cuerpos ajuntar también tan fuerte

que no pudiendo, como esponja el agua,
pasar del alma al dulce amado centro,
llora el velo mortal su avara suerte.'

The sonnet makes a philosophical point—the Neoplatonic doctrine that since true love is spiritual, physical union cannot in itself be wholly satisfying—but the physical intensity of the quatrains remains striking. The same atmosphere is to be found in Aldana's poem *Medoro y Angélica*, where the poet describes Cupid's gaze lingering over the beauty of the sleeping Angelica:

La sábana después quïetamente
levanta al parecer no bien siguro,
y como espejo el cuerpo ve luciente,
el muslo cual aborio limpio y puro;
contempla de los pies hasta la frente
las caderas de mármol liso y duro,
las partes donde Amor el cetro tiene,
y allí con ojos muertos se detiene.

Admirado la mira y dice: '¡Oh cuánto
debes, Medor, a tu ventura y suerte!'
Y más quiso decir, pero entre tanto
razón es ya que Angélica despierte,
la cual con breve y repentino salto,
viéndose así desnuda y de tal suerte,
los muslos dobla y lo mejor encubre,
y por cubrirse más, más se descubre.

Several other sonnets have an atmosphere of less explicit sensuality. Some of Aldana's most striking poetry is religious and ascetic, but in evaluating him the profane must also be taken into account; and indeed there is no necessary contradiction between them, since for a Neoplatonist the experiences can be complementary.

The terse vigour of Aldana's style is one of his most admirable and refreshing qualities. It can be judged in the excellent sonnet in which he declares his disenchantment with the endless warfare in which he spent his life.

Otro aquí no se ve que, frente a frente,
animoso escuadrón moverse guerra,
sangriento humor teñir la verde tierra,
y tras honroso fin correr la gente;
éste es el dulce son que acá se siente:
'¡España, Santïago, cierra, cierra!',
y por süave olor, que el aire atierra,
humo de azufre dar con llama ardiente;
el gusto envuelto va tras corrompida
agua, y el tacto sólo apalpa y halla
duro trofeo de acero ensangrentado,
hueso en astilla, en él carne molida,
despedazado arnés, rasgada malla:
¡oh sólo de hombres digno y noble estado!

In an epistle to his friend 'Galanio' Aldana describes the effect of grief on his heart, to which his vital spirits retreat, so that his body seems to swoon; until, seeing the danger of this state, his heart expels them again with an explosive sigh, so that the body settles to its normal state again. He develops a long comparison with an encamped army at night:

¿Vistes alguna vez en la campaña
ejército español, fiero y lozano,
cuando la noche con sus alas negras
esparce por el aire tenebroso
silencio, sueño, miedo y sobresalto?
¿Vístesle estar durmiendo y reposando
debajo la despierta vigilancia
de la real, nocturna centinela
que está con recatado azoramiento
mirando al derredor por sí y por otros?

The sentinel perceives danger:

mira y torna a mirar, se abaja y alza,
echa adelante un paso y vuelve al puesto;
se impone, se apercibe, se apareja,
se empina, para, parte, prueba y pasa
su paso a paso de una en otra parte
. . .

He sounds the alarm; the camp is thrown into turmoil; but at last calm is restored:

Estando en este error tumultuoso
y los cuerpos de guardia más cercanos
ya rebatido habiendo al enemigo,
pasa la voz que cada cual se vuelva,
y así, las centinelas reforzadas,
el belicoso pueblo y las cabezas
tornan a sus armados pabellones,
sus viudas chozas, tiendas y barracas,
y en lugar del rumor entra el silencio.

The description is vivid and interesting in itself, but it goes beyond the picturesque: it shows imagination and intellect working together with impressive coherence.

The poem of Aldana's which remains longest in the memory is another epistle: his *Carta para Arias Montano sobre la contemplación de Dios y los requisitos della,* written in 1577. The recipient, Benito Arias Montano, was one of the outstanding Spanish humanists of his day, a leading biblical scholar who directed the work on the great Antwerp Polyglot Bible (1569-73) and a friend of Luis de León. The epistle is the finest Spanish example of this important Renaissance genre.

The poem—a long one of 451 lines—exhibits all Aldana's excellences: his vigour, concentration, vivid imagery, and lyrical power. Its theme is his desire to lay aside wordly preoccupations and devote himself to the contemplation of his God.

> Y porque vano error más no me asombre,
> en algún alto y solitario nido
> pienso enterrar mi ser, mi vida y nombre
> y, como si no hubiera acá nacido,
> estarme allá, cual Eco, replicando
> al dulce son de Dios, del alma oído.
> Y ¿qué debiera ser, bien contemplando,
> el alma sino un eco resonante
> a la eterna Beldad que está llamando
> y, desde el cavernoso y vacilante
> cuerpo, volver mis réplicas de amores
> al sobrecelestial Narciso amante;
> rica de sus intrínsicos favores,
> con un piadoso escarnio el bajo oficio
> burlar de los mundanos amadores.
> En tierra o en árbol hoja algún bullicio
> no hace que, al moverse, ella no encuentra
> en nuevo y para Dios grato ejercicio;
> y como el fuego saca y desencentra
> oloroso licor por alquitara
> del cuerpo de la rosa que en ella entra,
> así destilará, de la gran cara
> del mundo, inmaterial varia belleza
> con el fuego de amor que la prepara;
> y pasará de vuelo a tanta alteza
> que, volviéndose a ver tan sublimada,
> su misma olvidará naturaleza,
> cuya capacidad ya dilatada
> allá verá do casi ser le toca
> en su primera Causa transformada.

Aldana's Neoplatonism is clear. From God, the celestial lover, emanates love, which is returned to him by his creation. God is like Narcissus because the world reflects his beauty. The discerning mind perceives spiritual beauty in the material world just as its essence may be extracted from the rose.

Aldana goes on to describe his hope to unite at last with God, in unfailingly vivid imagery, as in this striking tercet:

¡Oh grandes, oh riquísimas conquistas
de las Indias de Dios, de aquel gran mundo
tan escondido a las mundanas vistas!

Now he describes the retired life he hopes to lead, devoted not only to contemplation but to the observation of the wonders, large and small, of creation. He invites his friend to walk with him on the shore.

Verás mil retorcidas caracoles,
mil bucíos istriados, con señales
y pintas de lustrosas arreboles:
los unos del color de los corales,
los otros de la luz que el sol represa
en los pintados arcos celestiales,
de varia operación, de varia empresa,
despidiendo de sí como centellas,
en rica mezcla de oro y de turquesa.

The description breathes a sense of wonder at the manifold beauties of being. Aldana the Neoplatonist could love and admire the visible while yearning for what lay beyond.

He dates the letter 7 September 1577. Less than a year later he was dead.

So far only secular poets have been discussed. Two of the finest poets of the century are religious: Fray Luis de León and San Juan de la Cruz. Their poetry is very different in character and even theme: mystical experience, the sole theme of San Juan, is glimpsed only once or twice in Fray Luis's work.

The poetry of Fray Luis was not published in his lifetime.[4] He was known less as a poet in his own day than as a scholar and as the author of works such as *De los nombres de Cristo* (see above, Chapter 4). His poems—few in number: under forty, including doubtful attributions—were published by Quevedo in 1631 as examples of good poetry and pure style for the writers of that day. Fray Luis's dedication to Don Pedro Portocarrero begins: 'Entre las ocupaciones de mis estudios en mi mocedad, y casi en mi niñez, se me cayeron, como de entre las manos, estas obrecillas, a las cuales me apliqué, más por inclinación de mi estrella que por juicio o voluntad'. The poet's modesty is disingenuous: many of the poems are manifestly the fruits of maturity and painstaking application.

Fray Luis's style derives directly from that of Garcilaso, and his poetry displays some characteristically Renaissance themes. 'Vida retirada' is an example. At first sight it appears to be one more variation on Horace's *Beatus ille*, which inspired so many imitations during the Renaissance. Read in the light of Fray Luis's other works it acquires a deeper significance. The poet extols the simple life lived in the countryside, away from the cares of town and Court. The poem seems to end on an almost hedonistic note as the poet describes himself:

A la sombra tendido,
de hiedra y lauro eterno coronado,
puesto el atento oído
al son dulce, acordado,
del plectro sabiamente meneado.

The peace and beauty of nature are contrasted with the storms and terrors which afflict the merchant on the high seas. The contrasting scenes are expressive in themselves, but gain a deeper meaning in relation to the poem as a whole. The idyllic peace of nature is introduced by this stanza:

Oh monte, oh fuente, oh río,
oh secreto seguro deleitoso,
roto casi el navío,
a vuestro almo reposo
huyo de aqueste mar tempestuoso.

The poet flees from a metaphorical shipwreck in a metaphorical sea. The nature he finds refuge in had a special significance for the poet, as we see from a passage in the section called 'Pastor' in his *De los nombres de Cristo*. There, in a passage which makes manifest his Neoplatonism, he tells how the love of shepherds is made pure by their isolation from towns, and goes on:

> Y ayúdales a ello también la vista desembarazada, de que contino gozan, del cielo y de la tierra y de los demás elementos; que es ella en sí una imagen clara, o por mejor decir una como escuela de amor puro y verdadero. Porque los demuestra a todos amistados entre sí y puestos en orden, y abrazados, como dijésemos, unos con otros, y concertados con armonía grandísima, y respondiéndose a veces y comunicándose sus virtudes, y pasándose unos en otros y ayuntándose y mezclándose todos, y con su mezcla y ayuntamiento sacando contino a luz y produciendo los frutos que hermosean el aire y la tierra. Así que los pastores son en esto aventajados a los otros hombres.

Nature is morally instructive in that it confronts us with the harmony of the universe. It is the lesson of nature in the poem: the stream seems to offer itself to the garden in an act of love:

Y como codiciosa
por ver y acrecentar su hermosura,

desde la cumbre airosa
una fontana pura
hasta llegar corriendo se apresura.
  Y luego sosegada
el paso entre los árboles torciendo
el suelo de pasada
de verdura vistiendo
y con diversas flores va esparciendo.

The poet has found in nature the peace inspired by love. This in turn recalls the passages in the section 'Príncipe de la paz' in *De los nombres de Cristo* where peace, described as 'una orden sosegada o un sosiego ordenado', is said to be attained only through the subjection of the senses to Reason, and Reason to God. All men seek peace, but most by the wrong path. 'Porque si navega el mercader y si corre las mares, es por tener paz con su codicia, que le solicita y guerrea': but he succeeds only in feeding his inner strife. Only an inner harmony can bring peace.

> Porque no hay mar brava en quien los vientos más furiosamente ejecuten su ira, que iguale a la tempestad y a la tormenta que, yendo unas olas y viniendo otras, mueven en el corazón desordenado del hombre sus apetitos y sus pasiones.

The poet's description of the storm at sea now yields its full meaning: it is both the real storm endured by those who venture on the sea, and the inner storm suffered by those who have not found the true path to peace, the 'escondida senda'.

At last we see the poet listening to music stretched beneath a tree. The picture is an attractive one, but once again may conceal as much as it declares explicitly. The poem has described the harmony of the garden, where the elements conspire to produce and broadcast beauty. The wise man lives in harmony with this natural harmony. *De los nombres de Cristo* may help us again. In 'Príncipe de la paz' Fray Luis speaks of the need to acquire an inner peace, which itself depends on peace with God, before one can be at peace with others, and goes on:

> Así que, como la piedra que en el edificio está asentada en su debido lugar, o por decir cosa más propia, como la cuerda en la música, debidamente templada en sí misma, hace música dulce con todas las demás cuerdas, sin disonar con ninguna, así el ánimo bien concertado dentro de sí, y que vive sin alboroto y tiene siempre en la mano la rienda de sus pasiones y de todo lo que en él puede mover inquietud y bullicio, consuena con Dios y dice bien con los hombres, y teniendo paz consigo mismo, la tiene con los demás.

The lute to which the poet listens suggests similar implications to anyone acquainted with Renaissance Neoplatonism: it comes close to stating explicitly the theme of the entire poem—harmony, of man and of the universe.

With the poem 'A Salinas', a more explicit work, we are on surer ground, though once again a knowledge of the poet's ideology, especially his Neoplatonism, is necessary before the poem will yield its full sense. It is helpful to bear in mind that Salinas, a renowned organist (though blind), was the author of a well-known treatise on music and familiar therefore with the metaphysical speculations regarding the harmony of the universe which surrounded the study of music in the Renaissance.[5]

The poem opens with a description of the effect of Salinas's playing on the poet, whose soul is led to recall its origin and soars up to contemplation of God himself, the divine musician whose music is the universe. The poet swoons as if drowning in a sea of harmony. These experiences are governed by a logic which is not at first sight apparent to the modern reader.

The first effect of the music is to recall to itself the poet's soul sunk in forgetfulness, and make it remember its 'origen primera esclarecida'. This is Plato's Anamnesis, the soul's recollection of its celestial origin where it had gained its ideas. The harmonious spectacle of the stars at night——'este concierto y orden de las estrellas'——has the same effect on Fray Luis in 'Príncipe de la paz', where he describes how the soul, made harmonious by the contemplation of that spectacle of harmony, takes Reason as its sovereign, which

> como alentada con esta vista celestial y hermosa, concibe pensamientos altos y dignos de sí, y cómo en una cierta manera se recuerda de su primer origen, y al fin pone todo lo que es vil y bajo en su parte y huella sobre ello.

In this state of recollection, having glimpsed the eternal ideal beauty—the world of Plato's Ideas, of which earthly things are only an imperfect reflection—the poet's soul is incapable of finding value in earthly beauty, 'la belleza caduca engañadora'. The soul takes wing to the highest sphere and there hears another kind of music,

> y oye allí otro modo
> de no perecedera
> música, que es la fuente, y la primera.

This music is the music of God, the great Musician as imagined by Augustine and others.

> Ve como el gran maestro
> a aquesta inmensa cítara aplicado,

con movimiento diestro
produce el son sagrado
con que este eterno templo es sustentado.[6]

The progression—from heard music to contemplation of God—is not arbitrary. For such as Fray Luis, the whole universe is a harmony, its various parts united in sympathy by harmony or love, which ultimately emanates from God himself. Our heard music is only a pallid echo of that unheard music which underlies all things. This is how Sir Thomas Browne spoke of it in his *Religio Medici* (1643):

> For there is a musick where ever there is a harmony, order, or proportion . . . Whosoever is harmonically composed delights in harmony; which makes me much distrust the symmetry of those heads which declaim against all Church-Musick. For myself, not only from my obedience, but my particular genius, I do embrace it: for even that vulgar and Tavern-Musick, which makes one man merry, another mad, strikes in me a deep fit of devotion, and a profound contemplation of the First Composer. There is something in it of Divinity more than the ear discovers: it is an Hieroglyphical and shadowed lesson of the whole World, and creatures of God; such a melody to the ear, as the whole World, well understood, would afford the understanding. In brief, it is a sensible fit of that harmony which intellectually sounds in the ears of God. (Everyman edition, 1959, p. 79)

The soul, itself a harmony (as Pythagoras taught, and later Plato), echoes the music of God:

Y como está compuesta
de números concordes, luego envía
consonante respuesta,
y entre ambos a porfía
se mezcla una dulcísima armonía.

This is the moment of union with God, in which the smaller harmony is absorbed in the greater. Having brought our understanding logically to this point, the poet abandons himself to the emotional tides of ecstasy in the last three stanzas.

The poem is one of Fray Luis's finest. It is a characteristic illustration of how his mind works from the particular to the general, from a particular experience of beauty to what for him is the source of all beauty. It may seem strange to call one so emotional, and so responsive to beauty, an intellectual poet; but the adjective is justified: in the last analysis, the beauty that Fray Luis responds to is the beauty of the invisible world of metaphysical—sometimes mathematical—relationships which sustains the visible world. Unless the reader himself comprehends those relationships, the point of the poetry will often be lost, and the poet praised (or blamed) for irrelevant reasons. Fray Luis reacted keenly to nature, but in the end for him it was 'but a spume that plays upon the ghostly paradigm of things'.

'Noche serena' shows a similar movement of thought. It opens with a description of the night sky, resplendent with stars. The sight moves the poet to despise Earth. He calls on men to gaze on the heavens and turn their minds to the contemplation of eternal peace and beauty. The poet is not moved to despise his earthly prison just by the grandiose spectacle of the sky: the poem is ordered by a more precise logic. 'Príncipe de la paz' can again be helpful. There Marcelo, moved by the sight of the starry sky, begins:

> Cuando la razón no lo demonstrara, ni por otro camino se pudiera entender cuán amable cosa sea la paz, esta vista hermosa del cielo que se nos descubre agora y el concierto que tienen entre sí aquestos resplandores que lucen en él, nos dan de ello suficiente testimonio. Porque ¿qué otra cosa es sino paz, o, ciertamente, una imagen perfecta de paz, esto que agora vemos en el cielo y que con tanto deleite se nos viene a los ojos?

The stars are an image of peace because they are an image of order, since peace is 'una orden sosegada o un sosiego ordenado'. They are beautiful in themselves, but also in the order they reveal: 'el ejército de las estrellas puesto como en ordenanza y como concertado por sus hileras'. In 'Noche serena' it is the spectacle of supernal peace as well as of beauty which moves the poet to spurn the Earth, with its 'bien fingido'. When he calls on his fellows to contemplate the heavens, it is the mathematical perfection of the celestial mechanism which he describes, a mechanism which is also unaffected by change, unlike the Earth.[7]

> Quien mira el gran concierto
> de aquestos resplandores eternales,
> su movimiento cierto,
> sus pasos desiguales,
> y en proporción concorde tan iguales.

The movement of the heavenly lights is 'certain' because never-ceasing. They move at an unequal pace because the speed of revolution of each sphere is proportional to its distance from the centre of the system. The last line of the stanza is a reference to the harmony of the spheres, each of which was believed in Pythagorean theory to emit a note (inaudible to our gross hearing) proportionate to its distance from the centre; just as a vibrating string stopped half-way along its length will sound the octave above, or stopped two-thirds along its length will sound the fifth above, and so on.

The poet now invokes particular planets and, beyond them, the fixed stars in their 'reluciente coro', a term which picks up the allusion to harmony in 'el gran concierto'. Who can now be content with the lowliness of Earth? cries the poet, who exclaims in ecstasy as he contemplates the unfading beauty of Heaven, where are stored up the eternal Forms or Ideas of which on Earth we know only the shadows. That eternal realm is governed by love.

> Aquí vive el contento,
> aquí reina la paz; aquí asentado
> en rico y alto asiento
> está el Amor sagrado
> de glorias y deleites rodeado.

The spectacle of universal harmony, imaged in the spheres, has led by a completely logical process to the contemplation of Love, since for Fray Luis, in whom Christianity is fused with Neoplatonism, love and harmony are synonymous terms for the force which rules the universe. Here once again we have a poem shaped by a coherent structure of ideas; a poem born, we may suspect, of an excitement generated by the beauty of ideas rather than things.

In 'De la vida del cielo' the poet describes Christ, the Good Shepherd, leading his flock through heavenly pastures. He gives them music:

> Toca el rabel sonoro,
> y el inmortal dulzor al alma pasa,
> con que envilece el oro,
> y ardiendo se traspasa
> y lanza en aquel bien libre de tasa.

Music turns the soul away from temporal values since it is the harmony of the universe made audible, and harmony is love; and love is God himself. A poem about a loving shepherd culminates in music: once again a clear logic controls the poem.

Not all Fray Luis's poems are of this metaphysical character. One of his best known, 'Profecía del Tajo', is a vigorous reworking of Horace's Ode I, xv, applied to an episode in Spanish legend—the seduction of La Cava by King Roderick and the invasion of Spain by the Arabs. The poem is vigorous and builds up skilfully to a stirring climax.

The style of Fray Luis is terse and vigorous. He learned from Garcilaso (and echoed him on occasion) but leaned towards the drier, more epigrammatic style of Horace. His style has a distinctive bite of its own, as in lines like these from 'En una esperanza que salió vana':

> No pinta el prado aquí la primavera,
> ni nuevo sol jamás las nubes dora,
> ni canta el ruiseñor lo que antes era.
> La noche aquí se vela, aquí se llora
> el día miserable sin consuelo,
> y vence el mal de ayer el mal de agora.

San Juan de la Cruz (1542-91) is remembered chiefly for three poems: 'Cántico espiritual', 'Noche oscura', and 'Llama de amor viva', all of which, with their extensive prose commentaries, were published after his death (see above, Chapter 4).

The poetry of San Juan presents the reader with peculiar difficulties. The main difficulty is intrinsic to the subject-matter: mystical experience, whatever its real basis, is inevitably alien to most men. The poetry of San Juan is wholly about this experience: that is, its imagery symbolises the union of the poet's soul with his God. The prose commentaries are an essential aid if we hope to discover the poet's meaning, though the complexity of his exegesis creates further problems. In 'Noche oscura' the girl who symbolises the soul is described as 'segura' as she slips out to keep her assignation with her lover. San Juan tells us that she is 'segura' because she is free from the turbulence of the flesh and of earthly desires, and also because God is her guide. But also she is 'segura' because she follows the way of suffering, 'porque el camino de padecer es más seguro y aún más provechoso que el de gozar y hacer'. We are far from any meaning that the ordinary reader could divine by intuition alone, though the exegesis is not yet too complex to be borne in mind when we return to the poetry. But the commentary goes further: the girl is also 'disfrazada' which, we learn, signifies that she goes in the livery of Christ.

> Y así la librea que lleva es de tres colores principales, que son blanco, verde y colorado; por los cuales son denotadas las tres virtudes teologales, que son fe, esperanza y caridad, con las cuales no sólamente ganará la gracia y voluntad de su amado, pero irá muy amparada y segura de sus tres enemigos.

The ordinary reader has a right here to declare this to be irrelevant. We need the poet's assistance, but must feel entitled to dispense with the commentary when the poet manifestly begins to treat his poetry as a preacher treats his text: as an occasion for fine-spun lucubrations which, however edifying, have no necessary bearing on the text whence they sprang. Each reader must decide for himself when this point is reached in the commentary of San Juan.

Almost unquestionably, the finest of San Juan's poems is 'Noche oscura', which describes the soul's union with God in terms of a girl's escape from her hushed house by night to keep a secret assignation with her lover. The ostensibly erotic theme has to be borne in mind as we read if we are to sense anything of the emotion attaching to the poet's experience. The 'human' sense is easy to grasp, and only a minimum of information from the commentary is necessary to allow us to glimpse the 'real' meaning. The *declaración* of the first stanza sets us on the way.

> Cuenta el alma en esta primera canción el modo y manera que tuvo en salir, según la afición, de sí y de todas las cosas, muriendo por verdadera mortificación a todas ellas y a sí misma, para venir a vivir vida de amor, dulce y sabrosa, con Dios; y dice que este salir de sí y de todas las cosas fue una noche oscura, que aquí entiende por la contemplación purgativa . . . , la cual pasivamente causa en el alma la dicha negación de sí misma y de todas las cosas.

The hushed house is the body with its passions stilled: a moving and evocative image. The soul goes safely, guided in the darkness by 'la dicha luz o sabiduría oscura', the light of divine illumination. The 'secreta escala' she leaves by is the 'sabiduría secreta' of the mystic vision; and a stair leads up as well as down: contemplation can lead up to God and down to the humbling of self.

This is sufficient: the symbolism of the rest of the poem is not hard to penetrate. What is important is to yield to the poem's urgency as it flows rapidly to its climax. The repetition and echoing of certain words and phrases adds to the sense of urgency: 'noche oscura . . . oh dichosa ventura . . . a escuras . . . secreta . . . en secreto . . . luz y guía . . . guiaba . . . luz': a chain of words which carries us forward rapidly to the climax in:

> ¡Oh noche que guiaste!
> ¡oh noche amable más que el alborada!
> ¡oh noche que juntaste
> amado con amada,
> amada en el amado transformada!

The sexual union is allegorical, but unless we respond to the sexuality the poem must fail of its full effect. The repetitions of 'noche' convey a sense of excitement which in the fourth and fifth lines gives place to a helpless ecstasy: 'amado . . . amada . . . amada . . . amado . . . transformada'—it is as if words almost fail beneath the weight of emotion, as if the girl babbles in her ecstasy, on the verge of incoherence. The emotion expends itself and tension drops in the remaining stanzas. The poem ends in the tranquillity of fulfilment.

'Noche oscura' has an easily grasped unity and completeness. The same is true of 'Llama de amor viva'. This too has the appearance of a love-poem; and once again (with perhaps the exception of the third stanza), the reader can make his way without constant recourse to the commentary. The ecstatic air is sustained throughout. Even San Juan wrote few lines more delicately expressive or of more rapt intensity than the ecstatic oxymorons of the second stanza:

¡Oh cauterio sauve!,
¡oh regalada llaga!,
¡oh mano blanda, ¡oh toque delicado,
. . .!

'Cántico espiritual' poses greater difficulties than either of these since, though its subject is the same, the treatment is more complex and the symbolism (borrowed almost in its entirety from the *Song of Songs*) correspondingly more esoteric.

The poem describes how the soul, the *amada*, seeks the divine lover through the world until at last she sees his eyes reflected in a pool into which she gazes. The two join in love in an atmosphere of heightening ecstasy. The poem describes three stages on the mystic way, as San Juan explains: the purgative (stanzas 1-12), the illuminative (stanzas 13-21), and the unitive (stanzas 22 to the end). More often than in the case of the other two poems, the symbolism is impenetrable without the commentary; but equally often the commentary can enrich a word or a phrase *poetically* by a felicitous explanation. Sometimes the explanation, though doubtless doctrinally edifying, fails to animate the imagery, as in the case of the lines

Nuestro lecho florido
de cuevas de leones enlazado.

The explanation is rational enough: the flowery bed is the bosom of the divine Lover, and the lions' caves symbolise the strength in virtue of the fortified soul; but the image remains awkward and unhappy. Of instances where the commentary enriches, a few examples must suffice. In stanza 3 the soul, searching for her lover, declares

no cogeré las flores,
ni temeré las fieras,
y pasaré los fuertes y fronteras.

She will not be distracted by earthly pleasures (*flores*), will not fear enemies (*fieras*—the world), will pass beyond the reach of the Devil (*fuertes*) and beyond the boundaries of the flesh (*fronteras*). Intuition might have been sufficient help, but San Juan's comment on *fronteras* gives the image a sudden vividness.

> Dice también el alma que pasará las fronteras, por las cuales entiende . . . las repugnancias y rebeliones que naturalmente la carne tiene contra el espíritu . . .

The key word is *rebeliones*. For the poet a frontier is a place of disorder, of skirmishes and lawlessness. Although Spain was unified before San Juan was born, perhaps he felt something—through literature: *romances fronterizos* and the like—of the atmosphere which the old frontier war created. *Fronteras* acquires a particular aptness.

There is a more complex example in the stanza

Oh ninfas de Judea,
en tanto que en las flores y rosales
el ámbar perfumea,
morá en los arrabales,
y no queráis tocar nuestros umbrales.

The reference to nymphs in a poem of mainly biblical inspiration has been thought inappropriate by some. San Juan explains:

> Judea llama a la parte inferior del ánima, que es la sensitiva. Y llámala Judea, porque es flaca y carnal, como lo es la gente judaica. Y llama ninfas a todas las imaginaciones, fantasías y movimientos y afecciones de esta porción inferior. A todas éstas llama ninfas, porque así como las ninfas con su afición y gracia atraen para sí a los amantes, así estas operaciones y movimientos de la sensualidad sabrosamente procuran atraer a sí la voluntad de la parte razonal . . .

Though he does not say so explicitly, the reason for his choosing *ninfas* rather than the superficially more appropriate *vírgenes* or *doncellas* is patent: he needed to convey the sense of 'flighty girls' in the clearest way and found the seductive nymphs of classical and modern pastoral literature more disturbingly evocative than the maidens of the Bible. To feel the force of the poet's words, the profane reader need only draw on his own reading of secular literature.

This is also true of the stanza

Mi amado, las montañas
los valles solitarios nemorosos,
las ínsulas extrañas,
los ríos sonorosos,
el silbo de los aires amorosos . . .

The lines express the poet's sense of the marvels and mysteries of the inwardness of God. The strange adjective *nemorosos* suggests Garcilaso's shepherd to any reader of Spanish poetry (as Dámaso Alonso has pointed out[8]): it brings with it a world of poetic associations.

The *ínsulas extrañas* express the secrecy and strangeness of the soul's union with God:

> Las ínsulas extrañas están ceñidas con la mar, y allende de los mares, muy apartadas y ajenas de la comunicación de los hombres; y así en ellas se crían y nacen cosas muy diferentes de las de por acá . . . que hacen grande novedad y admiración a quien las ve.

Doubtless reports of Spanish explorations and discoveries had played a part in the conception of this image. But why *ínsulas* instead of the more usual *islas* (which had been good enough for the discoverers themselves, as we see from Columbus's first newsletter of 1493)? For the (almost self-evident) answer one has only to appeal to an ordinary knowledge of Spanish literature. San Juan wanted a word evocative of mystery and magic: *ínsula* brings this atmosphere with it from the romances of chivalry, as this passage from *Amadís* will show:

> Este gigante que el doncel llevó era natural de Leonís y había dos castillos en una ínsula, y llamábase él Gandalás, y no era tan hacedor de mal como los otros gigantes, antes era de buen talante, hasta que era sañudo, mas después que lo era hacía grandes cruezas. El se fue con su niño hasta en cabo de la ínsula a do había un hermitaño, buen hombre de santa vida . . .

Amadís himself reigns over the Ínsula Firme. It is literary associations of this kind which the reader of San Juan's poetry needs, as much as the poet's own commentary. The reader must, at all events, be prepared to use his imagination creatively; and indeed San Juan gives his reader encouragement of a sort to do this when he writes in the prologue of *Cántico espiritual* addressed to Mother Ana de Jesús, at whose request the commentary was written:

> Por haberse, pues, estas canciones compuesto en amor de abundante inteligencia mística, no se podrán declarar al justo, ni mi intento será tal, sino sólo dar alguna luz en general . . . ; y esto tengo por mejor, porque los dichos de amor es mejor dejarlos en su anchura, para que cada uno de ellos se aproveche según su modo y caudal de espíritu, que abreviarlos a un sentido a que no se acomode todo paladar. Y así, aunque en alguna manera se declaran, no hay para qué atarse a la declaración . . .

San Juan wrote other poems as well: ten spiritual *romances* and some other pieces, of which two stand out: 'El pastorcico', a version *a lo divino* of a secular lyric,[9] and 'Aunque es de noche'. The sources of San Juan's imagery in these and other poems have been expertly studied by Dámaso Alonso,[10] who has traced possible sources—apart from the Bible—as diverse as traditional ballads, *cancionero* love-poetry, and the poetry of Garcilaso as reworked *a lo divino* by Sebastián de Córdoba.

Devotional poetry of a more traditional and less esoteric kind continued to be written in abundance by men like Juan López de Ubeda (late sixteenth century) who published poetry by himself and others in his *Cancionero general de la doctrina cristiana* (1579) and *Vergel de floros divinas* (Alcalá, 1582); and Pedro de Padilla (later sixteenth century), who published *Tesoro de varias poesías* (Madrid, 1580), and *Jardín espiritual* (Madrid, 1585), as well as some secular works. The poetry of men like these is unsophisticated, often banal, but with moments of charm.

Side by side with the 'literary' poetry with which we have been concerned so far there existed a 'popular' poetry derived from or written in imitation of folk-poetry or folk-song. This poetry is historically an important feature of the Spanish Golden Age, as well as being poetically valuable in its own right.

The Renaissance revival of classical learning went hand-in-hand with the growth of a courtly culture which favoured refinement, urbanity, and education. There grew up at the same time a strong interest in the popular and primitive as a result of the new importance given to Nature in philosophy and art. The rise of pastoral literature is a reflection of this. Man was thought to have been at his best in the mythical Golden Age, a Renaissance commonplace treated over and over again by generations of writers. The new interest in popular poetry evident from the later fifteenth century onwards was probably related to this revaluation of the natural. True folk-songs began appearing in print in the early sixteenth century, first in *pliegos,* later in *vihuela* manuals such as Luis Milán, *El maestro* (Valencia, 1535); Luis de Narváez, *Los seis libros del Delfín de música* (Valladolid, 1538); Diego Pisador, *Libro de música para vihuela* (Salamanca, 1552); and song-books such as Juan Vázquez, *Recopilación de sonetos y villancicos* (Seville, 1560), and the so-called *Cancionero de Upsala* (Venice, 1556).

In the sixteenth century an increasing number of poets took traditional *estribillos* as the basis for *villancicos* of their own. By the later sixteenth century very many educated poets were regularly writing free imitations of the traditional folk-lyric. The main forms were the *villancico,* the *letrilla* (really only the *villancico* under another name), the *seguidilla* (four-line stanzas of alternate 6/7- and 5-syllable lines with rhyme or assonance scheme ABAB), and the octosyllabic four-line stanza. *Villancicos* and other poems of popular cut were collected in the anthologies which appeared more and more frequently from the later sixteenth century onwards: collections such as *Flor de enamorados* (Barcelona, 1562), *Flor de romances y glosas, canciones y villancicos . . .* (Saragossa, 1578), and their numerous successors. From the 1580s poems by men like Góngora and Lope de Vega, but usually printed anonymously, were the staple of these collections. The themes were very varied. In the seventeenth century satire and burlesque were to play an accentuated role.

Folk-poetry nourished Golden Age literature in another way too. Throughout the period, but with increasing frequency in the later sixteenth and the seventeenth centuries, folk-poetry and poetry in imitation of it was rewritten *a lo divino*. In addition, numerous poems on the nativity and other religious festivals were written by Lope de Vega and others in imitation of the traditional lyric.

The *romance* underwent an analogous history. It began to gain courtly favour in the fifteenth century and in the sixteenth grew enormously in prestige. From the early years of the century *romances* were printed in *pliegos sueltos*, and from these were drawn most of the *romances* collected in the famous *Cancionero de romances* (Antwerp, n.d., but probably 1548). The collection was an immediate success, and was reprinted several times. After 1550 collections abound, though as the century went on their character changes. The *Cancionero de romances* consisted mainly of traditional *romances*. In subsequent years the new *romances artificiosos* (or *artísticos*) grew in popularity and the last twenty years of the century saw the victory of this *romancero nuevo*, which was lyrical and novelesque in its themes and in its treatment of them. Pastoral ballads were very much in vogue, as also were *morisco* ballads playing on the romantic appeal of the Moors of Andalusia in the days of their independence. In these years Lope de Vega became firmly associated with the *romance morisco*, which made him famous before he became famous as a dramatist.

Between 1589 and 1598 a large number of collections, works like *Flor de varios romances nuevos* (Huesca, 1589) and its successive parts, gathered together the *romances* written by the younger poets of the day. These collections were in turn collected in the *Romancero general* (Madrid, 1600), which went into a considerably enlarged second edition in 1604. This was followed by a *Segunda parte* (Valladolid, 1605). New editions of these and subsequent collections testify to the ever-increasing popularity of the *romance artificioso*. There were changes of fashion and taste within the general vogue of the *romance*, however: the *romance morisco* was eclipsed in the early seventeenth century, and the *romance* in general tended away from the novelesque towards the more purely lyrical, no doubt under the influence of music, now more important for its own sake. A disconcerting contrary development is to be seen in the growing taste for satirical ballads and for ballads of low life.

* * *

One large field of Spanish verse has not so far been touched on: the *jocoso* tradition—light verse written for amusement, often satirical in character, but equally often simply facetious, and embracing subjects of all kinds, from flirtatious banter to gross indecency. (Women are commonly the butt of this kind of humour, an attenuated form of that repellent appendage of the Christian tradition, medieval misogyny, which even in its 'humorous' Golden Age version must be distasteful to a modern reader of any degree of sensibility.) Very many poets indulged their wit in this fashion: *jocoso* verse was as much a part of social ritual as the love-poetry spoken of earlier. Diego Hurtado de Mendoza was well known for his *jocoso* poems, such as his eulogy of horns, and of carrots; and his indecent 'Fábula del cangrejo'. Cetina wrote his share of such verse. Perhaps the best-known of sixteenth-century *jocoso* poets is the Sevillian Baltasar del Alcázar (1530-1606), deservedly celebrated for his wit and facility. These lines 'A uno muy gordo de vientre y muy presumido de valiente' show his neatness of wit:

> No es mucho que en la ocasión,
> Julio, muy valiente seas,
> Si haces cuando peleas
> De las tripas corazón.

His 'Cena jocosa' is probably his best-known piece.

The shadowy 'Licenciado Tamariz' is another of these *jocoso* poets. Nothing is known of him, though it has been surmised by his modern editor that he must have been a well-known figure in Seville and may have died around 1570. Tamariz's extant work consists of six (perhaps ten) piquant and wittily-told stories in verse which probably derive from some collection of Italian *novelle.*[11]

One genre remains to be discussed: the literary epic. Long poems have been out of favour since Poe declared them to be intrinsically unpoetic on the ground that the inspiration which is the essence of true poetry can be sustained only for the length of a short lyric. There has been a revolution in taste since the days when Dryden could affirm that 'a Heroic Poem, truly such, is undoubtedly the greatest work which the soul of man is capable to perform'.

In the sixteenth and seventeenth centuries well over one hundred and fifty literary epics were published in Spain, in imitation of a vogue which had started in Renaissance Italy. The literary epic, a heroic poem of some length divided into books or cantos, was modelled primarily on the *Aeneid,* not on the heroic poetry of post-classical Europe; though another classical influence was also at work: that of Lucan's *Pharsalia*, which recounted incidents from recent history (the Civil Wars between Caesar and Pompey). Two Italian works were equal to them in prestige and influence: Ariosto's *Orlando furioso* (1516), and Tasso's *Gerusalemme liberata* (1580). Both were influential in Spain: Lope de Vega, for example, wrote *La hermosura de Angélica* (1602) in imitation of the first and *Jerusalén conquistada* (1609) in imitation of the second. In imitation of the Italian *ottava rima*, the Spanish literary epic was generally written in *octavas reales* (eight hendecasyllables rhyming ABABABCC). The number of cantos varied: sometimes twelve (in imitation of the *Aeneid*), sometimes ten (in imitation of Lucan), sometimes twenty-four (in imitation of Homer), or some arbitrary number of the poet's choice.

One of the most famous of Spanish literary epics is *La Araucana* (in three parts: 1569, 1578, 1589) by Alonso de Ercilla, and it is probably the one most deserving of attention from modern readers. (The finest of such works written in the Iberian Peninsula is without question *Os Lusiadas* (1572) by the Portuguese Camões, but this is outside the scope of this history.) Ercilla (1533-94), a nobleman who had the added fortune to marry great wealth, himself fought in the conquest of Chile, which is the subject of his epic. The story he tells is an exciting one, albeit of horrifying brutality. He depicts the Araucanian Indians in noble terms (since after all an epic demanded noble treatment of a noble theme), saying of them in his prologue:

> Y si a alguno le pareciere que me muestro algo inclinado a la parte de los araucanos, tratando sus cosas y valentías más extendidamente de lo que para bárbaros se requiere, si queremos mirar su crianza, costumbres, modos de guerra y ejercicio della, veremos que muchos no les han hecho ventaja, y que son pocos los que con tan gran constancia y firmeza han defendido su tierra contra tan fieros enemigos como son los españoles.

The dignity with which Ercilla invests the Indians may be seen in his treatment of Caupolicán, their chief. Captured by the Spaniards, he is impaled—but only after conversion and baptism. He permits himself to be seated on the sharpened stake.

> No el aguzado palo penetrante
> por más que las entrañas le rompiese
> barrenándole el cuerpo, fue bastante
> a que el dolor intenso se rindiese:
> que con sereno término y semblante,
> sin que labio ni ceja retorciese,

sosegado quedó de la manera
que si asentado en tálamo estuviera.

En esto, seis flecheros señalados,
que prevenidos para aquello estaban
treinta pasos de trecho desvïados
por orden y de espacio le tiraban;
y aunque en toda maldad ejercitados,
al despedir la flecha vacilaban,
temiendo poner mano en un tal hombre
de tanta autoridad y tan gran nombre.

(Canto XXXIV, stanzas 28, 29)

Ercilla sustains a remarkably high level of narrative verse in this poem. He is clearly no lyric poet, but the subject does not call for lyricism. The intercalated story of Dido in Canto XXXII, where Ercilla attempts a sentimental mode, is not successful poetry. Neither is he capable of a poetic account of nature. Ercilla is at his best with feats of arms, courage, and endurance, in describing which his verse can rise to a rugged grandeur. The opening stanzas of Canto I display his characteristic strength.

No las damas, amor, no gentilezas
de caballeros canto enamorados,
ni las muestras, regalos y ternezas
de amorosos afectos y cuidados;
mas el valor, los hechos, las proezas
de aquellos españoles esforzados,
que a la cerviz de Arauco no domada
pusieron duro yugo por la espada.

Cosas diré harto notables
de gente que a ningún rey obedecen,
temerarias empresas memorables
que celebrarse con razón merecen,
raras industrias, términos loables
que más los españoles engrandecen:
pues no es el vencedor más estimado
de aquello en que el vencido es reputado.

Ercilla's was not the first Spanish heroic poem on a modern historical subject. Before him had come Jerónimo Sempere's *La Carolea* (Valencia, 1560) and Luis Zapata's *Carlo famoso* (Valencia, 1566).[12] The first literary epic of the Golden Age, however, was not historical or mythological in the usual sense. It was a poem on the life of Christ by Juan de Quirós: *Christo Pathia* (Toledo, 1552). One of the finest of Golden Age literary epics was to be on the same subject: Diego de Hojeda's *La Christiada* (Seville, 1611). There is no classical precedent for works like these, naturally: they are probably a fusion of two traditions—the literary epic proper, and the medieval verse lives of Christ such as Fray Íñigo de Mendoza's *Vita Christi* and Diego de San Pedro's *Pasión trobada.* Devout Spanish poets saw an opportunity of turning the profane Renaissance literary epic to moral profit: hence the large numbers of epics on religious subjects, particularly in the seventeenth century, which abounds in works like Antonio de Escobar y Mendoza's *San Ignacio* (Valladolid, 1613).

The burlesque heroic poem was not neglected in Spain. Two outstanding examples are José de Villaviciosa's *La Mosquea* (Cuenca, 1615) and Lope de Vega's *La Gatomaquia* (Madrid, 1634), the first about a war between ants and flies, the second about cats.

* * *

A distinction is commonly made in the history of Golden Age poetry between the so-called schools of Salamanca and of Seville, the first being distinguished by its Horatian sobriety, the second by its colour and grandiloquence. Fray Luis de León has been taken as the representative of the first, Herrera of the second. The truth is that no valid distinction can be sustained, and the notion of 'schools' is best abandoned.[13]

NOTES

1. For the poets discussed in this chapter, it is useful to consult A. Terry, *An Anthology of Spanish Poetry 1500-1700*, Part I (Oxford, 1965). A. Rodríguez-Moñino reminds us in his *Construcción crítica y realidad historica en la poesía española de los siglos XVI y XVII* (Madrid, 1965) that most Spanish poets of the Golden Age did not see their works printed in their lifetime. Some of the poets most highly valued now were unknown to their contemporaries.

2. See L. Forster, *The Icy Fire. Five studies in European Petrarchism* (Cambridge, 1969).

3. See R. O. Jones, 'Renaissance Butterfly, Mannerist Flea: Tradition and Change in Renaissance Poetry', *MLN*, LXXX (1965).

4. The best studies of the poetry are by Dámaso Alonso (in *Poesía española*; Madrid, 1950) and by Oreste Macrí (introduction to his edition; Salamanca, 1970).

5. For a brief account of these speculations see R. O. Jones, *Poems of Góngora* (Cambridge, 1966), pp. 30-1. For a more comprehensive account see Christopher Butler, *Number Symbolism* (London, 1970).

6. This stanza does not appear in the Quevedo edition but is now commonly accepted as authentic.

7. His cosmology is Ptolemaic, according to which the universe is composed

of invisible concentric spheres, on which the planets (including the sun and the moon) as well as the stars are held in place. At the centre—that is, in the lowest place—is the earth, round which the whole system revolves.

8. In *La poesía de San Juan de la Cruz* (3rd ed., Madrid, 1966).

9. See J. M. Blecua, 'Los antecedentes del poema del "Pastorcico" de San Juan de la Cruz', *RFE*, XXXIII (1949).

10. Dámaso Alonso, op. cit.

11. See *Novelas y cuentos en verso del Licenciado Tamariz*, ed. A. Rodríguez-Moñino, Duque y Marqués VIII (Valencia, 1956).

12. *Carlo famoso* is dull. Zapata (1526-95) is now remembered chiefly for his entertaining and even informative *Varia historia*, a miscellany of anecdotes drawn from a lifetime as a courtier. The work was first published as *Miscelánea* (Madrid, 1859) by Gayangos. It was published again in an edition by G. C. Horsman (Amsterdam, 1935). Selections were published by A. Rodríguez-Moñino as *Miscelánea, Silva de casos curiosos* (Madrid, 1931).

13. See Henry Bonneville, 'Sur la poésie à Séville au Siècle d'Or', *BH*, LXVI (1964).

Chapter 6

THE PICARESQUE NOVEL

THE WORD *pícaro* (whose etymology is still uncertain) is first encountered in a text of 1525 where it means 'scullion', a sense it was to retain. By 1545 it already connoted dishonesty. 'Delinquent' has been suggested as the appropriate rendering rather than the more usual 'rogue', which has now lost much of its force.[1] The typical *pícaro* in literature is dishonest and parasitic, but not often violent, a drifter, always seeking easy advantage, always evading responsibility.

Though it is customary to include *Lazarillo de Tormes* in the genre, the first literary character to be called a *pícaro* by his author is Guzmán de Alfarache. The vogue of the *pícaro* in fiction was created in fact by the publication of the first part of Mateo Alemán's *Guzmán de Alfarache* (Madrid, 1599), whose success with the public is indicated not only by the fact of its being immediately reprinted and pirated, but by the publication in 1602 of a second part by 'Mateo Luján de Sayavedra' (the pseudonym of the Valencian lawyer Juan Martí). Alemán's own *Segunda parte* appeared in 1604, to be followed over the next half-century by a great number of picaresque works contributing their variations on the theme of roguery or delinquency. Cervantes himself took up the theme in his *novela Rinconete y Cortadillo*, and touched on it elsewhere. Most of the picaresque novels, following the pattern of *Lazarillo* and *Guzmán*, were written in the form of autobiographies. They are all episodic in character, which has led to the term 'picaresque' being journalistically applied to any loosely rambling episodic fiction. This will not do: *Pickwick Papers* is not a picaresque novel: the term must be reserved, if it is to retain any meaning, for the fictional biography (usually autobiography) of a parasitic rogue. That being said, it must be added that the picaresque does not constitute a clear-cut genre like the pastoral novel: differences of form and intention are great, and must be allowed for in interpretation. To speak of one picaresque theme would be misleading. Quevedo's target is not Mateo Alemán's.

Not many literary historians would now attribute the rise of the picaresque novel solely to social conditions in Spain in the sixteenth and seventeenth centuries: this naïvely deterministic view left out of account the fact that up to 1600 Spain was not markedly different from the rest of Europe in her social conditions. Another factor must be sought. Américo Castro has put forward the view that the picaresque novel had its origin in the bitter resentment of the *conversos* who, because of their Jewish descent, found themselves regarded as aliens in their own country and, if their ancestry was not generally known, lived in constant dread of exposure and its social consequences. This explanation, supported principally by the supposed Jewish ancestry of Mateo Alemán, has been extended backwards to the anonymous author of *Lazarillo*, now alleged (without serious evidence) to be a *converso*. The genre thus created, the argument runs, was then exploited by Christians such as Quevedo. Marcel Bataillon has more recently argued that the important thing is not the ancestry of the authors but the role—explicit or covert—of *limpieza de sangre* in the novels themselves, whose ironic treatment of 'external' honour (as opposed to real worth) is related in some way to the social tension between ambition for honour and fear of genealogical inquiry with what it might reveal.[2]

When Guzmán becomes a porter or errand-boy in Madrid he rejoices in his freedom. 'No trocara esta vida de pícaro por la mejor que tuvieron mis pasados' (1, 2, ii). He speaks again of 'el almíbar picaresco'—the carefree life of one liberated from slavery to appearances. For such a one honour ceases to be a concern. Guzmán sees that in this repudiation of honour, a source of false values, there is a real virtue.

> ¡Oh, decía, lo que carga el peso de la honra y cómo no hay metal que se le iguale! . . . ¿Qué frenesí de Santanás casó este mal abuso con el hombre, que tan desatinado lo tiene? Como si no supiésemos que la honra es hija de la virtud y, tanto que uno fuere virtuoso, será honrado, y será imposible la honra, si no me quitaren la virtud, que es centro della. (1, 2, ii)

The shamelessness of the *pícaro* appears here to be equated with the true Christian's indifference to worldly honour. But this is ingenious paradox, not a serious eulogy of the life of the *pícaro*. In the serious picaresque works, the freedom of the *pícaro* is represented as a holiday from responsibility, not as a good.[3]

However, the theme of picaresque freedom was undoubtedly an alluring one. A poem on *La vida del pícaro* published in 1601 illustrates its attraction.

> ¡Oh, pícaros cofrades!, ¡quién pudiese
> sentarse cual vosotros en la calle
> sin que a menos valer se le tuviese!

¡Quién pudiese vestir a vuestro talle,
desabrochado el cuello y sin petrina
y el corto tiempo a mi sabor gozalle! [4]

Even Quevedo took up the theme in a sonnet:

. . .
¡Oh santo bodegón! ¡Oh picardía!
¡Oh tragos; oh tajadas; oh gandaya;
oh barata y alegre putería!
Tras los reyes y príncipes se vaya
quien da toda la vida por un día,
que yo me quiero andar de saya en saya.

Though such poems smack also of literary convention, a real envy of irresponsibility, of freedom from care, is probably present. Low life had a clear appeal for one side of Quevedo's complex character: his *jácaras* (poems in criminal slang) are a sufficient sign of that. The taste was widely shared at even the highest levels: in 1605 a masquerade 'disfrazado a lo pícaro' took place at Court.[5] The picaresque very soon turned into an entertainment in which the respectable might find amusement in the contemplation of the disreputable. Murillo's picturesque urchins were painted in this spirit.

Though the picaresque novel owes its origin to something more than social conditions, those conditions were nevertheless a rich source of novelesque material. The life of Captain Alonso de Contreras shows how rich.[6] He left home at the age of fifteen in a style worthy of any picaresque hero:

. . . quedé con mi madre, a quien dije:
'Señora, vuestra merced está cargada de hijos; déjeme ir a buscar mi vida con este Príncipe.'
Y, resolviéndose mi madre a ello, dijo:
'No tengo qué te dar.'
Dije:
'No importa, que yo buscaré para todos, Dios mediante'.
Con todo, me compró una camisa y unos zapatos de carnero, y me dio cuatro reales y me echó su bendición. Con lo cual, un martes, 7 de septiembre de 1597, al amanecer, salí de Madrid tras las trompetas del Príncipe Cardenal.

A novelist with any concern for verisimilitude would have hesitated to make up the episode in which Contreras, determining after a life of conscienceless violence to become a hermit when his hopes of promotion are disappointed, packs his bags with hair-shirt, scourge, skull, and other requisites of the devout life, and retreats for seven months to

Moncayo. It was probably his swashbuckling picturesqueness which interested Lope de Vega, who befriended him and supported him for eight months. *La vida y hechos de Estebanillo González, hombre de buen humor. Compuesto por él mismo* (Antwerp, 1646), almost certainly a genuine autobiography, should be read in the same spirit. The author recounts in a floridly facetious style the story of his adventures as he travelled all over Europe in a variety of occupations of a bizarre or picaresque character, at last finding employment as the jester of the commander of the imperial army, Ottavio Piccolomini, and then of the Prince-Cardinal Don Fernando, brother of Philip IV. He writes with disarming shamelessness of his cowardice and his misdemeanours. He tells, for example, how after hiding to avoid the fighting at Nördlingen he sallied forth after the battle to slash at the Swedish corpses.

> Sucedióme (para que se conozca mi valor) que llegando a uno de los enemigos a darle media docena de morcilleras, juzgando su cuerpo por cadáver como los demás, a la primera que le tiré despidió un ¡ay! tan espantoso, que sólo de oírlo y paracerme que hacia movimiento para quererse levantar para tomar cumplida venganza, no teniendo ánimo para sacarle la espada de la parte adonde se la había envasado, tomando por buen partido el dejársela, lo volví las espaldas, y a carrera abierta no paré hasta que llegué a la parte adonde estaba nuestro bagaje . . .

His account of his life was probably retouched: it sometimes has a very literary flavour. He may have been consciously addressing himself to the public's taste for unheroic adventure revealed by the success of the picaresque literature of entertainment. However, this is not a book to moralise over; if it is an autobiography the criteria applicable to a work of art are not to be applied here. The value of the book is as a human document which gives us a glimpse of the frequently horrifying callousness of the daily life which underlies the literature and art of the period.

* * *

La vida de Guzmán de Alfarache, atalaya de la vida humana[7], though it appeared in two parts, was conceived as one story from the beginning. The best summary is Alemán's own introductory 'Declaración':

> Para lo cual se presupone que Guzmán de Alfarache, nuestro pícaro, habiendo sido muy buen estudiante, latino, retórico y griego, como diremos en esta primera parte, después dando la vuelta de Italia en España, pasó adelante con sus estudios, con ánimo de professor el estado de la religión; mas por volverse a los vicios los dejó, habiendo cursado algunos años en ellos. Él mismo escribe su vida desde las

> galeras, donde queda forzado al remo, por delitos que cometió, habiendo sido ladrón famosísimo, como largamente lo verás en la segunda parte. Y no es impropriedad ni fuera de propósito si en esta primera escribiere alguna dotrina, que antes parece muy llegado a razón darla un hombre de claro entendimiento, ayudado de letras y castigado del tiempo, aprovechándose del ocioso de la galera.

The work consists of Guzmán's account of his escapades together with his moral commentary on them, so that we are given (as it were) a double view of things. The moral commentary is an integral part of the work as it was conceived from the start, for *Guzmán* is not primarily a work of entertainment. It was a tract for the times; and it was received as such. Its popularity was immense. It was one of the most frequently reprinted works of the seventeenth century. There were three separate translations into French which went into a total of eighteen editions in the seventeenth century. The German translation went into ten editions within the century, and the English translation by James Mabbe (1622-23) into six. There were also early translations into Dutch, Italian, and Latin. Clearly, Alemán expressed in *Guzmán* something important to a multitude of western Europeans and the book, to judge by the number of editions, may have been read at some time by a majority of the European reading public of that century.

In the eighteenth century the moral 'digressions' began to be found tedious by some readers. Lesage brought out a new French translation in 1732 'purgée des moralités superflues'. This was a success with the public, and, together with Lesage's own *Gil Blas*, helped to establish the modern view of the picaresque novel as essentially a tale of amusing adventures. Only in fairly recent years has *Guzmán* come to be seen again, and appreciated, as a unity.

Although not a great deal is known of him, the life and apparent character of Mateo Alemán have had an influence on interpretation of *Guzmán*. He was born in Seville in 1547, the son of a doctor. He himself studied medicine for a time. He came to hold positions of importance under the Crown: he was *Juez de Comisión* in 1583, charged with auditing certain provincial tax accounts, and he occupied similar positions over a number of years. In 1593 he was sent as judge to investigate conditions at the mercury-mines of Almadén. The transcripts of evidence make horrifying reading: here, if never before, Alemán saw into the depths of human degradation and suffering.[8] He himself was in prison for short periods more than once: in 1583 on a charge of exceeding his authority, in 1602 for debt. In 1608 he sailed for Mexico with his mistress and certain other members of his family. Nothing is known of him after 1613. In addition to *Guzmán* he published *San Antonio de Padua* (Seville, 1604), *Ortografía castellana*

(Mexico, 1609), and *Sucesos de D. Fray García Gera* [*Guerra*], *arzobispo de México* ... (Mexico, 1613).

Much has been made of Alemán's supposed Jewish ancestry. How flimsy and unreliable is the evidence for this has been demonstrated recently[9]. It cannot be reaffirmed unless new evidence appears. *Guzmán* was almost certainly not written out of some secret anguish: the evidence depicts Alemán as an influential and respected man of affairs.

One of the most influential modern interpretations of *Guzmán* is that of Enrique Moreno Báez, who has effectively restored the unity of the book by demonstrating the inseparability of incident and moral commentary. He sees the book as a response to the didactic ideals of the Counter-Reformation and an embodiment of its view of man. The fundamental proposition of the book is Original Sin, illustrated over and over again by examples of backsliding and villainy.

> Este camino corre el mundo. No comienza de nuevo, que de atrás le viene al garbanzo el pico. No tiene medio ni remedio. Así lo hallamos, así lo dejaremos. No se espere mejor tiempo ni se piense que lo fue el pasado. Todo ha sido, es y será una misma cosa. El primero padre fue alevoso; la primera madre mentirosa; el primero hijo ladrón y fratricida. (I, 3, i)

All men are enemies, united only in their mutual treachery: 'No hallarás hombre con hombre; todos vivimos en asechanzas ...' (I, 2, iv). When Guzmán as a boy on the road to Toledo meets another lad they question each other cautiously; Guzmán knows the other lies, 'que por mis mentiras conocí que me las decía' (I, 2, vii). Deceit is a constant in human society, but *engaño* is yet more universal than this.

> Es tan general esta contagiosa enfermedad, que no solamente los hombres la padecen, mas las aves y animales. También los peces tratan allá de sus engaños, para conservarse mejor cada uno. Engañan los árboles y plantas, prometiéndonos alegre flor y fruto, que al tiempo falta y lo pasan con lozanía. Las piedras, aun siendo piedras y sin sentido, turban el nuestro con su fingido resplandor y mienten, que no son lo que parecen. El tiempo, las ocasiones, los sentidos nos engañan. Y sobre todo, aun los más bien trazados pensamientos. Toda cosa engaña y todos engañamos ... (II, I, iii)

But though the world deceives, and man's own appetites and passions are a snare, a man is responsible for his actions: he cannot absolve himself by blaming his corrupt nature. 'Querer culpar a la naturaleza, no tendré razón, pues no menos tuve habilidad para lo bueno que inclinación para lo malo' (I, 3, ix). It is open to every man, no matter how deeply sunk in sin, to save himself by repentance, as Guzmán, meditating on a sermon he had heard, suddenly realises.

¡Válgame Dios!, me puse a pensar, que aun a mí me toca y yo soy alguien: ¡cuenta se hace de mí! . . . Sí, amigo, me respondía. A ti te toca y contigo habla, que también eres miembro deste cuerpo místico, igual con todos en sustancia, aunque no en calidad. (I, 2, iii)

Whatever his position, a man is given the means to save himself. 'Procura ser usufructuario de tu vida, que usando bien della, salvarte puedes en tu estado' (I, 2, iv).

This, then, is the fundamental theme of the book, which all Guzmán's experiences will illustrate. His mother was an adulteress, his real father a conscienceless villain. After leaving home Guzmán slides easily into a life of dishonesty and idleness. From petty thieving and gambling he graduates rapidly to major theft, the proceeds of which he squanders on cutting a fine figure. Crossing to Italy he becomes a sham beggar in Rome. There a Cardinal takes him into his household, but Guzmán, unable to shake off his old ways, is dismissed. Aided by Sayavedra, a confederate whom he takes into his service, Guzmán perpetrates an ingenious swindle in Milan, cheats his Genoese relatives out of a large sum, and returns to Spain with his wealth. He settles in Madrid as a wealthy merchant, marries, and in association with his father-in-law engages in a variety of dishonest business. At last he is discredited and ruined. On the death of his wife he decides to study for the priesthood, but only out of self-interest: 'tendré cierta la comida y, a todo faltar, meteréme fraile, donde la hallaré cierta' (II, 3, iv). At Alcalá he settles down to a virtuous life and continues in it for seven years, but almost on the eve of graduation he falls in love, abandons his studies, and marries again. He and his wife settle in Madrid, where he lives on her immoral earnings. They move to Seville, where his wife leaves him, taking with her all his money. He is reduced to a variety of desperate shifts, including stealing capes and linen. By imposing on the guilelessness of a friar he acquires a reputation for sanctity which secures him the post of steward to a rich lady. He robs her systematically, is found out, and sent to the galleys, where he suffers the extremes of degradation and misery. But there, a friendless outcast, he is led to reflect on his fate.

¿Ves aquí, Guzmán, la cumbre del monte de las miserias, adonde te ha subido tu torpe sensualidad? Ya estás arriba y para dar un salto en lo profundo de los infiernos o para con facilidad, alzando el brazo, alcanzar el cielo. (II, 3 viii)

A mountain of miseries, from whose top he can reach heaven: a striking paradox.

Seeing the futility of his previous life he repents, sleeps, and on waking 'halléme otro no yo ni con aquel corazón viejo que antes'. Now begin fresh trials: he is falsely accused of theft and brutally punished. At last his new-found virtue brings its reward: invited to join a conspiracy to mutiny, he denounces it to the commander and is rewarded by a return to favour and by being granted the freedom of the ship.

Original Sin is not, however, the sole theme of the book. It is the background against which the action takes place; but as Guzmán moves through different ways of life and levels of society many different topics engage his (or his author's) attention. 'Todo ha sido, es y será una misma cosa': no doubt; but Guzmán, in denouncing evils in the society of his day, has many reforms to propose. Mateo Alemán evidently believed that some things were capable of change. When robbed in Italy Guzmán discourses on thieves and how they should be treated. The usual sentence of exile is worse than useless since they will simply go and steal elsewhere.

> No, no: que no es útil a la república ni buena policía hacer a ladrones tanto regalo; antes por leves hurtos debieran dárseles graves penas. Échenlos en las galeras, métanlos en presidios o denles otros castigos, por más o menos tiempo, conforme a los delitos. Y cuando no fuesen de calidad que mereciesen ser agravados tanto, a lo menos debiéranlos perdigar, como en muchas partes acostumbran, que les hacen señal fuego en las espaldas, por donde a el segundo hurto son conocidos. (II, I, viii)

The frequent discussions of justice and its perversion doubtlessly reflect Alemán's professional concern with crime and punishment. In II, 2, ii-iii Guzmán discourses on the hazards of litigation, on the dishonesty of officers of the law, on the corruptibility of some judges (and how it may be guarded against) and the capriciousness of others. An unfortunate experience in Madrid leads him to discourse on false charges of rape and to propose a remedy against light and unscrupulous females: 'Si así se les respondiese con una ley en que mandase que mujer de once años arriba y en poblado no pudiese pedir fuerza, por fuerza serían buenas' (II, 3, ii). Describing the swindles in which he engaged, he proposes a change in the law of contracts and compares the laws of Castile unfavourably with those of Barcelona, where a man may set up as merchant only with the permission of the Consuls who regulate commerce. The sale of his house leads him to inveigh against the iniquities of the *censo perpetuo,* whereby an extortionate proportion of the proceeds of a sale are payable to the original owner. It is an arbitrary imposition.

> Y como fueron los que gasté tres mil ducados, pudiera ser trecientos,

> treinta a treinta mil y aquella casa pudo venderse treinta veces en un año. Que fuera un excesivo y exorbitante derecho. Y aquesto ni lo es de civil ni canónico ni tiene otro fundamento que nacer del que llamamos de las gentes y no común, sino privado, porque lo pone quien quiere y no corre generalmente, sino en algunas partes y término de cuatro leguas lo pagan en unos pueblos y en otros no. En especial en Sevilla ni en la mayor parte del Andalucía no lo conocen, jamás oyeron tal cosa. (II, 3, iv)

Guzmán's experience and indignation are undoubtedly Alemán's own: he himself had bought and sold property in Seville and Madrid.

When Guzmán becomes a sham beggar in Rome, no doubt we are to see in this too an exposure of an abuse, though this time no precise remedy is proposed. It is interesting that a letter purporting to be by Alemán deals at length with the problem of vagrancy and beggary.[10] Special prominence is given to the army of able-bodied beggars and vagrants, who (the author urges) should be put to work. 'Estos de florida edad y mejores fuerzas, ágiles y con salud, ¿no esgrimieran mejor un azadón en las manos, que andarse danzando con unas espuertas en los hombros o canasto en los brazos?'

Guzmán has a word to say on the proper running of hospitals, where the sick are often overfed by 'algunas piadosas mentecates'. 'Mi parecer sería que no se consintiese, y lo tal antes lo den al enfermero que al enfermo. Porque de allí saldrá con parecer del médico cada cosa para su lugar mejor distribuida, pues lo que así no se hace es dañoso y peligroso' (I, 1, ii). He comments on the proper treatment of servants (I, 3, ix). In short, *Guzmán de Alfarache* is more than a serious call to a holy life. It is a survey not only of the life of one man but of the society which contains him. Alemán no doubt hoped to bring sinners to repentance, but as a judge of long experience he had the wit to see that legislation has its importance; that Original Sin may be a constant, but that many things can be mended. Though the book does not deal explicitly with the larger social problems of Alemán's own time—the stagnation of the economy, the decay of agriculture, and depopulation of the countryside, etc.—the picture that Alemán gives us is the product of his own observation of a declining society diagnosed in the only terms familiar to him, those of Christian theology. He personifies the evils of the society he knows in a man who weakly yields to sin until sinning becomes his way of life; but who can at last will to be virtuous. The moralists of his day, blind to economic realities, attributed the decline of Spain to sloth, the national sin; could the idle be made again to work, prosperity would return. In his eulogy of *Guzmán* Alonso de Barros makes it clear that he read the book as, amongst other things, an attack on idleness (from which other vices flow):

> en la historia que ha sacado a luz, nos ha retratado tan al vivo un hijo del ocio, que ninguno, por más que sea ignorante, le dejará de conocer en las señas, por ser tan parecido a su padre, que como lo es él de todos los vicios, así éste vino a ser un centro y abismo de todos . . .

From Guzmán's punishment can be inferred, as its contrary,

> el premio y bienafortunados sucesos que se le seguirán al que ocupado justamente tuviere en su modo de vivir cierto fin y determinado, y fuere opuesto y antípoda de la figura inconstante deste discurso.

Wilful idleness, inconstancy, dishonest gain preferred to honest labour: these are the characteristics of society as surveyed in the book. *Guzmán* may in part be Alemán's diagnosis of the state of Spain.

Guzmán is undeniably rambling, but Alemán imposed coherence on his heterogeneous material by the ingenious device of making it the autobiography of a repentant sinner, so that picaresque adventure and moral commentary are both wholly in character. To the objection that we cannot know at the start of his repentance it is enough to point to the author's 'Declaración' (quoted above), which he can reasonably expect us to have read. The prolixity of the moralising is no less in character (though doubtless it is also a trait of Alemán himself). Guzmán's repeated apologies for long-winded moralising are not to be taken as Alemán's own: the author had well gauged his public's appetite for moral discourse. What Guzmán apologises for is the strangeness of morality in the mouth of a *pícaro* and galley-slave. 'Quiero callar . . . Pues aun conozco mi exceso en lo hablado: que más es dotrina de predicación que de pícaro' (I, 2, iii). Or again: '¡oh qué gentil disparate! ¡Qué fundado en teologia! ¿No veis el salto que he dado del banco a la popa? ¡Qué vida de Juan de Dios la mía para dar esta dotrina! (I, I, ii). He maintains on occasion the pretence that he is writing a work of entertainment, in which his moralisings are digressions (as he calls them in II, 3, iii). He can write:

> ¡Oh, válgame Dios! ¡Cuando podré acabar comigo no enfadarte, pues aquí no buscas predicables ni dotrina, sino un entretenimiento de gusto, con que llamar el sueño y pasar el tiempo! No sé con qué disculpar tan terrible tentación sino con decirte que soy como los borrachos, que cuanto dinero ganan todo es para la taberna. (II, 2, ii)

An urbane joke, no more: readers were not put off: they flocked to buy. All the same, Alemán was careful to provide sufficient entertainment to sustain interest in the weaker spirits. He incorporated three stories on the lines of the Italian *novelle*: that of Ozmín and Daraja, that of Dorido and Clorinia, and that of Dorotea. All three can be considered exemplary in that virtue is rewarded and villainy punished, but the main purpose is undoubtedly entertainment (as is made clear in the text). The main narrative itself is diversified with numerous anecdotes which the author brings ingeniously to bear on the point. The very first chapter establishes the pattern. He promises to tell his story without adornments, and promptly illustrates this with the anecdote of the man who commissioned two paintings of a horse, one of which he refused to buy because the painter asked too high a price, though he had painted less horse than landscape. Guzmán now tells something of his father, but the chance reference to an *escribano* prompts him to bring in a sermon on *escribanos* once heard by him in Madrid. A discourse on corrupt judges is illustrated by an anecdote about a *labrador* of Granada. We return to Guzmán's father, whose effeminate appearance reminds his son of a monster, born at Ravenna in 1512, which symbolised the vices for which Italy was about to be punished. And this in turn leads to the reflection that though sin is universal, so also is the opportunity for redemption: whereby we return to one of the book's main themes.

Alemán's style is both rich and vigorous. It is on the whole plain in vocabulary, but full of variety in its rhetorical figures, and also in its alternation between terseness and ampler, more Ciceronian, periods.

The success of the first part prompted Martí to write a continuation. This is not a distinguished work: it is clearly a commercial product designed solely to profit from the success of Alemán's first part. Alemán had his revenge: the Sayavedra who helps to defraud Guzmán in Italy becomes Guzmán's devoted servant, tells of his disreputable brother Juan Martí, and goes mad in a storm at sea, crying '¡Yo soy la sombra de Guzmán de Alfarache! ¡Su sombre soy, que voy por el mundo!'. He jumps into the sea and is drowned, unregretted by Guzmán.

The next picaresque work to be published was *Libro de entretenimiento de la pícara Justina* (Medina, 1605) by Francisco López de Úbeda. In spite of the author's affirmation that he had written it many years earlier, the book appears to be modelled on *Guzmán*: in form, that is, for in content it is very different, as its title suggests. The author claimed that he wrote with a moral intent, and that each chapter ends with a moralising *aprovechamiento* seems to bear this out, but the moral frequently bears no relation to the story, which on the whole is straightforwardly entertaining in character. However, there are puzzling features which have led M. Bataillon to the conclusion that the book is a *roman à clef*, full of allusions to figures well known in court circles, and that it satirises the obsession with *limpieza de sangre*. A full understanding of the book must await further research.

Historia de la vida del buscón llamado don Pablos by Francisco

Gómez de Quevedo y Villegas was published (probably without Quevedo's authority) in Saragossa in 1626, but internal evidence suggests that a first draft was written before 1604.[11] If that is so, Quevedo must have been stimulated to write by the success of *Guzmán de Alfarache*.

Quevedo was born in Madrid in 1580. He was of noble family. He studied at Alcalá, becoming one of the most learned Spaniards of his day. He corresponded with the neo-Stoic humanist Justus Lipsius. He moved in high circles and was much concerned in affairs of state. On the fall of his protector the duque de Osuna, Quevedo was banished in 1620, but his star rose again with the accession of Philip IV in 1621. He eventually incurred the enmity of the new *privado*, the conde duque de Olivares, and was imprisoned in 1639. He was released on the fall of Olivares in 1643, but his health was impaired and he retired to his seignorial property, la Torre de Juan Abad, where he died in 1645. He had married in 1634, but the couple separated in 1636. He wrote voluminously in prose and verse, and on a wide range of themes (see below, Chapters 7 and 9).

In his prologue to *El buscón* Quevedo writes:

> Aquí hallarás en todo género de picardía (de que pienso que los más gustan) sutilezas, engaños, invenciones, y modos nacidos del ocio para vivir a la droga, y no poco fruto podrás sacar dél si tienes atención al escarmiento . . .

This is not in itself proof that the book contains a serious moral: the claim was made for most books, even when it was in flagrant contradiction of the truth. Quevedo's claim, however, seems to be borne out by the book. Only the humourless would fail to see that the book is also an extraordinarily witty (though cruel) work of entertainment.

Pablos, its 'hero', tells that his mother was a bawd, witch, and whore. His ostensible father was a barber who combined this trade with theft. Pablos's little brother died in prison after a flogging for theft. Pablos himself, however, was ambitious since childhood to rise in society.

> Hubo grandes diferencias entre mis padres sobre a quién había de imitar en el oficio, mas yo, que siempre tuve pensamientos de caballero desde chiquito, nunca me apliqué a uno ni a otro. (I, i)

He is sent to school and is there befriended by the son of a *caballero*, Don Diego Coronel, whose favour Pablos sets himself obsequiously to win. Pablos's shame at his disgraceful origins, a shame frequently expressed in the book, drives him to seek to rise by any means in his power in order to escape from his shameful past. As a child his shame shows itself as an excessive desire to please, so that on one occasion, 'por darle gusto a mi amigo' (I, ii) he gets up to mischief and is punished.

This desire to please becomes later a determination to follow the way of the world and is the origin of his decision to turn *pícaro*. His sufferings at Alcalá, where he accompanies Don Diego when he goes there to study, lead him to say to himself: ' "Avisón, Pablos, alerta." Propuse de hacer nueva vida' (I, v). This is his turning-point.

> 'Haz como vieres', dice el refrán, y dice bien. De puro considerar en él, vine a resolverme de ser bellaco con los bellacos, y más, si pudiese, que todos. (I, vi)

He becomes the greatest rogue in Alcalá. Don Diego is forced by his father to dismiss the ever more unruly Pablos. The latter, however, has received a letter from his uncle, the public hangman of Segovia, announcing the execution of his father and imprisonment of his mother and summoning Pablos to come to claim his inheritance. Pablos therefore replies to Don Diego:

> Señor, ya soy otro, y otros mis pensamientos; más alto pico y más autoridad me importa tener. (I, vii)

Pablos's sense of shame had revived with the news—'No puedo negar que sentí mucho la nueva afrenta'—but he is glad to be rid of his parents and determines to collect his inheritance 'y conocer mis parientes, para huir dellos'. On arriving in Segovia he is greeted in the street by his uncle, who is flogging a procession of malefactors. 'Penséme morir de vergüenza' (II, iii). Consumed with shame and impatience all the time he is in his uncle's house, Pablos leaves secretly next morning to go to Madrid.

> Consideraba yo que iba a la corte, adonde nadie me conocía—que era la cosa que más me consolaba—, y que había de valerme por mi habilidad allí. (II,v)

On the way he encounters an impoverished *hidalgo*, Don Toribio Rodríguez Vallejo Gómez de Ampuero y Jordán, who offers to introduce Pablos to the fraternity of which he is a member, a fraternity of men living by their wits, cadging, stealing, keeping up an appearance of gentility by the most fantastic means. 'Somos gente que comemos un puerro y representamos un capón (II, vi). Pablos joins them. He goes to jail with them when they are all arrested for theft but bribes his way out. Now more determined than ever to rise, he strives to make a profitable marriage. He hires a horse by the hour, since a horse is a necessary badge of nobility. Calling himself Don Felipe Tristán he succeeds in enamouring a noble young lady who unfortunately proves to be a relative of Don Diego Coronel who, now reappearing, at once suspects that Pablos is indeed his old servant in spite of the latter's denials. Next day, Pablos falls off a borrowed horse outside Doña Ana's house and suffers the further ignominy of being upbraided by the horse's owner. Don Diego sees his suspicions confirmed and plots revenge. He arranges with some fellow-*hidalgos* for Pablos to be beaten and his face slashed open. As Pablos is left bleeding one of the *caballeros* cries: '¡Así pagan los pícaros embustidores mal nacidos!' (III, vii). Pablos's descent is now rapid. He takes to begging, joins a band of travelling actors, becomes a *galán de monjas*, and finally goes to Seville, where he joins a gang of ruffians. He takes part in the murder of two *corchotos*, takes up with a whore, la Grajal, and, at the end of the story, tells of his resolution to go with her to America in search of better fortune.

> Y fueme peor, como v.m. verá en la segunda parte, pues nunca mejora su estado quien muda solamente de lugar, y no de vida y costumbres. (III, x)

This is the only explicitly didactic note in the book, but the course of the story leaves the reader in no doubt of Quevedo's intentions. Pablos's immoral ambitions lead him to punishment after punishment from the time he goes to Madrid. Apart from the more obvious punishments, such as the beatings and slashings, he suffers ever-deeper humiliation in that, far from rising in the world, he descends to ever-deeper depths until at last he drifts to the very bottom of society. The book is clearly exemplary. Pablos, nursing a secret shame, is led from mischief to mischief as, despising humble diligence, he follows first the glamour of applause and later the hope of social ascent.

The book's didactic intention must not blind one to Quevedo's literary ambitions. There are insistent reminiscences of *Lazarillo*. Both Pablos and Lázaro are children of disreputable parents. Just as Lázaro is nearly starved to death by the priest of Maqueda, Pablos nearly dies of hunger at the academy of the Dómine Cabra. Lázaro's third master was a proud *hidalgo*, determined not to reveal his poverty or abate his honour; he is caricatured in Don Toribio. Both Lázaro and Pablos have dreams of honour and ambition. There are differences, of course. The sobriety and realism of *Lazarillo* are absent from *El buscón*, but the similarities remain. Quevedo evidently had the set intention of outdoing *Lazarillo*: to show the brilliance of his style and invention by excelling an acknowledged masterpiece of entertainment. Everything that he takes from *Lazarillo* emerges more brilliant, more fantastic, after passing through Quevedo's brain. Lázaro's hunger is credible; the hunger which Pablos and his companions suffer in Cabra's academy is fantastic. One boy has forgotten how to eat and tries to insert food at his ears and eyes. When Pablos and Don Diego are taken home and put to bed, their mouths have to be dusted out, so unused are they to eating. Cabra himself is pure fantasy, a sustained exercise in wit. His nose, half eaten away with 'bubas de resfriado', is described as 'entre Roma y Francia': snub-nosed but looking as if he had the pox. Lázaro's *escudero* picked his teeth in public to make it seem that he had eaten; one of Don Toribio's fraternity in Madrid keeps crumbs in a box to sprinkle on himself. The *escudero* was fully dressed at least; Don Toribio is dressed only where it shows: 'por la parte de atrás, que cubría la capa, traía las cuchilladas con entretelas de nalga pura' (II, v). One of the fraternity, Don Lorenzo Íñiguez del Pedroso, had been in bed a fortnight with 'mal de zaragüelles' (III, i). All this exhibits a literary ambition: a young man's wish (if the first version is as early as 1604) to astonish and to obliterate a model and rival.

This is perfectly compatible with a fundamentally serious didactic intention. *Lazarillo* represented for Quevedo, as for Mateo Alemán, an example and a suggestion of further narrative possibilities. To judge from the frontispiece of *La pícara Justina* (1605), *Lazarillo* was considered to be related to the new picaresque works, though remaining apart from them as their precursor: the engraving shows Lazarillo in a small boat being towed by (or towing) 'La nave de la vida pícara'.

The central strand of *El buscón* is Pablos's ambition to be a *caballero*. This was reprehensible: Pablos should (in the accepted belief of his day) know his station in life and stay in it. It was a constant complaint in those years that now all men wanted to be *don*. As Pedro Fernández Navarrete complained in his *Conservación de monarquías* (Madrid, 1626):

> apenas se halla hijo de oficial mecánico que por este tan poco sustancial medio no aspire a usurpar la estimación debida a la verdadera nobleza ... (*BAE*, 25, p. 472)

The desire to enter the ranks of the nobility was founded on three things: the perennial human craving for social honours, the exemption of the nobility from taxation for the payment of the royal *servicio* (taxation which fell only on *pecheros*), and the increasingly obsessive wish to display public proof of *limpieza de sangre*. Associated with the last was the widespread reluctance to engage in manual work or trade.

Quevedo was himself very conscious of his aristocratic pedigree. This is evident in *El buscón*. Pablos's attempt to associate with the nobility is savagely punished; and when he is beaten by Don Diego's noble friends one of them cries: '¡Así pagan los pícaros embustidores mal nacidos!'. Pablos is, of course, utterly immoral and can hardly be said to deserve to rise; but Quevedo's strength of feeling, betrayed in this incident, suggests that in Pablos and his kind he resents not just the immorality of the *pícaro* but the presumption of the base-born in attempting to enter the ranks of their 'betters'. Since the reign of

Ferdinand and Isabella the bestowal of patents of nobility allowed commoners to become *hidalgos*. This created resentment in the older nobility. The *Cortes* of 1592 complained:

> The sale of *hidalguías* is giving rise to numerous inconveniences, for they are generally purchased by wealthy persons of inferior quality . . . This is hateful to all classes. Nobles resent finding people of inferior condition obtaining equality with them simply through the expenditure of money, to the consequent disparagement of nobility . . . while *pecheros* are annoyed that people of no higher origin than themselves should secure precedence over them merely because of their wealth.[12]

Quevedo's intensity of feeling reflects a general aristocratic resentment of social pressure from below. In Pablos Quevedo caricatures a whole movement of social aspiration in order to expose what for him was its moral ugliness. On Pablos, the representative of a socially disruptive force, is hung every undesirable social and moral characteristic. Quevedo, like Alemán, is obliged to treat a social question in the only terms available to him, those of Christian morality.

Much in the society of his day was distasteful to Quevedo, in particular the ascendancy of money over true worth. He treated the theme in comic terms in his *letrilla* 'Poderoso caballero/es don Dinero', whose theme is that money is the great leveller.[13]

> Son sus padres principales
> y es de nobles descendiente,
> porque en las venas de Oriente
> todas las sangres son reales;
> y pues es quien hace iguales
> al duque y al ganadero,
> *poderoso caballero*
> *es don Dinero.*

With money anyone may be noble, without it no one. Money will make cowards fight ('al cobarde hace guerrero') and tramples on laws and privileges ('quebranta cualquier fuero'). It makes money-grubbing in time of peace more esteemed than courage in war:

> Más valen en cualquier tierra
> (mirad si es harto sagaz)
> sus escudos en la paz
> que rodelas en la guerra.

Quevedo, lamenting that in his degenerate times wealth was stronger than merit and commoners were enabled to mingle with their betters, looked back for his ideal society to poorer and sterner times, to the

Middle Ages, when merit was not overshadowed by money. This is one of the themes of his poem *Epístola satírica y censoria* (*c.* 1627) addressed to the conde—duque de Olivares.

> Joya fue la virtud pura y ardiente;
> gala el merecimiento y alabanza;
> sólo se codiciaba lo decente.
>
> No de la pluma dependió la lanza,
> ni el cántabro con cajas y tinteros
> hizo el campo heredad, sino matanza.
>
> Y España, con legítimos dineros,
> no mendigando el crédito a Liguria,
> más quiso los turbantes que los ceros.

The upstart Pablos, given his opportunity by money, was seemingly intended as the epitome of seventeenth-century Spaniards, active only in seeking unearned honour and unmerited glory. But for Quevedo it was not only the commoners who were degenerate; he evidently thought that the nobility themselves, represented in the *Epístola* as infected by the degeneracy of the times, were unfit to set an example. Pablos is an unworthy social climber, but in his progress his path crosses that of the *hidalgo* Don Toribio who, lacking an income to match his station and evidently unwilling to work, leads the life of a parasite in Madrid. For a short time the ascending upstart and the descending downstart keep company. Both are Quevedo's comment on his times. (It is worth noting that even Don Diego is not exempt from failings: after the exchange of capes Pablos is beaten by some thugs 'que lo aguardaban para cintarearlo por una mujercilla, entendiendo por la capa que yo era don Diego'; III, vii.)

El buscón is one of the three masterpieces of the Spanish picaresque novel: arguably the finest of the three. It is a brilliant work, but a cruel one, completely lacking in compassion.

The picaresque, once its appeal for the reading public was recognised, was soon exploited for the purpose of pure entertainment, as the next work in the series shows. *La hija de Celestina* (Saragossa, 1612) by Alonso Jerónimo de Salas Barbadillo (1581-1635) is a well-told tale of a light woman, Elena, and her complaisant husband Montúfar, who is finally murdered by one of his wife's lovers, for which Elena ends on the scaffold. It is a frank tale of disreputable adventure, though the author made the customary bow to morality in the prologue: 'Se pretende y muestra en la astucia y hermosura de Elena y trato de su compañía lo que ejecuta la malicia deste tiempo, y el fin que tiene la gente desalmada'.

Vicente Espinel (1550-1624)—priest, poet, and musician—published his *Relaciones de la vida del escudero Marcos de Obregón* in 1618 (Madrid). Though this is nowadays commonly called a picaresque novel, it is the story of a respectable and prudent man who recounts the adventures great and small which have filled his life, moralising and digressing freely as he does so. The book is a leisurely and soberly attractive portrait of a wise old student of human nature. It is largely autobiographical in content. Lesage took material from it for *Gil Blas*. Though it is not a great work of art, it is one of the most agreeable books of its period, full of curious lore and shrewd observation.

Alonso, mozo de muchos amos (Part I, Madrid, 1624; Part II, Valladolid, 1626) by Jerónimo de Alcalá Yáñez y Ribera (1563-1632) is the story of Alonso, in Part I a lay-brother in a monastery, in Part II a hermit, who recounts his life to a sympathetic priest. It is in dialogue form. Once again, this is not a picaresque novel, though often called one. Alonso is not a rogue, simply a harmless and garrulous man who has seen a good deal of life in the service of his many masters. Like Marcos de Obregón, Alonso moralises and digresses uninhibitedly: indeed the book greatly resembles Espinel's in structure and manner, though it is far inferior in interest.

A few years before a Spanish émigré, Carlos García, had published *La desordenada codicia de los bienes ajenos* (Paris, 1619) in which the author, purporting to be writing in a French jail, sets down the autobiography of a fellow-prisoner as recounted to him. It is a story of continuous robbery which the narrator, Andrés, prefaces with an account of 'la nobleza y excelencias del hurtar' and concludes with 'los estatutos y leyes de los ladrones'. Virtually nothing is known of Carlos García, who two years earlier had published in Paris *La oposición y conjunción de los dos grandes luminares de la tierra* in which he discusses the antipathy between Spain and France and voices his hopes for future concord.

Perhaps in emulation of García's book, another Spanish émigré, Juan de Luna, a Spanish language-teacher living in Paris, published in the following year a *Segunda parte de la vida de Lazarillo de Tormes, sacada de las corónicas antiguas de Toledo* ... (Paris, 1620), which he issued with a 'corrected' edition of the original *Lazarillo,* whose style he had 'improved' at various points. In his prologue Luna makes a fierce attack on the tyranny of the Inquisition, and his *Segunda parte* is written in a passionately anti-clerical spirit. It is an inventive and entertaining book.

The most voluminous contributor to picaresque literature, and arguably the most frivolous, was Alonso de Castillo Solórzano (1584-1648?) who amongst his other works of fiction (see below, Chapter 8) included a number of picaresque novels and shorter stories: *Las harpías en Madrid y Coche de las estafas* (Barcelona, 1631), *La niña de los embustes Teresa de Manzanares* (Barcelona, 1632), *Aventuras del bachiller Trapaza, quinta esencia de embusteros y maestro de embelecadores* (Saragossa, 1637), and *La garduña de Sevilla y anzuelo de las bolsas* (Madrid, 1642). The last, the best known, is a continuation of *Las aventuras del bachiller Trapaza.* It is representative of the whole group in its monotonous parade of would-be ingenious trickery and in its general shallowness.

Antonio Enríquez Gómez (1600?-60?), a Spanish Jew who chose to live abroad (see also below, Chapter 7), published a satirical survey of life purporting to be the account of a soul which transmigrates through many bodies: *El siglo pitagórico, y vida de don Gregorio Guadaña* (Rouen, 1644). The life of Don Gregorio Guadaña (in prose, the rest of the work being in verse) is a picaresque narrative. It has some entertaining moments but on the whole it is dull stuff.

And so the picaresque peters out as a distinct genre in Spain, being absorbed into the miscellaneous mass of light fiction which became the staple of the reading public in the seventeenth century.

NOTES

1. A. A. Parker, *Literature and the Delinquent* (Edinburgh, 1967), p. 4. This is the best account of its subject.
2. A. Castro, *La realidad histórica de España* (Mexico, 1954), pp. 514 ff. M. Bataillon, *Pícaros y picaresca* (Madrid, 1969), pp. 184-5.
3. Parker, op. cit., pp. 16-19.
4. Quoted from Bataillon, op. cit., p. 183.
5. ibid., p. 189.
6. Written in 1633 but not published until this century.
7. To give it its full title, which appeared only in Part II, though—as the royal privilege makes clear—it was also the intended title of Part I.
8. The documents have been summarised by Germán Bleiberg in *Actas* II, 25-49.
9. By E. Asensio in 'La peculiaridad literaria de los conversos', *Anuario de estudios medievales* 4 (Barcelona, 1967), 328-9.
10. E. Cros, *Protée et le gueux* (Paris, 1967), pp. 436-42. Some caution is needed: the letter appears to be dated 1597 yet refers to 'la primera parte del pícaro', perhaps finished but not yet in print. Is the letter authentically Alemán's?
11. F. Lázaro in his edition of *El buscón* (Salamanca, 1965), pp. LII-LV. This dating is disputed by A. A. Parker, op. cit., pp. 56-7. Against his objection, it can be pointed out that *El sueño del juicio final,* which appears to have been composed in the first decade of the century, is stylistically equally mature.
12. J. H. Elliott, *Imperial Spain* (London, 1963), p. 105.
13. But one must be wary of reading too much contemporary significance into the poem, whose theme is a traditional one. Even the name of Don Dinero may be traditional: a fifteenth-century English poem on 'Sir Penny' is subtitled 'Incipit narracio de domino denario' (*Secular Lyrics of the XIVth and XVth Centuries*, ed. R. Hope Robbins, Oxford, 1952, p. 51).

Chapter 7

POETRY IN THE SEVENTEENTH CENTURY

THE ACCELERATING ECONOMIC DECLINE OF SPAIN which began in the late sixteenth century was up to the middle of the seventeenth consistent with an extraordinary flowering of the arts, not least poetry. In the longer run, however, the decline affected all areas of life: the period of great literary brilliance had ended before 1650 (Calderón is a lonely eminence after that date). Góngora died in 1627, Lope de Vega in 1635, Quevedo in 1645: no poets of even remotely comparable stature rose to take their place. The display of creative brilliance in the first half of the century is itself not so paradoxical as it may seem on first consideration. Intelligent creative writers of the time were well aware of the symptoms of national decline and the growing national mood of disenchantment is often reflected in their work; but the potentially discouraging effect of this was compensated by other factors, such as the patronage extended by the aristocracy, for whom protection of the arts, though partly attributable to a genuine artistic interest, was to some extent part of the life of competitive ostentation and bounty thought fitting to the nobleman's station in society. The conde (later conde-duque) de Olivares, for example, surrounded himself with writers both before and after his rise to power as the *privado* of Philip IV. The flowering of the arts is, in fact, another aspect of the precariously brilliant world of the ruling élite of seventeenth-century Spain.

Writing was also fostered by the literary academies which in imitation of the academies of Renaissance Italy began to appear in Spain in the later sixteenth century and multiplied in the seventeenth. Among famous early academies was the Academia Imitatoria, established in Madrid perhaps as early as 1586, and the Academia de los Nocturnos, which met in Valencia from 1591 to 1594. In the early seventeenth century academies were established in most towns of any importance, commonly meeting in the palaces of their noble patrons. While it must be admitted that much of the poetry written for these academies is trivial, the existence of a group of like-minded friends must have provided encouragement for many writers who, lost in an indifferent provincial society, might otherwise have lacked a sounding board.

Another kind of literary gathering provided a similar stimulus with similar equivocal results: the *certamen* or *justa poética*: poetic competitions convened to celebrate an event, to honour a saint, or on some other like occasion. Some good poetry was written for *certámenes* by Góngora, Lope, and others, but the general standard is not high.

Literary theory, which began to flourish in Spain towards the end of the sixteenth century, was also fostered by the literary academies, though nothing came out of them to rival Herrera's *Anotaciones* or Alonso López Pinciano's *Filosofía antigua poética* (Madrid, 1596). This last, a basically Aristotelian treatise but with many points of originality, is mainly interesting for dramatic theory.

There is a clear continuity in the evolution of Spanish poetry of the Golden Age, but certain trends were accentuated in the course of time to such a degree that much seventeenth-century poetry is strikingly unlike the poetry of Garcilaso and his immediate successors. Two movements in particular account for this: *culteranismo* and the cult of *agudeza* or Wit (or, to use a modern term, *conceptismo*).

Culteranismo, a term coined early in the seventeenth century, connotes a style of extreme artificiality, which in practice meant Latinisation of syntax and vocabulary, constant use of classical allusion, and the creation of a distinctive poetic diction as far removed as possible from the language of everyday discourse. Herrera played an important part in this development. The *culto* or *culterano* poets of the seventeenth century went far beyond Herrera, however, and wrote in a style of deliberate difficulty in order to exclude the generality of readers. Góngora prided himself on his obscurity to the uninitiated: as he wrote in a letter to an unknown correspondent in 1613 or 1614 in reply to an attack on his *Soledades*: 'Demás que honra me ha causado hacerme escuro a los ignorantes, que ésa es la distinción de los hombres doctos, hablar de manera que a ellos les parezca griego . . .' His views were no novelty. In his *Libro de la erudición poética* (printed in his *Obras,* Madrid, 1611) Luis Carrillo de Sotomayor wrote in similar terms: 'Eternidad y valor prometen las Musas, joyas por cierto bien preciosas. . . . Presume el vulgo de entendellas, el mismo pretende juzgallas. . . . Engañóse por cierto quien entiende los trabajos de la Poesía haber nacido para el vulgo.' The *culterano* style evolved by Góngora came to be a dominant force in the poetry of the period, and Góngora himself the principal target of its detractors. Lope de Vega scolded Góngora and his imitators (and was scathingly derided for his *llaneza* by Góngora in return), but, like others, Lope succumbed eventually to the irresistible *culterano* fashion. Even Quevedo, Góngora's sternest (and most scurrilous) accuser, was not uncontaminated by his enemy's style.

Very frequently, in the case of lesser writers, *culteranismo* was undoubtedly a symptom of an empty-headed modishness, but in the poetry of Góngora and other poets with both intelligence and imagination it meant an enrichment of the expressive power of language. Hyperbaton (the separation of related parts of speech—article from noun, noun from adjective, and so on) could be used to throw a key word into relief by displacing it from its expected position. Classical allusion could, when used intelligently and not as empty adornment, add force and compression to poetry; as when in his *Polifemo* Góngora describes with great erotic effect how Galatea delicately eludes the caresses of Acis, who burns for her as passionately as Tantalus had thirsted for the water that eternally receded from his mouth, and who tries to touch her breasts as Tantalus had tried to taste the fruit that slipped for ever from his grasp.

Entre las ondas y la fruta, imita
Acis el siempre ayuno en penas graves:
que, en tanta gloria, infierno son no breve
fugitivo cristal, pomos de nieve.

Wit or *agudeza*—the use of conceits—was consciously cultivated by the majority of writers of the late sixteenth and the seventeenth centuries, both in prose and verse. *Agudeza* defies rigorous definition. Even Gracián, whose *Agudeza y arte de ingenio* (Huesca, 1648) is a manual of wit, was unable to arrive at a definition that would clearly distinguish a conceit from ordinary metaphors and similes. He wrote:

> Consiste, pues, este artificio conceptuoso en una primorosa concordancia, en una armónica correlación entre dos o tres conocibles extremos, expresada por un acto del entendimiento. . . . De suerte que se puede definir el concepto. Es un acto del entendimiento que exprime la correspondencia que se halla entre las cosas.

Ordinary tropes could well be included in this definition, which has its value, all the same, in emphasising the role of the intellect. Conceits were not primarily attempts to communicate sense-impressions, but to establish conceptual relationships. To the seventeenth-century mind the more extreme the terms thus related, the more satisfying the result. A conceit simultaneously affirmed likeness (through its appropriateness) and unlikeness (through the distance between the two things or terms compared). In the clash lay the wit. For our purpose we may take *agudeza* to be the ingenious exploitation of unexpected analogy. The conceit could be a joke of a quite trivial kind; it could even be meaningless, like the series of puns in the *romance* 'Picarilla, picarilla', once attributed to Quevedo,[2] addressed to a beautiful girl. The poet describes her breasts:

En dos cumbres los divides,
y las tienen coronadas
dos pezones tan chiquitos
que aún no saben decir 'mama'.

Her hands:

Tan transparentes las tienes
que cualquiera luz las pasa,
y en las puntas de tus dedos
hasta las yemas son claras.

These are intentionally absurd. At the other end of the spectrum the serious conceit could offer enormous compression of meaning, as well as beauty.

Agudeza was not a new phenomenon. It is present in Renaissance poetry: Garcilaso can show at least one conceit, in his *Canción* V:

Hablo de aquel cativo
de quien tener se debe más cuidado,
que está muriendo vivo,
al remo condenado,
en la concha de Venus amarrado.

The image springs from the name of the friend on whose behalf he writes: Mario Galeota, whose surname suggests *galeote*, a galley-slave condemned to row in Venus' shell. There is wit of this kind in Petrarch; and in later times Petrarchism undoubtedly fostered the European appetite for ingenuity.

Wit of this kind was one facet of the essentially analogical and metaphorical cast of much medieval thought, and it may have its roots ultimately in traditional biblical exegesis in which, as in very many medieval works, correspondences were sought between the most disparate matters in the interest of bringing to light a spiritual truth. Edification was found in the fact that *Eva* (Eve) when reversed gave *Ave*, Gabriel's greeting at the Annunciation to Mary, through whom was taken away the sin brought by Eve into the world. The conceit is to be found in the beautiful ninth-century hymn *Ave maris stella*:

Sumens illud Ave
Gabrielis ore,
funda nos in pace,
mutans nomen Evae.

Behind wit was a world-picture according to which, in medieval and Renaissance Europe, the universe was a system of signs, a kind of book in which the greatness of God might be read. The Jesuit Juan Eusebio

Nieremberg (1595-1658) compared it in his *Oculta filosofía* (Madrid, 1643) with the poetic *laberintos* (complex acrostics) written by Porphyry in praise of Constantine.

> Plotino llamó al mundo Poesía de Dios. Yo añado, que este poema es como un laberinto, que por todas partes se lee y hace sentido y dicta a su autor. . . .
>
> Así imagino yo al mundo ser un panegírico de Dios con mil laberintos de sus excelencias, trabándose unas naturalezas con otras, publicando por todas partes sus grandezas, ahora se consideren por los grados genéricos, ahora por las diferencias últimas, ahora por sus propios, ahora por sus accidentes; y de todas maneras hace su harmonía, y forman y componen algún himno divino. (pp. 308-9)

Turning to another analogy he describes Phidias' statue of Minerva, composed of many different pieces which separately were of no account but when assembled formed a whole of astounding beauty; and where they all met in the goddess's shield, there Phidias had carved his own face.

> Así pasa, que aunque cada naturaleza tenga mucho que admirar, pero juntadas todas, viendo cómo asientan y corresponden unas con otras, armada ya esta estatua del mundo, este simulacro de Dios, es cosa para pasmar, y mucho más cuando se considera que no sólo todas en una se eslabonan, sino todas en todas, y cada una en todas, y todas en cada una, respondiéndose de mil modos; y en cada una y en todas está esmaltado un bulto de Dios, un rostro de su Artífice, con diferentes visos de sus perfecciones, que por todas partes se ve y lee *Deus me fecit*. (p. 308)

For those who thought like this, a conceit might through its analogies give expression to the hidden affinities which permeate the universe and thereby give an insight into the underlying plan of things; might, in fact, be a means of knowledge, not simply a source of pleasure.

Medieval interest in symbol and allegory gave rise to the devices or *imprese*—symbolic pictures accompanied by a motto—which were fashionable in European courts by the later fifteenth century. Renaissance misunderstanding of the nature of Egyptian hieroglyphs (believed to be an ideographic writing whereby the priests of Egypt taught their wisdom) gave birth to emblems, allegorical pictures with explanatory verses (longer than mottos) designed to teach a moral truth.[3] The first were printed by the Italian Alciati in 1531. For the next two centuries Europe was inundated by such works. The emblem was credited with powers to convey truths to the mind more directly than words could do; and it would imprint itself indelibly on the mind as the eye wandered over the symbolic details of the illustration. It was considered a powerful instrument of instruction and for this reason was taken up eventually by the Jesuits who (not alone of the orders) made enthusiastic use of emblems in the seventeenth century.

The emblem could be regarded as a visual conceit. Each supported the other in forming the minds of generations of readers and writers. For minds formed in this way the universe itself seemed to be composed of emblems for our instruction, as Nieremberg will once again illustrate.

> Vengo pues al otro fin de la naturaleza, que es la enseñanza e instrucción de nuestro ánimo. En ella nos designió Dios toda la filosofía moral; ella es, como en otra parte probamos, un libro de virtudes y vicios, un sentenciario prudentísimo. Esto de dos maneras. Una es, muertamente en lo material de los animales, plantas y otras naturalezas, en su composición y fábrica. Otra es, vivamente en los ingenios de animales, propiedades y costumbres. Aquello es como una pintura y jeroglífico, esto como un ejemplo. . . . Del primer modo nos enseñan, como en cifra, la condición de algún vicio o virtud, no de otra manera que cuando un pintor hace un jeroglífico. (p. 353)

Much of the poetry of the seventeenth century shows the influence of the emblem in the use of symbolic imagery, so arranged as to reveal a truth implicitly or explicitly in the manner of juxtaposing the constituent elements. Many images are demonstrably derived from known emblems; but more generally, even when this is not the case, images will frequently reveal a habit of mind learned from a lifetime's acquaintance with emblem-books.[4]

The claim is still sometimes made that the Segovian poet Alonso de Ledesma (1562-1623) was the first *conceptista* poet in Spain. He was undoubtedly a prolific writer of conceited verse, as his books show: *Conceptos espirituales* (in three parts; Madrid, 1600, 1608, 1612); *Juegos de Noche Buena moralizados* (Madrid, 1611); *Romancero y monstruo imaginado* (Madrid, 1615); *Epigramas y hieroglíficos* (Madrid, 1625). The very titles show his interest in emblematics. The verse—all of it devotional—draws on a wide range of material. In the *Juegos*, for example, Ledesma draws edifying Christian doctrine out of children's games.

This use of secular material for doctrinal purposes was far from new, even in Spain. It derives from the preaching technique of medieval friars, particularly the Franciscans.[5] Neither did Ledesma create the conceit. What can be conceded is that he was more thorough-going in his exploitation of bizarre allegory than anyone before him. For example, one of his spiritual *romances* depicts Christ 'en metáfora de un reformador de una universidad'. Christ inspects the Chair of Grammar:[6]

En la Gramática halló
una mala concordancia,
que es acusar a quien hizo
cielo, tierra, cuerpo y alma.
Y no es gramática buena,
pues de solecismo pasa,
donde la persona que hace
en acusativo se halla.

The whole poem is in this vein. In another poem, St Stephen (who was stoned to death) is represented as a lapidary:

Esteban, un lapidario,
muerto por recoger piedras
. . .

Stephen works the stones with his blood (thought to soften precious stones) not with *hierros* (*yerros*).

Y no las labra con hierros;
que este artífice profesa
no tomar hierro en sus manos
ni colgarlo de su tienda;
sólo las labra con sangre
. . .

Ledesma's was manifestly a barbarous imagination. His cheerful brutality is again evident in these lines (written to accompany an emblem) 'A Santa Águeda, cortados los pechos':

Ya que no iguala la esposa
al dulce esposo que espera,
a lo menos no es pechera.

However distasteful to a modern sensibility, his verse was popular in his own age, even with men like Cervantes, Lope de Vega, and Gracián. The *kind* of imagination he possessed—drawing all manner of things together in his analogies—is the kind that underlies the best writing of the period. What we can legitimately object to is the *quality* of his imagination, at once coarse and shallow. In a poem on the conception of Christ he describes how a king enters a hermitage called Santa María.

Viene por cumplir un voto
que prometido tenía,
estando Adán a la muerte
de achaque de una comida.
No es voto de nueve horas,
ni aun de solos nueve días,
que nueve meses estuvo
sin salir de la capilla.

How like and unlike is George Herbert's brief poem which turns on an anagram of *Mary*!

> How well her name an *Army* doth present,
> In whom the Lord of Hosts did pitch his tent.

The variety of poetic forms in the seventeenth century is great. All the Italianate forms continued to be used, and alongside them traditional forms such as the *romance* and *letrilla*. Old stanza-forms like the *quintilla* (five octosyllabic lines of varying rhyme-scheme) come back into favour. There is great thematic variety also, between the two poles of ever more alambicated refinement of *culto* verse on the one hand and the growing taste for satirical and burlesque verse, often of extreme indecency, on the other.[7] All the poetic genres cultivated in the sixteenth century continued to flourish, including the literary epic (for which see above, pp. 117-20).

In general, as in the sixteenth century, a poet's collected work did not reach print in his lifetime. His contemporaries might see his work either in *pliegos sueltos*, in which some new work appeared side by side with older poetry[8]; or in one of the many printed *romanceros*. Pedro Espinosa's *Primera parte de las Flores de ilustres poetas* (Valladolid, 1605) was almost alone in including Italianate poetry, which was not again included in a printed anthology for nearly half a century: in José Alfay's *Poesías varias de grandes ingenios españoles* (Saragossa, 1654). Much of the finest poetry circulated in its authors' own day only in manuscript.

Though *culteranismo* and *agudeza* became the dominant modes of seventeenth-century Spanish poetry, there were so many exceptions that a history cannot be reduced to a clear-cut pattern. Madrid dominated the cultural life of Spain in the seventeenth century but a good deal of vitality was left in the provinces. Seville enjoyed the prosperity conferred by American trade and was the cultural capital of the south. Elsewhere, cultural life might flourish under the patronage of a cultivated nobleman. A tentative grouping by city or region is permissible, therefore, so long as it is recognised that though a group or coterie may exhibit certain common characteristics, most groups were fluid, and the notion of poetic 'schools' is on the whole an unhelpful oversimplification.

Juan de Arguijo (1567-1623), an immensely rich man who spent his wealth in extravagant patronage of the arts, was at the centre of the literary life of Seville in the early seventeenth century. He wrote some good poetry, particularly in sonnet-form. His classically chaste style has a lapidary quality which is sometimes moving though often chilly. His themes are in the main drawn from ancient Greece and Rome. Arguijo's 'archaeological' interest was shared by other Sevillian poets of his time, notably by Rodrigo Caro (1573-1647), an antiquarian in whom the interest may have originated. As a poet Caro is remembered for only one poem, his *Canción a las ruinas de Itálica,* impressive for its classical poise and restraint of diction as well as for the vividness of its evocation of dead glories. Its theme is not (of course) archaeology but transience and mutability, suggested by the ruins—a frequent subject of poetic meditation during the century—over which the poet moralises. Another Sevillian, Francisco de Rioja (1583?-1659) took up the theme in some finely-wrought sonnets, though he is now remembered more for his *silvas*[9] on flowers. His diction is as classical as Caro's. Italica reappears (for the same reasons) in the famous *Epístola moral a Fabio* by another Sevillian, Andrés Fernández de Andrada (contemporary with Rioja), who writes with Horatian pithiness of the vanity of human ambitions. An older Sevillian also showed this classical turn of mind: Francisco de Medrano (1570-1607), who left Seville young to be trained as a Jesuit and returned only on leaving the order in 1602. His poetry is classical in spirit and much of it consists of translations or paraphrases of classical originals. At his best he has Horace's vigorous directness. Juan de Jáuregui (1583-1641) was born in Seville but settled later in Madrid. He attacked Góngora in his *Antídoto contra la pestilente poesía de las Soledades* (first printed in 1899)[10] and in his *Discurso poético* (Madrid, 1624), but though his own early poems are relatively unadorned, his brilliant imitation of Ovid, *Orfeo* (Madrid, 1624), shows the full impact of *culteranismo.* Probably his finest work is *Aminta* (Rome, 1607), a translation of Tasso's original.

Another kind of poetry also flourished at Seville: the *jocoso.* Baltasar del Alcázar had a worthy successor in the witty cleric Juan de Salinas (1562?-1643), author in addition of a number of very fine *romances artificiosos* in the manner of Góngora.[11] Another cleric, Pedro de Quirós (1607?-67), continued the *jocoso* tradition; he also left some good poetry on moral themes.

Antequera was another flourishing centre of poetry. The outstanding poet in a group which included the interesting Luis Martín de la Plaza (1577-1625) was Pedro de Espinosa (1578-1650) who, turning to religion, for a time withdrew from the world to live as a hermit. He describes the consolations of nature and solitude in the beautiful *Soledad de Pedro de Jesús* and again in the later (and inferior) *Soledad del Gran Duque de Medina Sidonia.* The first *Soledad* shows the richness of imagination found also in his early *Fábula del Genil* and *A la navegación de San Raimundo,* this last a *tour de force* of marine imagery of a brilliance remarkable in an age of brilliance.

Granada had its group, of whom the most interesting is Pedro Soto de Rojas (1584-1658). His early poetry is in the tradition of Garcilaso, but his later work shows a complete assimilation of Góngora. His most striking work is *Paraíso cerrado para muchos, jardines abiertos para pocos*

(Granada, 1652), a poem in seven *mansiones* describing the formal garden which Soto made for himself at his home in the Albaicín in his later years. The poem lingers over the beautiful details of nature with a heady sensuous relish worthy of Góngora himself. It is unquestionably one of the finest poems of the period: Marvell's *Garden* under southern suns. In the last *mansión* the poet reveals his true subject, turning his praise of nature into a eulogy of its Creator. The poem is in the tradition of meditation on the creatures as symbols of God's beauty and greatness—'Nature's mystick Book' in Marvell's phrase—a tradition stretching back through Luis de Granada to the Neoplatonism of Bonaventure and Hugh of St Victor. It is a tradition which shows in the poetry of Espinosa also.[12] Francisco de Trillo y Figueroa (1618?-80?), a friend of Soto, wrote *culto* sonnets, *romances,* and *letrillas* inspired by Góngora's and, among other longer works, *Neapolisea,* a Gongoristic (and dull) heroic poem on Gonzalo de Córdoba.

Another Andalusian played an important part in the *culterano* movement: the Cordobese nobleman and captain of galleys Luis Carrillo de Sotomayor (1581/2-1610), author of the *Libro de la erudición poética* already mentioned. He wrote excellent *romances* reminiscent of Góngora, and some fine *culto* sonnets. He wrote also a *Fábula de Acis y Galatea* of considerable poetic power (though inferior to Góngora's *Polifemo*).

Salvador Jacinto Polo de Medina (1603-76) was born in and returned to Murcia after some years in Madrid and perhaps elsewhere. No doubt stimulated by friendship with the humanist Francisco de Cascales (1567?-1642), author of *Tablas poéticas* (Murcia, 1617) and *Cartas filológicas* (Murcia, 1634), both important works of criticism and literary theory, Polo de Medina declared himself an anti-*culterano,* even though distinct traces of the influence of Góngora are detectable in his work. This is mainly *festivo* in character, including satires on the *culto* poets; but his own *culto* poetry is often finely imaginative.

From Aragon came two poets of severely classical style and temperament, the brothers Lupercio (1559-1613) and Bartolomé Leonardo de Argensola (1562-1631). Lupercio Leonardo made his career in administration, spending the last three years of his life as Secretary of State to the conde de Lemos, viceroy of Naples, where Lupercio founded the Academia de los ociosos. His poetry, uncompromisingly classical and sometimes uncomfortably chilly, has an impressive sinewy strength. Bartolomé, who entered the Church, was appointed rector of Villahermosa, lived for a period in Madrid (where he knew Lope and others), was chaplain to the conde de Lemos in Naples, and returned at the end of his life to Saragossa. His poetry is strikingly like his brother's in general characteristics, but perhaps less coldly severe. Both excelled in urbane satire and the poetic epistle. Both were historians also: Lupercio wrote (among other things) *Información de los sucesos del Reino de Aragón en los años de 1590 y 1591* (printed Madrid, 1808), and Bartolomé *Conquista de las islas Malucas* (Madrid, 1609) as well as continuing (as Chronicler of Aragon) the *Anales* of Zurita for the period 1516-20. Though the notion of an Aragonese 'school' is an insecure one, the influence of the Argensolas may perhaps account for the classicism of Esteban Manuel de Villegas (1589-1669), whose single volume *Las eróticas o amatorias* (Nájera, 1618) contains many imitations of Horace, Anacreon, and others. There were, however, Aragonese poets who preferred the example of Góngora. One of these was Juan de Moncayo, marqués de San Felices (1614?-56 or later), whose *Rimas* (Saragossa, 1652?) and *Poema trágico de Atalanta e Hipomenes* (Saragossa, 1656) show the influence of Góngora quite clearly. Another was the priest Miguel de Dicastillo, author (under the pseudonym Miguel de Mencos) of a beautiful descriptive poem *Aula de Dios, Cartuja Real de Zaragoza* (Saragossa, 1637).[13]

In Madrid the most diverse styles and trends were found side by side as more and more writers gravitated to the centre of Spanish cultural life. Among the host of minor poets was Vicente Espinel (1550-1624), who spent his later years in Madrid and gave his name to the *espinela* or *décima*, a ten-line stanza in octosyllables. Pedro Liñán de Riaza (d. 1607)—important in the development of the *romance artístico*—was another. José de Valdivielso (1560?-1638), who came to Madrid in his middle years from his native Toledo, wrote *a lo divino* (like some fellow-*toledanos*) many fine *villancicos* and other poems in traditional forms.

Some of the best poetry of the time was written by courtier-poets, most of them associated with literary academies. Diego de Silva y Mendoza, conde de Salinas (1554-1630), wrote a considerable body of elegant and finely-turned Petrarchan poetry (most of it still unpublished) unmarked by the *culteranismo* of his day. Francisco de Borja y Aragón, príncipe de Esquilache (1577-1658), almost (though not quite) equally resistant to *culteranismo* (some say through the influence of his friends the Argensolas) combined elegance and a relative simplicity in his 'courtly' poems; and wrote in addition some excellent *romances artísticos* and *letrillas*. Juan de Tasis y Peralta, conde de Villamediana (1582-1622), was very different from either, both in the flamboyance (touched by scandal) of his life and death by assassination, and in his poetry, most (though by no means all) of which was printed in his *Obras* (Saragossa, 1629). He wrote excellent love-poetry in a relatively straightforward Petrarchan style but, captivated by the new style, came to be one of Góngora's most brilliant imitators, notably in his very difficult *Fábula de Faetón* (1617), one of the most ambitious poems of the period. The subject is almost emblematic of Villamediana's own recklessly adventurous career. Not less impressive, though more subdued, is his poetry of *desengaño*. In Villamediana's work a personal note rings through all conventions. This is true also of the poetry of Francisco López de Zárate (1580-1658), a lesser poet, but one whose *Obras varias* (1651) contain a handful of poems (principally sonnets) which are memorable for their colloquial—even idiosyncratic—directness: the quality strikingly present in (to take one example) the sonnet 'Después de una grande enfermedad'. Antonio Hurtado de Mendoza (1586?-1644) wrote copiously but without great depth. His satirical poems are wittily pointed. He owed a great deal to Góngora, whom he could imitate with sometimes charming effect, especially in his *romances*.

Into the orbits of the influential were drawn lesser *hidalgos* like Jerónimo de Cáncer y Velasco (?-1655), who wrote ingeniously witty light verse; and Antonio de Solís y Ribadeneyra (1610-86), better known as historian and dramatist, who wrote fashionably witty verse and some religious poetry, neither of much depth. Talented commoners were also taken up; men like Anastasio Pantaleón de Ribera (1600-29), who died young of the pox before fulfilling his early promise. He was an enthusiastic disciple of Góngora, with most success in his satirical and burlesque poetry but with a few excellent serious poems to his credit also. Also favoured for his talents was Gabriel Bocángel y Unzueta (1603-58), who took his stand as a poet on clarity and solid sense; as he wrote in the prologue to his *Rimas y prosas* (Madrid, 1627): 'porque el boato de las oraciones es muy ordinario ardid para suspender la atención en el sonido y paliar la falta de sentencias, que sólo deja ruido en los oídos, como el trueno'. What he attacked was not *culteranismo* but empty ostentation of it: he was himself a *culterano* who showed the influence of both Góngora and Jáuregui, notably in his *Fábula de Ero y Leandro*. In its sensuous texture (and particularly in its sharply visual images) his poetry has at times an immediacy achieved by few.

Several Hispano-Jewish poets may conveniently be mentioned together. João Pinto Delgado (*c*. 1585-after 1633), of Portuguese origin, joined his family in exile in France. He wrote in both Portuguese and Spanish. His most important poetry is embodied in three long poems published together, *Poema de la Reina Ester, Lamentaciones del Profeta Jeremías, Historia de Rut y varias poesías* (Rouen, 1627).[14] He is at his best in his meditative poetry, which is sometimes suffused with a quiet lyricism. Antonio Enríquez Gómez (1600?-60?) was born in Spain, served as a soldier, emigrated for a time but returned to Spain again. He wrote plays and other works as well as poetry. His satirical verse is witty, but he is seen to best advantage in his moral verse, whose grave simplicity can be moving.[15] Miguel de Barrios (1635-1701) also settled at last in Amsterdam. He was an immensely prolific writer (of poems, plays, and prose). His poetry reflects clearly the influence of Góngora. He wrote too much; but his best poetry—for example, some passages in the long *Imperio de Dios en el teatro universal*—has moments of brilliance. His 'sonetos dobles fúnebres' on the death of his wife are poignant.[16]

There are other Spanish poets of the seventeenth century: more than it would be useful to catalogue. Some are merely names without a biography. One such is the remarkable Adrián de Prado, evidently a Hieronymite friar, who in his *Canción real a San Jerónimo en Suria* (Seville, 1619) redeploys the pictorial resources of *culto* poetry to evoke vividly the pitiless harshness of the desert and its fauna as a setting for the austere saint. Not often was Spanish used with such brilliant (and horrific) effect. At times—for example, in its description of how the creatures of the desert prey voraciously on each other—the poem reads like a riposte to those who like Góngora saw harmony and beauty in nature: a *Soledad* written by a world-renouncing ascete.

So much for the general picture. The three greatest poets of the time demand separate consideration.

Don Luis de Góngora y Argote was born in Córdoba in 1561.[17] His family was ancient and noble. He entered the Church in order to accept a prebend renounced in his favour by an uncle. In 1617 he moved to Madrid with hopes of lucrative preferment which were to be disappointed. In his last years he suffered growing and extreme financial distress. In 1625 he had a stroke. In 1626 he returned to Córdoba and died there in 1627. The evidence of his life and works shows him to have been a worldly man; convivial and pleasure-loving; fond of music and at one time of women; given to the company of writers and players; addicted to cards; far from being a devout man; excellent company and devotedly generous to his family.

Góngora wrote in a variety of poetic forms, sometimes simply, sometimes in a style of extreme complexity. Too hard and fast a distinction should not be made between the two styles: few of the 'simple' poems are completely straightforward; and certainly a chronological division into early and late would be quite wrong.[18] Nevertheless, it is true that his *culto* verse became progressively more difficult until it reached its climax in the great poems of 1612-13.

One of the most characteristic features of Góngora's *culto* style (described in general above) was an intensified use of the poetic commonplaces of Renaissance poetry. When he speaks of the white limbs of a girl, turning simile into metaphor he calls them *nieve* or *cristal*: she is not just *like* snow, she *is* snow. Anything white—fleece, skin, snow—could be described by the same metaphors, which were interchangeable, so that any of the terms could stand for any other. Similarly, blood could be *rubí*, lips *claveles*, corn *oro*, etc. The system could be abused; but out of what coldly described may seem barren pedantry Góngora made some of the greatest poetry of seventeenth-century Europe.

Two themes stand out in his poetry: transience and mutability in human affairs; and the permanence and beauty of nature. They are intimately interrelated.

Góngora has a number of poems on the first theme, some light-hearted, some more sombre. Among them are the *letrilla* 'Aprended, Flores, de mí' and the *romance* 'Que se nos va la Pascua, mozas'. Mutability is also an underlying theme of some of his beautiful *romances* on separated lovers, such as 'Amarrado al duro banco'.

For Góngora the refuge from vicissitude and from the evils of the Court was nature (a highly idealised nature), protective of her children, and the abode of permanence. Court and country are brought together in the *romance* 'En un pastoral albergue' (1602), which retells an episode from Ariosto. The time is Charlemagne's. Angelica, a princess of Cathay, comes upon the body of the young Saracen Medoro, left for dead after a Christian ambush. She nurses him back to health, falls in love with him and he with her. They live a brief idyll before fleeing from the pursuing Orlando, who in his jealous fury lays waste the quiet scene. The poem is not a simple one. In it, Góngora uses his poetic artifice to contrast the values of Court and country, the first the source of strife, the second the home of love. Medoro lays aside his arms, Angelica her jewels; he follows now the banners of Venus; she, once a *diamante* for her hardness of heart, now adorns herself only with flowers.

The poem, like many others, exalts love. What then of the brilliant burlesque poems, such as the *romances* on Hero and Leander and on Pyramus and Thisbe, where Góngora seems to mock at love? That Góngora's target is not love itself but the folly of useless (and destructive) ideals is shown in the *letrilla* 'Ándeme yo caliente' (1581), where he writes:

Pase a media noche el mar,
y arda en amorosa llama
Leandro por ver su Dama;
que yo más quiero pasar
del golfo de mi lagar
la blanca o roja corriente,
y ríase la gente.

Pues Amor es tan cruel,
que de Píramo y su amada
hace tálamo una espada,
do se junten ella y él,
sea mi Tisbe un pastel,
y la espada sea mi diente,
y ríase la gente.

Góngora was to remain true to a vision of life that found value only in the natural and humble, and mocked at self-importance and useless heroics.

The supreme expression of this vision is in the *Soledades,* the first (like the *Polifemo*) written by 1613, the second never completed. According to his contemporary commentators there were to have been four *Soledades,* and according to the most acceptable account they were to treat of fields, shores, woods, and wasteland. The poem is in *silvas* (an irregular arrangement of seven- and eleven-syllable lines).

The story is tenuous. In the first *Soledad* a lovesick and shipwrecked young nobleman makes his way through the countryside and attends a rustic wedding; in the second he stays briefly with an old fisherman and his family before going on his way again. On the face of it the work has little unity, and the youth is too shadowy a figure for his story to be the centre of interest. The work is less about him, however, than about the spectacle of nature's richness, innocence, and permanence. The youth himself is only one element in this theme.

In a letter already referred to above (p. 142) Góngora appears to claim an esoteric content for the poem. Claiming that beneath the *corteza* of the *Soledades* a meaning may be found, he affirms that the hidden meaning, once discovered, will please and satisfy the mind, the more so since the mind, seeking truth and satisfied at last only by *la primera verdad,* will find it here: 'quedará más deleitado, cuanto, obligándole a la especulación por la obscuridad de la obra, fuera hallando debajo de las sombras de la obscuridad asimilaciones a su concepto'. Góngora's justification of his obscurity is itself somewhat obscure; but he appears to point to a general theme underlying the work, discoverable in resemblances (*asimilaciones*) to the idea (*concepto*) of the First Truth (signifying God). Góngora seems to suggest that in puzzling over the images of the poem the mind will be brought to perceive the underlying scheme of things.

The poem describes how the youth was vomited ashore by the ocean—inevitably suggesting an analogy with Jonah (the Vulgate has *evomuit*), whose sojourn in the belly of the fish was traditionally interpreted as a period spent in sin. Whatever the youth's errors (seafaring seems to be among them) the countryside will show him the way back to innocence. All he sees is instructive. A mouldering castle overtopped by trees once in its shadow is emblematic of the fall of artifice and the silent victory of nature. Later, Pyramids and life-giving Nile in similar juxtaposition teach the same lesson.

Seafaring impelled by greed is one of Góngora's targets. He represents it as not only debased but finally profitless: a moral order is broken as well as a physical one (by man's venturing on an alien element) and the result can only be disaster. This implicit theme becomes explicit in the speech by the old *serrano,* who alludes to wider calamities when he describes the Spice Islands.

> De firmes islas no la inmóvil flota
> en aquel mar del Alba te describo,
> cuyo número—ya que no lascivo—
> por lo bello agradable y por lo vario
> la dulce confusión hacer podía
> que en los blancos estanques del Eurota
> la virginal desnuda montería,
> haciendo escollos o de mármol pario
> o de terso marfil sus miembros bellos,
> que pudo bien Acteón perderse en ellos. (I, 481-90)

The lines express the intoxication with beauty of the first Europeans to see the islands, still virginal like Diana and her maidens, on whom Actaeon spied. He was turned into a wild beast for his curiosity and hunted by his own dogs: so, Góngora implies, discoveries inspired by greed destroy the discoverers.

The first *Soledad* culminates in the wedding. Góngora likens the young bride to the Phoenix flying over Nile and Pyramids: a verbal icon of the endlessly reborn life of nature contrasted with the dead works of artifice.

The second *Soledad* again depicts a life of humble concord with nature. In the garden tended by the old fisherman's daughters, the youth is shown scenes at once natural and symbolic: bees, more secure in their defenceless city than Dido within the walls of Carthage; a dying swan which sings as cygnets go out for their first swim.

References to music and rhythm abound: girls sing or play clappers; a grove becomes a rustic temple whose music is birdsong (I, 556-61); lapping water sounds as harmoniously as a theorbo while birds—*confusamente acordes*—sing in the ivy (II, 349-57), and so on. In these Góngora seems to allude to the music of the universe, the *musica mundana* of Boethius and all who wrote on music up to the seventeenth century: the vast symphony that governed the movements of the heavenly bodies, the coupling of the elements, the procession of the seasons, the generation, growth, and death of all living things. Perhaps here is to be found an answer to the apparent paradox that Góngora's praise of nature and the simple life is itself a work of extreme artifice. The all-pervading harmonies of *musica mundana* and the *laberintos* of the universe described by Nieremberg could be taken account of only in a poem which itself is a mirror of their complexities. His claim that he brought the reader to contemplate the First Truth—the pattern which underlies the apparently patternless multiplicity of the world—was not unjustified.

The *Fábula de Polifemo y Galatea* (in *octavas reales*) is a retelling of the story of Acis and Galatea in Ovid's *Metamorphoses,* XIII. The story is a simple one: it tells how Acis wins the love of Galatea, unsuccessfully wooed by the Cyclops Polyphemus who, enraged with jealousy, kills Acis, whom the compassionate gods turn into a stream. Góngora was probably moved to write a version of this widely treated subject by the posthumous publication of Carrillo's *Fábula de Acis y Galatea.* Góngora borrowed nothing from Carrillo, who followed Ovid closely, and radically reworked the subject, so that the freedom of his treatment and the originality of his style allow us to consider his poem as a personal creation, and to interpret it accordingly.

The poem is complex. The focus is Galatea and the love she inspires. All Sicily burns for her, who seems to preside like a goddess over love and fertility together. She and Acis together typify love and beauty.

Polyphemus, on the other hand, is a monster: a Cyclops for whom the stoutest pine is a weak staff. His hair is unkempt, his beard black as Lethe, his single eye a rival to the sun. But in his love-song to Galatea he is subtly humanised. Love has tamed his ferocity, and he tells how he has come to know pity. He remains inhuman in his stature; but he is human in his defencelessness against love. A momentary pathos brings him close to us. Though he is a monster, he too is a child of nature. His wealth—the wealth of the herdsman and farmer—associates him with the abundance of nature from his first appearance in the poem. He cannot be made to represent evil: he is an uncouth cousin of Acis.

The poem is a hymn to life. Love, beauty, and the succulence of nature's fruits are described in some of Góngora's finest poetry. The poem breathes a guiltless sensuality (though Góngora is sparing of carnal details).[19] Nature may be innocent, but what of the irruption of violence? The poem alludes to the precariousness of human happiness: the momentary joy of the lovers is abruptly dispelled. For a moment all is discord, but the discord is resolved: Acis is changed into a stream, beautiful in itself and a cause of beauty, and his reception in the arms of the sea culminates in what is distinctly a note of triumph:

> Sus miembros lastimosamente opresos
> del escollo fatal fueron apenas,
> que los pies de los árboles más gruesos
> calzó el líquido aljófar de sus venas.
> Corriente plata al fin sus blancos huesos,
> lamiendo flores y argentando arenas,
> a Doris llega, que, con llanto pío,
> yerno lo saludó, lo aclamó río.

Death enters, but life prevails. In his *Polifemo,* as in his *Soledades,* Góngora evokes a poetic atmosphere of optimism in which death is absorbed into the invincible harmony of the universe. Perhaps in this we glimpse a reflection of the Neoplatonism which exercised such an irresistible hold on the mind and imagination of the age.

Góngora's collected works were not printed in his lifetime: the first collected edition was published by Juan López de Vicuña as *Obras en verso del Homero español* (Madrid, 1627). The degree of interest which Góngora aroused—and his difficulty even for his contemporaries—is suggested by the number of commentaries his poetry inspired. The principal ones are: García de Salcedo Coronel, *Obras de don Luis de Góngora comentadas*... (3 vols. Madrid, 1636, 1644, and 1648—though the commentary on *Polifemo* had already appeared in 1629); José Pellicer de Salas, *Lecciones solemnes a las obras de don Luis de Góngora* (Madrid, 1630).

Among Góngora's many imitators one of the most successful is the most unexpected: the Mexican nun Juana Inés de la Cruz (1648?-95), a prodigy of beauty, learning, and talent. In addition to plays, sonnets, *silvas,* and poems in traditional metres she wrote a long *Sueño* (975 lines in *silvas*) in which she deliberately imitates the style of Góngora, echoing not only his characteristic tricks of style but often particular phrases. Its subject is an ambitious one: she describes how as the body sleeps at night the soul takes wing to contemplate and try (in vain) to comprehend the universe. The poem is a striking feat of intellect and imagination. In spite of Sor Juana's borrowings from Góngora she shows a real originality in her manipulation of his style, both in the expression of abstractions and the description of mental processes, and in describing the outside world. Here she often has the authentic Gongorine ring, as in her description of the sea at night:

El mar, no ya alterado,
ni aun la instable mecía
cerúlea cuna donde el Sol dormía;
y los dormidos, siempre mudos, peces,
en lechos lamosos
de sus obscuros senos cavernosos,
mudos eran dos veces;
... (86-92)

Lope Félix de Vega Carpio (1562-1635), one of the most astounding phenomena in the whole of Spanish literature, was so prolific in every genre that to attempt to describe his work in a few pages is a hopeless undertaking. He was born of humble parents, though he came to boast of *hidalgo* origins. He had some experience of soldiering and even sailed with the Armada. He was twice married and had numerous liaisons. In 1618 he met Marta de Nevares, his last love. Unable to marry, having been ordained a priest in 1614, he lived with her until—now blind, perhaps even insane—she died in 1632. His fidelity to her is one of his noblest traits.

His last years were clouded by more than Marta's plight. He had to bear the death of his son Lope Félix and the elopement of his daughter Antonia Clara. He himself was now leading a very devout life. He was, and had long been, a deeply pious man. His last illness was brief, brought on by a cold caught (by one account) while watering his garden.

The variety of his poetry is great.[20] He wrote several literary epics (*La Dragontea*, 1598; *La hermosura de Angélica*, 1602; *Jerusalén conquistada*, 1609), as well as other long poems such as *Corona trágica* (1627), *La Circe* (1624), *Isidro* (1599). He published several volumes of shorter poems: *Rimas* (Seville, 1604), *Rimas sacras* (Madrid, 1614), and *Rimas humanas y divinas del Licenciado Tomé de Burguillos* (Madrid, 1634). In addition he poured out *romances*, as well as lyric poems scattered throughout his plays.

It is a commonplace, but true, that Lope poured his life into his writing. He bared his soul in public like no other poet of his day. Much of his poetry for this reason has a peculiarly poignant pathos, as if we eavesdropped on private grief. In a verse epistle to Dr Matías de Porras in 1624 he recalls the happy time when his little son Carlos, who died in 1612 (and to whom he had earlier addressed a moving elegy), was still alive.

> Llamábanme a comer; tal vez decía
> que me dejasen, con algún despecho:
> así el estudio vence, así porfía.
>
> Pero de flores y de perlas hecho,
> entraba Carlos a llamarme, y daba
> luz a mis ojos, brazos a mi pecho.
>
> Tal vez de la mano me llevaba,
> me tiraba del alma, y a la mesa,
> al lado de su madre, me sentaba.

In the eclogue *Amarilis*, a profoundly moving work which he wrote on the death of Marta de Nevares, he described Amarilis now bereft of reason:

> Aquella que gallarda se prendía
> y de tan ricas galas se preciaba,
> que a la aurora de espejo le servía,
> y en la luz de sus ojos se tocaba,
> curiosa los vestidos deshacía,

y otras veces, estúpida, imitaba,
el cuerpo en hielo, en éxtasis la mente,
un bello mármol de escultor valiente.

Lope was one of the most gifted and prolific creators of the *romancero nuevo*, being particularly associated at first with the *romance morisco*.[21] In 1583 he achieved his first popular success with the *romance* about the Moor Gazul which begins 'Sale la estrella de Venus'. The poem may refer to Lope's love-affair with Elena Osorio, which began about that time. His *romance* 'La bella Zaida Zegrí' almost certainly refers to the affair. The famous 'Mira Zaide que te aviso' (now generally attributed to Lope) may refer to his banishment in 1588 for lampooning the family of Elena which had now intervened in the affair.

Like most *romances artísticos*, these appeared anonymously, and were printed as anonymous in the collections of the period. Numerous *romances* known to be by Lope or confidently attributable to him appear in the great *Romancero general* (Madrid, 1600), whose second edition (1604) bears an anonymous prologue which has also been attributed to him.[22] In it the *romance* is praised as 'natural' poetry:

> . . . porque como este género de poesía (que casi corresponde a la lírica de los griegos y latinos) no lleva el cuidado de las imitaciones y adorno de los antiguos, tiene en ella el artificio y rigor retórico poca parte, y mucha el movimiento del ingenio elevado, el cual no excluye el arte, sino que la excede, pues lo que la naturaleza acierta sin ella es lo perfecto.

Whether or not these words are by Lope, they express a belief he reiterated frequently, partly perhaps to justify his own superabundant and sometimes careless prodigality of composition, partly undoubtedly out of a genuine conviction. For with one part of himself he evidently did feel that the best poetry was simple and natural. Throughout his life he poured out not only his spontaneous-seeming *romances* but also songs and lyric poems so sensitive to the spirit of folk-poetry that it is often hard to tell which he borrowed and which he composed himself.

But Lope wrote not only simple poetry. Piqued by the *éclat* with which Góngora's 'new' style in his *Soledades* and *Polifemo* burst on the town in 1613, Lope's first reaction was satirical; but, perhaps wounded by Góngora's manifest appeal to the educated, and always eager to show his own erudition, Lope eventually succumbed to fashion, and, as Dámaso Alonso has shown,[23] wrote on occasion poetry as hermetic as anything of Góngora's. A mistake: his talents were different. But when not trying merely to dazzle, he could write *culto* and *conceptista* poetry of peculiar beauty: as, for example, in the sonnet 'Pastor que con tus silbos amorosos' (*Rimas sacras*), or the sonnet 'Ir y quedarse, y con quedar, partirse' (*Rimas*), whose antitheses tellingly convey the torment of the separated lover. The same restrained *agudeza* is the strength of one of his most successful religious poems, the poignant sonnet:

> ¿Qué tengo yo que mi amistad procuras?
> ¿Qué interés se te sigue, Jesús mío,
> que a mi puerta, cubierto de rocío,
> pasas las noches del invierno escuras?
> ¡Oh, cuánto fueron mis entrañas duras,
> pues no te abrí! ¡Qué extraño desvarío
> si de mi ingratitud el hielo frío
> secó las llagas de tus plantas puras!
> ¡Cuántas veces el ángel me decía:
> Alma, asómate agora a la ventana,
> verás con cuánto amor llamar porfía!
> ¡Y cuántas, hermosura soberana:
> Mañana le abriremos—respondía—,
> para lo mismo responder mañana!

Lope's last book of poems (though not his last work) was *Rimas . . . del Licenciado Tomé de Burguillos*. The pseudonym was one he had used sometimes before. The volume contains mainly (but far from exclusively) burlesque verse, including the burlesque epic *La Gatomaquia*. The humour is on the whole benign—an old man's indulgent view of life.

Lope, 'monstruo de la naturaleza' to his contemporaries, prodigal in all he did, no doubt wrote too much; but his powers of invention are astounding, and in reading through the many volumes of his verse one is continually surprised to find that so much of what he wrote is good.

Francisco de Quevedo y Villegas (1580-1645: see above, p. 133), one of Spain's greatest poets, left a large and complex body of verse which, like the man—learned, devout, frivolous, amorous, and foully scurrilous—is not easy to get into focus.[24]

In style Quevedo is above all a *conceptista*. His poetry, both light and serious, makes constant demands on the reader's agility of mind.[25] At its most characteristic, even in much of his love-poetry, his tersely epigrammatic style is at the opposite pole from Góngora's luminous sensuousness. Though here and there one catches echoes of Góngora in his work, Quevedo was Góngora's sternest critic, satirising him and his followers in some of the most pungent verse of that age of uninhibited literary warfare. When in 1631 Quevedo published the poetry of Luis de León, he made his dedicatory epistle to Olivares an attack on the *culteranos*. It reads like a manifesto of his own poetic intentions (at least in his serious poetry).

> Todo su estilo con majestad estudiada es decente a lo magnífico de la sentencia, que ni ambiciosa se descubre fuera del cuerpo de la oración, ni tenebrosa se esconde—mejor diré que se pierde—en la confusión afectada de figuras, y en la inundación de palabras forasteras. La locución esclarecida hace tratables los retiramientos de las ideas, y da luz a lo escondido y ciego de los conceptos.

The key to some of Quevedo's contradictions and to much else in him may be found in his Stoicism.[26] He aspired (without achieving it) to detachment from things, as a prerequisite for immunity from Fortune, and as a preparation for death. It is not far-fetched to see in Quevedo's Stoicism the root of his austere stylistic ideals, and also of his antagonism to Góngora. If his ideal was detachment from things, he could not but be offended, morally and aesthetically (if there is a distinction to be made), by Góngora's all too manifest attachment to this world.[27] It would be wrong to insist on this too absolutely; there are moments when Quevedo shows himself sensible to beauty (as in the exquisite *silva* 'Este de los demás sitios Narciso'), and then his language acquires a Gongoristic hue; but a clear difference of temperament and outlook separates the two men. It comes out expressively in the late *canción* 'El escarmiento', one of Quevedo's most austerely impressive poems, in which he rejoices bleakly at having learned to live as if already dead. For an instant the poetry grows warm and seems to echo Góngora as Quevedo describes the pleasures of nature:

> Orfeo del aire el ruiseñor parece,
> y ramillete músico el jilguero
> . . .

But the diction abruptly retreats again to cold sobriety as Quevedo, rejecting the world those images seemed for a moment to caress, veers towards his closing injunction:

> Vive para ti solo, si pudieres;
> pues sólo para ti, si mueres, mueres.

The momentary confrontation of two styles is the confrontation of two views of life.

One of Quevedo's most memorable poems is his 'Epístola satírica y censoria contra las costumbres presentes de los castellanos' addressed to Olivares, where his austere and elliptical style—the antithesis of Góngora's—expresses perfectly the harshly comfortless life which Quevado looks to as his ideal. The poem, probably written about 1627, expresses the hopes which Quevedo placed on Olivares, whose early years as Philip IV's favourite seemed to promise reform and national revival. Quevedo contrasts the degenerate present with the idealised

Spartan virtue of the Middle Ages. He writes with invigorating terseness, as when he praises the frugality of those times.

> Caducaban las aves en los vientos,
> y espiraba decrépito el venado:
> grande vejez duró en los elementos.
> . . .
> No había venido al gusto lisonjera
> la pimienta arrugada, ni del clavo
> la adulación fragrante forastera.
>
> Carnero y vaca fue principio y cabo
> y con rojos pimientos, y ajos duros,
> tan bien como el señor comió el esclavo.

Terseness and word-play make this a difficult poem, but there are few difficulties in it which do not yield to patience and a knowledge of history. It is worth persisting: here Quevedo is sometimes near his best.

Quevedo's resistance to poetic adornment leads him on occasion to a sinewy colloquialism which lends force and urgency to some of his most memorable poems, as in this striking sonnet:

> '¡Ah de la vida!' . . . ¿Nadie me responde?
> ¡Aquí de los antaños que he vivido!
> La Fortuna mis tiempos ha mordido;
> las Horas mi locura las esconde.
> ¡Que sin poder saber cómo ni adónde
> la salud y la edad se hayan hüido!
> Falta la vida, asiste lo vivido,
> y no hay calamidad que no me ronde.
> Ayer se fue; mañana no ha llegado;
> hoy se está yendo sin parar un punto;
> soy un fue, y un será, y un es cansado.
> En el hoy y mañana y ayer, junto
> pañales y mortaja, y he quedado
> presentes sucesiones de difunto.

In one way or another, a great part of Quevedo's poetry seeks to strip life of its dangerous enchantment. In a sonnet which is a *tour de force* of cacophonous rhyme Quevedo describes deflatingly the ages of man. It runs:

> La vida empieza en lágrimas y caca,
> luego viene la *mu*, con *mama* y *coco*,
> síguense las viruelas, baba y moco,
> y luego llega el trompo y la matraca.

En creciendo, la amiga y la sonsaca:
con ella embiste el apetito loco;
en subiendo a mancebo, todo es poco,
y después la intención peca en bellaca.

Llega a ser hombre, y todo lo trabuca:
soltero sigue toda perendeca;
casado se convierte en mala cuca.

Viejo encanece, arrúgase y se seca;
llega la muerte, y todo lo bazuca,
y lo que deja paga, y lo que peca.

Quevedo was fascinated by the nastiness he found in life. Góngora too could satirise and ridicule; but one never feels that for him life itself was hateful: for Quevedo everything teaches *desengaño*, disenchantment with the things of this world. This is the theme of one of his most famous sonnets, 'Miré los muros de la patria mía'. In the *romance* 'Son las torres de Joray' the mouldering castle, described as a corpse of its former self, is a lesson in stone which teaches the folly of love and ambition. The sardonic style of the opening gives way for a moment to a mellifluous Petrarchan mood, abruptly dispelled and made ironic by the refrain.

Yo, que mis ojos tenía,
Floris taimada, en los tuyos,
presumiendo eternidades
entre cielos y coluros;
en tu boca hallando perlas,
y en tu aliento calambucos,
aprendiendo en tus claveles
a despreciar los carbunclos;
en donde una primavera
mostró mil abriles juntos,
gastando en sólo guedejas
más soles que doce lustros,
con tono clamoreado,
que la ausencia me compuso,
lloré los versos siguientes,
más renegados que cultos:
'*Las glorias de este mundo
llaman con luz, para pagar con humo*'.

This is characteristic: Quevedo is master of the sudden reversal, the twist which turns appearances inside-out to reveal the sobering or ridiculous reverse. In the 'Epístola' to Olivares Quevedo derides the bullfighting in which modern youth wastes its time:

> Pretende el alentado joven gloria
> por dejar la vacada sin marido,
> . . .

Glory in killing the husband of a herd of cows? Abruptly undermined, altisonance collapses into bathos.

In his burlesque and satirical poems Quevedo's targets are usually the faults and follies of mankind, including falsity and deceit—old women posing as young, cowardly braggarts, and so on. But not all his satire has this moral basis: human weakness and misfortune attract his venom no less. Quevedo undoubtedly had less than his share of the milk of human kindness; but his command of ingenious absurdity makes even some of his most malign poems funny. One outstanding example must suffice: his satire, 'Corrido y confuso me hallo', on a woman who had spurned him for one alleged by Quevedo to be a eunuch. The cumulative effect of absurdity is overwhelming as with dazzling inventiveness metaphor is piled on metaphor.

> ¿De qué sirven tantos bríos,
> si en vuestro jardín de gloria
> han de subir de su noria
> los arcaduces vacíos?
> . . .
> Con más que palabras malas
> no hayáis miedo os acometa
> y si apunta la escopeta,
> reíos, que está sin balas.

Quevedo wrote some of the finest love-poetry in the Spanish language, particularly in the sequence addressed to 'Lisi'. Quevedo writes within the Petrarchan tradition,[28] whose vocabulary and imagery he reanimates so that his poems speak with a voice distinctively his own. A sonnet addressed to 'Floralba' offers a good example. It begins:

> ¡Ay Floralba! Soñé que te . . . ¿Diréló?
> Sí, pues que sueño fue: que te gozaba.

The poem expresses an experience common enough in the Petrarchan tradition, but Quevedo strikes a novel note at the very beginning: his dream of going to bed with Floralba is startlingly bold and threatens to disrupt the euphemistic Petrarchan conventions; but after all it was only a dream, so the conventions are uneasily preserved. The carnal immediacy of the scene, however, creates a tension between real desire and the discreet language of poetic convention which brings the whole poem sharply to life. The best of Quevedo's love-poems—for example, the sonnet 'Cerrar podrá mis ojos la postrera'— reuse traditional elements in an equally creative fashion.

But Quevedo's love-poetry is sometimes complicated with other moods. The sonnet 'A fugitivas sombras doy abrazos' expresses a sense of futility at pursuing what he can never finally possess. The final mood of the sonnet 'En crespa tempestad del oro undoso' is also one of despairing recognition of futility. Poems like these express the tension between the lover and the Stoic in Quevedo, yearning for communion in love but hating what diminishes his self-sufficiency by attaching him to the world. The disgust not far from the surface in poems like these is related to the offensively brutal demythification of love in obscene poems like the sonnet

> Quiero gozar, Gutiérrez; que no quiero
> tener gusto mental tarde y mañana
> . . .

Quevedo wrote a number of *jácaras, romances* written in *germanía* (criminal slang), which were famous in his time.[29] They are characteristically ingenious and, utterly lacking in moral content, express nothing but high-spirited pleasure in invention. Evidently, too, low life had an attraction for its own sake—an attraction expressed again in the eulogy of the picaresque life in 'Mientras que tinto en mugre sorbí brodio'.

During his lifetime Quevedo's poetry circulated only in anthologies, *pliegos*, and manuscript. The first substantial collection was published as *El Parnaso español* in 1648 by his friend José Antonio González de Salas. A further collection, *Las tres Musas últimas castellanas*, was brought out in 1670 by his nephew Pedro Aldrete Quevedo y Villegas.

NOTES

1. The reader would find it helpful to consult A. Terry, op. cit., II: *1580-1700* (Oxford, 1968). For *culteranismo* and *conceptismo*, discussed below, much clarification may be got from a cautious use of Andrée Collard, *Nueva poesía: conceptismo, culteranismo en la crítica española* (Waltham, Brandeis University, 1967).

2. See Quevedo, *Obras en verso*, ed. L. Astrana Marín (Madrid, 1943), p. 320.

3. See Mario Praz, *Studies in Seventeenth Century Imagery* (London, 1939).

4. Among Spanish emblem-books were: Juan de Horozco y Covarrubias, *Emblemas morales* (Segovia, 1589); Hernando de Soto, *Emblemas moralizadas* (Madrid, 1599); Sebastián de Covarrubias Orozco, *Emblemas morales* (Madrid, 1610); Diego de Saavedra Fajardo, *Idea de un príncipe político cristiano* (Amsterdam, 1659). All are incorporated in A. Henkel and A. Schöne, *Em-*

blemata. Handbuch zur Sinnbildkunst des XVI und XVII Jahrhunderts (Stuttgart, 1967).

5. See K. Whinnom, 'El origen de las comparaciones religiosas del Siglo de Oro: Mendoza, Montesino y Román', *RFE*, XLVI (1965), 263-85.

6. All my examples are taken from *BAE*, 35.

7. Some wrote only burlesque and satirical verse, like Jacinto Alonso Maluenda, author of *Cozquilla del gusto* (Valencia, 1629) and *Tropezón de la risa* (Valencia, n.d.) among other works.

8. See E. M. Wilson, 'Quevedo for the masses', *Atlante*, 3 (1955), 151-66.

9. The *silva* is composed of an irregular sequence of seven- and eleven-syllable lines of varying rhyme-scheme.

10. In E. J. Gates, *Documentos gongorinos* (Mexico, 1960).

11. See H. Bonneville, *Le poète sévillan Juan de Salinas* (Paris, 1969).

12. See A. Terry, 'Pedro de Espinosa and the Praise of Creation', *BHS*, XXXVIII (1961), 127-44.

13. I am indebted to Miss Aurora Egido for drawing my attention to these last two. Miss Egido is preparing an edition of *Aula de Dios*.

14. Published by I. S. Révah (Lisbon, 1954).

15. See *BAE*, 42. For his biography see I. S. Révah in *REJ*, CXXI (1962).

16. See K. Scholberg, *La poesía religiosa de Miguel de Barrios* (Columbus, Ohio, 1962).

17. For a fuller exposition—and justification—of some of the interpretations outlined here, see R. O. Jones, *Poems of Góngora* (Cambridge, 1966).

18. Fortunately, there is a reliable chronology of Góngora's poetry in the famous Chacón manuscript.

19. The sensuality of his imagination can be seen at its most striking and beautiful in the poem 'Qué de invidiosos montes levantados'. R. Jammes (*Etudes sur l'oeuvre poétique de Góngora*, Bordeaux, 1967) has an interesting discussion of this aspect of Góngora, especially on pp. 533-47.

20. This is not a complete list. There is no comprehensive study of Lope's poetry. For excellent partial studies see Dámaso Alonso, *Poesía española*; J. F. Montesinos, introductions to the two volumes of *Poesías líricas*, CC (Madrid, 1926-27); and J. M. Blecua, introduction to Lope de Vega, *Obras poéticas*, I (Barcelona, 1969).

21. See R. Menéndez Pidal, *Romancero hispánico*, II (Madrid, 1953), 126-30.

22. ibid., 159.

23. Alonso, op. cit., pp. 472-87.

24. There is no comprehensive study of his poetry. Dámaso Alonso in *Poesía española* is illuminating, as is J. M. Blecua's introduction to Quevedo, *Obras completas*, I: *Poesía original* (Barcelona, 1963). See also the introduction by R. M. Price to his *Anthology of Quevedo's Poetry* (Manchester, 1969).

25. See A. A. Parker, 'La agudeza en algunos sonetos de Quevedo', *Estudios dedicados a Menéndez Pidal*, III (Madrid, 1952), 345-60.

26. As is suggested by A. Mas in his interesting (but sometimes misleading) *La caricature de la femme, du mariage et de l'amour dans l'oeuvre de Quevedo* (Paris, 1957). For Quevedo's Stoicism, see below, pp. 189-90.

27. In view of the Neoplatonism reflected in Góngora's poetry, it is interesting to find Quevedo attacking 'la doctrina de Platón, con la cual . . . todos los herejes informaron sus errores' (*Providencia de Dios*, in *Obras en prosa*, ed. L. Astrana Marín, Madrid, 1932, pp. 1042-3).

28. See Otis H. Green, *Courtly Love in Quevedo* (Boulder, Colo., 1952).

29. For this peculiar genre see J. M. Hill, *Poesía germanesca* (Bloomington, 1945).

Chapter 8

CERVANTES: PROSE FICTION AFTER CERVANTES

BOOKS AND ARTICLES ON CERVANTES would fill a library. Since it would be absurd to attempt to give a comprehensive view of Cervantine scholarship here, it seems more profitable to ignore most of his interpreters and outline instead the simplest possible view which will make sense of his work, though subtlety and nuance must inevitably be sacrificed.

Miguel de Cervantes Saavedra (1547-1616) was the son of an obscure surgeon. Much of his own life remains obscure. He went to Italy in or about 1569, served as a soldier, and fought at Lepanto (1571) where he was wounded, losing the use of his left hand. He was captured by corsairs in 1575 while returning to Spain from Naples, and was ransomed five years later after several attempts to escape. After drifting for a time, while he tried to live by his pen, he became a commissary charged with purchasing and requisitioning provisions for the Armada. He remained in similar government service for a number of years. He was in frequent trouble over his accounts, and was several times imprisoned; from the evidence it is clear that the worst he can be accused of is imprudence. He had married in 1584; the marriage was to all appearances an unhappy one. Cervantes knew poverty for much of his later life, and all his hopes of advancement were disappointed. His works show no bitterness on this account; the character mirrored in them is in fact a singularly attractive one, and far more humane than that of most of his contemporaries.

Cervantes had begun writing even while still in captivity in Algiers, where he wrote plays to amuse his fellow-captives, and some verse. On his return to Spain he wrote a number of plays, only two of which have survived (*Numancia* and *El trato de Argel*, both published in the eighteenth century). He continued throughout his life to write poetry; most of his poems are eulogies of other men's books, or are scattered throughout his own prose-works. *El viaje del Parnaso* (Madrid, 1614) is a mock-heroic survey of the state of poetry. He took pride in being a poet, but not much of his verse rises far above a solid mediocrity.

In order of publication his other works are: *Primera parte de la Galatea* (Alcalá, 1585); *El ingenioso hidalgo Don Quijote de la Mancha*

(Madrid, 1605); *Novelas ejemplares* (Madrid, 1613); *Ocho comedias y ocho entremeses nuevos* (Madrid, 1615); *Segunda parte del ingenioso caballero Don Quijote de la Mancha* (Madrid, 1615); *Los trabajos de Persiles y Sigismunda, historia setentrional* (Madrid, 1617).

It is clear from his writings that Cervantes was a very cultivated, even bookish, man; but he was also a man of action, mentioned for bravery at Lepanto, and displaying unusual courage in captivity. It is one more of the paradoxes of the age that his first book was a pastoral novel, *La Galatea*. It is clear that Cervantes felt a special affection for it: he promised a second part in the prologue of *Don Quixote*, Part II, and repeated the promise in the dedication of *Persiles*, when he was already on his deathbed. The book is quite a good example of its genre; it is more serious and consistent than many; and it has more of a structure than has generally been noticed.[1] But it also has *longueurs*, and it certainly does not show Cervantes's powers of invention at their best.

One of the attractions of the pastoral novel for him was probably the opportunity it offered for accommodating numerous short stories within its easy-going looseness of form. Cervantes, who had probably become interested in the Italian *novella* during his years in Italy, remained attached to the short narrative all his life. In spite of *El Abencerraje* and the stories in *Guzmán de Alfarache*, Cervantes was nearly right when he claimed in the prologue of his *Novelas ejemplares* that 'yo he sido el primero que he novelado en lengua castellana'. He was the first to take a serious and sustained interest in the *novella* as a form, and it was he who established it as a flourishing genre in Spain.

Although his *Novelas ejemplares* were not published until 1613, some of them had certainly been written many years before. *Rinconete y Cortadillo* is mentioned in *Don Quixote* I, xlvii, and some time in the years 1605-09 it and *El celoso extremeño* were copied into a manuscript collection of entertaining miscellanea by one Francisco Porras de la Cámara. There are *novelas* embedded in *Don Quixote* (*El curioso impertinente*, the story of the captive, etc.); and it has been suggested that *Don Quixote* itself was to have been a *novela* until Cervantes saw its richer possibilities: certainly, the knight's first sally, which occupies the first five chapters, is self-contained. For these reasons it seems appropriate to discuss the *Novelas ejemplares* before *Don Quixote*.

In the prologue Cervantes wrote of the stories:

> Heles dado nombre de *Ejemplares*, y si bien lo miras, no hay ninguna de quien no se pueda sacar algún ejemplo provechoso; y si no fuera por no alargar este sujeto, quizá te mostrara el sabroso y honesto fruto que se podría sacar, así de todas juntas como de cada una de por sí.

The claim that there is a hidden 'fruto' is a common one in works of the time, but it is borne out by the character of the *novelas* themselves.

What is difficult to decide is the precise significance of 'así de todas juntas'. Is Cervantes claiming that there is a collective moral to be drawn from the collection as a whole?

However that may be, the stories were intended also (or even primarily) as entertainment. He writes:

> Mi intento ha sido poner en la plaza de nuestra república una mesa de trucos, donde cada uno puede llegar a entretenerse sin daño de barras . . .

Entertainment is a necessity in life—'que no siempre se está en los templos, no siempre se ocupan oratorios'—but it must be moral; and Cervantes affirms that sooner than publish his *novelas* if they were likely to suggest evil thoughts or desires he would cut off the hand that wrote them.

There are twelve *novelas*. Their order does not appear to have any special significance; except that *El coloquio de los perros*, which presents a wide panorama of life, is appropriately the last. All the *novelas* are concerned in some way with good and evil; and most of them are concerned with love, or at any rate sexual relations. They are exemplary in that they show examples to avoid and to imitate, but not in all is the moral wholly explicit. Cervantes disliked preaching in works of entertainment, though he also believed firmly that they should be morally profitable, or at least harmless. In the prologue to *Don Quixote* I, he wrote of the book:

> . . . ni tiene para qué predicar a ninguno, mezclando lo humano con lo divino, que es un género de mezcla de quien no se ha de vestir ningún cristiano entendimiento.

This is probably a veiled reference to *Guzmán de Alfarache*, whose buttonholing familiarity with the reader and insistent preaching may have seemed to Cervantes to make a hybrid of it: part entertainment, part work of devotion.

The *novelas* show Cervantes's concern for verisimilitude, which we may take to mean credibility, not realism. It was held (following Aristotle) that whereas the proper matter for history was the particular (things as they were, however singular), the proper matter for art was the probable, the typical, the universal. This applies as much to characters as to events. The characters who people the *novelas* are not individuals (though there are some rare touches of individual psychology): they are characteristic of their types—high-minded lover, hot-headed youth, etc. What Cervantes has to tell humanity is general not particular. The entertainment he offers is not to be sought in psychological realism but in formal aspects of narrative: strange (but not impossible) situations; surprising (and hence ingenious) turns of events; unexpected encounters and recognitions; cunning patterns of narrative, unobvious and so the more pleasing when perceived.[2] Cervantes evidently intended the book to be a show-case of the art of narrative. Then there is the pleasure of style: elegant, varied—now plain, now rhetorical—appropriately solemn or humorous. And, finally, the pleasure of edification, on the whole less impressive to modern readers than Cervantes's serene and humane attitude to life.

Nine of the *novelas* deal with love—its nature and its consequences, including marriage—or parodies of love. Three depict perfect love. *La gitanilla* is one of these. It tells how a noble youth falls in love with Preciosa, a gipsy girl famous for her beauty, her *desenvoltura*, and her virtue. She promises to marry him if he lives for two years as a gipsy in order to discover if his love is real or merely infatuation. She will be a sister to him in the meantime, but she will accept no restraint on her freedom: 'Sepa que conmigo ha de andar siempre la libertad desenfadada, sin que la ahogue ni turbe la pesadumbre de los celos'. Already some main themes of the book are announced: love is not temporary, and its proper end is in marriage; it is incompatible with jealousy; and virtue will preserve itself from corruption in the most inauspicious surroundings if the will to be virtuous is there, since virtue is a positive quality and not the mere absence of its opposite. For the source of Cervantes's moral ideas we do not need to look further than Christian teaching, together with the Neoplatonic treatises on love.

The youth, who adopts the name Andrés, undertakes the test. Cervantes contrives an apparent impasse, but at the last minute Andrés is saved from execution for murder by the discovery that Preciosa is the long-lost daughter of the *corregidor* who, learning that Andrés is really Don Juan de Cárcamo, has him released without further ado. (The *alcalde*, uncle of the dead man, is given two thousand ducats for overlooking the affair.)

Preciosa is one of Cervantes's most animated creations and, in her mixture of *desenvoltura* and chastity, a perfect embodiment of his conception of active virtue. She is immune to the temptations her way of life exposes her to. But Cervantes is reluctant to give her too low a background: though he represents gipsies as thieves, he also represents them as more strict in their own morality in some ways than the socially more respectable. They observe complete chastity and fidelity; adultery in women is punished with death; all possessions (except women) are held in common. The account of their free and natural life has a pastoral quality. As children of nature they display a stern and primitive virtue. However, there is a superior code, and at the end the lovers come under the higher law of Christianity (through the sacrament of marriage) and the obligations of nobility.

La ilustre fregona is a variation on the same theme. It tells how two noble lads run away to become *pícaros*. One, Avendaño, falls in love with Costanza, a beautiful girl brought up as the daughter of an innkeeper. After many vicissitudes it is discovered that Costanza is the natural child of the father of Carriazo (Avendaño's companion) by an unnamed but extremely high-born lady. The lovers are married and all ends happily.

There is no novelty in the theme: Costanza and Avendaño are the counterparts of Preciosa and Andrés; but the circumstances are sufficiently different to sustain interest. For one thing, Avendaño is given a companion quite unlike him: Carriazo's mind is more gross—being blind to beauty, all he wants is to get back to the tunnyfisheries. Avendaño is the perfect Neoplatonic lover, so susceptible to beauty that a mere report of Costanza's beauty fills him with longing to see her. The contrast between the two lads both points the theme and gives Cervantes opportunity for the invention of incident.

La española inglesa concerns again the Neoplatonic doctrine that love, though awakened initially by beauty, attaches itself to a higher beauty than the physical. Isabel retains the love of Recaredo even when she temporarily loses her beauty.

El amante liberal tells of an imperfect love perfected. Ricardo's love is marred by jealousy; love and adversity teach him selflessness. Though it is interesting in many respects, this is one of Cervantes's less mature *novelas*. He strains coincidence, and the double attraction of surprise and symmetry led him too far when he made two boatloads of Turks annihilate each other almost to the last man, whereby lovers and Christian captives recover their freedom.

La fuerza de la sangre is a story of the power of beauty. Stirred by her beauty, Rodolfo abducts and rapes Leocadia. Years later she identifies the house where she was taken and tells her story to Rodolfo's parents, who bid Rodolfo, now in Italy, to come home to marry a bride they have chosen for him. He is allowed to meet Leocadia without knowing she is the chosen bride. Her beauty causes him to fall in love with her. They marry, so that marriage at last removes the stain on Leocadia's honour. The story is of a perverted love (Rodolfo's lust) redeemed: appropriately, a crucifix which Leocadia sees on recovering consciousness after the rape and then takes with her from the house, serves to corroborate her story when she tells it to Rodolfo's parents. An image of divine love helps to prepare the way for a victory of human love.

United in love, Leocadia and Rodolfo will make a happy marriage. In *El celoso extremeño* we are shown a parody of marriage. The rich *indiano* Carrizales returns to Spain at the age of sixty-eight and marries a girl of barely fourteen. Jealous with no cause, and determined to protect her at all costs, he immures her in a house which becomes her prison. In spite of his precautions a young rake, Loaysa, gets in. Repenting almost too late, Leonora resists him.[3] Finding them asleep in the morning Carrizales believes the worst. He dies of grief. His error was to believe that innocence can be guarded by locks and bolts if virtue is not active in its own defence, and to imprison Leonora instead of guiding her to virtue. Hardly less grave is the error of marrying a young girl to an old man. Like all those in Cervantes's works who commit grave moral error, he cannot but die.

Carrizales's precautions are ridiculous (their absurdity is aptly matched by the meaningless oath whereby Loaysa eludes them) and he himself comes close to being funny. But at the end he transcends all this when on his deathbed he forgives Leonora—possibly the first example in Spanish literature of the period of a wronged husband abstaining from vengeance on his (apparently) adulterous wife.

Rinconete y Cortadillo, quite different in theme from these, is at once one of the most enjoyable and one of the most cleverly didactic of the *novelas*. It probably reflects Cervantes's own observations of Seville during one of his many stays there. The plot—which is rudimentary: the *novela* is really a succession of tableaux—tells of two young *pícaros* who on arrival in Seville are enrolled in a guild of thieves whose head is Monipodio. The thieves and prostitutes who belong to the guild are all, to the boys' surprise, profoundly devout, and are even obliged by Monipodio to contribute to keeping a lamp perpetually burning before an image of their special devotion. Their devotions are exaggerated, and irrational: a whore remarks of her earnings 'que el trabajo y el afán con que yo los había ganado ruego yo a los Cielos que vayan en descuento de mis pecados'. Misplaced piety is in fact the central theme of the *novela*. It would be naïve to believe that Cervantes is satirising only thieves and prostitutes: his target is mindless piety at all levels of society. For example, when their informant tells the boys 'ni tenemos conversación con mujer que se llame María el día del sábado', it is a clear allusion to the extreme and superstitious devotion to the Virgin which characterised Seville at that time. The doctrine of the Immaculate Conception was espoused there with extraordinary fervour. Pedro de Castro, who became archbishop of Seville in 1610, shared the fervour of his flock. 'It is even said that in this holy Marian cause he had the official brothel closed on days consecrated to the Virgin and insisted that girls called Mary should not be employed there'.[4] This was some years after the composition of *Rinconete*, but the atmosphere was already there. Although real life provided him with his material, probably Cervantes's attack on empty formulas and ceremonies owed a good deal to Erasmus.[5]

There is more in the *novela* than this; more, even, than an exposure of the lawlessness of Seville (which was well enough known). The guild of criminals may be intended as a distorted mirror-image of respectable society: it has its laws, a parody of taxes and tithes, even government of a kind. Pickpockets are jealous of their honour and address each other as *vuesa merced*. Perhaps what is being satirised is a society which lived only according to external forms, a society in which the shadow of honour, devotion, and industry is mistaken for the substance.

El licenciado Vidriera tells how a clever youth, deranged by a love philtre, becomes famous for the witticisms he utters while mad. Sane again, and no longer funny, he is shunned. Whatever Cervantes's purpose in writing this *novela* it must be accounted a failure: interesting elements of a story, but unrealised.

Two other *novelas, Las dos doncellas* and *La señora Cornelia,* are pleasant but have little depth.

In the interlinked stories *El casamiento engañoso* and *El coloquio que pasó entre Cipión y Berganza* (better known as *El coloquio de los perros*) Cervantes is at his best. In the first, Campuzano, back from the wars in Flanders, tells how he tried to provide for his retirement by marrying the apparently rich Doña Estefanía, who is herself attracted by the two thousand ducats he claims he is worth. After the marriage she disappears with his gold chain and other valuables. But it is doubly a case of the biter bit, for the chain was not gold and the value of the lot is only some ten or twelve ducats. She has left him something to remember her by: the pox, which he had just been sweating out when the story opened. From a parody of marriage—entered into through a cold calculation of material profit—the fruits which Campuzano gathers are a parody of what we normally think of as the fruits of marriage.

While in the hospital at Valladolid, Campuzano wrote down an imaginary conversation between the two dogs Cipión and Berganza (real, and well known in the town). Berganza recounts his life, while Cipión comments. The story of Campuzano is a special case of what is a general state, for all the humans Berganza has known are deceitful and hypocritical (with the exceptions of the Jesuit fathers of Seville). Shepherds kill the sheep they are employed to protect; an *alguacil* connives at the perversion of justice. The worst hypocrite of all is the witch Cañizares, by whom Berganza is adopted, and whom he exposes.

Cañizares had told Berganza that he was in reality one of twins born to her sister-witch la Montiela, transformed into dogs by the malignant arts of la Camacha. Some verses prophesy their return to human form:

Volverán a su forma verdadera
cuando vieren con presta diligencia
derribar los soberbios levantados
y alzar a los humildes abatidos
por poderosa mano para hacello.

Is the true sense that things will always remain the same? Probably: it is in accord with the seventeenth-century Christian view of things. It is always open to the individual to repent, but men in general do not: there will be injustice and inequality as long as men are men. Doubtless the verses mean that dogs will become men when men become just: which is to say, when pigs fly.

The theme of the *novela* is hypocrisy. Appearances count more in the world than real worth. (Cipión's comment on the lot of the poor man is heartfelt: Cervantes knew what it was to be poor and neglected.) The fundamental irony of the story is this: that dogs, though lacking reason, are wiser than man who, possessing it, has fallen so low that animals appear superior to him. (There are moments in *Don Quixote* where Cervantes makes a similar point: for example, the exemplary friendship between Rocinante and Sancho's ass, or the prudence of the lion in II, xvii, who refuses to be provoked by Don Quixote and replies to the challenge by displaying his hindquarters.) But Cervantes, though a moralist, will not moralise to excess. Cipión continually reproves Berganza for *murmuración* (even when his criticisms are general). At one moment, when Cipión expatiates on the difference between earthly masters and the Lord of Heaven, it is Berganza's turn:

Berganza.—Todo eso es predicar, Cipión amigo.
Cipión—Así me lo parece a mí, y así callo.

For this, after all, is entertainment, as Cervantes seems to be trying, with increasing difficulty, to remember.

Though the example in most cases is clear enough, some remain doubtful. *Las dos doncellas* and *La señora Cornelia* may be meant to illustrate indiscretion retrieved by discretion, but this is far from clear; and *El licenciado Vidriera* (which will be touched on again below) may satirise the crowd's readiness to laugh at a madman when in some ways he may be less mad than they, but if this is the point, it is well hidden. What of the *fruto* which may be gathered *de todas juntas*? Perhaps *El coloquio* is our guide. The bleak picture of life it gives is relieved almost solely by the dogs' virtue. As Cipión says of dogs, 'nos suelen pintar por símbolo de la amistad'. Perhaps this is the theme of the book. Love is man's surest guide in his darkness: true love, which looks beyond possession to companionship, to *caritas*.

Its absence leads to disaster in private life (*El celoso extremeño*) and to chaos in social life (*Rinconete, El coloquio,* both of them panoramas of compassionless self-seeking).

The Porras de la Cámara manuscript contains another *novela* which has been attributed to Cervantes, *La tía fingida.* The attribution has been hotly contested by some, principally on the grounds that such an immoral story could not be by Cervantes. There is nothing to preclude the possibility: it is an entertaining and well-told story, which the author of the *entremés* of *El viejo celoso* might well have told. The question remains open.

Don Quixote has given rise to such numerous, varied, and contradictory interpretations that a modern reader may well despair of seeing the book for its critics, though Cervantes declared his intentions in unequivocal terms in the prologue to Part I, where his friend declares of the book 'todo él es una invectiva contra los libros de caballerías', and makes the point three times more. Cervantes reminds us periodically of his intent, and affirms it again at the end of Part II. The work is, then, a burlesque of the romances of chivalry, for Cervantes a literature of lies, and aesthetically absurd in addition.[6]

Don Quixote, an elderly *hidalgo* living a humdrum life in a sleepy village of La Mancha, is sent mad by his passion for romances of chivalry. Once mad, he transforms everything into chivalresque terms. The knight he models himself on is Amadís, but the book contains allusions to or reminiscences of many other romances. The name 'Caballero de la Triste Figura' comes from the third book of *Don Clarián* (1524) and 'Caballero de los Espejos' (applied to Sansón Carrasco) from the fourth (1528).[7] When Don Quixote tells of his adventures in the Cave of Montesinos, he describes his distant glimpse of Dulcinea:

> . . . me mostró tres labradoras que por aquellos amenísimos campos iban saltando y brincando como cabras . . . (II, xxiiii)

Dulcinea's damsel leaps so vigorously that 'se levantó dos varas de medir en el aire'. They leap in Don Quixote's imagination because the peasant girl whom Sancho passed off as Dulcinea in II, x, leapt on her donkey with singular agility; but Don Quixote may also have been recalling something he had read in Bernardo de Vargas's *Cirongilio de Tracia* (1545)—a book referred to twice by Cervantes—in which the Maid of the Fountain, held in thrall by a wicked knight, is discovered 'dando muy grandes saltos y deshonestos, así que las piernas descubría por cima de la rodilla'. Two things are evident to a reader of *Don Quixote*: that at some time in his life Cervantes had read many romances of chivalry, and that the humour of *Don Quixote* is to a large extent dependent on a knowledge of these books. Modern critics who confidently set out to interpret *Don Quixote* ignorant of—or wilfully ignoring—its literary background are likely to mislead more than they help.

All the evidence indicates that in the seventeenth and eighteenth centuries *Don Quixote* was seen only as a masterpiece of comedy.[8] Not until the Romantics was Don Quixote himself regarded as a figure of noble pathos: for his contemporaries—for whom *triste figura* connoted an object of ridicule—*El Caballero de la Triste Figura* was anything but pathetic. As for the general sense of the work, much modern interpretation from the Romantics to the present day goes far beyond what is historically credible; and much of it is patent nonsense.[9] The most prudent course is to be guided in the first instance by Cervantes's declared intention, and go beyond it only to the extent that it fails to account for the work as a whole. And it does fail: it does not cover episodes like the story of Marcela in Part I; and it does not cover Don Quixote's many apparently sane moments.

Don Quixote is the story of a madman; it seems necessary therefore to determine the view of insanity taken by Cervantes and his contemporaries. Cervantes probably took some of his ideas from *Examen de ingenios* (1575, enlarged edition 1594) by Dr Juan Huarte de San Juan who, following an ancient tradition, accounted for all the variety of human psychology in terms of the theory of humours. The four elements of which the world was thought to be composed—earth, air, fire, water—had their counterparts on the constituent humours of the human body: melancholy, blood, choler, and phlegm. Differences of temperament were thought to be caused by the different proportions in which the humours are mixed in individuals. A perfect balance of the humours produced a mediocre all-round competence; some 'distemper' or disproportion was necessary for any outstanding mental development or aptitude. Conversely, any outstanding mental power argued a certain imbalance:

> . . . por donde dijo Platón que por maravilla se halla hombre de muy subido ingenio que no pique algo en manía (que es una destemplanza caliente y seca del celebro).

To illustrate how great intelligence may be (indeed must be) associated with derangement of one of the other faculties, Huarte tells how Hippocrates was asked to treat the philosopher Democritus, now mad:

> el cual vino a tanta pujanza de entendimiento allá en la vejez que se le perdió la imaginativa, por la cual razón comenzó a hacer y decir dichos y sentencias tan fuera de términos que toda la ciudad

> de Abderas le tuvo por loco.... Y haciéndole [Hipócrates] las preguntas que convenían para descubrir la falta que tenía en la parte racional, halló que era el hombre más sabio que había en el mundo. . . . Y fue la ventura de Demócrito que todo cuanto razonó con Hipócrates en aquel breve tiempo fueron discursos del entendimiento y no de la imaginativa, donde tenía la lesión.

This is in fact what we find in Don Quixote: manifestly mad, but capable of impressing with his wisdom those who come upon him in his lucid intervals.[10]

This tradition is allied to another: the ancient attitude to the fool, regarded on the one hand as an entertaining figure of fun, on the other hand as a receptacle of unusual wisdom.[11] Court fools commonly had both functions. Court fools or jesters were often moralists in disguise, and criticisms were often tolerated in the mouth of a fool which would not be accepted from ordinary men. In short, mental abnormality—and in this connection little or no distinction was made between madness and folly—was regarded ambivalently: it was comic, but simultaneously it was felt that the fool might be wiser than his fellows.

This mixed attitude is at the basis of one of the masterpieces of the Renaissance, Erasmus's *Praise of Folly* (1509), which had a wide and incalculable influence throughout Europe. Folly, personified, praises all manifestations of folly among men as acts of homage to her, thereby permitting Erasmus to satirise a wide range of human behaviour. Most men are mad, Folly asserts: they must surely be mad who are obsessed with hunting, or gaming, or similar irrational pursuits—though the most mad are those who think that by empty religious observances they can save their soul though they make no attempt to live according to the law of Christ. 'But in the meantime, one madman mocketh another and not seldom you shall see the more mad man the loudlier laugh the less to scorn'.[12] This is the heart of Erasmus's argument: all men may indeed be mad, but the least mad are often those whom the world derides. Folly goes on to affirm that the simple-minded are preferred by God to wise men (by which she means those wise in the ways of the world). 'This by Paul's words is confirmed, where he saith, "God hath chosen him out those that the world reputed for fools" '.

Once seen in this light (though it need not be supposed that Cervantes had read Erasmus) Don Quixote's mixture of lunacy and wisdom ceases to be contradictory and becomes profoundly meaningful. He is funny when he deludes himself and is deluded by others; but there are moments when the apparently sane are madder than he. When he charges windmills, takes an innkeeper for a warden of a castle, or mistakes the slatternly Maritornes keeping a midnight assignation with a muleteer for a love-struck damsel bent on tempting his virtue and losing her own, matters are straightforward and the humour is uncomplicated. When he is deluded by others, laughter becomes uneasy since it is hard not to feel that he rises in moral stature above his deceivers. As Marcos de Obregón remarks in Espinel's novel:

> y para mí tengo por mejor y más seguro el estado del engañado que la seguridad del engañador: porque al fin lo uno arguye sencillez y buen pecho, y lo otro mentira y maldad profunda.

This is particularly true in Part II, where so much of the deception of Don Quixote has only frivolous entertainment as its object; which causes Cervantes (as 'Cide Hamete Benengeli') to remark:

> que tiene para sí ser tan locos los burladores como los burlados, y que no estaban las Duques dos dedos de parecer tontos, pues tanto ahinco ponían en burlarse de dos tontos. (III, lxx)

This sounds like an echo of Erasmus's words: 'and not seldom you shall see the more mad man the loudlier laugh the less to scorn'.

Many of Don Quixote's discourses—on the Golden Age of man, on Arms and Letters, etc.—are unquestionably meant to be taken seriously. On these occasions Cervantes directs the reader's feelings by remarking how admirable Don Quixote's words seemed to his hearers. On other occasions, his actions are not less admirable. An episode early in Part I (xi-xiv) shows him both sane and mad, in word and deed. He and Sancho are given hospitality by some goatherds. Moved to eloquence by his surroundings Don Quixote seizes a handful of acorns and begins:

> Dichosa edad y siglos dichosos aquéllos a quien los antiguos pusieron nombre de dorados, y no porque en ellos el oro, que en esta nuestra edad de hierro tanto se estima, se alcanzase en aquella venturosa sin fatiga alguna, sino porque entonces los que en ella vivían ignoraban estas dos palabras de 'tuyo' y 'mío'.

Then commerce and injustice were alike unknown, but now injustice reigns—and here he plunges back into his mania—so that knight-errantry became necessary to redress wrongs. (In the meantime the goatherds listen with stupefaction to the speech—'que se pudiera muy bien excusar'—while Sancho drinks on the sly.) The episode serves to introduce on the following day a 'real-life' pastoral episode: the burial of Grisóstomo, who had killed himself in despair on being rejected by the beautiful Marcela, who, as if attempting to recreate the innocence and freedom of the Golden Age of which Don Quixote spoke, had turned shepherdess. She appears at the funeral to defend herself against the charge of cruelty and to reaffirm her free will. There is a threatening move towards her by the friends of the dead man, whereupon Don Quixote stands forth effectively in her defence. The pattern of his discourse is reflected in his actions: he is mad (he acts as a knight errant) but he is wise enough to see what others cannot, that Marcela is right.

Immediately afterwards Don Quixote spoils the effect by engaging in ridiculous adventure, beginning with his encounter with the *yangüeses*, followed by other episodes which culminate in the battle for 'Mambrino's helmet'. There follows an incident—the freeing of the galley-slaves—which contains at least one puzzling moment. In general it is an act of folly, and hence funny; but the case of one prisoner stands out; that of the procurer, condemned to four years in the galleys. As he himself points out, this is in effect a sentence of death: he is old, ill, and not likely to last long in the cruel life of the galleys. Even Sancho has pity on him and gives him a *real*. Don Quixote is moved to utter a solemn defence of the office of bawd. Whether or not we are expected to laugh, the point seems to be made that justice must be tempered with mercy, that some crimes are punished with more savagery than the little real harm they do would warrant.

This is not the first time that the theme of justice has appeared. In I, iv, Don Quixote rescues the boy Andrés from a beating. We learn later that his intervention made matters worse. This is Don Quixote the madman, boasting of more than he can fulfil. The whole affair is a joke: no wisdom here.

In I, xxiii, Don Quixote enters the Sierra Morena, and the book enters a new phase. Almost the whole of the remaining portion (xxiii-li) is as much concerned with the stories of others as with Don Quixote. By devious ways and with many interruptions we are led into the story initiated by Don Quixote's encounter in the Sierra with another madman, Cardenio, whose subsequent meeting with Dorotea is the encounter of two interlocking stories and the contrast of four characters: the irresolute Cardenio; the impetuous and unscrupulous Fernando; the timid Luscinda; and the boldly enterprising and discreet Dorotea.[13] It is Dorotea who by her discretion (and eloquence) happily resolves the affairs of all four. The beginning of their story is separated from its resolution by the *novela* of *El curioso impertinente* (perhaps to exemplify disaster caused by indiscretion), which is itself interrupted by Don Quixote's battle with the wineskins. This intricate interweaving of 'real' and fictional stories, comic and serious, is a *tour de force* of narrative, a piece of virtuosity which is evidently intended by Cervantes as an exhibition of his skill as a writer; like a juggler keeping a dozen assorted objects in the air at once. Once this sequence is concluded, a new story begins, that of the escaped captive. It is a story of prudence and fortitude rewarded. Don Quixote introduces it with a long discourse on Arms and Letters, a common Renaissance theme here given new life by the fervour of Cervantes's style (the autobiographical bearing is clear) and by Don Quixote's application of it to his own case. At the close the discourse collapses again into madness, but up to that moment Don Quixote's words are seriously intended and he himself arouses admiration for his 'buen entendimiento y buen discurso'.

In short, *Don Quixote* I—fundamentally a tale of a comic madman with lucid intervals—is a medley in whose second half Don Quixote himself diminishes in importance, his story now forming a background for a series of ingeniously interwoven tales and incidents, evidently intended as a triumphant example of literary artifice. Appropriately, now follows the discourse on fiction by the Canon of Toledo, who argues for a literature which is both rational and moral. Burlesque of the romances of chivalry—of which we are not allowed to lose sight—is supported by a reasoned critique of them and an account of an alternative kind of fiction directed towards 'el fin mejor que se pretende en los escritos, que es enseñar y deleitar juntamente'. No doubt *Don Quixote* itself is intended as an example.

Part II is different, both in its general tone and to some extent in form. In the discussion of Part I (now in print) which takes place in II, ii-iv, Cervantes shows his awareness of criticism and implicitly undertakes to avoid irrelevancies in Part II. Though his success was only partial, Part II is more unified to the extent that Don Quixote is concerned in or witnesses most of the important events, and there are no intercalated *novelas*. Thematic unity is given by a somewhat more fully realised alternation of Don Quixote's mad and lucid moments, and also—more tenuously—by the persistence of the theme of deception: Don Quixote twice deceived by Sansón Carrasco (though for his own good), by Sancho, by the Duke and Duchess; Sancho himself deceived when he is made 'governor'; Doña Rodríguez and her daughter deceived by the Duke's cruel joke. This may have no special significance: it may simply reflect a more disillusioned view of life on the part of Cervantes, now ten years older, perhaps more poignantly aware of his own decline, and his country's. More probably it is a solution to the difficulty of inventing new material. Don Quixote's 'spontaneous' feats of madness in Part I were not easily repeatable; Cervantes may have tried to find a formula which would assist invention. A series of practical jokes (for which 'deception' is perhaps too solemn a word: they are after all meant to be funny) may have seemed the most fertile solution.

Whatever the reason, the consequence is an increase in Don Quixote's moral stature by contrast with his deceivers. When Don Quixote is first challenged by the disguised Sansón Carrasco and unexpectedly wins, Tomé Cecial comments: 'Sepamos, pues, ahora: ¿cuál es más loco: el que lo es por no poder menos, o el que lo es por su voluntad?' 'Cide Hamete' will later make a similar comment on the Duke and Duchess.

As he rides away triumphant from his encounter with *El Caballero de los Espejos*, Don Quixote meets with Don Diego de Miranda, 'un discreto caballero de la Mancha', who stands in everything for the golden mean, and is the embodiment of prudence and rational piety. When Don Quixote describes his calling, the other exclaims with astonishment:

> No me puedo persuadir que haya hoy en la tierra quien favorezca viudas, ampare doncellas, ni honre casadas, ni socorra huérfanos, y no lo creyera si en vuesa merced no lo hubiera visto con mis ojos. (II, xvi)

Don Quixote spoils the effect by challenging a caged lion, which refuses to fight:

> Pero el generoso león, más comedido que arrogante, no haciendo caso de niñerías ni de bravatas, después de haber mirado a una y otra parte, como se ha dicho, volvió las espaldas y enseñó sus traseras partes a Don Quijote, y con gran flema y remanso se volvió a echar en la jaula. (II, xvii)

Don Quixote discourses lucidly on poetry in Don Diego's house. On leaving, he is drawn into a wedding party, where he defends (with manifest justice) the lovers Basilio and Quiteria against the anger of Camacho. Later he sets an example of wisdom and Christian spirit in attempting to reconcile the warring villages, though (through Sancho's folly) he is stoned for his pains. He displays the same mixture of madness and wisdom at the Duke's palace. Though mad—perhaps because he is mad—he is the only person to feel compassion for the wronged daughter of Doña Rodríguez, whose plight is made the occasion of another heartless joke by the Duke.

Sancho is like his master: shrewd and foolish. Though in general the second quality is uppermost, he displays the first in his brief reign as governor of his 'island', where he dispenses justice with an acuteness which astonishes all—except the reader, prepared by earlier hints, like the exchange in II, xii:

> —Cada día, Sancho—dijo don Quijote,—te vas haciendo menos simple y más discreto.
>
> —Sí, que algo se me ha de pegar de la discreción de vuestra merced —respondió Sancho.

Sancho's departure from the 'island' leaves even his tormentors astonished by his dignity.

At last, defeated by *El Caballero de la Blanca Luna*, Don Quixote returns home; returns, in fact, to die. But before he dies he recovers his sanity. Perhaps Cervantes felt it intolerable that a man, even in fiction, should approach death with his wits deranged and so be unable to prepare his soul. Then there is an artistic reason: Don Quixote began sane, and symmetry requires that he end sane. Finally, by this means Cervantes—with whom Avellaneda's spurious second part rankled—effectively prevented any attempt to write another continuation.

So ends Don Quixote, who had been amusing in his madness and instructive in his folly. Perhaps 'el licenciado Vidriera' had been conceived as just such another, but if so Cervantes failed to bring him to life. Don Quixote has much to teach in his lucid moments, but the book remains a comic one. No doubt Cervantes would have agreed with Democritus, the laughing philosopher, who (as Juan Huarte tells in *Examen de ingenios*) explained to Hippocrates why he laughed. Look at men, he says: they wish to rule others and cannot rule themselves; they love and hate; they make war; they kill; they dig the earth for gold . . . how is this different from madness?

> Y concluyendo le dijo que este mundo no era más que una casa de locos, cuya vida era una comedia graciosa representada para hacer reír a los hombres; y que ésta era la causa de que se reía tanto.

For Cervantes too the whole human spectacle seemed more fit for laughter than for tears.

There are undoubtedly other themes in *Don Quixote*. Probably Joaquín Casalduero is right in seeing in the person of Don Quixote a more than half-nostalgic, though ironic, evocation of the heroic past (Spain's and Cervantes's own) which, after reaching its climax for both at Lepanto, now seemed so sadly distant and outmoded in the more sober light of seventeenth-century reality. There may be other themes, though certainly fewer than the sum-total of what the book's exegetes have claimed. But a reader has the right to refuse invitations to pursue an author's intentions into subliminal regions, where monsters lurk, as often as not imaginary.

Both parts of *Don Quixote* were a great success with the reading public, and they went into numerous editions. Translations soon followed. For Cervantes had created the most ingeniously diversified work of entertainment in any of the modern literatures. Don Quixote belonged to a type familiar enough to students of psychopathology, but Cervantes had made him more than a casebook figure. Sancho too was not wholly new; the shrewd and foolish peasant was a familiar figure; even Sancho's stringing together of proverbs is a comic device taken from the sixteenth-century imitations of *La Celestina*. But in sending the two Fools abroad together to amuse, disturb, and question, Cervantes created a book which was not only a masterpiece of entertainment in itself but a pattern for the future European novel.

Don Quixote's success with the public may be judged by the appearance of a spurious second part in 1614, over the name Alonso Fernández de Avellaneda, probably a pseudonym. The author was evidently no friend of Cervantes, whom he castigates and even insults in the prologue. The work is crude in invention and lacks the sparkle of Cervantes. The conception of Don Quixote himself is a very simple one: his madness is unrelieved by wisdom or learning; his adventures mostly knockabout farce; and he ends in a madhouse. Cervantes was sufficiently irritated by the book to criticise it in his own Part II and to send Don Quixote to Barcelona instead of Saragossa to emphasise the falsity of the other 'history'.

When in I, xlvii, the Canon of Toledo denounced the absurdities of the romances of chivalry, he also spoke of the opportunities for variety of invention offered by their conveniently loose form:

> . . . que era el sujeto que ofrecían para que un buen entendimiento pudiese mostrarse en ellos, porque daban largo y espacioso campo por donde sin empacho alguno pudiese correr la pluma, describiendo naufragios, tormentas, rencuentros y batallas, pintando un capitán valeroso con todas las partes que para ser tal se requieren . . .; pintando ora un lamentable y trágico suceso, ahora un alegre y no pesado acontecimiento; allí una hermosísima dama, honesta, discreta y recatada; aquí un caballero cristiano, valiente y comedido; acullá un desaforado bárbaro fanfarrón. . . . Ya puede mostrarse astrólogo, ya cosmógrafo excelente, ya músico, ya inteligente en las materias de estado, y tal vez le vendrá ocasión de mostrarse nigromante, si quisiere. . . .

In this he laid down a literary programme which was fulfilled by Cervantes in his *Persiles y Sigismunda*, a work cast in the mould of the Byzantine novel, and hence concerned above all with love. *Persiles* is set in the far North, and concludes in Rome, having passed through Portugal and Spain. Numerous characters and their stories are interwoven, the whole being stage-managed with considerable skill. Cervantes strains his narrative and inventive talents to their utmost. He never loses sight of his ideal: 'enseñar y deleitar juntamente': for the tale appears to concern man's spiritual pilgrimage, illustrated by a profusion of story and incident exemplary of virtue and depravity.[14] The work is not realistic except to the extent that it deals with real human problems and motives, albeit given an unrealistic setting.

Persiles has intensely interesting moments, but as a whole it is disappointing. It does not fulfil either the hopes or fears of Cervantes for it, expressed in the dedication of *Don Quixote* II: 'el cual ha de ser o el más malo o el mejor que en nuestra lengua se haya compuesto . . .' It is very far from being 'el más malo': it is inventive, entertaining, well-written, and occasionally deeply perceptive; but it is very far from being the best, even if we compare it only with fiction of its own day.

Although *Don Quixote* was widely read, Cervantes exercised greater influence on Spanish literature through his *Novelas ejemplares*, which naturalised the *novella* in Spain. There was a flood of acknowledged and unacknowledged imitations, as well as more direct imitations of the Italian *novellieri*. Lope de Vega tried his hand at the form, and wrote four *novelas*, the first printed in his *La Filomena* (Madrid, 1621) and the remainder in *La Circe* (Madrid, 1624). They were written for Marta de Nevares (here called Marcia Leonarda) in a simple and familiar style (which sometimes smacks of condescension). The plots are very intricate: evidently Lope hoped to eclipse his model; but the intricacy becomes tedious, and the stories can hardly be counted among Lope's most inspired works. Alonso Jerónimo de Salas Barbadillo published several collections of stories, such as *Casa del placer honesto* (Madrid, 1620), the first Spanish imitation of the *Decameron*. Juan Cortés de Tolosa published *Lazarillo de Manzanares, con otras cinco novelas* (Madrid, 1620). Among other collections were: Juan Pérez de Montalbán, *Sucesos y prodigios de amor en ocho novelas ejemplares* (Madrid, 1624); José Camerino, *Novelas amorosas* (Madrid, 1624); Doña María de Zayas y Sotomayor, *Novelas amorosas y ejemplares* (Saragossa, 1637) and *Desengaños amorosos* (Barcelona, 1647). Tirso de Molina had embodied *novelas* in his intricate miscellany *Cigarrales de Toledo* (Madrid, 1621), and included several religious *novelas* in his *Deleitar aprovechando* (Madrid, 1635). Gonzalo Céspedes y Meneses (1585?-1638) strove for novelty in his *Historias peregrinas y ejemplares* (Saragossa, 1623) by setting each story in a different city of Spain, of which he gives a brief account. He wrote also a long tale of amorous adventure and misadventure, *Poema trágico del español Gerardo, y desengaño del amor lascivo* (Part I, Madrid, 1615; Parts I and II, Barcelona, 1618), and *Varia fortuna del soldado Píndaro* (Lisbon, 1626). Alonso de Castillo Solórzano (1584-1648), undoubtedly the most prolific writer of fiction in seventeenth-century Spain, published numerous volumes of *novelas*. The stories are set in a *Decameron*-like framework, as is clear from the very titles of the collections, such as (for example): *Tardes entretenidas* (Madrid, 1625); *Jornadas alegres* (Madrid, 1626); *Noches de placer* (Barcelona, 1631); *Fiestas del jardín* (Valencia, 1634). He also composed longer narratives (apart from the picaresque novels already touched on). His work—like most seventeenth-century fiction after Cervantes—is escapist. The so-called *novela cortesana* is an endless set of variations on one theme, amorous intrigue of the most vapid kind. The decline of fiction into triviality is a reflection of the society for which it was written: a society declining into irresponsibility and frivolity, though clinging ever more tenaciously to social appearances and ceremonies, including a more and more hollow sense of honour.

One work of fiction remains to be discussed here: Lope de Vega's *La Dorotea* (Madrid, 1632). It is not a novel (Lope called it an *acción en prosa*): it is in dialogue, and divided into five acts, each of which ends with a *Coro*, a versified moral comment on the action. The form of the work is inspired by *La Celestina*. Its content is autobiographical: Lope's youthful love-affair with Elena Osorio. Though Lope alleged that he wrote it 'en mis primeros años', the *Dorotea* we have is manifestly a work of Lope's last years. What is true is that Lope had been obsessed for half a century with memories of Elena Osorio (and no doubt his own unattractive role in the affair).

Whatever its autobiographical basis, *La Dorotea* matters now as a work of art, not history. It tells how the beautiful Dorotea, who loves and is loved by the penniless and egotistic young poet Fernando, is pushed by her mother and her Celestina-like friend Gerarda into the arms of the rich *indiano* Don Bela. Dorotea is abandoned by Fernando, and she loses Don Bela, who is murdered. The theme of the work is the hollowness of earthly pleasures and hopes. As the last Coro expresses it:

> todo deleite es dolor,
> y todo placer tormento.

But the moral is not what gives *La Dorotea* its value. Lope, passing judgment on himself, wrote in so doing a profoundly compassionate and moving study of human motivation and self-deception. The lovers, caught up in a dream of love and attempting to live as if life were literature, invite disenchantment. Though Lope's compassion embraces all the characters, his deepest feelings are reserved for Dorotea, and it is she whose portrayal is the most moving.

Given his choice of form, Lope has to convey in dialogue everything that a novelist would put in description and commentary: action, character, his own attitude to his characters, etc. Since everything has to be explained in endless talk, there are inevitable *longueurs*, but in spite of that *La Dorotea* is unquestionably one of the masterpieces of its time. But equally unquestionably a flawed work, marred by the pedantries and irrelevance which Lope was never able to keep out of his writing for long.

NOTES

1. In addition to the works listed in the Bibliography see: Jennifer Lowe, 'The *Cuestión de amor* and the structure of Cervantes' *Galatea*', *BHS*, XLIII (1966), 98-108.

2. See, for example, Jennifer Lowe, 'The structure of Cervantes' *La española inglesa*', *RN*, IX (1968), 1-4.

3. In the manuscript Leonora is actually seduced. The explanation of Cervantes's second thought given by Casalduero in *Sentido y forma de las Novelas ejemplares* (Buenos Aires, 1943) is the most satisfying.

4. Sir Thomas Kendrick, *St James in Spain* (London, 1960), p. 93. The whole account is instructive. Clearly life improved on art. Nothing in Cervantes excels in robust humour some of the incidents recounted by Kendrick.

5. See Bataillon, op. cit., II. But A. G. de Amezúa expresses disagreement in his *Cervantes, creador de la novela corta española* (Madrid, 1956), pp. 139-99.

6. In *De Cervantes y Lope de Vega* (Madrid, 1940) R. Menéndez Pidal suggests that the conception of Don Quixote was inspired by an *Entremés de los romances* (*c.* 1591) in which a simple peasant goes out of his mind after reading too many *romances*.

7. F. Rodríguez Marín, *Estudios cervantinos* (Madrid, 1947), pp. 373-9.

8. See P. E. Russell, ' "Don Quixote" as a funny book', *MLR*, 64 (1969), 312-26, one of the most illuminating pieces ever written on the book.

9. There are critics who discuss *Don Quixote* in terms more appropriate to an epistemological treatise. Cervantes has a curiously extinctive effect on the sense of humour of most of his critics.

10. See M. de Iriarte, *El doctor Huarte de San Juan* . . . (Madrid, 1939).

11. See Enid Welsford, *The Fool, His Social and Literary History* (London, 1935). There are interesting (though sometimes strained) general reflections on folly in W. Willeford, *The Fool and his Sceptre* (London, 1969).

12. I quote from the Chaloner translation of 1549.

13. For the important concept of *discreción* see M. J. Bates, *'Discreción' in the Works of Cervantes: A Semantic Study* (Washington, 1945).

14. See J. Casalduero, *Sentido y forma de 'Los trabajos de Persiles y Sigismunda'* (Buenos Aires, 1947), and also Jennifer Lowe, 'Themes and structure in Cervantes' *Persiles y Sigismunda*', *FMLS*, III (1967), 334-51.

Chapter 9

MORALISTS AND SATIRISTS

WITHIN CERTAIN DOCTRINAL LIMITS the sixteenth century was in Spain a period of considerable intellectual ebullience, and this persisted into the early seventeenth century. A number of distinctive contributions were made to European thought. Juan de Valdés left a mark for a time on the religious life of Italy; Juan Luis Vives left a more enduring mark on European thought in several fields. Dr Juan Huarte brought the traditional psychological theories based on Galen's classification of the humours to an original application in his *Examen de ingenios para las ciencias* (Baeza, 1575),[1] which circulated widely in its French, English, and Italian translations. The sixteenth-century Spanish Thomist revival had important repercussions. Vitoria gave an important impetus to the development of a concept of international law. The Jesuit Francisco Suárez (1548-1617), 'el único gran filósofo escolástico después de Ockam',[2] made a significant contribution to European philosophy in his *Disputationes metaphysicae* (1609), in which he addressed himself to the task of synthesising a system of metaphysics (carefully distinguished from theology) based on Aristotle interpreted in the light of scholastic tradition. The *Disputationes*, an important work of philosophy in their own right, were widely studied in European universities in the seventeenth and eighteenth centuries. To turn to more local matters: the active and frequently highly original analysis of economics which began in the sixteenth century continued into the seventeenth, and the host of *arbitristas* who proposed a variety of solutions, some fantastic, for the social and economic problems of Spain included men of outstanding ability.

The picture changed as the seventeenth century advanced. Although in fields other than theology and allied matters there was no formal discouragement to free speculation, there was a general self-limitation, a refusal to go beyond familiar horizons. And those horizons began to close in. Intellectual curiosity declined, or narrowed its field. The new scientific and philosophical explorations of seventeenth-century Europe passed Spain by. There is little sign in the literature of the period that among Spaniards interest in these fields extended beyond received ideas. In spite of its artistic brilliance, in the realm of intellect it was not for Spain an age of novelty but of restatement and redefinition of the orthodox. Spain had closed in on herself.[3]

Within those narrowed limits, however, the educated élite were cultivated enough. They were well grounded in classical literature, with which the *culto* writing of the time takes for granted an easy familiarity. The study of history—a gentlemanly pursuit—engaged the interest of many. In all this a man like José Pellicer de Salas Ossau y Tovar (1602-79) acquires in retrospect the air of a representative figure—'el siglo XVII hecho hombre' as he has been called. His classical learning is displayed in his commentary on the works of Góngora. His wide and miscellaneous historical lore is manifested in his genealogical and other works, which show, however, more the spirit of an antiquarian than of a historian, and one not over-critical (or even over-scrupulous) in his attitude to evidence. The more serious side of seventeenth-century learning is seen at its best in the Sevillian Nicolás Antonio (1617-84), whose two large bibliographies—*Bibliotheca hispana vetus* (listing works by Spanish writers from ancient times to 1500) and *Bibliotheca hispana nova* (works from 1500 to 1670) (Rome, 1672 and 1696)—are monuments to an honest erudition displayed in a different way in his *Censura de historias fabulosas* (Valencia, 1742), which destroyed the authority of the false chronicles fabricated earlier in the century by the Jesuit Jerónimo Román de la Higuera and others.[4]

Another aspect of the literary culture of the period stands impressively displayed in the dictionary of the Spanish language compiled by Sebastián de Covarrubias y Orozco (1539-1613): *Tesoro de la lengua castellana o española* (Madrid, 1611), justly characterised by the humanist Pedro de Valencia[5] in his *censura* as 'lleno de varia y curiosa lección y doctrina'. It is unsystematic and its etymologies usually suspect, but it is still an invaluable work of reference. A similar concern with the language led Gonzalo de Correas, a professor at Salamanca, to compile his *Vocabulario de refranes y frases proverbiales y otras fórmulas comunes de la lengua castellana* (finished in 1627 but first printed in 1906), a gold-mine of idiom and proverb. He also composed a grammar, *Arte de la lengua española castellana* (dated 1625; first printed complete in 1954). In addition he wrote a short treatise on orthographic reform.

Though the genius of Francisco de Quevedo was too great and too individual for him to be regarded as a representative figure, his themes and attitudes, both as moralist and satirist, are characteristic of his time. Most of his writings are moral or devotional. A typical example is *La cuna y la sepultura para el conocimiento propio y desengaño de las cosas ajenas* (Madrid, 1634) which, as its title adequately indicates, is a homily to remind man to take timely heed of the fugacity of life and the need to prepare for death. Some Stoic ideas may be detectable in the book. Quevedo was strongly drawn to the Neo-Stoic movement born in sixteenth-century Europe; he even exchanged a few letters in 1604-05 with the acknowledged leader of the movement, the great Flemish scholar Justus Lipsius of the University of Louvain. Quevedo's attraction to Stoicism, evident in a great part of his work, is explicit in his translation of Epictetus, to which is appended *Nombre, origen, intento, recomendación y descendencia de la doctrina estoica* (Madrid, 1635). For Quevedo Stoicism fell short of perfection only in that its proponents lacked the Christian revelation: 'No saliera defectuosa la doctrina de nuestros estoicos si como Epícteto la escribió a la luz de su pobre candil la hubiera estudiado a los rayos puros de la vida y palabras de Jesucristo Nuestro Señor' ('Carta a un amigo'). Although as a Christian he was obliged to reject *apathia*—the cultivation of insensibility to things outside oneself—Stoic doctrine was clearly congenial to Quevedo: its harsh asceticism chimed with the undertone of misanthropy in his character and his general suspicion of the world.[6]

Quevedo was an avidly-read author. For a time at least, one of his most widely-read works was *Política de Dios, gobierno de Cristo* (Part I, Madrid, 1626; Part II, Madrid, 1655), a work on Christian statecraft whose first part (begun *c.* 1617) is addressed to Philip IV and the second (written 1634-39) to the Pope, Urban VIII. Part I was reprinted more often in its first year than any other Spanish book of its time: nine editions appeared in 1626. The work was evidently felt to have an urgent relevance. It is in fact a thinly veiled commentary on the reign of Philip III, whose ineptitude and infirmity of purpose Quevedo had had ample opportunity to observe. Treatises on kingship commonly appealed to Christian principles for general guidance; Quevedo boldly took the life of Christ himself as an example to set before the new king. He starts from the premise that Christ was king: the only true king in that he alone devoted himself wholly to his people, and in being free from sin and tyranny of the passions.

> No admitió lisonjas de los poderosos, como se lee en el Príncipe que le dijo *Magister bone*, ni se retiró en la Majestad a los ruegos y a los necesitados, ni atendió a cosa que fuese su descanso o su comodidad; toda su vida y su persona fatigó por el bien de los otros; ... Cristo solo supo ser Rey, y así sólo lo sabrá ser quien le imitare.[7]

Quevedo takes quotations from the Bible and forms from them a pattern of just and vigilant government to offer the king. Some qualities of Christ as king have a straightforward application; others Quevedo applies in a metaphorical sense. He recounts (for example) how Christ felt someone touch his garment, and then applies the lesson:

> El buen Rey, Señor, ha de cuidar no sólo de su reino y de su familia,

> mas de su vestido y de su sombra, y no ha de contentarse con tener este cuidado: ha de hacer que los que le sirven y están a su lado y sus enemigos vean que le tiene . . . El ocio y la inclinación no ha de dar parte a otro en sus cuidados . . . Quien divierte al Rey le depone, no le sirve. (pp. 56-7)

This is very pointed: neither Philip III nor his son played much part in government: both handed over responsibility to their *privados*, whose intermediacy surrounded the king with an invisible wall. Quevedo harps constantly on the king's duty to make himself accessible. Commenting on the text 'Suffer little children to come unto me' he writes:

> El Rey es persona pública, su Corona son las necesidades de su reino, el reinar no es entretenimiento sino tarea; mal Rey el que goza sus estados, y bueno el que los sirve. Rey que se esconde a las quejas, y que tiene porteros para los agraviados y no para quien los agravia, ése retírase de su oficio y obligación, y cree que los ojos de Dios no entran en su retiramiento, y está de par en par a la perdición y al castigo del Señor, de quien no quiere aprender a ser Rey. (p. 100)

Quevedo's metaphorical application of Scripture is sometimes ingenious. Of Christ's miracles of healing he writes:

> Verdad es que no podéis, Señor, obrar aquellos milagros; mas también lo es que podéis imitar sus efectos. Obligado estáis a la imitación de Cristo.
>
> Si os descubrís donde os vea el que no dejan que pueda veros, ¿no le dais vista? Si dais entrada al que necesitando della se la negaban, ¿no le dais pies y pasos? (p. 165)

Política de Dios is not a theoretical work but one addressed to reform. However, it may be that the choice of a model impossible of attainment expressed, beneath the energy of the writing, an invincible despair of the possibility of change.

Most treatises on kingship and statecraft—a genre abundantly represented in Spain—struck a different note in that they attempted to reconcile principle and necessity. Next to Quevedo's, the finest example in seventeenth-century Spain is unquestionably *Idea de un príncipe político cristiano* (Munich, 1640) by Diego Saavedra Fajardo (1584-1648), nobleman and diplomat. He was also the author of (amongst other works) a history of the Goths, *Corona gótica, castellana y austríaca* (Munster, 1646), and *República literaria* (Madrid, 1655), a witty survey of the republic of letters, ancient and modern, provoked by the spectacle of the ever-growing sea of print.

The *Idea* is in the form of 101 *empresas* or symbolic devices, each accompanied by a commentary, whose purpose is 'criar un príncipe desde la cuna hasta la tumba' (p. 172).[8] Saavedra, being concerned with the realities of politics and diplomacy, and recognising that prudence in a ruler means guile as well as goodness, attempts to chart a course between principle and opportunism. A prince (he affirms) must learn to separate public and private roles, to play a part.

> Entonces más es el príncipe una idea de gobernador que hombre; más de todos que suyo. . . . Los particulares se gobiernan a su modo; los príncipes según la conveniencia común. En los particulares es doblez disimular las pasiones; en los príncipes, razón de estado. (p. 199)

Policy may thus lead at times to dissimulation, but only when it cannot discredit the prince's majesty. Saavedra concedes that it is permissible to dissemble the truth, but not to suggest a falsehood (except perhaps to make an interrogation more effective; p. 492); for though a prince must strive for glory, it must be the enduring glory that is grounded in virtue.

> No hay fiera más peligrosa que un príncipe a quien ni remuerde la conciencia ni incita la gloria; pero también peligra la reputación y el Estado en la gloria; porque su esplendor suele cegar a los príncipes y da con ellos en la temeridad. . . . Ponen los ojos en altas empresas, lisonjeados de sus ministros con lo glorioso, sin advertilles la injusticia o inconvenientes de los medios; y hallándose después empeñados, se pierden. (p. 239)

In all this, Saavedra is perfectly orthodox. His treatise may be regarded as a Christian reply to Machiavelli.

The work is written with luminous intelligence, but as doctrine it has (after all) no radical novelty. Its value to modern readers lies not in what it teaches but in its exhibition of an intelligence engaged in discourse: in the widest sense, its style. Saavedra prided himself both on the book's ingenuity of form and on its style. Of the latter he writes:

> Con estudio particular he procurado que el estilo sea levantado sin afectación, y breve sin oscuridad; empresa que a Horacio pareció dificultosa, y que no la he visto intentada en nuestra lengua castellana. (p. 168)

His style is admirable: lucid, pithy, and energetic. These qualities may be seen in this characteristic passage:

> Dudoso es el curso de la culebra, torciéndose a una parte y otra con tal incertidumbre que aun su mismo cuerpo no sabe por dónde la ha de llevar la cabeza; señala el movimiento a una parte, y le hace

a la contraria, sin que dejen huellas sus pasos ni se conozca la intención de su viaje. Así ocultos han de ser los consejos y desinios de los príncipes. (p. 370)

Saavedra's style inclines to the epigrammatic, in imitation of the Senecan style which in the seventeenth century displaced the more leisurely Ciceronian as a model.[9]

* * *

The seventeenth century's intense preoccupation with the backslidings of erring mankind turned easily to satire, in which Spain is rich. Since there was a general disposition to stop short of radical novelty, criticism of society necessarily took the form of an attack on contemporary behaviour rather than the postulation of an alternative social model. There are no Spanish *Utopias*, since these are essentially products of a freely-questioning mind. Dissatisfaction with society in seventeenth-century Spain ran off therefore into the channels of homily and satire.

We are given a particularly interesting picture of Spanish society, especially of its follies and vices, in *El pasajero* (Madrid, 1617) by Cristóbal Suárez de Figueroa (1571?-1639?), author of a number of works of very varied character, among them a translation of Guarini's *Pastor fido* (Valencia, 1609); *La constante Amarilis* (Valencia, 1609), a pastoral novel; *España defendida* (Madrid, 1612), an epic on Bernardo del Carpio; *Plaza universal de todas las ciencias y artes* (Madrid, 1615), largely a translation from the Italian. *El pasajero,* written in the form of conversations between four travellers going from Madrid to Barcelona and Italy, is an improving miscellany which ranges over a great variety of subjects. Much of the book is satirical in character. Suárez de Figueroa ridicules the craving for *hidalguía*, foppery, presumption, and a host of other follies great and small. Among his targets are the new drama and *culteranismo*. The book's elastic frame embraces a picaresque *novela* and some good verse (including an excellent *romance* on the bucolic life). In his prologue the author gives it as his purpose to bring his readers to *desengaño* and knowledge of themselves, in order to effect 'alguna reformación de costumbres'. Whatever his success in this, he produced a most readable portrait of his times.

Some years later Antonio Liñán y Verdugo published his *Guía y avisos de forasteros que vienen a la corte* (Madrid, 1620), in which three interlocutors discuss the perils of the capital, illustrating their homilies by means of exemplary *novelas*. Though far from sparkling the book is interesting in a sober way. A similar intention inspired Baptista Remiro de Navarra's more frothy *Los peligros de Madrid* (Saragossa, 1646). In the same line of descent came Juan de Zabaleta's *El día de fiesta por la mañana* (Madrid, 1654) and *El día de fiesta por la tarde*

(Madrid, 1660), both of them mingling the satirical with the picturesque, the latter constantly threatening to gain the upper hand. Francisco Santos, a prolific writer of satire, continued the line with his *Día y noche de Madrid* (Madrid, 1663), a general satire on Madrid life and manners cast in a loosely novelesque form.

Quevedo's *Sueños* are among the most brilliant and are certainly the most inventive satires of the seventeenth century. In the main the *Sueños* proper were early works. *El sueño del juicio final* and *El alguacil endemoniado* date from 1607, *El sueño del infierno* from 1608, *El mundo por de dentro* from 1612. *El sueño de la muerte* was written in 1621-22. The five were published as *Sueños y discursos descubridores de abusos, vicios y engaños en todos los oficios y estados del mundo* (Barcelona, 1627), at once reprinted under a new title (Saragossa, 1627), and reissued as *Juguetes de la niñez y travesuras del ingenio* (Madrid, 1629), this time considerably altered under pressure from the censors of the Inquisition: amongst other changes references to Christian figures and institutions were removed (God becomes Jupiter, etc.), and the titles of the first three and last changed to *El sueño de las calaveras, El alguacil alguacilado, Las zahurdas de Plutón,* and *Vista de los chistes*. Other lighter pieces were added to fill out the volume.

The *Sueños* have no plan: each is a freely-evolving fantasy providing a panorama of a variety of social types and misdeeds. *El sueño del juicio final* describes the awakening of the dead at the last trumpet. All Quevedo's favourite butts—among them women, doctors, tailors, innkeepers—are seen going to judgment. The work is grounded in *agudeza*: otherwise commonplace points are made keener by unexpected strokes of wit. Some Genoese merchants arrive and ask for *asientos* ('seats' and 'contracts'). A devil comments: '¿Aun con nosotros piensan ganar en ellos? Pues esto es lo que les mata. Esta vez han dado mala cuenta, y no hay donde se asienten, porque ha quebrado el banco de su crédito'. The play on *asientos*, *cuenta*, and *banco* is ingenious but not profound. The next incident shows Quevedo's wit to better advantage. A dandified and ceremonious *caballero* arrives. 'Preguntáronle qué pretendía, y respondió: Ser salvado'. He wishes to be saved, but *salvado* is also 'bran', a fitting reply from one who is all husk and no substance. 'Y fue remitido a los diablos para que le moliesen ['grind' and 'beat']; y él sólo reparó en que le ajarían el cuello'. Each of these two short incidents is complete in itself; each is an extended conceit developed from an initial pun. All the *Sueños* are similar structureless successions of strokes of wit. According to the devil by whom the *alguacil* is possessed in *El alguacil endemoniado* the damned are sorted by witty analogy: a blind man is put among lovers, a murderer among doctors, and 'los mercaderes que se condenan por vender están con Judas'. *El sueño del infierno*, longer and more complex, follows the same free development. On two occasions this *Sueño* plumbs deeper depths of seriousness than any of the others. The first is when Quevedo encounters a man tormented not by devils but by his understanding, memory, and will: a scene poignantly presented. The other is when a devil ridicules the pretensions of a vanity-ridden *hidalgo*, pouring scorn on his empty notion of honour. The climax of the devil's harangue shows Quevedo's gift for disconcerting bathos at its most pungent.

> ¿Pues qué diré de la honra? Que más tiranías hace en el mundo y más daños, y la que más gustos estorba. Muere de hambre un caballero pobre, no tiene con qué vestirse, ándase roto y remendado, u da en ladrón; y no lo pide, porque dice que tiene honra; ni quiere servir, porque dice que es deshonra. . . . Por la honra se muere la viuda entre dos paredes. Por la honra, sin saber qué es hombre ni qué es gusto, se pasa la doncella treinta años casada consigo misma. . . . Y porque veáis cuáles sois los hombres de desgraciados y cuán a peligro tenéis lo que más estimáis, hase de advertir que las cosas de más valor en vosotros son la honra, la vida y la hacienda; y la honra está junto al culo de las mujeres, la vida en manos de los dotores y la hacienda en las plumas de los escribanos.

In *El mundo por de dentro* Quevedo is conducted along the street of Hypocrisy by an old man, *Desengaño*, who reveals people and things as they really are. In *El sueño de la muerte* we are shown Death herself holding court. Among those who come before her are the originals of a number of proverbial names or catch-phrases: Juan del Encina, *el rey que rabió*, and others. The *jeu d'esprit* is ingenious but of little depth. The last is, in fact, the most frivolous of the *Sueños*, as if Quevedo had at last been carried away by the exuberance of his fancy, always a danger he had manifestly found hard to resist.

Discurso de todos los diablos, o infierno emendado (Gerona, 1628) is another work of a similar kind, and Quevedo returned to the genre with *La hora de todos y la Fortuna con seso* (according to Quevedo's dedication of 1636, but printed as *La Fortuna con seso y la hora de todos*, Saragossa, 1650). This is the profoundest of the series. Quevedo characterises it well in his dedication: 'El tratadillo, burla burlando, es de veras. Tiene cosas de las cosquillas, pues hace reír con enfado y desesperación.' It is the bitter humour of a moralist exasperated by the universal spectacle of hypocrisy and self-seeking. 'Universal' indeed: the mood is established by the classical gods with whose description the work opens. Jupiter and the rest are jumped-up ruffians whose speech is the low jargon of criminals and whores. If burlesque of classical mythology were not such a fashionable device at the time[10] it would be tempting to see in the gods an oblique comment on the degradation of values glaringly manifest in the ruling caste from the slothful and licentious Philip IV down. The theme of the work is that Fortune, at Jupiter's command, gives all men their deserts at four o'clock on 20 June. Upon the hour justice is done and frauds exposed. Some incidents are simple: a prisoner being flogged through the streets suddenly changes places with his tormentor; a *casamentero* finds himself married to the ill-favoured woman he had tried to palm off on another. Even in some of these, chains of elaborate conceits lead into unsuspected depths of seriousness.[11] Quevedo goes on to survey the scene of international politics and, in the section called *La isla de los Monopantos*, the machinations of Olivares and his party.[12] Finally, we are shown a general assembly of the subjects of all lands met together to discuss their grievances. The assembly breaks up in uproarious discord. Jupiter concludes that men are incapable of reform: 'El abatimiento y la miseria los encoge, no los enmienda; la honra y la prosperidad los hace hacer lo que, si las hubieran alcanzado, siempre hubieran hecho'; whereupon he commands Fortune to revert to her former ways. In this work Quevedo reveals himself as conservative even for a conservative age. He ridicules all aspiration for change: for example, the reasonable plea for some emancipation of women (XL). His distrust and contempt for anything which threatened the archaic values he embraced are expressed in no. XXXI, in which a Spanish soldier on his way to Flanders first upbraids and then assaults some French merchants entering Spain. Whatever one's view of his ideas, however, no one can reasonably dispute that Quevedo's disciplined virtuosity of imagination makes this one of the masterpieces of the Spanish language.[13]

The high-spirited fantasy and linguistic ebullience of these works inspired other satirical fantasies, among them Rodrigo Fernández de Ribera's *Los anteojos de mejor vista* (Seville, n.d., but *c.* 1630), in which the author encounters at the top of the Giralda a certain Licenciado Desengaños whose glasses show men as they really are. The same author's *El mesón del mundo* (Madrid, 1631)—a series of satirical and picaresque sketches set in the Inn of the World—may also owe something to Quevedo. The most noteworthy satirical fantasy after Quevedo's is *El diablo cojuelo* (Madrid, 1641) by Luis Vélez de Guevara (1579-1644), who was also a prolific dramatist. *El diablo cojuelo* is a rambling story which gives a satirical panorama of Spanish life in the course of recounting the adventures of Don Cleofás Leandro Pérez Zambullo and his confederate, the lame devil. The book is written with a sustained witty *éclat*, of which the description of Don Cleofás's midnight escape over the rooftops from the officers of justice pursuing him on a false charge of rape provides a good example:

> . . . no dificultó arrojarse desde el ala del susodicho tejado, como si las tuviera, a la buharda de otro que estaba confinante, nordesteando de una luz que por ella escasamente se brujuleaba, estrella de la tormenta que corría, en cuyo desván puso los pies y la boca a un mismo tiempo, saludándolo como a puerto de tales naufragios . . .

However, brilliant though the book is in style, its contents are the banalities of seventeenth-century satire, and the work as a whole must be judged superficial. But its brilliance made it popular; it was several times reprinted, translated into several languages, and adapted by Lesage as *Le diable boiteux.*

Among other satirical fantasies may be noted *El Arca de Noé y campana de Belilla* (Saragossa, 1697) by Francisco Santos, a laboriously contrived and heavy-handed book.

Among the most agile minds of his time was that of Baltasar Gracián, one of the most interesting writers—though also one of the narrowest in range—of the Spanish seventeenth century. He was born at Belmonte, near Calatayud, in 1601. In 1619 he entered the Jesuit Order, and studied successively at Tarragona, Calatayud, and Saragossa. He was ordained in 1627. After some years in Valencia, Lérida, and Gandía he was sent to the Jesuit College at Huesca. There he came to know and enjoy the friendship of Don Vincencio Juan de Lastanosa, an erudite nobleman of cultivated tastes whose house in Huesca contained an excellent library and an extensive collection of works of art, antiquities, and natural curiosities of all kinds. Stimulated by intellectual companionship, Gracián published in Huesca his first book, *El héroe* (1637). This and a number of his later works were published under the patronage of Lastanosa. In 1640 Gracián left Huesca for Saragossa. Though until his disgrace his later career in his order was a relatively distinguished one, for the rest of his life he looked on Huesca, and Lastanosa's house in it, as his spiritual home.

Gracián's was not an easy nature. Early in his career there was friction between him and his colleagues. When he began to publish he did so under the pseudonym Lorenzo Gracián, and without the permission of his superiors. A blind eye was turned, even when he went on to publish *El político don Fernando el Católico* (Saragossa, 1640); *Arte de ingenio* (Madrid, 1642), its revised version retitled *Agudeza y arte de ingenio* (Huesca, 1648); *El discreto* (Huesca, 1646); and *Oráculo manual* (Huesca, 1647) in the same way. However, when in spite of warnings he proceeded to bring out the three parts of *El Criticón* (Saragossa, 1651; Huesca, 1653; Madrid, 1657) without permission and under the old pseudonym—though, perhaps hoping to mollify his superiors, he carefully submitted his devotional work *El comulgatorio* for approval before publishing it in 1655 (Saragossa)—he was severely reprimanded, deprived of his Chair of Scripture, and sent to do penance in Graus in 1658. Though his later transfer to Tarazona meant some degree of rehabilitation, his disgust was such that he sought to leave the order. Permission was refused. He died in December 1658.

Gracián's persistence in disobedience, in defiance of his vows, was doubtless an expression of inordinate pride. It has been suggested that (the Aragonese province of the order being intellectually poverty-stricken) he was unwilling to submit his works to the censorship of colleagues whom he despised.[14]

Gracián's life helps us to understand his books. The importance he attached to superiority of mind and the display of it; to the need for incessant watchfulness, even distrust; to manoeuvre and calculation—all this reflects the loneliness of a man of unusual gifts lost in what he considered a cultural desert, subordinate to men whose minds he could not admire, chafing against the narrowness of provincial life. Huesca was an oasis, where he could escape from mediocrity and mingle with men of his own sort.

Gracián declares in the prologue to *El héroe* his purpose in writing the book:

> ¡Que singular te deseo! Emprendo formar con un libro enano un varón gigante, y con breves períodos, inmortales hechos; sacar un varón máximo, esto es milagro en perfección; y, ya que no por naturaleza, rey por sus prendas, que es ventaja.[15]

His recipe for greatness is set out pithily in twenty short chapters (or *primores*: 'excellences'). The first emphasises the need to dissemble one's true powers: 'Excuse a todos el varón culto sondarle el fondo a su caudal, si quiere que le veneren todos. Formidable fue un río hasta que se le halló vado, y venerado un varón hasta que se le conoció término a su capacidad' (p. 7). Or, as he puts it later: '¡Oh, varón candidado de la fama! Tú, que aspiras a la grandeza, alerta al primor: Todos te conozcan, ninguno te abarque' (p. 8). The aspirant must gain and preserve an ascendancy over other men. He will need intelligence, nimbleness of mind, and fastidious taste; but excellence is not enough: it must be displayed: 'Empleo plausible llamo aquel que se ejecuta a vista de todos y a gusto de todos . . .' (p. 19). Perhaps the hero's greatest gift is good fortune: 'Gran prenda es ser varón afortunado . . .' (p. 20). The hero must have *despejo* (an effortless grace): 'Consiste en una cierta airosidad, en una indecible gallardía, tanto en el decir como en el hacer, hasta en el discurrir' (p. 25). He must have 'un señorío innato, una secreta fuerza de imperio' (p. 26), and that 'simpatía sublime' which wins men to one's cause. The final *primor*, and the chief, is virtue.

Gracián's next book, *El político don Fernando*, is a eulogy of Ferdinand of Aragon, praised for his sagacity, decision, and energy.

Ferdinand—for Gracián an embodiment of the qualities set out in *El héroe*, and a silent contrast with Philip IV, to whom that work had been dedicated in its manuscript version—was also one of the princes admired by Machiavelli, to whom this book, like other Spanish works on statecraft, is probably intended as a Christian reply; though between Machiavelli and Gracián there is more than one point of similarity in temperament and outlook.

El discreto is directed to the same general end as *El héroe* (though written in a more varied form): to instruct in successful living. Gracián returned yet again to the theme in his *Oráculo manual y arte de prudencia*, written in the form of three hundred commented aphorisms into which is distilled the essence of his previous works of the kind. It is the most brilliant of the series.

The book teaches prudent management of one's affairs so as to achieve success, which appears to be measured in exclusively social terms. Life is represented as a tacit struggle for influence and esteem. Gracián is much concerned with appearances, since these are important in that struggle.

Gracián believed that in his day the arts of living had reached a higher pitch than ever before, so that now more was required of a man than formerly: '*Todo está ya en su punto, y el ser persona en el mayor.* Más se requiere hoy para un sabio que antiguamente para siete' (1).[16] One pursuing success must arouse expectation, wonder, admiration; and he must keep his own counsel. Other men must be kept on a string, for the expectant are more submissive than the satisfied: '*Hacer depender.* . . . Más se saca de la dependencia que de la cortesía; vuelve luego las espaldas a la fuente el satisfecho, y la naranja exprimida cae del oro al lodo' (5). However, one must be careful not to overreach oneself: to dazzle inferiors is useful, to outdo superiors is merely stupid: '*Excusar victorias del patrón.* Todo vencimiento es odioso, y del dueño o necio o fatal' (7). Life is a war which requires stratagems and cunning: '*Obrar de intención, ya segunda y ya primera.* Milicia es la vida del hombre contra la malicia del hombre' (13). Wiliness is needed, even duplicity; and just as one must reveal nothing of one's own mind to other men, another's weakness must be sought out to use to one's own advantage: '*Hallarle su torcedor a cado uno.* Es el arte de mover voluntades' (26).

A prudent man will not get entangled in the misfortunes of others: '*Conocer los afortunados para la elección, y los desdichados para la fuga.* . . . La mejor treta del juego es saberse descartar: más importa la menor carta del triunfo que corre, que la mayor del que pasó' (31). Related to this injunction is another: '*Nunca por la compasión del infeliz se ha de incurrir en la desgracia del afortunado*' (163). The rejection of a quixotic compassion is no doubt excellent good sense, at least in the world of affairs, but together with it goes a more ordinary virtue, pity. A similar social *Realpolitik* informs many other aphorisms: for example, '*Saberse excusar pesares*' (64), which teaches a ruthless allegiance to self. Appearances are important in this world of manoeuvre: '*Todo lo favorable, obrarlo por sí; todo lo odioso, por terceros*' (187).

The book is not (of course) a treatise on morality: its subject is the prudent management of affairs, and in this opportunism must have a place. Gracián is concerned less with ends than with means. But successful manoeuvre can be directed as much to a good end as to a bad one, and there is nothing intrinsically wrong with the baldly opportunistic advice '*Entrar con la ajena para salir con la suya*' (144). Indeed, some of his aphorisms are misleading in that a bold injunction is sometimes tempered in the ensuing commentary. '*Sentir con los menos y hablar con los más*' (43 is quietly qualified; and so is '*Antes loco con todos que cuerdo a solas*' (133), on which Gracián comments:

> Hase de vivir con otros, y los ignorantes son los más. Para vivir a solas, ha de tener, o mucho de Dios, o todo de bestia. Mas yo moderaría el aforismo diciendo: 'Antes cuerdo con los más, que loco a solas'. . .

What Gracián seems here to be saying is that only by being social is rightmindedness preserved: the solitary and the wilfully singular fall into eccentricity. This is the theme of '*No condenar solo lo que a muchos agrada*' (270), not an injunction to hypocrisy but a warning against crankiness.[17]

This is a worldly book, but it concludes: '*En una palabra, santo, que es decirlo todo de una vez*' (300). This may seem to modern readers an abrupt change of direction, but it did not in Gracián's day. The book's subject is worldly prudence; the divine is taken for granted.

Much of the advice Gracián gives is wise by any standards: appearances are important, the ability to win approval is a merit in a good cause, excessive guilelessness can be a defect, the golden mean is a worthy ideal; but there is a chilly calculation in Gracián which dismays. We belong to a different tradition, one which values spontaneity more than did our ancestors. For Gracián Nature had to be improved by Art: '*Naturaleza y arte, materia y obra*' (12). And he is right; but from art to artfulness is a dangerously short step.

The book is written, like all Gracián's works, in a style which is terse, pithy, constructed in short phrases with much use of antithesis: Senecan, in short. An *aprobación* written by Don Manuel de Salinas for *El discreto* describes it well: 'El estilo es lacónico, y tan divinizado, que a fuer de lo más sacro, tiene hasta en la puntuación misterios'.

Agudeza y arte de ingenio is an anatomy of Wit, the most comprehensive in Spanish.[18] Gracián writes with feeling of what lay close to his heart: 'Es la agudeza pasto del alma' (*Discurso* I). He emphasises at the start of his account of *agudeza* the need not only for ingenuity but for beauty, and the aesthetic aspect is implicit throughout in his insistence on harmony and proportion.

He defines *agudeza* as follows:

> Consiste, pues, este artificio conceptuoso en una primorosa concordancia, en una armónica correlación entre dos o tres cognoscibles extremos ['terms'], expresada por un acto del entendimiento. (II)

That is, wit establishes quasi-logical relationships which Gracián now proceeds to categorise and define. Gracián proposed, however, not only to analyse but to teach: the book is a recipe for the creation of *agudeza*, a rhetoric of wit. Gracián begins his instruction with a general statement which contains the essence of the matter:

> Es el sujeto sobre quien se discurre . . . uno como centro, de quien reparte el discurso líneas de ponderación y sutileza a las entidades que lo rodean; esto es, a los adjuntos que lo coronan, como son sus causas, sus efectos, atributos, calidades, contingencias, circunstancias de tiempo, lugar, modo, etc., y cualquiera otro término correspondiente: valos careando de uno en uno con el sujeto, y unos con otros entre sí; y en descubriendo alguna conformidad o conveniencia, que digan, ya con el principal sujeto, ya unos con otros, exprímela, pondérala, y en esto está la sutileza. (IV)

The subject of one's discourse will suggest all manner of associated ideas linked with the first as cause, effect, and so on. Exploration of these will provide material for witty (but logical) extensions of the subject. The *adjuntos* here enumerated are the 'topics' set out in Cicero's *Topica*: a repertoire not of themes but of the different kinds of logical relationships on which an argument may be based. In his version of the Ciceronian scheme Gracián offers a matrix which may be used for generating wit. The remainder of his treatise is a detailed and copiously illustrated examination of the various kinds of relationships (by similarity, dissimilarity, etc.) which are possible. But though the exposition is couched in the traditional logical terminology appropriate to the subject's origin in dialectics, Gracián's concern is always more with beauty than with truth. Both in his choice of examples—a wide-ranging anthology of wit—and in his analysis he gives an insight into the working of the *conceptista* mind such as can be got from no one else.

El Criticón, Gracián's finest work and one of the supreme masterpieces of seventeenth-century Spanish literature, is an allegorical narrative which shows its author's conception of prudence in action. Its three parts trace the journey through life of Critilo and Andrenio; the first part is entitled 'En la primavera de la niñez y en el estío de la juventud', the second 'Juiciosa cortesana filosofía, en el otoño de la varonil edad', and the third 'En el invierno de la vejez'.[19]

The book opens with a description of the castaway Critilo being washed ashore on the island of St Helena. There he encounters a solitary young inhabitant whom he calls Andrenio and whom he teaches to speak. The symbolic significance of their names soon becomes clear: Critilo represents judgment and prudence, Andrenio man's natural impulses.

Andrenio tells how he was released by an earthquake from the cave in which he spent his earliest days, and tells of his wonder at the splendour of the world which was revealed to him. Critilo provides a running commentary of explanation and symbolic interpretation. Andrenio observed the antagonism between sea and land, that flowers bloomed and quickly died, and that the harmony of so much beauty was paradoxically composed of conflict. Critilo explains that the discords of the universe contribute to a larger harmony.

> Mas, ¡oh maravillosa, infinitamente sabia providencia de aquel gran Moderador de todo lo criado, que con tan continua y varia contrariedad de todas las criaturas entre sí, templa, mantiene y conserva toda esta gran máquina del mundo!
> —Ese portento de atención divina—dijo Andrenio—era lo que yo mucho celebraba, viendo tanta mudanza con tanta permanencia, que todas las cosas van acabando, todas ellas perecen, y el mundo siempre el mismo, siempre permanece.
> —Trazó las cosas de modo el Supremo Artífice—dijo Critilo—que ninguna se acabase que no comenzase luego otra, de modo que de las ruinas de la primera se levanta la segunda. Con esto verás que el mismo fin es principio; la destrucción de una criatura es generación de la otra. Cuando parece que se acaba todo, entonces comienza de nuevo. La naturaleza se renueva, el mundo se remoza, la tierra se establece y el divino gobierno es admirado y adorado. (Pt. I, III)

The universe is harmonious and the natural scene idyllic; but they are now rescued by a Spanish fleet and so enter the world of men. Critilo warns Andrenio that they are now among enemies—'ya es tiempo de abrir los ojos, ya es menester, vivir alerta. . . . Oye a todos y de ninguno te fíes' (I, IV). In this now more sombre setting, Critilo tells of his earlier life. Andrenio's story was of an innocent idyll, Critilo's of imprudence, misfortune, injustice, and treachery. In Goa he loved the beautiful Felisinda but was prevented from marrying her by their difference in fortune. He is imprisoned for killing a rival and spends many years in jail. In the meantime Felisinda has been taken back to Spain and he has heard no more of her or of the child she was pregnant with. Sailing back to search for her he is thrown overboard by the ship's captain, a friend of Critilo's enemy. It is evident that the name of Felisinda is as symbolic as Critilo's own: she stands for the elusive happiness which is every man's goal.

They disembark. Now begins their allegorical progress through the world and through life. They see an army of children—'un ejército desconcertado de infantería' (I, v)—led by a smiling woman who showers them with loving attentions. But she leads them into a valley where she summons forth wild beasts to devour them. Only a few are rescued, by another woman of great beauty. The first woman is 'nuestra mala inclinación', the second Reason.

They come to a town, a spectacle of universal folly and deceit. Andrenio joins in the laughter of a crowd enjoying the sight of a ragged stranger being heartlessly tricked. But Critilo weeps, saying: 'Y dime . . . y si fueses tú ése de quien te ríes, ¿qué dirías? . . . Sabe, pues, que aquel desdichado estranjero es el hombre de todos y todos somos él'. We are tricked and abused from birth to death. Andrenio will not learn: he accepts an invitation to stay in the palace of Falimundo—the palace of worldly deception—where Critilo leaves him, while he himself presses on to the palace of Artemia: Reason, whose art can improve on untutored human nature. She is a more benign Circe. 'No encantaba las personas, antes las desencantaba. De los brutos hacía hombres de razón' (I, VIII). Andrenio, won away from Falimundo, is brought to her Court. There he, Critilo, and Artemia discourse on the greatest marvel of creation, Man, whose every limb and feature is a living sermon. The entire episode is an excellent illustration of that pursuit of ingenious analogy and recondite significance which lies at the heart of the *conceptista* imagination. They comment (for example) on the supremacy of the head:

> —Y aquí he notado yo con especial atención—dijo Critilo—que aunque las partes desta gran república del cuerpo son tantas, que solos los huesos llenan los días del año, y esta numerosidad, con tal armonía que no hay número que no se emplee en ellas, como, digamos, cinco son los sentidos, cuatro los humores, tres las potencias, dos los ojos; todas vienen a reducirse a la unidad de una cabeza, retrato de aquel primer móvil divino a quien viene a reducirse por sus gradas toda esta universal dependencia. (I, IX)

Nature is harmonious, a copy of the harmony of its Maker. Every detail teaches a profitable lesson. Even hair, which to Andrenio seems only adornment: 'Son raíces deste humano árbol—dijo Artemia—; arráiganle en el Cielo, y llévanle allá de un cabello; allí han de estar sus cuidados y de allá ha de recibir el sustancial sustento'.

They proceed on their way. At the palace of Falsirena, Andrenio learns that Felisinda (her cousin) is his mother, and Critilo his father. Andrenio falls a victim to the charms of Falsirena (the enchantment of women) and has to be rescued by his father. They go forward to the Feria del Mundo, 'aquel gran emporio que divide los amenos prados de la juventud de las ásperas montañas de la edad varonil', where all manner of things both vain and useful are on sale.

In Part II, having passed through the heart of Spain, they enter the most austere Aragon, where they encounter Argos the keen-sighted, who leads them to the 'Aduana general de las edades'. Those who enter come out changed as if by enchantment. '¿Qué mayor encanto—dijo Argos—que treinta años a cuestas?'. Argos, all eyes, has already taught them to distrust all things and all men.

> ¿No sabes tú que casi todos los arrimos del mundo son falsos, chimeneas tras tapiz, que hasta los parientes falsean y se halla peligro en los mismos hermanos? Maldito el hombre que confía en otro, y sea quien fuere. ¿Qué digo amigos y hermanos? De los mismos hijos no hay que asegurarse, y necio del padre que en vida se despoja. (II, I)

The lesson of distrust is a constant in Gracián, to which his friendship for Lastanosa (eulogised in II, II as 'Salastano') seems to be the sole exception.

The two travellers go forward, admire the palace of Salastano and, being unable to find the palace of Virtelia (Virtue), pass by the 'yermo de Hipocrinda' (Hypocrisy) instead (II, VIII). At last they come upon the palace of Virtue, ugly without but beautiful within (II, X). Virtelia directs them on their way to find Felisinda. They observe how many try to cross to the Court of Honoria by the 'puente de los peros', but tripping over the *peros* ('¡qué valiente soldado, pero gran ladrón!'), fall into 'el río del reír' (II, XI). Momo affirms that true honour does not now exist, but another character offers to lead the travellers to it, and takes them to 'el trono del Mando' (II, XII). They learn that true dominion lies only in virtue.

Now in Part III they come to old age.

> Estaban ya nuestros dos peregrinos del mundo, los andantes de la vida, al pie de los Alpes canos, comenzando Andrenio a dar en el blanco, cuando Critilo en los dejos de cisne. (II, I)

Andrenio, who throughout has plunged unrestrainedly into folly after folly, is beginning to learn prudence as his first white hairs appear ('dar en el blanco'), while Critilo grows wholly white. Among those they meet is 'el Descifrador', who offers to teach them to decipher the book of the world, and the human heart, the hardest book of all. He shows them some who seem men but who are diphthongs: 'diptongo es un hombre con voz de mujer, y una mujer que habla como hombre. . . .

Diptongo es un niño de sesenta años, y uno sin camisa crujiendo seda' (III, IV). Others are parentheses: ¿Que os diré de las paréntesis, aquellas que ni hacen ni deshacen en la oración, hombres que ni atan ni desatan? No sirven sino de embarazar el mundo'.

Seeking the palace of 'Saber coronado' the two come to a fork in their path: Critilo follows one road, which leads to the land of the excessively guileful, Andrenio the other, which leads to 'el país de los buenos hombres', the land of excessive guilelessness. The two meet again where the two paths join (suggesting the Golden Mean). At one place they come upon 'la Cueva de la Nada', where all worthless people and things end. They come at last to Rome, 'término de la tierra y entrada católica del Cielo' (III, IX), where they hope to find Felisinda at last, but learn that she is not to be found on earth.

> En vano, ¡oh peregrinos del mundo, pasajeros de la vida!, os cansáis en buscar desde la cuna a la tumba esta vuestra imaginada Felisinda, que el uno llama esposa, el otro madre; ya murió para el mundo y vive para el cielo. Hallarla heis allá, si la supiéredes merecer en la tierra. (III, IX)

They are threatened by Death, but told how they may escape to 'la Isla de la Inmortalidad' (III, XII):

> Eternízanse los grandes hombres en la memoria de los venideros, mas los comunes yacen sepultados en el desprecio de los presentes y en el poco reparo de los que vendrán. Así, que son eternos los héroes y los varones eminentes inmortales. Este es el único y el eficaz remedio contra la muerte ... (III, XII)

These two succeed; most fail. The book, composed of conceits, is itself a large conceit, developed with brilliantly sustained ingenuity. Gracián teaches, not manipulation and manoeuvre as in his earlier books, but *desengaño* and prudence, which make a man a *persona* and lead him to that happiness which is to be found only in Heaven. But this is not *The Pilgrim's Progress*: Gracián is not concerned with unassuming virtue content with obscurity. He is concerned with excellence, distinction; and the book ends not with a vision of Christian salvation but with the arduous passage to the Isle of Immortality. Who wishes to follow Critilo and Andrenio thither,

> tome el rumbo de la Virtud insigne, del Valor heroico y llegará a parar al teatro de la Fama, al trono de la Estimación y al centro de la Inmortalidad.

This is not to say that it is an un-Christian book. On the contrary, though there is no formal reference to it, the Christian view is everywhere taken for granted. But Part III makes it plain that Gracián had not changed: he preached virtue, and always affirmed that it is the source and basis of everything of value, but what still caught his imagination was distinction. *El Criticón* teaches how to live well; but it is addressed above all to those who wish to stand out above their fellowmen.

Gracián's frequent use of terms like 'Supremo Artífice', 'Divino Arquitecto', and so on rather than plain 'Dios' has deluded some into believing that *El Criticón* anticipates eighteenth-century deism, but this is untenable. Gracián was an orthodox Christian of his time: the terms he used were commonplace. The book does not speak explicitly of the Christian revelation because Gracián's theme is the prudence that may be learned by the light of natural reason: the prudence which Segismundo learns in Calderón's *La vida es sueño*.

Gracián's world is frosted with distrust. Lean on nothing and no one, he teaches; everything in this world is treacherous, 'chimenea tras tapiz' (II, 1). Nothing is what it seems. He teaches us to get through life with the least harm to ourselves. There is little hint of charity. Gracián is bleak; but undeniably bracing. It is little wonder that he was avidly read in Spanish and in translation in seventeenth-century Europe and later. As late as the nineteenth century Schopenhauer was sufficiently taken with *Oráculo manual* to translate it.

NOTES

1. See M. de Iriarte, *El doctor Huarte de San Juan y su 'Examen de ingenios'*... (Madrid, 1948).
2. Julián Marías, *Historia de la filosofía* in *Obras*, I (Madrid, 1958), 203.
3. There were signs of national revival in the last years of the reign of the feeble-minded Charles II. There was probably a more active intellectual life in Spain in those years than is traditionally acknowledged, but information is scanty and more research is desirable. See, for example, J. M. López Piñero, *La introducción de la ciencia moderna en España* (Barcelona, 1969).
4. Among seventeenth-century historians and histories may be mentioned Juan de Mariana (1536-1624), *Historia general de España* (Toledo, 1601)—translated by Mariana from his own *Historia de rebus Hispaniae* (1592-1605); Garcilaso de la Vega el Inca (1540-1615), *Los comentarios reales* (Lisbon, 1609); Francisco de Moncada, *Expedición de los catalanes y aragoneses contra turcos y griegos* (Barcelona, 1623); the Portuguese Francisco Manuel de Melo who among his Castilian works wrote a *Historia de los movimientos y separación de Cataluña*... (Lisbon, 1645); Antonio de Solís y Rivadeneyra, *Historia de la conquista de Méjico*... (Madrid, 1648). For interesting comments on Spanish historiography at this time, see Jesús M. Ruiz, 'La primera acción literaria de la Academia de la Historia', *BBMP*, XLVI (1970).
5. A highly interesting figure. See M. Solana, *Historia de la filosofía española*, vol. 3 (Madrid, 1941), 357-76.
6. Amédée Mas has interesting remarks on this aspect of Quevedo. See *La caricature de la femme... dans l'oeuvre de Quevedo* (Paris, 1957).

7. *Política de Dios*, ed. James O. Crosby (Madrid, 1966), p. 51. All references are to this edition.

8. All references are to *Obras completas*, ed. A. González Palencia (Madrid, 1946).

9. There is no adequate study of this phenomenon in Spanish literature. For English see George Williamson's excellent *The Senecan Amble* (London, 1951).

10. See T. W. Keeble, 'Some Mythological Figures in Golden Age Satire and Burlesque', *BSS*, XXV (1948).

11. See an excellent analysis of one passage in A. A. Parker, '*La buscona piramidal*: aspects of Quevedo's *conceptismo*', *Iberoromania*, 3 (1969).

12. The notes by A. Fernández-Guerra to his edition in *BAE*, 23 are essential to an understanding of this episode.

13. Quevedo's fame was European and his satires, like some of his serious works, much translated.

14. M. Batllori, *Gracián y el barroco* (Rome, 1958), p. 92.

15. All quotations are from *Obras completas*, ed. A. del Hoyo (Madrid, 1960).

16. *Persona* for Gracián was the man mature in wisdom, self-controlled educated in prudence.

17. *Oráculo manual* is a portable oracle, and oracles require interpretation. There is good sense on this point in T. E. May's review article 'Romera-Navarro's Edition of Gracián's *Oráculo manual*', *BHS*, XXXII (1955), but excessive zeal to defend Gracián against the charge of worldliness leads the author into unsustainable interpretations.

18. For an excellent analysis of the basis of Gracián's scheme in this work, and for some account of its relationship with other treatises on wit, see the articles by M. J. Woods given in the Bibliography.

19. It has been suggested that Gracián derived the idea for *El Criticón* from a philosophical romance by the twelfth-century Andalusian Ibn Tufail, but this was not printed until 1671 (with a Latin translation). Another hypothesis has been put forward by E. García Gómez in 'Un cuento árabe, fuente común de Abentofail y de Gracián', *RABM* (1926).

BIBLIOGRAPHY

THIS BIBLIOGRAPHY IS NOT, and could not be, exhaustive. Some important works (especially older ones) difficult of access are excluded. For further inquiry reference should be made to specialised bibliographies in some of the works listed.

General

J. Simón Díaz, *Manual de bibliografía de la literatura española*, 2nd ed. (Barcelona, 1966)

Otis H. Green, *Spain and the Western Tradition*, 4 vols. (Madison, 1963-66)

J. H. Elliott, *Imperial Spain 1479-1716* (London, 1963)

——, *The Old World and the New 1492-1650* (Cambridge, 1970)

Américo Castro, *La realidad histórica de España*, 3rd ed. (Mexico, 1966)

Note: many of the editions listed below contain important introductory studies.

Chapter 1

Studies

F. J. Norton, *Printing in Spain 1501-1520* (Cambridge, 1966)

A. A. Parker, 'An Age of Gold. Expansion and Scholarship in Spain', in *The Age of the Renaissance*, ed. D. Hay (London, 1967)

Marcel Bataillon, *Erasmo y España*, 2nd ed. (Mexico, 1966)

E. Cione, *Juan de Valdés' la sua vita e il suo pensiero religioso* (Bari, 1938)

D. Ricart, *Juan de Valdés y el pensamiento religioso europeo en los siglos xvi y xvii* (Mexico, 1958)

José C. Nieto, *Juan de Valdés and the Origins of the Spanish and Italian Reformation* (Geneva, 1970)

R. Hamilton, 'Juan de Valdés and some Renaissance theories of language', *BHS*, XXX (1953)

L. Terracini, 'Tradizione illustre e lingua letteraria nella Spagna del Rinascimento', in *Studi di letteratura spagnola*, 1, 2 (Rome, 1964 and 1965)

René Costes, *Antonio de Guevara. Sa Vie* and *Son Oeuvre* (Bordeaux, 1925 and 1926)

María Rosa Lida, 'Fray Antonio de Guevara. Edad media y Siglo de oro español', *RFH*, VIII (1945)

J. Gibbs, *Vida de fray Antonio de Guevara* (Valladolid, 1960)

J. Marichal, 'La originalidad renacentista en el estilo de Guevara', in *La voluntad de estilo* (Barcelona, 1957)

Texts of principal works and authors

Erasmus, *El Enquiridión o manual del caballero cristiano*, ed. Dámaso Alonso (Madrid, 1932)

Antonio de Nebrija, *Gramática castellana*, ed. P. Galindo Romeo and L. Ortiz Muñoz, 2 vols. (Madrid, 1946)

Alfonso de Valdés, *Diálogo de las cosas ocurridas en Roma*, ed. J. F. Montesinos, CC 89 (Madrid, 1928)

——, *Diálogo de Mercurio y Carón*, ed. J. F. Montesinos, CC 96 (Madrid, 1929)

Juan de Valdés, *Diálogo de la lengua*, ed. J. F. Montesinos, CC 86 (Madrid, 1928); also ed. J. M. Lope Blanch, C Ca (Madrid, 1969)

——, *Diálogo de doctrina cristiana*, ed. D. Ricart (Mexico, 1964)

Juan de Mal Lara, *Filosofía vulgar*, ed. A. Vilanova, 3 vols., Selecciones bibliófilas (Madrid, 1958)

Pedro Mejía (Pedro Mexía), *Silva de varia leción*, ed. J. Garcia Soriano, 2 vols., Sociedad de bibliófilos españoles (Madrid, 1933)

Melchor de Santa Cruz, *Floresta española*, ed. R. Benítez Claros, Sociedad de bibliófilos españoles (Madrid, 1953)

Juan Rufo, *Las seiscientas apotegmas*, ed. A. González de Amezúa, Sociedad de bibliófilos españoles (Madrid, 1923)

Antonio de Torquemada, *Jardín de flores curiosas*, ed. A. G. de Amezúa, Sociedad de bibliófilos españoles (Madrid, 1943)

Antonio de Guevara, *Menosprecio de corte y alabanza de aldea*, CC 29 (Madrid, 1915).

——, *Libro áureo*, ed. R. Foulché-Delbosc, *RH* (1929)

——, *Epístolas familiares*, ed. J. M. de Cossío, 2 vols. (Madrid, 1950)

——, *Una década de Césares*, ed. J. R. Jones (Chapel Hill, 1966)

Libro de la vida de D. Alonso Enríquez de Guzmán, ed. H. Keniston, *BAE* (Madrid, 1960)

Diego Hurtado de Mendoza, *Guerra de Granada*, ed. B. Blanco González, C Ca (Madrid, 1970)

Fernán Pérez de Oliva, *Diálogo de la dignidad del hombre*, ed. J. L. Abellán (Barcelona, 1967)

Chapter 2

Studies

M. Menéndez Pelayo, *Boscán* in *Antología de poetas líricos castellanos*, X, Edición nacional (Santander, 1945)
Dámaso Alonso, *Poesía española* (Madrid, 1950)
A. Rodríguez-Moñino, *Poesía y cancioneros (Siglo XVI)* (Madrid, 1968)
——, *Diccionario bibliográfico de pliegos sueltos poéticos* (*Siglo XVI*) (Madrid, 1970)
M. Arce Blanco, *Garcilaso de la Vega: contribución al estudio de la lírica española del siglo XVI* (Madrid, 1930; 2nd. ed. 1961)
P. N. Dunn, 'Garcilaso's Ode *A la Flor de Gnido*', *ZRPh*, 81 (1965)
R. O. Jones, 'Ariosto and Garcilaso', *BHS*, XXXIX (1962)
——, 'Bembo, Gil Polo, Garcilaso. Three Accounts of Love', *RLC*, XL (1966)
H. Keniston, *Garcilaso de la Vega: a Critical Study of his Life and Works* (New York, 1922)
R. Lapesa, *La trayectoria poética de Garcilaso* (Madrid, 1948; 2nd ed. 1968)
E. L. Rivers, 'The Pastoral Paradox of Natural Art', *MLN*, 77 (1962)
M. J. Woods, 'Rhetoric in Garcilaso's first eclogue', *MLN*, 84 (1969)
A. Gallego Morell, *Garcilaso de la Vega y sus comentaristas* (Granada, 1966)

Editions of principal works and authors

Cancionero general, facsimile edition with introduction by A. Rodríguez-Moñino (Madrid, 1958)
Pliegos poéticos góticos de la Biblioteca Nacional, 6 vols. (Madrid, 1957-61)
P. Gallagher, *The Life and Works of Garci Sánchez de Badajoz* (London, 1968)
Juan del Encina, *Cancionero* (1496), facsimile edition, Real Academia Española (Madrid, 1928)
——, *Obras completas*, ed. R. O. Jones and H. López Morales (Madrid: to appear shortly)
Pedro Manuel de Urrea, *Eglogas dramáticas y poesías desconocidas*, ed. E. Asensio, *Joyas bibliográficas*, V (Madrid, 1950)
Cristóbal de Castillejo, *Obras*, ed. J. Domínguez Bordona, 4 vols., CC 72, 79, 88, 91 (Madrid, 1926-28, and later editions)

Juan Boscán, *Obras poéticas*, ed. M. de Riquer, A. Comas, and J. Molas (Barcelona, 1957)
Garcilaso de la Vega, *Obras completas*, ed. E. L. Rivers (Madrid, 1964)
——, *Poesías castellanas completas*, ed. E. L. Rivers, C Ca (Madrid, 1969)

Chapter 3

Studies

H. Thomas, *Spanish and Portuguese Romances of Chivalry* (Cambridge, 1920)
A. Rodríguez-Moñino, 'El primer manuscrito del "Amadís de Gaula" . . .' *BRAE*, XXXVI (1956) and in *Relieves de erudición* (Madrid, 1959)
Frida Weber de Kurlat, 'Estructura novelesca del *Amadís de Gaula*', *RLM*, 5 (1967)
I. A. Leonard, *Books of the Brave* (Cambridge, Mass., 1949)
B. W. Wardropper, 'The *Diana* of Montemayor: revaluation and interpretation', *SPh* (1951)
——, 'La novela como retrato: el arte de Francisco Delicado', *NRFH*, VII (1953)
——, 'El trastorno de la moral en el *Lazarillo*', *NRFH*, XV (1961)
J. B. Avalle-Arce, *La novela pastoril española* (Madrid, 1959)
A. Solé-Leris, 'The theory of love in the two *Dianas*: a contrast', *BHS*, XXXVI (1959)
Jennifer Lowe, 'The *Cuestión de amor* and the structure of Cervantes' *Galatea*', *BHS*, XLIII (1966)
M. Menéndez Pelayo, *Orígenes de la novela*, 4 vols. (Santander, 1943)
Bruno M. Damiani, ' "La lozana andaluza": bibliografía crítica', *BRAE*, XLIX (1969)
Francisco Rico, 'Problemas del *Lazarillo*', *BRAE*, XLVI (1966)
A. Rumeau, 'Sur les "Lazarillo" de 1554. Problème de filiation', *BH* (1969)
F. Lázaro Carreter, 'La ficción autobiográfica en el *Lazarillo de Tormes*', *Litterae Hispanae et Lusitanae*, ed. Hans Flasche (Munich, 1968)
——, 'Construcción y sentido del *Lazarillo de Tormes*', Abaco 1 (Madrid, 1968)
R. W. Truman, 'Lázaro de Tormes and the "Homo novus" tradition', *MLR*, 64 (1969)
F. Durand, 'The author and Lázaro: levels of comic meaning', *BHS*, XLV (1968)
M. Bataillon, *Novedad y fecundidad del 'Lazarillo de Tormes'* (Salamanca, 1968)

H. A. Deferrari, *The Sentimental Moor in Spanish Literature before 1600* (Philadelphia, 1927)

Texts of principal works and authors

Amadís de Gaula, ed. E. B. Place, 4 vols. (Madrid, 1959-69)
Libros de caballerías, ed. P. de Gayangos, *BAE*, 40 (numerous editions)
Libros de caballerías, ed. A. Bonilla y San Martín, 2 vols. (Madrid, 1907 and 1908)
Jorge de Montemayor, *Los siete libros de la Diana*, ed. F. López Estrada, CC 127 (Madrid, 1946)
Gaspar Gil Polo, *Diana enamorada*, ed. R. Ferreres, CC 135 (Madrid, 1953)
M. de Cervantes, *La Galatea*, ed. J. B. Avalle-Arce, 2 vols. CC 154, 155 (Madrid, 1961)
Francisco Delicado, *La lozana andaluza*, ed. Bruno M. Damiani, C Ca (Madrid, 1970)
La comedia Thebaida, ed. G. D. Trotter and K. Whinnom (London, 1969)
Feliciano de Silva, *Segunda comedia de Celestina*, ed. M. I. Chamorro Fernández (Madrid, 1968)
Sancho de Muñón, *Tragicomedia de Lisandro y Roselia*, Colección de libros españoles raros o curiosos 3 (Madrid, 1872)
Alonso de Villegas, *Comedia llamada Selvagia*, Colección de libros españoles raros o curiosos 5 (Madrid, 1873)
La vida de Lazarillo de Tormes, ed. R. O. Jones (Manchester, 1963)
——, ed. J. Caso González (Madrid, 1967)
Cristóbal de Villalón (attributed to), *El Crotalón*, ed. A. Cortina, Colección Austral (Buenos Aires: numerous editions)
Juan Timoneda, *El Patrañuelo*, ed. F. Ruiz Morcuende, CC 101 (Madrid, 1930, and subsequent editions)
Juan de Segura, *Proceso de cartas de amores*, ed. E. B. Place (Evanston, 1950)
El Abencerraje y la hermosa Jarifa, ed. F. López Estrada (Madrid, 1957)
Ginés Pérez de Hita, *Guerras civiles de Granada*, ed. P. Blanchard-Demouge, 2 vols. (Madrid, 1913 and 1915)

Chapter 4

Studies

A. F. G. Bell, *Luis de León. A Study of the Spanish Renaissance* (Oxford, 1925)
K. Vossler, *Luis de León*, Colección Austral (Buenos Aires: numerous editions)

A. Guy, *La pensée de Fray Luis de León* (Limoges, 1943; Spanish translation, Madrid, 1960)
E. A. Peers, *Studies of the Spanish Mystics*, 3 vols. (London, 1927-60)
H. Hatzfeld, *Estudios literarios sobre mística española* (Madrid, 1955)
J. Baruzi, *Saint Jean de la Croix et le problème de l'expérience mystique* (Paris, 1924; 2nd ed. 1930)
F. Ruiz Salvador, *Introducción a San Juan de la Cruz: el escritor, los escritos, el sistema*, *BAC* (Madrid, 1968)
B. W. Wardropper, *Historia de la poesía lírica a lo divino en la Cristiandad occidental* (Madrid, 1958)
M. Bataillon, 'El anónimo del soneto, "No mi mueve, mi Dios"', in *Varia lección de clásicos españoles* (Madrid, 1964)

Texts of principal works and authors

Luis de León, *Obras castellanas completas*, ed. F. García, *BAC* (Madrid, 1944, and later editions)
Luis de Granada, *Obras completas*, *BAE*, 6, 8, 11 (Madrid; numerous editions)
——, *Obra selecta*, *BAC* (Madrid, 1952)
P. Malón de Chaide, *La conversión de la Magdalena*, ed. F. García, 3 vols., CC 104, 105 (Madrid, 1930, and later editions)
Santa Teresa de Jesús, *Obras completas*, ed. Efrén de la Madre de Dios and O. Steggink, *BAC* (Madrid, 1962)
San Juan de la Cruz, *Vida y obras de* . . ., ed. Lucinio del SS. Sacramento, *BAC* (Madrid, 1946, and later editions)
Juan de los Ángeles, *Obras místicas*, ed. Fr. J. Sala, 2 vols., (Madrid, 1912-17)
——, *Diálogos de la conquista del reino de Dios*, ed. A. González Palencia (Madrid, 1946)
Sebastián de Córdoba, *Las obras de Boscán y Garcilaso trasladadas en materias cristianas* . . ., ed. Glen Gale (Madrid, 1970)

Chapter 5

Studies

Dámaso Alonso, *Poesía española*, 5th ed. (Madrid, 1970)
A. González Palencia and E. Mele, *Vida y obras de don Diego Hurtado de Mendoza*, 3 vols. (Madrid, 1941-43)
J. G. Fucilla, *Estudios sobre el petrarquismo en España* (Madrid, 1960)
J. M. Blecua, 'De nuevo sobre los textos poéticos de Herrera', *BRAE*, XXXVIII (1958)
A. D. Kossoff, *Vocabulario de la obra poética de Herrera* (Madrid, 1966)

O. Macrí, *Fernando de Herrera* (Madrid, 1959)
E. Orozco Díaz, 'Realidad y espíritu en la lírica de Herrera. Sobre lo humano de un poeta "divino" ', *BUG* (1951)
E. L. Rivers, *Francisco de Aldana, el Divino Capitán* (Badajoz, 1955)
R. Lapesa, 'Las odas de Fray Luis de León a Felipe Ruiz', *Homenaje a Dámaso Alonso*, II (Madrid, 1961)
Dámaso Alonso, *La poesía de San Juan de la Cruz. (Desde esta ladera)* (Madrid, 1942; 3rd ed. 1966)
J. M. Blecua, 'Los antecedentes del poema del "Pastorcico" de San Juan de la Cruz', *RFE*, XXXVI (1949)
Jorge Guillén, 'The Ineffable Language of Mysticism', in *Language and Poetry* (Cambridge, Mass., 1961) (Spanish edition: *Lenguaje y poesía*, Madrid, 1961)
Margit Frenk Alatorre, *La lírica popular en los Siglos de Oro* (Mexico, 1946)
——, 'Dignificación de la lírica popular en el Siglo de Oro', *Anuario de letras*, II (Mexico, 1962)
J. M. Alín, *El cancionero español de tipo tradicional* (Madrid, 1968)
A. Sánchez Romeralo, *El villancico. (Estudios sobre la lírica popular en los siglos XV y XVI)* (Madrid, 1969)
R. Menéndez Pidal, *Romancero hispánico*, 2 vols. (Madrid, 1953)
Frank Pierce, *La poesía épica del Siglo de Oro*, 2nd ed. (Madrid, 1968)

Texts of principal works and authors

Diego Hurtado de Mendoza, *Obras poéticas*, ed W. I. Knapp, Colección de libros españoles raros o curiosos (Madrid, 1877)
Francisco Sá de Miranda, *Obras completas*, ed. M. Rodrigues Lapa, 2 vols. (Lisbon, 1942)
Francisco de Figueroa, *Obras*, ed. A. González Palencia, Sociedad de bibliófilos españoles (Madrid, 1943)
Hernando de Acuña, *Varias poesías*, ed. E. Catena de Vindel (Madrid, 1954)
Gutierre de Cetina, *Obras*, ed. J. Hazañas y la Rúa, 2 vols. (Seville, 1895)
Jorge de Montemayor, *El cancionero*, ed. A. González Palencia, Sociedad de bibliófilos españoles (Madrid, 1932)
Fernando de Herrera, *Algunas obras*, ed. A. Coster (Paris, 1908)
——, *Poesías*, ed. V. García de Diego, CC 26 (Madrid, 1914, and later editions)
——, *Rimas inéditas*, ed. J. M. Blecua (Madrid, 1948)
——, *Anotaciones . . .* : in A. Gallego Morell, *Garcilaso y sus comentaristas* (Granada, 1966)
——, *Controversias sobre sus Anotaciones a las obras de Garcilaso de la Vega*, ed. J. M. Asensio (Madrid, 1870)

Francisco de Aldana, *Poesías*, ed. E. L. Rivers, CC 143 (Madrid, 1957)
——, *Obras completas*, 2 vols. (Madrid, 1953)
Luis de León, *Obras castellanas completas*, *BAC* (Madrid, 1944, and later editions)
——, *La poesía* . . . , ed. O. Macrí (Salamanca, 1970)
San Juan de la Cruz, *Vida y obras de* . . . , *BAC* (Madrid, 1946, and later editions)
Margit Frenk Alatorre, *Lírica hispánica de tipo popular* (Mexico, 1966)
Dámaso Alonso y J. M. Blecua, *Antología de la poesía española. Poesía de tipo tradicional* (Madrid, 1956)
A. Rodríguez-Moñino (general editor), *Floresta*, 9 vols. (Valencia, 1953-63). Reprints, with valuable introductions by Rodríguez-Moñino and others, of sixteenth- and early seventeenth-century verse-collections)
Frank Pierce, *The Heroic Poem of the Golden Age: Selections* (Oxford, 1947)
Alonso de Ercilla, *La Araucana*, ed. Concha de Salamanca (Madrid, 1968)
Fr. Diego de Hojeda, *La Christiada*, ed. M. P. Corcoran (Washington, 1935)

Chapter 6

Studies

Marcel Bataillon, *Pícaros y picaresca* (Madrid, 1969)
A. A. Parker, *Literature and the Delinquent* (Edinburgh, 1967)
F. W. Chandler, *Romances of Roguery* . . . I. *The Picaresque Novel in Spain* (New York, 1899 and 1961)
A. Castro, *La realidad histórica de España* (Mexico, 1966)
E. Moreno Báez, *Lección y sentido del 'Guzmán de Alfarache'* (Madrid, 1948)
E. Cros, *Protée et le gueux* (Paris, 1967)
F. de Haan, *An Outline of the History of the Novela Picaresca in Spain* (New York, 1903)
F. Lázaro Carreter, 'Originalidad del "Buscón" ', *Homenaje a Dámaso Alonso*, II (Madrid, 1961)
C. B. Morris, *The Unity and Structure of Quevedo's 'Buscón': desgracias encadenadas* (Hull, 1965)
A. del Monte, *Itinerario del romanzo picaresco spagnuolo* (Florence, 1957)
G. Haley, *Vicente Espinel and Marcos de Obregón* (Providence, 1959)

Texts of principal works and authors

Mateo Alemán, *Guzmán de Alfarache*, in Francisco Rico (ed.), *La novela picaresca española* (Barcelona, 1967)

Mateo Luján de Sayavedra, *Segunda parte de . . . Guzmán de Alfarache*, *BAE*, 3 (numerous editions)

F. de Quevedo, *La vida del buscón llamado don Pablos*, ed. F. Lázaro Carreter (Salamanca, 1965)

Alonso de Contreras, *Vida de . . .* (Madrid, 1965)

La vida y hechos de Estebanillo González . . ., ed. J. Millé y Giménez, 2 vols., CC 108, 109 (Madrid, 1946, and later editions)

Juan de Luna, *Segunda parte de la vida de Lazarillo de Tormes* in M. de Riquer, *La Celestina y Lazarillos* (Barcelona, 1959)

F. López de Ubeda, *Libro de entretenimiento de la pícara Justina . . .*, ed. J. Puyol y Alonso, 3 vols. (Madrid, 1911)

Vicente Espinel, *Vida de Marcos de Obregón*, ed. S. Gili Gaya, 2 vols., CC 43, 51 (Madrid, 1922-25, and later editions)

J. de Alcalá Yáñez y Ribera, *Alonso mozo de muchos amos*, *BAE*, 18 (numerous editions)

A. de Castillo Solórzano, *La garduña de Sevilla*, ed. F. Ruiz Morcuende, CC 42 (Madrid, 1922 and later editions)

Chapter 7

Studies

Andrée Collard, *Nueva poesía: conceptismo, culteranismo en la crítica española* (Waltham, Brandeis University, 1967)

José F. Montesinos, introduction to *Primavera y flor de los mejores romances* [1621], *Floresta*, V (Valencia, 1954)

Dámaso Alonso, *Poesía española*, 5th ed. (Madrid, 1970)

——, *La lengua poética de Góngora*, 3rd ed. (Madrid, 1961)

——, *Estudios y ensayos gongorinos* (Madrid, 1955)

R. Jammes, *Études sur l'oeuvre poétique de Góngora* (Bordeaux, 1967)

C. C. Smith, 'La musicalidad del "Polifemo" ', *RFE*, XLIV (1961)

E. J. Gates, *Documentos gongorinos* (Mexico, 1950)

J. de Entrambasaguas, *Estudios sobre Lope de Vega*, 3 vols. (Madrid, 1946-58)

Otis H. Green, *Courtly love in Quevedo* (Boulder, Colo., 1952). Spanish version: *El amor cortés en Quevedo* (Saragossa, 1955)

A. Mas, *La caricature de la femme, du mariage et de l'amour dans l'oeuvre de Quevedo* (Paris, 1957)

A. A. Parker, 'La agudeza en algunos sonetos de Quevedo', *Estudios dedicados a Menéndez Pidal*, III (Madrid, 1952)

J. O. Crosby, *En torno a la poesía de Quevedo* (Madrid, 1967)

Otis H. Green, *Vida y obras de Lupercio Leonardo de Argensola* (Saragossa, 1945)
H. Bonneville, *Le poète sévillan Juan de Salinas (1562?-1643). Vie et oeuvre* (Paris, 1969)
D. Alonso, *Vida y obra de Medrano,* I (Madrid, 1948); II (with S. Reckert) (Madrid, 1958)
G. A. Davies, *A Poet at Court: Antonio Hurtado de Mendoza (1586-1644)* (Oxford, 1971)
F. Rodríguez Marín, *Pedro de Espinosa* (Madrid, 1907)
A. Gallego Morell, *Pedro Soto de Rojas* (Granada, 1948)
E. Orozco Díaz, 'Introducción a un poema barroco. De las "Soledades" gongorinas al "Paraíso" de Soto de Rojas', in *Paisaje y sentimiento de la naturaleza en la poesía española* (Madrid, 1968)
L. Rosales, *Pasión y muerte del Conde de Villamediana* (Madrid, 1969)
K. Scholberg, *La poesía religiosa de Miguel de Barrios* (Columbus, Ohio, 1962)

Texts of principal works and authors

Luis de Góngora, *Obras completas,* ed. J. and I. Millé y Giménez (Madrid, 1932, and later editions)
——, *Letrillas,* ed. R. Jammes (Paris, 1963)
——, *Sonetos completos,* ed. B. Ciplijauskaité, C Ca (Madrid, 1969)
——, *Soledades,* ed. Dámaso Alonso (Madrid, 1927, and later editions)
——, *Fábula de Polifemo y Galatea,* in Dámaso Alonso, *Góngora y el 'Polifemo',* 2 vols. (Madrid, 1961)
L. Carrillo y Sotomayor, *Poesías completas,* ed. Dámaso Alonso (Madrid, 1936)
Lupercio y Bartolomé L. de Argensola, *Rimas,* ed. J. M. Blecua, 2 vols. (Saragossa, 1950 and 1951)
Lope de Vega, *Obras poéticas* I, ed. J. M. Blecua (Barcelona, 1969)
——, *Poesías líricas,* ed. J. F. Montesinos, 2 vols., CC 68, 75 (Madrid, 1926-27, and later editions)
F. de Quevedo, *Obras completas* I. *Poesía original,* ed. J. M. Blecua (Barcelona, 1963, 2nd ed. 1968)
——, *Obra poética,* ed. J. M. Blecua, 4 vols. (Madrid, 1969-; two volumes published so far)
Juan de Tasis, Conde de Villamediana, *Obras,* ed. J. M. Rozas, C Ca (Madrid, 1970)
F. López de Zárate, *Obras varias,* ed. J. Simón Díaz, 2 vols. (Madrid, 1947)
V. Espinel, *Diversas rimas,* ed. D. Clotelle Clarke (New York, 1956)
Pedro Espinosa, *Obras,* ed. F. Rodríguez Marín (Madrid, 1909)

Pedro Soto de Rojas, *Obras*, ed. A. Gallego Morell (Madrid, 1950)
Juana Inés de la Cruz, *Obras completas*, 4 vols. (Mexico, 1951-57)
——, *Antologia*, ed. E. L. Rivers, Biblioteca Anaya (Salamanca, 1965)
J. M. Hill, *Poesía germanesca* (Bloomington, 1945)

Chapter 8

Studies

L. Astrana Marín, *Vida ejemplar y heroica de Miguel de Cervantes Saavedra*, 7 vols. (Reus, 1948-58)
Américo Castro, *El pensamiento de Cervantes* (Madrid, 1925)
——, *Hacia Cervantes*, 2nd ed. (Madrid, 1960)
J. Casalduero, *Sentido y forma de las Novelas ejemplares* (Buenos Aires, 1943)
——, *Sentido y forma del Quijote*, 2nd ed. (Madrid, 1966)
——, *Sentido y forma de 'Los trabajos de Persiles y Sigismunda'* (Buenos Aires, 1947)
H. Hatzfeld, *El 'Quijote' como obra de arte del lenguaje*, 2nd ed. (Madrid, 1966)
E. C. Riley, *Cervantes's Theory of the Novel* (Oxford, 1962)
A. González de Amezúa, *Cervantes, creador de la novela corta española*, 2 vols. (Madrid, 1956-58)
M. J. Bates, *'Discreción' in the Works of Cervantes: a Semantic Study* (Washington, 1945)
J. B. Avalle Arce, *Deslindes cervantinos* (Madrid, 1961)
Manuel Durán, *La ambigüedad en el Quijote* (Xalapa, 1961)
R. L. Predmore, *The World of Don Quixote* (Cambridge, Mass., 1967)
A. A. Parker, 'El concepto de la verdad en el Quijote', *RFE*, XXXII (1948)
——, 'Fielding and the structure of *Don Quixote*', *BHS*, XXXIII (1956)
Suma cervantina [essays on all Cervantes's works by leading scholars], ed. J. B. Avalle-Arce and E. C. Riley (London; expected shortly)
P. J. Waley, 'The Unity of the *Casamiento engañoso* and the *Coloquio de los perros*', *BHS*, XXXIV (1957)
Jennifer Lowe, 'Theme and Structure in Cervantes' *Persiles y Sigismunda*', *FMLS*, III (1967)
P. E. Russell, ' "Don Quixote" as a funny book', *MLR* (1969)
P. N. Dunn, *Castillo Solórzano and the Decline of the Spanish Novel* (Oxford, 1952)
J. M. Blecua, introduction to Lope de Vega, *La Dorotea*, ed. Blecua (Madrid, 1955)

Texts of principal works and authors

Miguel de Cervantes Saavedra, *Obras completas*, ed. R. Schevill and A. Bonilla y San Martín, 9 vols. (Madrid, 1914-31)

——, *El ingenioso hidalgo don Quijote de la Mancha*, ed. F. Rodríguez Marín, 8 vols., CC 4, 6, 8, 10, 13, 16, 19, 22 (Madrid, 1911-13, and subsequent editions)

——, *Novelas ejemplares*, ed. F. Rodríguez Marín, 2 vols., CC 27, 36 (Madrid, 1914-17, and subsequent editions). (This edition is only a selection.)

——, *El casamiento engañoso y el coloquio de los perros*, ed. A. González de Amezúa (Madrid, 1912)

——, *Rinconete y Cortadillo*, ed. F. Rodríguez Marín (Seville, 1905)

——, *La Galatea*, ed. J. B. Avalle-Arce, 2 vols., CC 154, 155 (Madrid, 1961)

——, *Los trabajos de Persiles y Sigismunda*, ed. J. B. Avalle-Arce, C Ca (Madrid, 1970)

Alonso Fernández de Avellaneda, *El Quijote apócrifo* [*El ingenioso hidalgo don Quijote de la Mancha*] (Barcelona, 1968)

La tía fingida, ed. A. Bonilla y San Martín (Madrid, 1911)

Colección selecta de antiguas novelas españolas, ed. E. Cotarelo y Mori, 12 vols. (Madrid, 1906-09)

Alonso Castillo Solórzano, *La garduña de Sevilla*, ed. F. Ruiz Morcuende, CC 42 (Madrid, 1942)

——, *Lisardo enamorado*, ed. E. Juliá y Martínez (Madrid, 1947)

Alonso Jerónimo de Salas Barbadillo, *Dos novelas* [*El cortesano descortés* and *El necio bien afortunado*], ed. Francisco A. de Uhagón Sociedad de bibliófilos españoles (Madrid, 1894)

——, *La peregrinación sabia* and *El sagaz Estacio marido examinado* ed. F. A. de Icaza, CC (Madrid, 1924, and subsequent editions).

——, *Casa del placer honesto*, ed. E. B. Place, University of Colorado Studies, vol. XV, no. 4 (Boulder, 1927)

——, *El caballero perfecto*, ed. P. Marshall, University of Colorado Studies, Series in Language and Literature 2 (Boulder, 1949)

María de Zayas y Sotomayor, *Novelas amorosas y ejemplares*, ed. A. González de Amezúa (Madrid, 1948)

——, *Desengaños amorosos*, ed. A. González de Amezúa (Madrid, 1950)

Gonzalo de Céspedes y Meneses, *Historias peregrinas y ejemplares*, ed. Y.-R. Fonquerne, C Ca (Madrid, 1971)

Lope de Vega, *La Dorotea*, ed. Edwin S. Morby (Madrid, 1958)

——, *Novelas a la señora Marcia Leonarda*, ed. F. Rico (Madrid, 1968)

Chapter 9

Studies

A. Rothe, *Quevedo und Seneca. Untersuchungen zu den Frühschriften Quevedos* (Geneva-Paris, 1965)
A. A. Parker, '*La buscona piramidal*: aspects of Quevedo's *conceptismo*', *Iberoromania*, 3 (1969)
R. D. F. Pring-Mill, 'Some techniques of representation in the *Sueños* and the *Criticón*', *BHS*, XLV (1968)
J. C. Dowling, *El pensamiento político-filosófico de Saavedra Fajardo* (Murcia, 1957)
F. Murillo Ferrol, *Saavedra Fajardo y la política del barroco* (Madrid, 1957)
J. P. W. Crawford, *The Life and Works of Cristóbal Suárez de Figueroa* (Philadelphia, 1907)
A. Coster, 'Baltasar Gracián (1601-1658)', *RH*, XXIX (1913). Also published in book-form in 1913. Spanish translation 1947.
M. Batllori, *Gracián y el barroco* (Rome, 1958)
Klaus Heger, *Baltasar Gracián* (Saragossa, 1960)
Monroe Z. Hafter, *Gracián and Perfection. Spanish Moralists of the Seventeenth Century* (Cambridge, Mass., 1966)
T. E. May, 'An Interpretation of Gracián's *Agudeza y arte de ingenio*', *HR*, XVI (1948)
M. J. Woods, 'Sixteenth-Century Topical Theory: some Spanish and Italian Views', *MLR*, 63 (1968)
——, 'Gracián, Peregrini and the Theory of Topics', *MLR*, 63 (1968)
E. Moreno Báez, *Filosofía del Criticón* (Santiago, 1959). (A lecture.)

Texts of principal works and authors

José de Pellicer, *Avisos históricos*, ed. E. Tierno Galván (Madrid, 1965)
F. de Quevedo, *Política de Dios*, ed. J. O. Crosby (Madrid, 1966)
——, *Obras completas. Prosa*, ed. L. Astrana Marín (Madrid, 1932, and later editions)
D. Saavedra Fajardo, *Obras completas*, ed. A. González Palencia (Madrid, 1946)
——, *República literaria*, ed. John Dowling, Biblioteca Anaya 79 (Salamanca-Madrid-Barcelona-Caracas, 1967)
Cristóbal Suárez de Figueroa, *El passagero*, ed. R. Selden Rose, Sociedad de bibliófilos españoles (Madrid, 1914)
Antonio Liñán y Verdugo, *Guía y avisos de forasteros* (Madrid, 1923)
Luis Vélez de Guevara, *El diablo cojuelo*, ed. R. Rodríguez Marín, CC 38 (Madrid, 1918, and later editions)
Rodrigo Fernández de Ribera, *El mesón del mundo* (Seville, 1946)

Francisco Santos, *El Arca de Noé y campana de Belilla*, ed. Fernando Gutiérrez (Barcelona, 1959)

See E. Correa Calderón (ed.), *Costumbristas españoles* (Madrid, 1950), I, for the following: Bautista Remiro de Navarra, *Los peligros de Madrid*; Juan de Zabaleta, *El día de fiesta por la mañana* and *El día de fiesta por la tarde*; Francisco Santos, *Día y noche de Madrid.*

Baltasar Gracián, *Obras completas*, ed. A. del Hoyo (Madrid, 1960)

——, *Agudeza y arte de ingenio*, ed. E. Correa Calderón, 2 vols., C Ca (Madrid, 1969)

——, *El Criticón*, ed. M. Romera-Navarro, 3 vols. (Philadelphia, 1938)

——, *Oráculo manual*, ed. M. Romera-Navarro (Madrid, 1954)

——, *The Oracle*, translated by L. B. Walton (London, 1953). (This edition includes the Spanish text.)

S. de Covarrubias Orozco, *Tesoro de la lengua castellana*. ed. M. de Riquer (Barcelona, 1943)

Gonzalo Correas, *Vocabulario de refranes y frases proverbiales* . . . (Madrid, 1924)

——, *Vocabulario* . . . etc., ed. Louis Combet (Bordeaux, 1967)

INDEX

Names of authors and titles of books discussed in the text are included, but not names of modern critics

D

Q

R